I0607252

The Further Adventures of...

Krög, The Battle Prince

Volume 2
The Waning Days of Summer

Ryan Cipriani

Published by Guardian Reaper Publications, LLC

What Readers said about "The Mythical, Mystical, Magnificent Adventures of Krög, the Battle Prince: Beyond the Great Hall"

"A refreshing new entry in the genre of high fantasy, Cipriani steers clear of the high language and lofty characters commonly associated with fantasy..."

"A coming of age story without all the melodramatics; a fantasy tale without the over-seriousness that often plagues the genre..."

"The author's writing contains humour in the style of David Eddings, a richness in vocabulary not often seen in this genre, character value systems similar to those found in the writings of Anne McCaffrey and R.A. Salvatore, and the magical fantasy style of Terry Brooks' Shannara Series..."

"The attitudes and humor brought by the supporting characters is what really stood out..."

"A great adventure into a mystical world that is written with amazing images, witty dialogue and a touch of humor..."

"These are Achilles awkward teenage years..."

Read the reviews and find Volume 1, 3 and 4 on Amazon, available in paperback and for Kindle!

About the Author

Ryan Cipriani originally hails from northwest Ohio, but has since made adventure a part of his existential fabric. While originally that call drew him to a life on stage, both as a physical performer and a heavy metal guitar player, his one, true creative passion remains, inextricably, writing and storytelling. Over the years, Ryan has moved from Ohio to Florida, California, Indiana and Tennessee, in constant pursuit of the next tale to weave. While Krög, the Battle Prince represents his most ambitious project to date, Ryan has penned a number of other written works across genres. His science fiction horror novel, *A Fathom Infinite*, is lauded as a claustrophobic, Lovecraftian thrill ride, and he was one of the contributing writers on the ill-fated *Lemonade Stand Massacre*, originally conceived to be a collection of tongue-in-cheek pulp-fiction a la *Strange Tales*. He is currently working on follow-ups to several of his works, and is compiling a collection of short stories to be called *The Wrong Universe*. In his spare time, Ryan enjoys "adventure races," hard rock music, retro video games, and schlocky horror movies. Eagle eyed readers will be able to spot references and in-jokes for all of these sprinkled throughout his narratives, and Ryan always enjoys it when a reader reaches out having picked up on a particularly silly or well hidden homage. Ryan currently lives and works in Nashville, but always has his eye on the next horizon.

<u>Contents</u>

The Waning Days of Summer

Acknowledgements and Thanks

It is a remarkably difficult thing to properly and appropriately offer gratitude to all the unbelievably supportive people who were party to my decision to move forward with self-publishing the annals of Krög, the Battle Prince. Volume 1 offered a short, but very significant list of individuals who were directly responsible for the absolute genesis of this project, as it relates to the saga as a whole. Essentially, these were the few who helped to spark, encourage or enable the work I did to bring the story of the Battle Prince out of the remote corners of my mind, and commit it to paper. They deserve more recognition than I am able to give.

The continuing quest to share Krög's story with a larger audience has become a personal struggle to maintain the focus and motivation necessary to break into an extremely challenging realm of the media industry. So often the draw to writing, for myself at least, is the solitary nature of the project, and the immense amount of intrinsic desire required to articulate and author a saga on the scope of the Battle Prince's totaled adventures. For those of you who have connected with me over the years, you already know that I spent just under twenty four months between 2014 and 2015 writing the eight volumes that would comprise Krög's legacy, and trust me when I say it takes a certain degree of inward discipline to pen a story that spans nearly nine hundred thousand words. So too, the path to becoming published absorbs a great deal of my time out of the view of others, and requires singular focus on my part as an individual.

That said, I would be completely remiss in dismissing the continued encouragement of my readers and Krög's newfound fans, and the impact it has had on my crafting the Battle Prince's saga. Let's be honest- not every day is a good day, even in a fairytale kingdom of your own making. I have only so much control over the ultimate fate of Krög as he relates to the, so called, "real world," even if I ultimately decided how his adventures would play out long ago. In the moments I felt this project was not as worth pursuing, or that I had forgotten the initial passion that drove along the writing process when I first began, I was thankfully called back to a place of excitement by a new reader taking their first steps along the path of the Battle Prince.

So, it is a much more difficult thing to name names and point to individuals that stoked the continued fire of this project, as it has transformed into a community of voices who have become enchanted with Krög and his companions. To those of you who read Volume 1 and immediately clamored for the next installment, to those of you who have reached out to me personally to discuss and delve into the characters and their motivations, and to those of you who have shared your equal excitement at seeing the Battle Prince slowly come into the world, I offer this:

In no uncertain terms, unequivocally and irrevocably, Thank You. I very literally could not have continued to create what I did without your support and interest.

Decidedly there are still little moments or quirky happenings that are direct influences of those whom have inspired me most directly. Yes, Aaron and Lindsay, I absolutely did write the argument on the proper pronunciation of Krög's name to settle the argument between you two. Lee's weapons lesson, word for word, almost directly mirrors things my ballroom dance instructor, Hannah, says to me when we practice- and things I would stupidly say in response. And Mike, if you had not referred to the saga as my "magnificent octopus" at that street corner cafe almost three years ago, literally one of the most hilarious and fantastical stories of the saga might never have come to be.

It would be easy to carry on like this, and continue to point out all the subtle influencers and inspiration sources. I could keep on raving about the unbelievable works of art Jon creates for the covers of these books, or share the rousing discussions of fantasy and fiction I held with Garrett at my favorite coffee shop that shaped some of my later decisions in Krög's world. At the end of the day though, so much of these influences have been so woven into the fabric of the story, separating all of them out would be a rather frolic task.

So again, I will say this to the body of readers who have adopted my junior warlord, and are looking forward to another series of ridiculous, preposterous, sarcastic, eye-rolling, cringe-inducing misadventures...

Thank you.   Thank you all, sincerely and earnestly. I hope you find the stories contained herein a suitable followup, and that you are left with an equally excited desire to see what is yet to come as we sail on towards Volume 3 and beyond...

Krög's stories have only just begun, and his road to heroism is a long one. As one reader said "it's like seeing the awkward teenage years of Achilles."   So buckle up everyone- have fun, laugh readily and face-palm heartily. Welcome to that mystical place at the edge of autumn... welcome to The Waning Days of Summer.

Cover Illustrations, Layout and Artwork Courtesy of
Jonathan Hunt, Copyright 2016

There is only one person I trust to get it right when I say
"I want to do a book cover that looks like a combination
of a 1950's monster movie poster, and an H.P. Lovecraft
nightmare."

His name is Jon Hunt. He is the man.

And so begins our tale…

Regarding An Unfortunate Picnic In Troll Country

Not long after taming Raicleach, the last Grand Dragon of the Southern Reach, Krög, the Battle Prince, found himself unfortunately without adventure and sorely at want for travel. He was restless and suffered greatly from wanderlust, an affliction that went largely untreated within the heavy stone walls of his father's Great Hall. North of their borders, over the raging Swordsong River, a war was taking place in the Ivory City of Fanfarra. Though Krög had begged to be allowed to take part in the campaign and lead the barbarian hordes against the pirate invaders and their eccentric Captain, Mordenall, the prince had been denied the escapade in favor of more seasoned leaders. This, of course, only served to antagonize the young ruler's fidgety moods further. Coupled with a strange company of odd characters he had recently acquired as "friends," all of whom were just as bored to hell as he was, Krög found unease gnawing at his consciousness while the long days of summer waned towards the prowling chill of autumn.

At first, the prince tried to fill his time with tasks of a dutiful nature... if begrudgingly so. He engaged in activities that served to better prepare him for the day he might at last take to the front lines, and would also make the Battle King proud. War School welcomed Krög back with ringing steel and flashing swords. Teachers that once found him a disinterested and detached student discovered the youthful prince had returned from his recent travels a more focused and determined warrior. The young ruler's humiliating defeat at the hands of one of his own captains notwithstanding, the Battle Prince was encouraged to greater skill by a swelling confidence garnered from a few haphazard victories in the face of true danger. Well, true-ish danger. All the same, he swung swifter, struck truer and stood stronger against every sparring partner, grizzled instructor or anxious challenger that crossed blades with him. It was all, however, practice, and Krög badly wanted to bury his family's sword in the skull of something big and mean- for real. He was one of the very few barbarians in the whole of the frontier nation who had never actually killed anything. The skulls and trophies of the Great Hall taunted him to add to the grisly collection.

When the Battle Prince was under the most scrutiny to be productive with his time, his other chores helped him to burn daylight while appearing to work towards the betterment of the kingdom. He held court with the Battle Queen and the Council of Elders to review the affairs of the land. He and the Battle King discussed the status of treaties and accords with their neighboring countries. When he was not in class, Krög maintained his family's estate and belongings; mostly the work entailed shoeing horses, sweeping leaves out of the Great Hall or polishing the artifacts hanging about the mighty fortress- all menial tasks his father insisted upon him performing to keep the young royal humble and grounded. Occasionally, the prince would find an odd job around town he sincerely enjoyed assisting with, such as working alongside the local blacksmiths, cutting lumber with the carpenters and laying mortar for the masons. It was all a routine of some of the more useful tasks that were meant to imbue him with the necessary knowledge to be a warrior-cunning-in-battle, and a frontiersman-strong-in-ability.

However, on the rare day occurred a perfect storm of boredom, which left the Battle Prince bereft of anything constructive do with his time- or even something mundane to accomplish for his kingdom. Usually these were the days War School gave its students off for rest and recuperation, and the Council of Elders and Warlords were away busying themselves with the colossal task of reassuring one another's self-importance. The Battle King refused to let Krög have a moment to himself for fear of what madcap adventure the wild-eyed prince might end up contriving on his own. Accordingly, during those periods of emptiness, the old man always heaped tasks on his son that precipitated monumental amounts of eye-rolling and foot-dragging. None were more loathsome, none more terrifying, none more heart-stopping than when the old man told Krög to spend time with the young ruler's betrothed: the stunningly gorgeous and perilously vapid Lady Ydal, who was still taking refuge in the Southern Reach while her home was under siege.

It was during the late morning hours of one such day when the Battle Prince quickly realized he had almost entirely run out of tasks to muddle through. The fear of being commanded to court Ydal started to burble up in Krög's chest. From their first meeting, the two had *exactly* nothing to say to one another. It was an awkwardness that was only exacerbated by the prince's growing attraction to the lithe, impish Lee, who had in turn realized how uncomfortable her presence made the engaged pair. Naturally, the spritely young woman liked to crash in on Krög and Ydal's interactions as often as possible. To make matters worse, the disgusting little dragon, Scale, had all but abandoned Krög's shoulder for a fairer perch on the arm of the princess, and had it in his mind to devour anyone who dared insult or look sideways at the Lady- including the prince. At one time, the young ruler found Scale's insistence on dining on human flesh simply an unseemly facet to the miniature dragon's increasingly questionable charm, and often felt the little monster's, mostly, empty threats towards Lee were the universe's way of getting even with her for annoying Krög at every turn. However, as soon as the prince realized he had made the short list for menu items, he stopped finding it funny. At all.

Frantically, Krög tried to settle on some way to occupy himself so the Battle King would not find the young ruler in the completely unacceptable position of having free time on his hands. His choices were limited to digging up a sparring partner for the charade of pretending to spend extra time on his weapons handling- but it was unlikely given most of his classmates were using the day to catch up on their own chores or resting. Alternatively, the prince could disappear from the Fortress City for the day and think up a convincing lie on his way home as to the absence of his presence. The later was far more likely, though he also reasoned having a few accomplices might allow for a better fabricated alibi.

If nothing else, he could feed off the creativity of his fellow conspirators to come up with a solid fib. There was really only one person Krög trusted to brew up the best mischief and cook up the wildest, yet believable, tall tales- which was odd given how short she was.

Of course, as the Battle Prince strode swiftly through the streets of the Fortress City, he did everything his mental acrobatics could possibly allow to convince himself he was not seeking out her company to squeeze in some alone time with the girl. Now, Lee was already exceedingly good at catching the young ruler in his most uncomfortable moments with Ydal, to add her own sweet venom to the situations. However, the sly, athletic woman had become positively talented at finding ways to get Krög by himself- mostly to laugh at the prince's befuddlement over how smitten he was with her. As irksome as her trademark brand of snark and wit was, Lee did have some legitimate sway over the young ruler's head and heart... as well as other regions he would rather not mention in front of her for fear of turning deep crimson. So, despite all the trouble she caused, Krög would seek out her attention when it did not seem *too* obvious, and find ways to spirit Lee away somewhere they could be out from under the judging eyes of those expecting him to marry Ydal.

For good measure, the Battle Prince also decided he would need to find his burly and towering Honor Guard, the troll Ashley. Apart from the fact Krög just did not feel safe anymore leaving the protection of the Great Hall without his nigh-invincible shield knight, Ash was hands down his sincerest friend, and the prince refused to go adventuring without the gentle giant in tow. On reflection, the young ruler realized he sort of understood why Lee liked to make him squirm so much, as Krög delighted in involving the upright and earnest troll in his own troublemaking- only to watch Ash sweat it out as he tried to fumble his way through an explanation as to why he had allowed the prince to waltz into such bouts of youthful rebellion. And youthful rebellion was really straining what youth Krög actually had left. Being more than two and a half decades old the young ruler detested being looked after, but if he had to have any babysitter, Ashley would always be his first, last and only choice.

The order in which the Battle Prince located his two most stalwart and ridiculous companions would be critical to accomplishing the morning's newly planned disappearing act. Ash would almost certainly be training with Val Gavisorm, one of the standing Honor Guards to the Battle King. Val, being the junior of the old man's knights, had been charged with passing on the duties and responsibilities of an Honor Guard to the troll. The lessons were always an unwieldy experience between the two. Val had been practically nursed on stories of how Röm, the First Battle King, lead the burgeoning barbarian nation to victory over the bloodthirsty monsters of the forests in the Great Troll War. Couple that with the fact Ashley was so titanic he was already dramatically stronger, faster and more powerful than the battle-hardened shield knight he was supposed to be learning from, and it quickly became difficult to tell who was learning from who. Interrupting such a cumbersome session meant Krög would have to find a way to casually engage both in conversation, before lying through his teeth to Val to get the troll away. Once again, there was really only one person charming enough to pull it off, and it was not the prince. He had to find Lee.

Looking for Lee and actually locating the pint-sized hellion were two entirely different, disparate and often incongruent activities. It was akin to the difference in stacking bricks and building a towering monument- the undertakings were similar in principle, but colossally different in practice. Krög could just as often find her traipsing through the Fortress City's town square and dancing around the maypole, as he could practically bang heads with the girl as she hung upside down from some odd anchoring just for the fun of seeing the world from a different angle. Oftentimes, if he could at least pick up her trail, the prince just had to follow the only footprints in the dust on the streets that were not heavily treaded boots, but tiny impressions of toe pads and the crescent moon shape of her soles. It assumed, of course, she had been walking on the streets when Lee was often given to skipping along fences, rooftops and walls with her uncanny balance. Krög decided to try one of her favorite haunts: the stable where the Griffin Riders put up their mounts when paying a visit to the Battle King's Great Hall.

For the most part, the Battle Prince had pretty much come to peace with the fact Lee had a girlish, though not completely misplaced, crush on the dashing, muscular, mildly arrogant, Captain of the Riders, Iolar. Krög was also willing to bet half his father's kingdom and a third of his mother's crown jewels the very reason the lithe young woman liked the stable so much was the chance she might run into the badlands flyboy as he returned from the front lines in the Ivory City. Though he could not really hide his jealousy, the young ruler also had found his way to a certain decidedness that Lee only fawned over the Captain so much so as to get a rise out of the prince. The two had discussed exactly those conditions in the deep reaches of the Grand Dragon's cave, but the Battle Prince was yet unsure she actually meant what she said in entirety. Lee was full of convincing half-truths, if she felt like holding back the full story would help her get her way, something that made it very difficult for Krög to believe a single word out of her mouth. Still, he was slowly learning to trust there were some topics she did not beat around the bush. She and the prince were gravitating towards one another, and she largely expected their attraction alone to carry him through her more frustrating traits. Then, one of the prince's own frustrating traits was his complete and total inability to act reasonably on that edict. It often left them on shaky ground, at best.

Another reason the young ruler believed Lee liked the stable so much was the peace and solitude it afforded when the Griffin Riders were away. It had been constructed only to house the great onyx birds, and when they were not taking residence, there was little to no use for the structure. It often stood silent and empty. As much as Lee loved being the absolute center of attention, Krög had begun to notice there was a much more reserved and softer side to her, which she largely kept for herself. The young woman occasionally slipped away to quiet contemplation in the open roofed stable, or sometimes even miles from the bustling Fortress City. He had said enough in the way of envious, churlish and downright stupid things to Lee to learn that when he had legitimately hurt her feelings, which was exceedingly rare, she usually retreated to one of her hushed thinking places. The Battle Prince decided the stable was his best bet.

Ah, to clarify, the prince did not think it was his best bet because he had recently offended Lee- it just seemed like a likely place to start. At least, he was fairly certain he had not recently offended her. Then, as Lee would tell you, he was rather stupid, so it was entirely possible. The Battle Prince proceeded with caution.

As soon as Krög stumbled into the raptor's stalls, he greeted with the familiar whistle-thump of a knife spinning through the air and burying its blade in a target. Of course, he was barely two steps into the building when the singing of the knives went suddenly silent and a heavy mute swallowed the room. The Battle Prince stiffened and darted his eyes around the chamber, trying to catch a glimpse of a floating shadow that might betray Lee's presence. All he heard was the rustle of the breeze as it breathed its way through the hay on the floor of some of the griffin's stalls. He had learned all too well a sound as faint as wind in straw was just deafening enough to mask the movement of the stealthy girl, and the young ruler kept his senses alert and muscles tense for her to spring on him. Several very long, very taut moments passed as Krög stood in the entrance, searching the cracks and corners of the stable for any sign of the tiny woman.

"Hi, prince!" Lee's bright, bubbly voice about made the Battle Prince jump out of of his skin.

"Lee, damn!" Krög stuttered in reply as he tried to calm his heart rate. He spun around to find her, assuredly, hanging upside down, fair hair falling in a goofy mane, smiling widely at him.

"Oh my," she crossed her arms in mock disapproval, "Somebody needs to relax a bit. Too much stress being waited on hand and foot?"

"Can you please talk to me like a normal person," the Battle Prince pleaded, "You know, face-to-face. Right side up."

"Fine," Lee huffed, disappointed, before performing a spectacular dismount from the beam she was dangling from and landing only inches away from Krög, "Is that better Mr. Rules-of-Society? You know, for a barbarian, you have an awfully strange sense of conventional decorum."

"Don't come at me sideways just because I'm halfway normal," the prince threw up his hands defensively.

"I'm normal too!" Lee responded, chipper, "I'm just *me* normal, just like you are *you* normal. Of course, when compared to the general tone of *normal* normal, neither one of us looks particularly so- wouldn't you agree?"

Krög narrowed his eyes and tried to follow her zippy speech, "Yes?"

She laughed musically, "So, what brings you to my castle?" she gestured grandly at the stable around her, "I heard you have been searching far and wide for me, the princess fair," Lee batted her eyes dramatically at Krög and pressed herself up into his personal space.

"How did you hear that? I haven't told anyone," the Battle Prince took a nervous step back.

"A little mouse told me a tall, mopey, broody prince was stomping about my kingdom searching high and low for me, the Viscountess of Vivaciousness," she announced as she lilted in circles around the young ruler, "And besides... you're *always* looking for me."

"I'm not always looking for you," Krög snorted, trying to disguise his all too transparent intentions.

"That was not an outright denial," Lee winked and smirked, "So, prince, now you have found me. What do you wish of me?" the mischievous young woman stroked his cheek with a stray shed griffin feather, "Or, what do you wish *with* me?"

The Battle Prince did his best to hold the intense stare of her crystalline eyes, "What are you up to today, Lee?"

"Me? I'm bored," she tousled his hair both playfully and patronizingly, "Tragically bored. Mortally bored. I have bored rot. If I do not find some way to amuse myself, I shall decay like a crawling fungus mold of bored."

"How graphic," Krög pushed her hand away, which only made her try harder to annoy him. She promptly set about trying to undue the clasps and buckles of his belts and armor, an easy feat for her small, lightning-quick hands against his frustrated and much slower attempts to stop her.

"You better have something amusing to say before I get all of these undone," Lee cautioned, "Or I imagine someone might just walk in on us in a rather comprising position, hm?"

The Battle Prince squirmed away, "I was going to ask if you wanted to go on a walk in the forest or something."

"Picnic!" Lee squealed, "Picnic, picnic, picnic, picnic!" she clapped her hands loudly with each exclamation, "Oh please, please can we go on a picnic?"

"Whoa, okay!" Krög put up his hands to quiet her, but was hindered in calming the young woman by the fact his armor, and some of his clothes, were falling off thanks to her efforts, "Keep it down! I'm trying to sneak out."

The girl's eyes went wide and she looked absolutely delighted, "Secret picnic! Even better. You bring the wine, and I'll bring the *more* wine. Maybe we can go for a secret swim afterwards," she raised her eyebrows bawdily at the young ruler.

"Yeah, so, that might be kind of weird with Ash around," the Battle Prince said slowly.

Lee's face dropped and she pouted at him, "So, secret picnic, just not secret *alone*?"

"More or less," Krög agreed.

She sighed, "I guess it's better than hanging around here all day."

"Literally," the young ruler joked, smiling slightly.

The bright young woman squinted at him, "You do know I don't hang upside down all the time, right? What do I look like, a bat?"

Krög shrugged, "I wasn't going to say anything."

Lee nodded slowly and pursed her lips, "Keep it up. You'll pay for that."

"Just, help me get Ash away from Val so we can get going," the Battle Prince huffed.

"Oh, *now* I see why I'm invited," the girl crossed her arms, "You can't charm the big barbarians yourself, and you needed someone who could."

"No, I wanted you to come along too," Krög defended unconvincingly.

Lee chewed at her tongue and considered his fumbling attempt to apologize, "You're lucky you're stupid, otherwise I might have been insulted."

"You're never insulted," the Battle Prince pointed out, half right.

"You're right!" she brightened considerably, "So, where *is* the big guy? Come on, let's get to this, I want to get out of here!"

"You know if you didn't always put up such a fight," Krög began.

Lee's eyes widened, daring the Battle Prince to finish his subjective appraisal of her free spiritedness.

"Yeah, never mind," the young ruler concluded, "Ash is in the training yards by the Warbrands' camp. He and Val are working on defensive stances and-"

"Right, that's interesting," Lee feigned boredom, "This way then?"

Krög rolled his eyes, "Yes, that way."

"Ladies first," the impish young woman swept her arms out for the young ruler to lead the way.

The Battle Prince paused, "I'm going to go first, but only because I have to get out of the city before someone finds me while you're grabbing Ash- not because you're telling me to go first."

Lee gave him a look of amusement and derision, "Gods, how old are you?! Besides, your life will get a lot easier once you accept I just win."

"You're not *always* right," Krög grumbled as they left the stable.

She pretended to think for a few moments about what he said, "You might be right. Oh wait, then if you were, I wouldn't be. Nope, I'm always right."

"You're impossible," the young ruler threw up his hands.

"And that's why you like me," Lee's voice was nothing short of bouncingly chipper.

Krög watched her swaying, dancing walk as she slipped between barbarians twice her size, darting in and out of their marching number, and wondered just what it was that went on inside her head during their conversations- or ever, really. It was almost funny: from a distance the flitting gal might have just fit in with the wild, unbridled municipality of the Fortress City. She had chosen to start dressing in the Southern Reach's manner, but with her own particular twist on the drab browns and heavy leathers of their world. In the heat of summer, Lee opted for garb that was a little cooler to don but decidedly more risqué and, in certain companies, dramatically inappropriate. All the same, were it not for her fair hair and extraneous bare skin, she would have appeared a childlike warrior of the barbarian nation with just a bit too much energy. Somehow, Lee managed to fit in wherever she went- whereas Krög found it difficult to look even part-way comfortable around the Council of Elders he was supposed to lead one day. He would say it was unfair, but his age and maturity had already been challenged by the lithe young woman, and he did not want to concede another point to her... even if it was only in his head.

Once he lost sight of Lee, which did not take long given her size and speed, Krög veered off the main roads of the Fortress City and made for its towering stone walls. His intention was to wait for the guards on the parapets to rotate, which occurred with a fair degree of routine, scale the wall, and drop off the other side before someone got wind of his passage. While the Battle Prince was far from as skilled as Lee when it came to sneaking around, it would not be the first time he had slid by the city watch to escape the Fortress City undetected. He was actually pretty good at it, although usually Krög was trying to duck out at night, which was a considerably easier feat given the cover of darkness. In broad daylight it was something of a more challenging endeavor, especially since the protective walls of the city were taller than most every structure within them. It would leave him in a position of being quite exposed as he climbed the bricks. Still, he could not worry about the consequences of getting caught. After all, if he gave them any credence, he would not be trying to slip out in the first place.

The Battle Prince tucked himself into the shadowy corner where the city walls met one of the guard towers, and watched the bouncing helmets of the patrolling barbarians at the top of the parapets wander back and forth accompanied by a dull click of boots. After a short time, it was followed by the excited scurrying of the group being relieved of their morning duties by some fellow warriors. During the dawdling trading of duties, the young ruler quickly found a toehold and finger-grip on the wall, and hauled himself up towards the sky. Braced between the tower and the rampart, Krög scaled its reaches rather quickly thanks to a fair degree of athletic strength and at least a modicum of talent. He quickly found his way to the patrol path between barricades, waited for the new guards to turn away, and skittered over the other side. It did not take the Battle Prince long to clamber down the opposite wall and slink around towards the city gates where he intended to meet up with Lee and Ash.

In the back of his mind, the young ruler wondered if he could so easily slip out of the city, how easy would it be for an Assassin Emissary like Lee to slip in? The Southern Reach's relationship with the mysterious Eastern Collective had been tenuous at best as of late, and the prince did not like the idea of a shadow warrior, or even several perhaps, stealing into the Fortress City undetected. Always Ganithen had been regarded as an impenetrable castle brimming with battle-crazed barbarians- a grim prospect for an invading force. But, times were changing, and so was warfare. No one had tried to assault the Fortress City directly in well over four decades from what Krög understood, but that precluded attacks of another persuasion. The prince wanted to bring the guards' lax surveillance to his father's attention, but if it actually meant a tightening of security27 then he would have to find a new way to sneak out. Finally, he just pushed the thought aside altogether- no one was stupid enough to attack the Great Hall. Why worry about it?

With his focus turned upwards at the guards on the walls above, Krög had barely taken three steps when he tripped on something low to the ground. Whatever he stumbled upon shrieked as it fell over, and the prince realized he had accidentally kicked a person sitting against the parapets of the city. The Battle Prince spun around and was met with the sight of an all too familiar face.

"Hi," Ydal said brusquely, a disgusted look on her countenance as she righted herself and brushed the dirt off.

"Ydal?" Krög whispered loudly, "What in the nine hells are you doing out here!?"

"Sitting," she crossed her arms and turned her gaze back towards wherever it had been before the prince tripped on her.

Krög grit his teeth in frustration, trying to reign in his discontent, but attempted to be thoughtful and concerned, "Okay. Why are you sitting out here?"

"Because," was all the princess offered in haughty explanation.

The young ruler tensed, but tried again, "Is there something wrong, maybe?"

"Nobody here likes me," the Lady spouted off rather vociferously.

Krög blinked his eyes a few times, "Are you being for real?"

"All my friends are back home, and my nice things are back home, and everything here is dirty and smells and nobody likes me," Ydal ranted with blazing abandon.

"Now, that's not *entirely* true," the Battle Prince faltered out his hazard at being comforting.

"Yes it is," the princess pouted, before turning a suspicious gaze at Krög, "What are *you* doing here."

The young ruler flitted his eyes away, "Going somewhere."

"Are you sneaking out?" Ydal stood abruptly and followed a few steps after the prince.

"Well…" Krög drifted.

"You *are* sneaking out, aren't you?!" the Lady accused rather accurately.

"Yes, okay? Yes!" the Battle Prince raised his hands to try and quiet her, "And it would be going much, much better if you weren't making so much noise."

Ydal opened her mouth as though about to scream an objection at his obtuse statement, before quickly relaxing with a demand, "Take me with you."

"Excuse me?" the prince asked.

"Take. Me. With you," she repeated with staccato jaggedness to her words, "We're supposed to be engaged, or something like that," she regarded Krög like he was a putrid puddle she did not want to touch, "So, take me with you."

"This isn't a good time," it was exactly what the Battle Prince was trying to avoid: spending the day with Ydal. Although, he was starting to feel bad at how depressed and lonely she was in their city.

"So I guess we'll only spend time together when we're married?" the princess shot back.

"That's kind of the idea," Krög said a little insensitively, before quickly following with, "Don't take it personally."

"See?!" Ydal almost screamed, "Nobody likes me!"

She sat down again, and immediately began bawling. It was, perhaps, a little forced.

The Battle Prince yanked at his hair and stifled a groan in exasperation, "Look, it's just, I kind of need some time away from everyone."

"I bet you're taking the big, stinking troll and not me," Ydal wailed louder, "He's ugly and nasty and you'd rather take walks in the forest with *him*. What is wrong with you?! What's wrong with *me*?"

The prince had never actually seen someone cry so heartily without producing any tears whatsoever. It was borderline fascinating.

"There's nothing wrong with you," Krög's tone turned pleading.

The Lady immediately halted her, mostly, false weeping, "Then take me with you."

"I'm just going somewhere you'll end up dirty," the Battle Prince tried to appeal to her vanity.

Ydal switched to threats, "Take me with you or I'll tell your father you snuck out and left me behind."

"I'll just tell him I was on an errand," Krög tried unconvincingly.

"Really?" the princess raised an eyebrow, "What kind of errand?"

The young ruler narrowed his eyes, "An important one."

"Such brilliance," Ydal scoffed, "Who do you think he's going to believe: his troublemaker son who ducks out of every responsibility he can, or the beautiful diplomat from a nation he's negotiating with?"

She had a point. She knew it, Krög knew it.

"Walk fast," he relented.

The princess did not smile or give thanks. She just shot him a curt look and followed as close to Krög as she could without actually looking like she had any association to the Battle Prince.

Together, the Lady and the prince skirted around the gargantuan walls of the Fortress City towards its northernmost gate where Ash and Lee were sure to be waiting. It had only been a few minutes, and already Krög was resenting Ydal's interruption, whose presence alone assured they would be taking the whole trip much slower than he had meant to. One thing the Battle Prince liked about adventuring with Lee and the troll, was the fitness and exhilaration of their movement. They liked to run. A lot. And so did Krög. Not over long distances, really, but in short, excited bursts just to let off some steam and feel the rush of the wind. Ydal did everything with slow purpose, which lent her an undeniable regality, but made her an irritatingly slow traveling partner. He did not foresee any hurried, excited sprints through the tangles of the Thorn Rift Forest as they set out across the fields.

Predictably, Ashley and the spritely young woman were milling about just outside the gate, trying to look like they were out for a nonchalant stroll in the late afternoon sunshine. Lee did not even try to mask her sarcastic contempt when Krög walked up with Ydal.

"I see you brought another friend," Lee clasped her hands together and feigned romanticism, "Secret picnic is turning into *crowded* picnic."

"You were going out for the day with *her*?! And not me?!" Ydal did not miss the uncomfortable realization it implied.

"Let's all try and play nice, huh?" Krög muttered back at her.

"I'm not leaving without dragon," Ydal stopped in place as the group met up.

Ashley tried to be as diplomatic as possible, like always, "Good day, Lady. Is nice for to see you again."

"See?" the princess gestured at the troll, "If you get to bring *your* monster, I get to bring *mine*."

"Ydal, Ash is not a monster," the Battle Prince defended his large friend, "He's my Honor Guard. And we don't have time to go looking for Scale anyway."

"Will make conversation with you, if want," Ash offered the Lady.

Ydal completely ignored the troll, "I want dragon."

"She is just a treat," Lee clapped and chuckled, "And for the record, the next patrol rotates this way pretty soon, so we might want to pick up the pace if we're not looking to get caught."

"How do you know that?" Krög asked.

Lee just gave him a knowing look.

"Look, Ydal," the Battle Prince turned back towards the princess, "I'm guessing the reason I found you hiding outside the wall is you're avoiding something too. So it's probably a good bet *you've* got no interest in getting caught either. What's it going to be? We go back in and try and find Scale, or get this fun little circus on the road?"

"Circus is right- you always bring out the freaks," Ydal huffed loudly, before relenting, "Fine, let's go."

Ignoring her gall, Krög faked a bow, "Thank you," he then looked around, a little confused, "Where is your pet anyway?"

"Eating someone," the princess said offhandedly, examining her fingernails.

"Great," the Battle Prince snorted, before turning to his shield-knight, "Nice to you see you, buddy," he rapped the troll on the shoulder.

"Greetings, Battle Prince," Ash grinned between his tusks at seeing his friend.

"Hooray, everyone is happy! Or at least only moderately annoyed," Lee celebrated, "Getting bored again, and I was promised a picnic."

"And we're off," Krög swung his arms and started to hustle the group away from the city walls, anxious to be hidden in the tree-line.

The late afternoon was warm and pleasant, and the heat of summer was trying to push its way to noontide dominance- even though the season was growing late. Days were still long and lazy, the sun was high in the sky, there was not a cloud in sight, and the radiant warmth of the great yellow fire above cascaded pleasantly across Krög's face and arms as a slight breeze ruffled his hair about.   A few weeks still remained until autumn's true chill began to creep its grasping fingers into their country, but the prince could already sense the changing the of the season from that one errant breeze. He could practically smell the drying of the leaves and feel the mountain's cold on the back of an eastern wind. The Southern Reach yet belonged to summer's embrace, though.   Krög's group most certainly had a hot, beautiful day in front of them as their little troupe tramped across the rolling fields north of the Fortress City and made for the tree-line.

Thankfully, even Ydal respected the silent sanctity of the hushed region of the Thorn Rift Forest Ashley called 'The Quiets' enough to shut right up when they passed into the soundless jungle.   There was a blessed lack of conversation between the squabbling friends as they wandered into the arbor sanctuary.   The Battle Prince always liked the way the sun dappled its way through the leaves to speckle the floor of the glade. He stepped carefully as they crunched through the wicked carpet of ferocious thorns that covered the ground. Lee climbed to her perch on Ashley's shoulder in an effort to preserve her own skin, and Ydal tiptoed around daintily to avoid the severe points.   Only the troll could crash through the sharp brush with little regard, so thick was his hide and heavy his boots. He still moved with a surprising amount of noiselessness- especially given his size. Within hours they were beyond the bizarre, magical realm of The Strange and had descended into the calmest, least haunted region of the forest: River Glen.

Lee dismounted from the troll and stretched, longingly eyeing a pool of water off the main river, clearly interested in diving into its crisp, cool depths. Ydal settled herself next to a tree on a patch of ground clear of thorns and considered their surroundings with a certain amount of disdain- although, she did not appear altogether incensed by the lovely oasis they had found. Krög wiped the sweat off his forehead and made idle conversation with his guardian while the others relaxed.

"How're you doing today, Ash?" the Battle Prince stretched his own limbs and took in the opulence of the rushing Swordsong River.

"Little tired. Honor Guard Val have very good workout this morning," Ashley said, "Him very strong warrior, would make excellent friend in battle."

"Yeah, he taught me everything I know," Krög nodded in agreement, just glad to be away from home, "And if you're tired, I bet he's exhausted."

Ash shrugged, not wanting to admit the truth of it and nominalize a warrior he had deep respect for, "Am sure him energy strong too. How you affairs of kingdom?"

"Oh, you know," the prince shrugged, "Fine, I guess. I'd rather be back on the road or helping Uncle Gögan with the campaign in the Ivory City. There's more excitement there."

"War not so exciting," the troll furrowed his brow, "Just lot of pain and death. There better adventures to be had."

"You're probably right," Krög admitted, always preferring Ashley's lessons and wisdom over the bunk he had to swallow from the elders, "Still, tell me you wouldn't want another shot at that Mordenall character. I'd love to go five rounds with that maniac again."

"Him maybe more cunning than you give credit," Ash cautioned, "Manage to escape first time, after all. Is probably not easy get become head of so many pirates- probably have to take control by force, which make him powerful foe."

"You know, if it weren't for you, I would probably have tripped into my own grave by now," Krög laughed.

"Fighting all concern Battle Prince with kingdom?" the troll queried.

"No, the rest just isn't as interesting," the young ruler sighed, "Or maybe interesting is the wrong word for the war."

Ashley followed Krög's gaze towards Lee wading around in the pool of water, "You attention divided. You focus off."

"Can you blame me?" the Battle Prince lowered his voice, "I mean, look at her, Ash. I've never even heard of a girl like her before, much less actually seen one."

"Battle King say she not to be yours," the troll said quietly, an edge of disappointment in his own voice. Though he tried to get along with everyone, even Ashley drastically preferred the company of Lee on his shoulder, far more than the judging eyes of Ydal on his face.

"Yeah. Dad made that pretty clear," Krög scoffed.

"Did not mean to offend," Ash backed off a bit.

"No, it's not you," the Battle Prince sighed, "It's him. Or, it's her," he gestured at Lee, "Or, neither of them really. Just this whole 'you're going to be king and tell everyone what to do one day, but until then you have to do everything *we* tell *you*' act," the young ruler jabbered, full of snark, "I'm closer to thirty than I am to fifteen, but everyone still treats me like some ornery teenager."

"Is certainly difficult being brought to have such power, but not feeling like any of it yours yet," the troll supported his friend, rather than making a deprecating remark about Krög's actual lack of sophistication.

"I mean, we've had this conversation before," the Battle Prince shifted his stance, "How am I supposed to lead one day if I'm never given a chance to do anything on my own?"

"Battle King will give you chance when him ready," Ashley assured the young ruler.

"Whenever that is," Krög snorted, "He still looks at me like I get out of everything I get into on sheer luck and stupid happenstance."

"Well," even the troll could not ignore it, "Him does have certain precedent."

Instead of being cut, the Battle Prince laughed, "Alright, fine. But, I give you my word- I will 'hero' my way out of the next predicament we get into."

"Would very much like to see that," Ashley chuckled.

"You're not the only one," Ydal was standing directly behind the two, "Did we come out here for any particular reason? Isn't there supposed to be food, or something?"

"Someone's been spending too much time with Scale," Krög joked.

"Will find Lady something to make humble lunch offering more appetizing," Ashley bowed his head to her, "Return soon with maybe berries or fruit."

The mighty troll took his bag off his shoulder and presented it as dutifully as he could to Ydal. She reached out, suspicious at first, but when she opened it to find the sack full of breads, meats and cheeses Ash and Lee had clearly packed for a group meal, the princess softened insomuch as she was capable.

"That would be very kind of you," her pompous air was only half present, "Now then. On your way."

Ash, who technically saw himself as reporting to the Battle Family, looked quickly to Krög for approval.

"Go ahead, big guy," the Battle Prince motioned his friend off.

The troll nodded swiftly, and strode off into the brush to forage for some sweeter additions to their lunch.

"Good to see him being useful for once," Ydal held her head a little too high.

"Thanks for at least *trying* to be nice," Krög mumbled back. He brushed past the Lady and headed down towards the pool beneath them where Lee was still mucking about.

"Where are you going?" the princess whined after him.

"For a swim," the prince motioned to the clear waters a little ways below.

"You can't," Ydal insisted, "Men and women should not bathe together in decent company."

"Who said anything about bathing?" Krög snickered, "I'm swimming. You know, splashing about, playing in the water- you have been swimming right?"

The princess gave him a look, "Of course. It still means you'll have to be," she struggled to find the right word, "Without proper clothing."

"Naked, right. Generally one is when swimming," the Battle Prince agreed, his tone unsure where the problem was.

"It's not appropriate," Ydal came back.

"Yeah, well," Krög gave her a mock helpless gesture, "I'm a barbarian. Inappropriate is practically my middle name."

The Lady rolled her eyes and shouted after him, "I bet your middle name is really something like Chester or... or... Leopold!"

"It's what they'll put on my epitaph," the young ruler called back, "Röm, the First. Lödrek, the Conqueror. Krög, the Inappropriate."

Ydal crossed her arms and planted herself, "Jerk."

The Battle Prince loped downhill towards the oasis pool where Lee had started kicking about in the water playfully, splashing as much as she could just to see the clear diamonds spring off the surface and glitter in the sunlight. Her hair was matted rather adorably against her head, the bright, fair mane sticking out at odd ends. She giggled to herself as she waded around and waved Krög down to her.

"It's cold!" the young woman exclaimed, "But it feels nice on a day like this. Come on in."

"Hold on, let me put my sword down," the young ruler answered.

Lee laughed, "Honestly, prince, your priorities- such a barbarian."

"Would you prefer I bring the lighting-making sword into your giant puddle?" Krög challenged sarcastically as he undid the buckles on his baldric that held Thundersteel in place.

"Nah," she shrugged and winked, "I can think of some better ways to get the sparks going."

"You're incorrigible," the Battle Prince laughed.

Lee spotted Ydal standing at the top of the little ridge, pouting, but too proud to actually give in and join the other two, "Awe, is the pretty princess not going to join us?"

"I don't think Ydal can get wet," Krög joked, "It's like with wool: I think she'd shrink or something."

The spritely girl laughed hard enough to fall over backwards into the pool, "Well, we can't have that," she said as she pushed herself out of the shallows, soaking wet, "Then she and I would be on the same level, and she'd actually have to look me in the eye. Where's big guy?"

"Ashley's getting us some fruit or berries for lunch I think," the Battle Prince told her, "He just left."

Lee pricked up, mischievously, "Did he? So, crowded secret picnic is back to just secret picnic."

Krög laughed, "Not really. Ydal's still right up there."

"She is, she is," the impish girl agreed, "But I bet she can't run so fast in that dress."

The Battle Prince tensed, "What did you have in mind?"

Lee flashed a brilliant smile and lowered her gaze a bit, "Catch me if you can, prince."

In a flash, the young woman burst out of the pool and bounded deeper into the forest, leaving only a splash of water and a trail of laughs behind her. Krög watched for a moment in awe as Lee high-stepped through patches of angry thorns, kicked off the trunks of trees to leap higher over the larger brambles, and swung from dangling vines or trotted across long limbs to stay off the ground completely. She was like watching a jungle predator in pursuit of its prey, sprinting, dancing and springing from one clear patch to the next in an extraordinary display of acrobatic talent and general free-spirited jubilation. Within the space of only a few well placed jumps and dashes, Lee was almost already far enough into the dense Thorn Rift Forest she had nearly vanished from sight.

Krög hung back a moment. He cast his eyes rapidly back and forth between the disappearing sprite who had challenged him to race to exactly nowhere, and the statuesque but very prissy princess who was standing at the lip of the oasis also watching Lee run deeper into the brush, her own jaw dropped open. The Battle Prince was torn between his rather limited sense of duty, and his bolstered desire for adventure offered by the two women. On the one hand, his father would probably skin him alive if he found out the young ruler had left the Northern Empire's heir and his own betrothed standing alone in the middle of an admittedly dangerous timberland. On the other, Lee always had the most fun of anyone he knew, and the whole reason he had tried to sneak out of the Fortress City was to spend time with her anyway. His responsibility to crown and kingdom, and the part of him who just wanted to do whatever he wanted and damn the consequences, were playing a match of tug-of-war with his sense of action.

In the end, Krög's less than altruistic and noble side won out, and he scampered up the opposite side of the oasis to give chase after Lee. He turned and shrugged at Ydal in a weak attempt to offer some kind of apology, but the Battle Prince just ended up opening his mouth stupidly for a moment without saying anything, before racing after the young woman still floating through the bush. Without her lithe athleticism, the young ruler was reduced to crashing his way through the carpet of thorns, stumbling and tripping along the way, always half a step away from falling face first into the wicked points jutting up out of the ground. Behind him, Krög could hear Ydal screeching some vehement objection to his latest caper and most recent plot to leave her behind, but his senses were quickly overwhelmed with just trying to keep sight of Lee as he tried desperately to catch up to her.

The Battle Prince had the longer, lean frame of a sprinter, and was naturally suited to quick bursts of acceleration and surprising speed- when he was on flat terrain unchallenged by jagged roots and brambles. Ever the acrobat, Lee was far more able-bodied for skirting the small spaces and slipping between narrow gaps. Though the young ruler was much taller and probably physically stronger than the small woman, she was infinitely more dexterous and in much better condition than he was, and Krög had a very difficult time closing the gap between them. It felt like every other step he took he was tripping on something or stumbling over something else, whereas she took to the formidable terrain like it were a playground she was just skipping through. The Battle Prince moved like a boulder tumbling down a mountainside, whereas Lee flowed like a breeze through the branches. In no time at all, Krög's heart was racing and his lungs heaving as he hurtled after the wild girl always ten steps ahead of him.

Much to the young ruler's shock and amazement, he found his steps being matched suddenly by an absolutely livid, but extraordinarily graceful Ydal. Even in her long Battle Maiden dress fashioned for her by the Battle Queen's house of waiting, the princess had a considerable stride that carried her over the thorns in the way a deer might prance along. Her long, flowing chestnut hair carried in a train behind her like some kind of shimmering banner at the start of a parade. As she effortlessly bounded up next to him Ydal fixed Krög with a look of infuriated fervor and spoke, unfaltering, no trace of effort in her breath.

"You are NOT leaving me behind!" the princess's words were even, not ragged like the young ruler felt assured his own would be.

"Ydal," Krög kept his sentences short, "Just wait for Ash!"

"No!" she screamed back at him, "I'm not getting left with the troll just so you can go play with her!"

"Suit yourself," the Battle Prince gasped, "Just, keep up if you can."

"I'm not the one out of breath, barbarian," the Lady hollered at him.

Ahead, Lee had heard Ydal's shouting and had poured on an extra burst of speed to try and outdistance the other woman. Krög pushed himself faster and harder hoping his lungs would not give out before he and the small girl had a chance to put some serious space between them and the pursuing princess. He fixed his concentration on Lee as she rushed on quicker and tried to steady his heart rate to keep up the effort. Greenery and tree trunks flashed by in the edges of his vision as he snorted for air and struggled to keep his feet beneath him. Not Krög, nor Ydal, nor Lee, in their blazing race, seemed to notice a rotting, splintered, ominous sign planted in the ground almost totally overgrown with thorns. Wreathed by human skulls and dangling with other bones, the plank was carved with only two words that should have made all three of them turn back immediately and retreat to the safety of River Glen, or even the weird atmosphere of The Strange.

The sign read: "Troll Country."

Lee was gaining ground on Krög and Ydal, and she laughed errantly as she flitted faster into the horizon before them. The princess was having no trouble keeping up on the Battle Prince's heels, but neither one had quite the leg speed to run down the spritely young woman ahead. Through fevered pants, Krög watched Lee dance about as she leapt over brambles and bounced off tree trunks, just absolutely having a hysterically fun time racing away into the brush. The young ruler snorted loudly to clear his lungs and charged on, determined to not only stay after the bobbing blonde mane before him, but to somehow lose Ydal in the process as well. It was a difficult task, and it made him sorely wish he had spent more time in War School focusing on conditioning and strength training, rather than just combat. What happened next, however, defied Krög's imagination and turned an otherwise pleasant afternoon romp in the forest into an inexplicably strange fight for survival.

Something nearly imperceptible to the human eye whipped out of the jungle ahead, and slapped Lee off her feet. Whatever it was, it sent the small girl flailing end over end through the air. Krög, astonished and concerned, immediately changed course to chase after where he thought she had landed, his eyes searching the forest for whatever it was that struck her in the first place. He was barely a few paces farther on when the trees above exploded with activity, and a great black thing came hurtling out of the branches. It, too, was a blur of movement so furious the prince could barely tell what it was. The young ruler heard Ydal scream as the creature in the trees landed on her. Krög wrenched his head around to see what had happened to the princess as he sprinted, and saw the Lady disappear under the mass of what could only be described as a six foot long, flat bodied beetle. Before he could decide whether to run to her aid or Lee's, Krög smashed into something tough and immobile.

At first, the young ruler assumed he had run headlong into a moss covered tree trunk, such was the girth and sturdiness of the object he struck, though there was a certain softness to it as well. The Battle Prince tumbled clumsily to the ground and looked up through dazed eyes to meet three staring faces, bulbous and crooked, drooling before equally vacant gazes. As his vision cleared, the young ruler realized he had bounced off the gut of an ogre, and was consummately surrounded by a few of its fellows. Krög largely ignored the throbbing pain in his head and sharp agony in his hands and back from landing in a patch of jagged thorns to take in his new predicament, as fears and concerns for both Lee and Ydal raced through his mind.

Ogres were the smallest of the Giant Kin, though still quite large. Most stood a little taller than the Honor Guard Val, somewhere around seven and a half to just below eight feet tall. They were closest in relative to the trolls, but quite a bit more primitive and far less physically developed. Whereas trolls were broad-shouldered, stout and square-jawed, ogres were slope-backed and narrow-armed, with bulging bellies and stumpy legs. While the majority of trolls were not especially known for extraordinary wit, ogres were notoriously stupid and dull, easily distracted by shiny objects or tasty smelling foods. Ogres also had faces that were blobby and misshapen, unlike the atavistic but ultimately symmetrical countenances of trolls, usually punctuated by drooping noses, flapping ears and warped jaws full of teeth pointing at all angles. They were also quite rare to come across- the trolls had enough foresight to retreat from the Southern Reach when the tides of the Great Troll War turned on them, but the ogres fought almost to their last, and their entire population had been summarily decimated. Mostly, they existed as errand-runners and miners for their larger cousins, and it was exceedingly unique to encounter them outside the company of other giants.

For all their shortcomings and oddities, ogres were none the less extremely strong and extremely dangerous, and Krög was faced with three of them without his sword. The Battle Prince reasoned he was faster than them, but he was tired already from sprinting after Lee and there was also the impossible choice of whether to first save the athletic young woman, or the princess who had been overtaken by the huge bug. Indecision and hesitancy struck the young ruler like a blow to the stomach, and he lay there in the brambles like an idiot, staring up at the slobbering ogres who were staring blankly right back at him. Krög decided the most obvious answer had to be the best one, and he scrambled to his feet and took off like a shot between the towering monsters. He got about three steps before a heavy fingered, two foot long hand slapped him back to the ground.

"Him stupid," one of the ogres burbled, scratching its head as though confused, "You think affect taste?"

"Hrm," another one reckoned, "That for Tongue to decide."

"Cow stupid," the third suggested, "Them taste good."

"Like pig more," the first rejected the idea, "And pig smart."

"How smart thing sleep in mud?" the second asked.

"*You* sleep in mud," the third pointed out.

"Sleep in mud *because*," the second replied as though it answered everything.

"We wait for Tongue. Him say whether use for food or for skins," the first decided.

Krög was beginning to get the distinct impression the ogres were trying to determine whether or not to eat him or skin him, two prospects that were equally grisly and undesirable. He did not like being talked about like he could not respond, especially by idiots like ogres, and he did not like being talked about like a source of sustenance or hides.

"If you think you're going to take me down without a fight, you're wrong!" the Battle Prince shouted as bravely and powerfully as he could.

The second ogre raised a fleshy eyebrow, "Why it squeak like that?"

"Shell understand Little Speak," the first responded, "Him explain."

The young ruler stood up and raised his fists in a fighting stance, and thought if he could not run past the ogres, maybe he could punch his way past them.

"What it do now?" the third asked confused.

Krög slugged the beast right in its round belly as hard as he could. The ogre coughed.

"Maybe should tie up, going to hurt itself," came the suggestion.

"Will get rope. Watch it careful," the first said.

The Battle Prince was not about to be bound by beasts of lesser intelligence than him, and especially not while they weighed in on whether or not to turn him into lunch. He tried again to run.

Within only a few strides, Krög was again stopped dead in his tracks, but not by a heavy blow- rather it was by the sight of Ydal being held, four-cornered, by the enormous beetle creature that had come down out of the tree tops. She was struggling violently against the grip of its spindly legs, but it held on tight. With a voice that rasped sinisterly, the huge bug spoke.

"Every step you take, I pull off one of her limbs," it threatened.

The Battle Prince tensed all his muscles and refused to even let his breathing show. Walking on two of its six legs, and holding the princess with the other four, the giant insect, which resembled the roaches Krög occasionally had to brush off his pillow at night, stood just as tall as the ogres, but spoke with remarkably more articulation.

"That's it, pretty boy," the huge cockroach spoke again, "Nice and easy. Take a few steps slowly back."

Krög did as he was told, eyes never leaving the crimson, furious expression of Ydal.

"Hands behind your head, kneel down and don't move until my very thick headed compatriot returns, understand?" the roach demanded.

The Battle Prince knelt down and tucked his hands into his hair as calmly as he could.

"You're not as stupid as you look," the roach quipped, "Got a voice, pretty boy?"

"Him squeak something, Legs," one of the ogres offered, "Not sure what say."

"That's because your ears are filled with candle wax, Lurch," the roach snapped, "And I'm not talking to you, I'm talking to him."

"What do you want with us?" Krög asked softly.

"Ah, he does have words in that skull," the roach chittered, "And, to your question, very little- I'm just hired help."

"We're royalty!" Ydal screamed, "Release me immediately and I promise you riches beyond your wildest dreams!"

"How dumb do you think I am?" the roach snorted, "Royalty wandering around in Troll Country without an escort?"

An escort! Krög realized he did not necessarily need to figure out a way to escape, he just needed to wait for Ash to track them down.

"When my Honor Guard returns, he'll be scraping you off the bottom of his boots," the Battle Prince growled.

"Brains and guts," the roach laughed, "Just no real grip on reality."

"Where Tongue be, Legs?" one of the ogres asked, "Getting hungry."

"Are you Legs?" Krög asked sharply to the roach, "Why does he call you Legs?"

"Because I've got more than he does," the giant bug, presumably Legs, snapped, "They're ogres, not wizards."

"And Shell and Tongue?" the Battle Prince realized he had been listening to the ogres rattle off names earlier.

"Why do you care?!" Ydal screeched, "Rescue me!"

"I'll get right on that," Krög scoffed, still on his knees hands behind his head.

"You're the Battle Prince! Now do something heroic like you said you would!" the princess demanded at the top of her lungs.

"Like what?!" the young ruler hollered back, "I'm a little low on options right now!"

"Never fear, I'll save you!" Lee's voice broke in.

Krög wrenched his head around and saw the small girl being carried over, entangled in a grotesquely long tongue attached to a disproportionately large toad.

"Right after I figure out my own situation, of course," she crossed her arms as the slimy tongue gripping her tightened a little more.

"Tongue back, now we get eat," one of the ogres said excitedly.

The Battle Prince did not have a difficult time determining why the giant toad was called Tongue.

Most toads Krög had ever come across were small enough they could fit in the palm of his hand. In contrast, the approaching amphibian could have very nearly held the Battle Prince in its hand- if it had hands, anyway. Its massive, bubbled eyes sat atop an enormously wide mouth, and when it finally came to rest after loping up to them, the young ruler could see it sat taller than he stood- well over six feet. Warty, dry, drab brown skin covered its body loosely, and it plodded around on broad, webbed pads slowly and ponderously. Most striking about the monstrous toad, other than a mouth wide enough to swallow a pony, was the long, rubbery, slimy tongue it had wrapped around Lee. There was a disturbing agility to it, and it was downright prehensile, moving around like a heavy limb shifting the small girl from side to side as it sauntered. On the end of it, the tongue split off into four smaller, more slender appendages like fingers of a hand.

"Hi, prince!" Lee said brightly, "Quite the picnic we're having isn't it?"

"Let her go!" Krög snarled at the enormous toad.

"You weren't HALF that upset when tall, dark and buggy here showed up with me!" Ydal keened.

"I'll get you both out of this, I promise," the Battle Prince hollered boldly.

"I can't wait to see that happen," Lee rolled her eyes, "By the way, the sooner the better, this thing is gross," she glanced disgustedly at the tongue gripping her lithe body.

One of the ogres, the one Legs had called Lurch, spoke up, "They make too much noise! We eat them now?"

"Patience, my dubious and ravenous companion, patience," the toad, Tongue, spoke with remarkable eloquence and a smart accent, "We must first determine their culinary quality before preparation can begin. Do bring the other two a bit closer, my good man, thank you kindly now."

One of the other ogres roughly shoved Krög forward towards the looming toad, and Legs trotted lightly over, carrying Ydal along though she struggled.

"Has, ahem, Shell joined yet?" Tongue used the name like it tasted sour in his mouth, "I need somewhere to put this," he waved Lee about.

"Coming now," another voice joined.

Krög snapped his head around to see a snail easily the size of an ox slowly sliming its way through the brambles. Sinister, beady black eyes sat atop the yellow, squirming creature's eyestalks, and a toothy maw completely foreign to most snails chomped and sucked constantly. Shell, the Battle Prince surmised, had an absolutely gorgeous shell of glittering pearl, which was unfortunately overshadowed by its unnaturally immense size and the gruesome appearance of the creature protruding from it.

"Wonderful!" Tongue exclaimed as the snail approached, "Then we are all gathered!"

"We get eat now!" the single minded ogre clapped his heavy hands joyfully.

"Easy, Snort," Legs chuckled, "Maybe make yourself useful and go get some firewood."

"Okay, Legs, will get firewood," the ogre- Snort the prince supposed- shuffled off into the brush.

"What do you think?" Legs asked Tongue, "Think they'll do?"

"They better," Shell said breathlessly, "That's enough chasing for one day. I'm bushed."

"You're always tired," Legs accused, "You just slow us down. Literally."

"Gentleman, gentleman, please some manners and civility," Tongue pleaded drawly, "We may be changed of form, but need not be changed of etiquette."

"What in the nine hells is going on?!" Krög shouted over top of the arguing, oversized vermin.

"Ah, do forgive me," Tongue said as though just noticing the prince and his companions, "I forget myself. Allow me to introduce my associates and I. Shell, if you please."

"You got it, boss," the snail rocked backwards and exposed its long, grotesque underside.

As soon as Shell had 'stood' up, Tongue placed Lee against the snail's gooey, sticky belly and retracted his tongue. The athletic young woman squirmed and struggled against the clutch of Shell's viscous form, but the glutinous fluids bonded her tightly in place.

Tongue smacked his lips a few times, "There, that's better. Now we're all comfortable."

"Speak for yourself," Lee said snidely as slime started to drip into her hair.

"Somebody better get this bug off of me right now!" Ydal screeched.

"She's spirited," Legs said luridly, "Maybe we can have a go with this one before lunch."

"I forbid it!" the princess protested shrilly.

"Now, now," Tongue chastised, "We mustn't play with our food."

"Stop talking about us like we're food!" Krög shouted.

"Ah my dear boy, I must regrettably inform you it is in fact the reason we have gathered your cadre," Tongue said almost remorsefully, "I know it is a rather grim prospect, but there you have it."

"There I have it?!" the Battle Prince exclaimed, "You're enjoying the *prospect* of devouring us!"

"Oh yes, quite so," Tongue replied brightly, "Certainly you feel a degree of pity for the cows you slaughter, but it need not mean you enjoy the steak any less."

"We are not steak!" Ydal shrieked.

"Keep using that volume, they're about to change their minds," Lee snorted.

"Steak, no indeed," Tongue appraised, "A delicacy without question, however. Perhaps it would be easier to understand after introductions. I am Gaston Crapaud, and these are my fellows, sous chef Stefan Escargot and mercenary hunter extraordinaire, Julian Cafard."

The toad bowed low as though what he had just said was extremely impressive.

"Is that supposed to mean something to me?" Krög asked dryly.

"You… you've not heard of me?" Tongue queried.

"Not especially," the Battle Prince shrugged.

"I operated one of the finest restaurants in all of Fanfarra!" Tongue said, a little offended, "We specialized in the most exquisite and exotic of dishes."

"Somehow I don't see you fitting in with the decor of the ivory city," Lee cast off with a load of snark.

"Certainly we did not always appear as such," Tongue explained, "We were about on an expedition with Monsieur Cafard in search of some new, strange and wonderful dish to serve for a grand celebration after our city was made safe again. I suppose we have you to thank for it," the toad recognized Krög as a warrior of the Southern Reach and chuckled, "All the same. Our little safari was most rudely interrupted when a decidedly unpleasant creature magically swapped our minds with those of these beasts you see before you. We gave chase, of course, but were unable to capture the terrible imp. So, we have been forced to remain in such ridiculous and exaggerated form wandering these forests grand, in search of our bodies and in search of the next palate tingling dish," he finished proudly.

"Well how sad for you," Lee huffed, "I'd like to not be eaten now."

"My sincerest apologies, little mistress," Tongue patted her on the head with his tongue, "I am most afraid it does not work as such."

"You won't get away with this," Krög growled.

"Ha, my dear boy," Tongue laughed, "I appreciate your pluck, however, it would perhaps be best to simply resign yourself to the eventuality. We sought a tasty new dish, and you shall most hopefully suffice. Such is the way of things."

"It most certainly is not!" Ydal's voice reached fever pitch.

The ogre, Lurch, spoke up, "Which one we going eat first? Can be that one? It noisy."

"I have to admit, she is starting to get on my nerves," Legs agreed darkly, "I like a little less feisty and a little more submissive."

"Ugh, your sordid fantasies, honestly Julian," Tongue scoffed, "Nevertheless, we have indeed put off our lunch far too long. Allow me to taste each and determine where in the courses they should be."

"You have got to be kidding," Krög struggled against the grip of the ogre holding him in place.

"Why not at all," Tongue was clearly put out, "Certainly you would not begin a meal with something which had a sweet note to it. Nor conclude on a saltier dish. No, my dear boy, everything has its place in the courses, and without question each of you shall have yours as well. It simply need only be determined."

"I have a feeling things are about to get extra, super gross," Lee said, her normally fearless self turning eight shades of squeamish.

"Your taste is still rather fresh on my palate," Tongue turned towards her, "Though there are hints and notes which still need to be sussed out. Shell, if you would please."

The snail inched itself forward, still holding the small, athletic girl pulled tight against its gooey underside. Tongue let out his unpleasantly long tongue, and the members on the end of it wiggled like fingers preparing to probe an interesting specimen.

"If you touch me with that thing," Lee warned, "I swear from here to the Everfrost, I will personally feed it to you."

"Oh, the spirit in all of you!" Tongue chuckled, "Honestly, I could not have picked a better lunch. Now then, hold still my dear. Ha! As though you had any choice."

Lee tried in vain to jerk away as the toad's tongue slithered through the air and began to poke, prod and slide along all her exposed skin. The kaleidoscope of emotions and expressions that burned across her face as she was tasted by the enormous toad would have been humorous were the situation not so disgusting. All the little fingers on the end of the tongue traced slimy paths about Lee's form, slobbering on her neck, digging here and there on her ribs and stomach, slapping up and down her arms and even lapped down her heels to dive in and out of her toes. Krög was certain she would have shivered in revulsion had she not been stuck so completely in place to the underside of Shell. As Tongue finally withdrew, the final look of abject abhorrence the small girl fixed the giant amphibian with was one the Battle Prince knew well, and also knew it would not bode well for the toad in the end.

"Mm," Tongue ran the fingers of his tongue along his broad lips and sucked each one clean of Lee's taste,

"Yes, indeed," he muttered to himself, "Ah, of course. Next."

The ogre holding on to Krög elbowed him forward.

"In your dreams, pal," the young ruler snorted, "No way."

Not waiting for the Battle Prince to object a second time, the massively strong, dimwitted beast picked Krög up almost by the scruff of his neck and held him out to Tongue.

The experience was just as repugnant to live through as it seemed watching. As soon as the fingers on the tongue started to grasp at the Battle Prince, he immediately tried to writhe away. It was not warm as he assumed it would be, but rather each member was cold and wet, and they had a suction to them every time they would latch to his skin. He remembered a time he had to pull a leech from his arm after an early morning swim in the Swordsong, and being tasted by Tongue felt like a handful of the bloodsucking critters puckering up to his flesh and tugging away every second, their icy mouths squirming along every bared inch of him. The toad licked and lolled along the ridges of his muscles, climbed down the Battle Prince's vest and across his chest, and dug his way down his tall riding boots. Krög could not recall a single more invasive, reviling incident.

After what certainly seemed like much longer than it was, the ogre set the sticky, humiliated young ruler down and Tongue withdrew, "Oh, my, I never should have suspected," the toad sounded pleased as he ran the fingers of his tongue around the inside of his mouth, "Such nuances, such subtlety."

Krög looked over at Lee who raised her eyebrows expectantly and sarcastically at him. The Battle Prince gave her a look of nauseated defeat.

"If we die today," he said dryly, "Can you punch me right before? Just so that I have a final memory more pleasant than that," he nodded at the toad's tongue, which was stroking the great amphibian's chin as though deep in thought.

"Oh, sweetheart," Lee cooed, "I'll not only punch you, I'll pummel the absolute shit out of you for getting me into this in the first place."

"Great," Krög shook a glob of slime from Tongue's tasting out of his hair, "Thanks."

"No, thank you, prince, for inviting me on this swell picnic," the bright young woman said in a singsongy tone laden with derision.

"You could help me think of a way out of this," the young ruler grumbled out of the side of his mouth, as though his captors might not hear him.

"Oh! Right! Because it's always up to me to save our collective asses! Hang on just one second," Lee threshed back and forth a moment, but remained patently attached to Shell's underside, "Sorry, looks like I'm still stuck!"

Before Krög could open his mouth to fire back, Tongue announced, "Wonderful! Next!"

Ydal was fit to be tied. She screamed and flailed, twisted and shouted and made an absolute scene of herself as Legs walked her towards the awaiting toad, its wide maw open and grandiose tongue already beginning to snake out to test the princess. Eventually the huge cockroach got tired of her shrieking and wrapped his antennae tightly around her face to stifle her cries, which only made the Lady try and reach an even more piercing timbre. Sincerely, if looks could kill, Tongue would have died ten thousand agonizing, terrible, virulent deaths in a split second, but fortunately for him, Ydal's murderous stare was contained to her eyes. Krög actually felt bad for the vapid woman as she was explored like the rest of them.

When the princess was suitably dripping with slop, and exhausted from her struggles, the toad took a long, protracted moment to consider her many flavors as well, "Fascinating," his eyes searched the sky for inspiration, "How novel. Unlike anything else. Exquisite."

Ydal's head rocked in the Battle Prince's direction, and through ragged breaths, she made a mumbling threat between Leg's antennae, "You're going to save me from this. And after you do, I'm going to tell your father what happened. If he doesn't kill you, I will."

"Why is everyone suddenly blaming me for this?!" Krög exclaimed.

"Because, King Mopey, it was your idea!" Lee yelled back, "If you hadn't gone all, 'princely castle life bores me, I need excitement beyond being waited on all day,' we wouldn't be out here!"

"You didn't have to come along," the prince snorted.

"Neither did she!" Lee motioned with the tips of her fingers, essentially all she could motion with, at Ydal.

"How dare you?!" the Lady screeched, her words still largely muffled by the cockroach's tentacles "You contrive to usurp my position as his betrothed!"

"I *contrive* to let him make his own choices!" the small girl snapped back.

"This is really not the time or place for this conversation," Krög jumped between them.

"SHUT UP!" both women yelled at him at once.

"I deserved that," the young ruler carped to himself.

Tongue cleared his throat loudly, "I have made the decisions!"

"Oh, goody," Lee rolled her eyes, "Now we get to find out what order we die horribly in."

"Yum, tasty," the ogre Lurch smacked loudly, eyes glittering with hunger lust, "Which one we get first, which one we get first?!"

Tongue raised himself up to full height as though about to make a proud proclamation, "Good gentleman of Troll Country, friends and compatriots of the Northern Empire and the Strange, I wish to present today's course of fare! Lightly salted and spiced with prufrock, princess flambé," he gestured with his tongue's hand at Ydal, "Followed, after a palate cleanser, by slow roasted warrior flank accompanied with a Neverwilt fruit basting," the tongue's fingers pointed at Krög, "And completing the afternoon's festivities, our dessert, a light wafer of waif tartare," the toad concluded by presenting Lee.

Both of the ogres clapped lightly and giggled, a sound that came across a deep burbling in their fleshy throats and only underscored their incredible capacity for absolute stupidity.

"Thank you, thank you," Tongue brandished his hand-tongue and bowed his head as he took in the applause, "Now then, there are many preparations to make. A number of my garnishes and seasonings are away at our other camp, and I shall need to retrieve them. Crunch, if you will accompany me, the rest please do await Snort's return and begin our cooking fire. I require tall flames that will recede to red coals, please- the flambé is a high heat composition so let's not spoil its flavor with a weak broil."

"Okay, boss," one of the ogres, presumably Crunch, shuffled forward towards Tongue, "We carry heavy stuff. Then gets eat right?"

"Honestly, dear boy," the toad chuckled, "Such single mindedness. How your kind persists, the very idea."

The two disappeared into the shadows of the forest, Tongue lightly chastising his ogre companion for being uninformed in the schools of so many, many things, leaving the three friends and their captors in awkward, extraordinarily uncomfortable silence.

"Hey, prince!" Lee's bright voice broke the settled quiet, "Do you want to know how many times something tried to eat me before I met you? I'll give you a hint, it rhymes with 'hero,'" she then added after a beat, "One of which I could very much use right about now!"

"I'm working on it," Krög said somewhat impotently.

"If he's saving *anyone*, I'm first!" Ydal lashed out. Legs had finally released his grip around her mouth, the exercise being futile in the first place.

"Oh, of course, princesses before peasants," the athletic blonde girl scoffed.

"It only makes sense," the Lady huffed, "Did you not hear the chef? I'm an appetizer, they're going to eat me first!"

"They have to cook you!" Lee argued back, "They're eating me tartare! Raw! That means you'll take longer to prepare, so *I* should go first, *before* they decide to just kill me and throw me on a plate!"

"Actually," Shell interjected drawlingly, "*Chilled* tartare is served in the appetizer position, desserts are most traditionally a warm tartare. Deceased flesh cools too quickly for an appropriate end of course platter, so it needs to be served at its freshest."

"You're going to eat her alive?!" Krög burst out.

"For the most part," Shell agreed, bored, "Though generally speaking, the dish rarely survives past the upper flanks. A shame really."

Lee raised her eyebrows and nodded sarcastically at Ydal, "They're eating me alive, feet first. Still think you've got it so bad, Madam Dramatic?"

Ydal shot back a burning look of unmistakable fury, "If someone doesn't rescue me by the time I count to three, I am going to start screaming and I won't stop screaming until-"

"Until what?" the athletic woman cut her off, "Until you die?! Because that's looking like a solid possibility!"

"This is really not productive," the Battle Prince scoffed.

"One," the princess counted.

"Thanks for noticing that, King Mopey," Lee laughed derisively, "How about throwing out an idea or two, because the Lady and I doing all the talking isn't exactly going to end in flowers and rainbows."

"Two," Ydal said more drawn out and purposeful.

"Well what in the nine hells do you want me to do here?!" Krög snapped back, "It's not like I'm in the best position myself either. In case you weren't listening, they're going to SLOW roast me, and that doesn't exactly sound so great!"

"Two and a half," Ydal grit her teeth in frustration at being ignored.

"Maybe we could move past who's being eaten *how*, and *when*, and move on to *how* we're going to get out of here... and *when*," the bright girl suggested sardonically, biting down on the symmetry.

"Well I'm open for suggestions," the Battle Prince snorted, "But unless you're somehow hiding a size fifty-two war hammer somewhere in that skimpy outfit, I submit we're all in a bit of a bind!"

Lee squinted her eyes at his sideways comment, "When I get unstuck, I'm going to slap you for that. Hard."

Ydal huffed, "Three."

"Awe, did you hear that?" the bright young woman rocked her head mock sympathetically, "Princess made it to three."

"I'm shivering with terror," Legs chuckled in his own unseemly manner.

"I," the Lady took in a deep breath, "Warned you."

"Oh, come off it," Krög dismissed, "Like screaming is really going to make a difference!"

"She seems to think," Lee began.

Ydal unleashed an absolutely blood-curdling, ear-shattering, brain-bursting banshee howl, which not only made the Battle Prince's skin crawl, but his eyes sear and his ears want to tuck themselves up inside his skull and never come out. The princess screamed. And she screamed, and she screamed, and she screamed. And just when it seemed she would turn blue, run out of breath and pass out, somehow she made it to an even more symphonic level that challenged the realm of human vocals capabilities. From the lungs of the Lady belched forth cacophony incarnate, an utterly mind-numbing blast of sonic itching powder, which tore everybody's thoughts into tiny shreds and left them weeping for merciful release from the terrible sound. Krög had no idea people could sound in such a way.

Almost immediately Legs buckled and beveled, trying desperately to keep a grip on all four of Ydal's limbs, but also just as interested in finding a way to plug his ears shut so he did not have to spend his remaining days deaf as a post. After squirming about a bit, the gigantic cockroach stuck his antennae into his head, blessedly depriving himself of the sound, but leaving everyone else stuck with her screech. Lee and Shell were worst off- her arms were stuck upright to the underside of the snail and Shell had no means of covering wherever it was he heard from. They could do little but struggle, bug-eyed, while the princess shouted herself hoarse... something she was showing little proclivity towards. Krög was wildly thankful he had not yet been tied up, and as soon as the ogre Lurch released him to stuff out the sound, the Battle Prince immediately clapped his own hands to the sides of his head to dampen the screech.

Most certainly, if nothing else had, the amount of time it took the Battle Prince to realize the ogre had released him earned the young ruler Lee's favored nickname for him: stupid prince. He sat there grimacing against the unnatural yowl being unleashed by the princess, teeth ground and eyes squeezed shut as though it would make a difference, just about completely oblivious the ogre holding him captive was doing the same. His very thoughts rattled as the shriek went on and on, until his sudden freedom cautioned the young ruler to open one eye and glance around slowly.

Lee was staring intently at him, and the pained look on her face was barely able to mask her exasperated contempt, "What in the nine hells are you waiting for?!" she yelled over the din, "Run!"

Krög was on his feet and bolted faster than he ever had ever in his life before. At first he was shaky, his legs numb and tingly from him kneeling for so long. The Battle Prince took an unfortunate, headlong dive into the thorny brambles as he tried to escape. Without thought, the young ruler pressed his hands against the biting vines and jumped back up, blood dripping down his fingers and shoulders where the thorns of the forest had embedded themselves. He never felt a thing as he surged forward again, the only thought on his mind was how to eventually find his way back to the two girls before they met an indescribably untimely end. All he could hope was the awful beings would not begin their stomach-churning feast until they had rounded up the main course-him- again. If nothing else, it would buy him some time to achieve his first goal.

Foremost in the Battle Prince's mind was his companion, guardian and super-strong friend, Ashley, had to be somewhere fairly nearby in the trees. The mighty troll had not been gone too long when Lee first raced off, and they had not been sprinting through the woodland all too long before being captured. It stood to reason Ash had to be close and was on his way. And given the troll's preternaturally sharp senses he had to have heard the noise, smelled the creatures, or felt the ripples of the conflict- or however his sixth sense worked. As far as Krög was concerned, all he had to do was basically run headlong into his exceptionally large best friend which, operating under the assumption Ashley was also looking for him, did not seem like it would be too terribly difficult. Of course, the Thorn Rift Forest was a sprawling and expansive desert of trees, and the lean possibility did exist the Battle Prince and the rest of his troupe had managed to put quite a bit of distance between themselves and their protector.

It did little good to worry about the odds of whether or not he would actually find Ashley, Krög decided. He needed to count on running into the troll, or Ydal and Lee would meet a fate that was exponentially more terrible than any he could otherwise imagine. Besides, Ashley had yet to fail the young ruler in his post as Honor Guard, and had gone so far as to turn a dragon inside out like a jacket to defend the Battle Prince. The troll was powerful, swift, and aware. In fact, the more Krög thought about it, the more it seemed a near certifiable guarantee he would track down his guardian, and the two would triumphantly rescue the captured girls.

A slight smile drew across the Battle Prince's exhausted lips as he pumped his legs harder and he thought of the exuberant Lee and how thankful she would be at being saved from the jaws of doom. Perhaps she might even go so far as to think of him as an actual, semi-competent, at least partially-able, would-be hero. His chest swelled with pride at her imagined accolades and his heart beat faster at the thought of her gratitude. It would probably mean the chance for the two of them to be alone, for her to express her joy at being alive in her own particularly delightful fashion, and for him to sink into the pleasure of her company. The more Krög thought about it, the faster he ran if for no other reason than to hurry along, what he had decided would be, her inevitable gracious debt at being saved by he, the Battle Prince, future lord sovereign of the Southern Reach, champion and legend.

Of course, reality caught up to the young ruler faster than he could catch up to Ashley, redemption, or salvation. Krög's fantasies about Lee were brought to a crushing halt when something heavy, wet and strong struck him in the chest. The Battle Prince flew off his feet, practically out of his boots, and sailed through the air before a tree limb ended his flight violently and painfully. Before he could pick himself up and dust off, the thick, wet thing grabbed him tightly and wound round his arms and legs. It lifted the Battle Prince off the ground and brought him face to face with two sets of unbelieving, but ultimately unfortunately familiar, eyes, blinking in the dappled sunlight and from astonished surprise.

At the other end of the gross thing holding on to the young ruler, was the mouth and face of Tongue, next to whom stood the ogre, Crunch. The two considered Krög for a while, puzzled at what it was he was doing with them, instead of where they had left him. Crunch scratched his head with one finger as though legitimately skeptical of what he was looking at, his bulbous, crooked face wrenching into an even more ridiculous countenance of wonderment and chagrin. He was legitimately dumbstruck they had to capture their meal a second time. Tongue's shock faded quicker, and he was the first to speak.

"My dear boy, whatever are you doing away from our picnic site?" the massive toad asked rather calmly.

"This is going to come as a real blow," Krög said, dripping with snark, "But I'm not really keen on being eaten today."

"How him get away?" Crunch questioned as though still trying to put the puzzle together.

"A question for our merry little band, to be certain," Tongue acknowledged, "However we are most fortunate to have once again acquired our main course. I do not fancy spending the afternoon indulging myself on, ahem, fast food."

"What that?" Crunch looked sideways at the toad.

"Never mind," Tongue dismissed, "Now then, dear boy," he addressed Krög again, "Just as the cow lows before the slaughter and the chicken clucks as its head is removed, I appreciate your endeavors to extend the length of your life, pathetic and fruitless though they may be. However, the time for foolery and playing is at its conclusion. I do not wish to be of a winded disposition when I begin preparing the afternoon's meal. If it is not too much, please, enough with the running and noise-making."

"If it's not too much, how about you *not* eat me and my friends?" Krög spat back.

"My dear boy," the toad sighed, "If you insist upon continuing this argument, I shall have to insist my rather large friend here strike you violently and repeatedly until you are either no longer interested, or no longer capable, in prattling on."

"Wouldn't want that now, would we?" the Battle Prince capped off, "Might spoil the flavors if you beat your meal about too much."

"Decidedly, it will be an element of preparation anyway," Tongue spoke of thrashing the young ruler tender as though one might discuss how much water to use in boiled oats, "However to do so too early will only over saturate the meat with its natural juices. I have no interest in spoiling you."

Krög was just aghast, "Weren't you a person once?! Doesn't this in some way qualify as cannibalism?"

If a toad could shrug, Tongue would have, "I suppose it never much did cross my mind. Then, none of the other courses have made quite so much of a fuss as you and your fellows. My thanks, dear boy! You have given me a topic of conversation to introduce during lunch!"

The Battle Prince smiled falsely, "Glad to be of assistance."

"Now then," Tongue concluded, "Back to camp with us all. The others must be waiting. Crunch, if you will bring the seasonings, I will carry the dish."

Krög was shocked at how titanically strong the grip of the toad's tongue was. Being wrapped up in it was akin to being constricted by a rubbery, sticky vine with the hugging power of a troll. The toad did not bind him so tightly he could not breathe, but the young ruler would have been very surprised learn to his organs had not been rearranged, or a few bones cracked under the member's crushing grasp. What was even more disconcerting was the sensation Tongue was only holding him lightly- Krög was fairly certain the immense amphibian could have squeezed him to the point his head burst... if it had crossed the toad's mind. Which, given the fate awaiting the Battle Prince back at the camp, seemed like a pretty good trade off, all things considered.

It also gave the young ruler pause when he took a moment to reflect on the odd variety of beasts he had encountered in such a short time with such bizarrely unnatural tongues. There was of course Scale, the cat-sized dragon with not one forked serpentine tongue, but rather three separate ones he liked to flit about as menacingly as he could manage- or use as substitute for a mature comeback. There was the encounter with the cavelings, who seemed to be able to practically unzip themselves and unleash a pulsing, yellow whip-like tongue that went far beyond being prehensile and landed it in the exclusive realm of being a truly combat effective instrument. And then there was the matter of the near six foot tall bull toad that had a slobbery, putrid, extension with a damn hand replacement on the end of it, built into the underside of his jaw. Krög swore, if he kept running into monsters with enormous tongues, provided he survived the ordeal, he was going to let Ash deal with them- he was tired of giant tongues.

The young ruler's thoughts were completely interrupted when the toad carrying him broke back through the tree-line and waddled back into the camp. Things had not changed much, but enough to make Krög's stomach drop out of his chest and into his boots. Snort had returned and had managed to start a roaring fire, to which he was adding more and more fuel, stoking the angry, hungry flames to greater heat. Lurch, having lost the main course, was trying to make himself useful again by arranging a suggestively person-shaped cage over the fire, dangling from a chain swung over a powerful tree limb. Ydal must have had shouted herself mute at last, and she was hanging, defeated, from the grip of Legs' claws, chest heaving and head down. Even Lee had lost her trademark boundless sunny attitude, and had a look of intense anxiousness carved on her face. Until, however, she laid eyes on Krög.

Immediately, the bright young woman burst out laughing, "Oh savior! Oh champion! Oh bringer of salvation, hero of our generation! Do tell me- was it a ferocious battle, or did you just hand yourself over to them again?"

"Not exactly helpful," the Battle Prince huffed, ashamed and embarrassed.

"Well, neither are your exploits," Lee giggled, "When we get to hell, if the demons don't make your afterlife miserable, then I will."

"It's not over yet," Krög hissed at her, "We still have a chance."

Ydal took notice of the young ruler's unexpected and unwelcome return, "You're useless! Some Battle Prince you are!"

Legs shot Krög a suspicious look, "You're the Battle Prince? Really? Are you sure?"

"Pretty sure," the young ruler rolled his eyes, but then got an idea, "Is that something you want to bring down on your heads? The full might and wrath of the Southern Reach? Do you have any idea what the Warbrands would do to you if they found out you murdered and ate the heir to the throne?"

Legs narrowed his gaze a moment and then relaxed, "They don't know where you are."

"Beg pardon?" Krög choked, astonished.

"If they knew where you were, they would have been here by now," the massive cockroach pointed out, "Since we're not dead and in pieces, I'm guessing it's a good bet you either snuck out and they haven't noticed you're gone, or you're not actually the Battle Prince. Either way, doesn't give you much space for negotiations, eh?"

The Battle Prince pulled a stupid face.

Lee was beside herself with laughter, "And now you're zero for two attempts, stupid prince. Anything else you'd like to try?"

Krög just shot her a look and receded into his mind to come up with a more feasible escape and rescue plan, though what few options he had were quickly dwindling to a place of pathetic desperation.

As the Battle Prince poured over options in his head, Tongue ordered the ogres about in further preparation for the incipient feast. Mostly they added more branches to the bonfire they had begun, the enormous toad insisting on there being a bed of red coals at the base of nearly white hot flames in order for the cooking to go as planned. They also shifted about grim looking cutting boards, carving utensils that Krög had no desire to feel on his own skin, and large crates and bags of spices and seasonings. Some of them were stamped with names so exotic, the Battle Prince had only heard of them when the Assassin Emissaries of the Eastern Collective spoke of the most fragrant and exquisite delicacies of their mysterious empire. Others were so commonplace as to be almost ridiculous in the heaping proportions the ogres had them in. One burlap sack nearly four feet in length was marked with plain black lettering reading simply "salt." The whole mess of it made Krög sick.

It did not take long before the fire reached a point that seemed to deeply please Tongue, and it became painfully clear he was ready to begin. Legs marched Ydal over to one of the tables the ogres had set up, and both he and Crunch held the princess taut by her wrists and ankles across the planks while Tongue went to work. The toad handed Krög off to Lurch so he could use the hand on the end of his tongue to season the princess. Against her struggles, the hulking amphibian sprinkled all manner of spices up and down Ydal's form, and the air above her became cloudy and fragrant with their wafting. Tongue chuckled and mumbled to himself all the while, selecting this shaker or grabbing a pinch of that, sickeningly engrossed in turning the Lady into a well seasoned appetizer for their picnic of the macabre.

Whether the titanic toad had never used such a powerful mix of spices before, or whether they really were not used to their food squirming and writhing so much and kicking up a sincere dust storm of seasonings, Krög could not be certain. However, the scene that played out before his horrified, amused eyes was not short of a comedy of errs much to the detriment of the hungry pack of beasts. In fact, it bordered on the ludicrously absurd.

From the moment Tongue had started to wantonly sprinkle Ydal's body with spices, Crunch was under visible distress. He kept working his face like trying to itch a scratch on it, but with both hands occupied by gripping the girl's wrists, he was left to helplessly bug out his eyes, twitch his nose and undulate his lips to dismiss the offensive sensation. Apparently, it did eventually become to much for him to handle, and the ogre loosed a truly heroic sneeze, which blasted a legendary amount of snot and seasoned powders out of his bulbous, blobby nose. A mass of sticky, thick green mucous struck Legs right in the face, and before he could think the action through, the huge cockroach loosed a disgusted roar and moved to wipe the gunk out of his eyes. In doing so, he released one of Ydal's ankles. The princess kicked across her body with such furious gusto that when the blow landed in the throat of the toad spicing her, Tongue choked and coughed violently. His hacking succeeded in expelling the shaker he was holding in his tongue with extraordinary force, and the container hurtled through the air before striking Lurch in the head. A red powder dumped out of it into the ogre's eyes, who then quickly released Krög as he screamed and screamed, clawing at his face to clear the unimaginably hot seasoning from his vision.

Again, the Battle Prince was momentarily frozen in place despite his freedom, though more from abject awe than anything else. Crunch was sneezing uncontrollably, and had released Ydal's hands completely as he batted at his nose. Legs had managed to clean the muck off his face, but he was being somewhat overwhelmed by the shrieking, livid princess who had both hands and one foot free from the grip of her captors and was fighting with everything she had. Lurch was still howling in pain, blinded from whatever corrosive powder had landed in his eyes, and Snort had abandoned his fire building to spit on the face of his fellow ogre repeatedly in an attempt to help wash the spices away. Tongue was still coughing too hard from Ydal's unimaginably strong kick to be able to issue any kind of order or recrimination. Pandemonium took the camp when a blinded Lurch stumbled into the cooking fire and knocked a particularly large clump of coals frighteningly close to the slow moving Shell, and the flames of the ember started to climb through the vines near him.

Krög recovered his faculties much quicker the second time, and took off like a shot back into the woods. He knew Ash could not be far anymore. In fact, something in him could almost feel it, as though he could sense the troll coming closer. Then again, it may have only been powerfully wishful thinking, but for what it was worth the Battle Prince was convinced his protector was drawing near enough to tilt the odds back in their favor. The young ruler only needed to keep his footing just long enough to find his guardian, and blunder their way through a rescue. There was no tangle of brambles or pain of gnashing thorns that could slow his charge. He was possessed and driven, single-minded and purposed. The Battle Prince was focused beyond measure, his thoughts and considerations were only on the finding of his Honor Guard and bringing the girls to safety. He would not fail. He could not fail.

A burning exhaustion nagged in Krög's legs, slowing his pace a hair. They were so worn from chasing Lee through the underbrush and his first attempt to escape their captors. Every breath seared in his lungs like he had sucked in a great gasp of smoke and it was scorching his throat. Thirst cracked his lips from exertion and his heart beat like a war drum, threatening to eject itself from his chest and go fluttering away. Even his arms were tired from pumping back and forth as he sprinted, and the Battle Prince wondered what state he would be in when the fighting began, and whether he would even be able to lift his sword. It was something he could not worry about. He could worry about nothing more than finding Ashley, getting a weapon, and gutting every one of the revolting beasts that had beset him and his friends. The young ruler was determined to be the hero.

Of course, as it so often did, fantasy separated swiftly and painfully from the real world for the would-be champion. Instead of finding himself surging towards victory and the enumerated, valorous rescue he had built up a *second* time in his head, the Battle Prince ran headlong into Legs, who had come crashing down out of the canopy like the first time he had caught Ydal. The giant cockroach quickly folded his wings into his carapace, and used the harder, outer covering of his shell to smack Krög into the thorns. Legs struck with such force that the blow knocked the wind out of the Battle Prince, and the young ruler gasped for ragged breaths while trying to scramble bracingly out of the barbed carpet. His skin tore open as he was raked against the spines, and stinging blood oozed to the surface on his arms and hands. The young ruler barely felt it- he was totally focused on the huge insect towering over him.

"Give it up, kid," Legs chittered, "It's not your day today."

"If you knew one damn thing about my family," Krög shakily found his way to a stand, "You'd know how stupid it is to ask one of us to give up."

The roach laughed, "How far you really think you're going to get out here? There's nowhere to run, boy."

"Then I hope you don't mind if I go down swinging," the Battle Prince raised his fists and set his stance.

Legs eyed him suspiciously, "Suit yourself, kid."

The two combatants squared off as Legs raised four of his limbs in a fighting pose as well. For a few moments they just danced back and forth in the brambles, circling each other and daring the other to take the first swing. Krög had only a moment to reflect on the sheer lunacy of getting into a fist fight with a six foot tall cockroach, but then the day had been anything but normal. It had been, start to finish, an absolutely vociferous practice in insanity, and rounding out the whole thing with a bout of fisticuffs against an oversized example of household vermin only seemed like a fitting cap. The Battle Prince determined he would never sneak out of the house again if he beat Legs and rescued the girls- there was too much potential for the weird.

Now, Krög had never been much of a hand-to-hand fighter- he was rather untrained in unarmed combat. Occasionally, the Assassin Emissaries of the east would teach him a few things about how to properly throw a punch or deflect an enemy's blow, but the young ruler was largely inexperienced. He could handle a sword or an axe, or a spear or a lance, but when it came to putting his fist against an opponent, he knew about as much as a baker knew about molding candles. Granted, he was fairly athletic and possessed at least above average strength, and he had occasioned a few drunken brawls as a hot-headed, irresponsible teenager, but against skilled opposition Krög knew his chances were slim. All the same, he was ready to knock heads.

The young ruler's first punch glanced off of Legs' armored head, and his following uppercut was a knuckle-stinging affair that he planted against the cockroach's hard gut. Legs barely grunted at the strike and swung back in succession, driving three quick jabs and a full-tilt haymaker at the Battle Prince. Krög managed to duck and dodge away from the jabs and, to his own shock, blocked the powerful swing with his forearm. With gusto, the young ruler struck again, hammering his fists against the huge bug's body, and taking a shot at the underside of Legs' jaws. The cockroach swept most of the Battle Prince's attacks aside, but missed the one coming for his head. With barbarian strength, Krög managed to rock Legs back on what would have been his heels, and the bug took a few teetering steps backwards.

Renewed in his confidence at stunning the verminous beetle, the Battle Prince stepped in and pressed forward with his attack, endeavoring to bowl the nasty creature over. Legs caught his balance faster than Krög expected, however, and sent a flurry of swings at the young ruler. The last punch caught the prince in the stomach and folded him over. Doubled with pain and gasping for air, Krög could only stumble out of the way of Legs' next onslaught, which came at lightning speed given the number of limbs the cockroach had at his disposal. An absolute hailstorm of strikes barely whizzed by the Battle Prince, who could only return by putting his shoulder down and hard-checking Legs. The cockroach crumpled against the young ruler's force, but quickly recovered and blasted Krög in the jaw with two successive blows.

Stars floated through his vision and everything sounded like it was underwater as the Battle Prince staggered backwards. A third strike rumbled against his head and a fourth hit his chest, but the young ruler barely seemed to notice. He just watched the world flip slowly upside down, his boots kick up over his head, and the clouds spin above. Everything moved slowly, like time had been drawn out to an absolute crawl, and each event strung into the next by long, languid seconds that were at once completely peaceful and entirely chaotic. There was a settling content in Krög's mind as he tumbled backwards, a sort of qualified acceptance he was sailing through the air and eventually the ground was going to catch up to him, which would mark nearly the fifth time he had fallen in the thorns in one day alone. Of course, he had no fear of the biting, gnawing sting of the brambles, and he largely suspected he would not feel it when he struck the earth.

He was wrong. As soon as the young ruler collided roughly with the ground he was snapped out of the stupor Legs had pummeled him into, and the Battle Prince was all too aware of the precariousness of his position.   The near knockout blow had rendered him weak-kneed and glassy-eyed, and though the world was no longer moving in slow motion and things were not flailing about him in every conceivable direction, he was still a great deal incapable of gathering his faculties. Krög knew he was in serious trouble, and though he possessed great will, he no longer had the capability to fight back.   His head lolled from side to side as he tried to clear the ringing in his ears and the blankness in his gaze. It did little good.

"Sorry, kid," Legs reached out and lifted the Battle Prince off the ground, "You've got spunk, but I can't take that to the bank."

Even if Krög could have struggled, it would have been feeble.   The giant cockroach slung the Battle Prince over his shoulder like a satchel, and crawled back towards the camp.   With about as much regard as one has for bundle of weeds, Legs dropped Krög in the middle of the gathering, and skittered off to take care of whatever it was giant cockroaches took care of when they were not eating people, or holding them hostage.

Tongue was incensed at the state of their return, "What have you done?!   It is far too early to prepare the main course yet!   How dare you!   Is he damaged?!"

"Not especially," Legs' tone was disinterested, "And it's not my fault- the little punk actually has a lot of fight in him.   I hope that means he'll be spicier."

Lee was slack-jawed and beyond amazed, unable to even laugh out of shock, "You have got to be kidding me!   Twice?!   Twice!   You got away, and they caught you back TWICE!"

"Are you the most useless hero in the whole realm?!" Ydal screeched offensively, though Krög was very much glad to see her still alive and out of the flames... if ruffled and covered in odd dusts and seasonings.

Tongue was not done chastising, "Dear boy! Now, I am a patient man-"

Krög cut him off, "You're not a man you slimy, bug-eyed bastard."

"Shut. Up!" the toad hollered, "You have very nearly managed to spoil this entire afternoon for my compatriots and myself! Never has there been circumstances I have been so rudely interrupted at every turn! The audacity! The gall! The reprehensible boldness!"

"In case it had very much slipped your mind," the Battle Prince began breathlessly, "YOU'RE TRYING TO EAT US!"

"A task you are making exceedingly difficult!" Tongue shouted back, "I do not fancy playing with my food, and this has been a truly taxing lunch!"

"I won't stop fighting," the young ruler growled, "I'll never stop trying to rescue my friends."

"You tell him, prince!" Lee quipped, still quite uselessly stuck to the underside of Shell, "I think he's almost thinking about being nervous!"

"Gods, I can't believe I'm siding with her," Ydal huffed, in the charge of the ogres during Legs' absence, "But, really- do something more violent and get us out of here."

"Yeah," Legs chuckled, "Let's see some more fisticuffs out of the great Crog the Battle Prince."

Krög could not remember when he had given the roach his name, but felt compelled to correct him all the same, "It's not Crog, it's Krög."

Legs gave him an annoyed look, "Crug?"

"Oh for the sake of the gods," the prince huffed, "No, not Crog, not Crug, Krög."

"Crog," Legs repeated.

"Krög," the young ruler said again.

"Crog," the roach was just not getting it.

"Krög!" the prince shouted, "It's not like Frog, it's like Crow! Krög! Listen to how I'm saying it! Krög!"

"Enough!" the toad exclaimed, "All of you! Mercy be to the powers above and below and chefs everywhere- ENOUGH! Never, in the history of recorded cooking, has there ever been a meal that has given its preparers such grief! You try not only my patience, but also my skill, and I'll not stand for it!"

"Truly," the slow spoken Shell, interjected, "My hunger waxes so. It has been an unbearable burden to mind the dessert so tantalizingly, and be so long deprived of something to satiate my ravenousness."

"Do you see?!" Tongue went on, "Do you see what you are doing to our number?! The suffering you are causing us!"

"What do you think WE'VE been complaining about?!" Lee cried incredulously back, "You think your suffering is bad?! You're not on the damn menu!"

"A minor qualm given our current state of famine," Tongue dismissed.

"Indeed," Shell agreed, "I am very nearly beyond waiting. Perhaps I will begin ahead of the rest," his eye stalks pulled inward and his maw disappeared into his slime, only for both to emerge again at the bottom of his body below Lee's heels, "Just a morsel or two to quell the growling of my belly," an unreasonably long, whip-like tongue appeared, wrapped itself around the girl's small ankle and wound up to her knee, slowly pulling her towards his open mouth, "Just a taste. A few bites."

Lee burned a hole through the back of Krög's head with her stare, "This is the second time today something has had its tongue on me, and if it doesn't stop soon, you'll never be lucky enough to do the same again."

"WHAT?!" Ydal yowled, "I'LL HAVE YOU THROWN TO THE DOGS FOR DEFILING MY BETROTHED!"

"Relax, princess," Lee chuckled, "If we live long enough for that to happen, I promise to clean him up before I turn him back over to you."

"Can we all stop talking about me like I'm not here," Krög scoffed.

"If Shell get eat now, can we?" Lurch eyed Ydal hungrily, insanely jealous of the snail gradually pulling Lee towards his teeth.

"Maybe just one or two bite," Crunch added, his belly growling.

"No! Stop! Everyone!" Tongue screamed, "You shall not ruin this picnic any more than it already has been! No one is eating early!"

"Speak for yourself," Shell yawned his mouth even wider as he dragged the girl closer, "I have had enough of your edicts for one day. I am eating, prepared or not."

"Hey, prince!" Lee said brightly, "Do you remember what I said to you when we first met and I was tied up and had a dragon clinging to my legs about to sink his teeth into my toes?"

"Get him off me?" Krög replied questioningly.

"Well what do you think I'm about to say now?" the spritely girl shot back as she inched towards the jaws of Shell, pulled down by his revolting tongue.

"Stop this at once, Monsieur!" Tongue hollered at his sous chef, "You were never patient enough to be a master at the culinary arts and you only prove it further! Gods, you would never be able to properly age a steak if you can't even wait for lunch!"

"Oh stuff it with a fine anise truffle!" Shell halted in his attempts to slowly bite into Lee, to instead argue with the giant toad, "You simply cannot stand there is someone else here who might be more skilled than you! Nor can you stand the idea of anyone else being in charge!"

"Well, I never!" Tongue argued, "When I found you, you could barely chop an onion, much less wine glaze a mignon cutlet! I turned you into what you are!"

"No- an imp with an axe to grind turned me into what I am!" the huge snail shouted, "I was a man before I met you, if you recall, and your incessant, insane quest for the 'next great flavor' lead us to this abominable state we find ourselves in!"

"A small price to pay in the search for culinary greatness," the toad screeched in retort, "A minor toll on the road to cooking perfection!"

"I liked having hands!" Shell bellowed.

"Look, if you two are just going to argue," Legs said dryly, "I'm going to join the goon squad over there and eat the princess. I can't taste much of anything anyway- she could be trash for all my mouth is concerned, and I'd still eat her."

The huge cockroach moved towards Ydal and the ogres, who had all begun to drool profusely, great globs of their saliva landing on her head, much to her disgusted objection.

"Fine!" the Lady shrieked, "Eat me! Just stop messing up my hair! It will take me weeks to get this junk out!"

"You really think that's going to matter once they're digesting you?" Lee chortled.

"Speaking of digestion," Shell's tongue snaked back out.

"Let them go!" Krög screamed amidst the infighting and arguing of their captors.

"Brilliant, prince," Lee just kept laughing as she moved another inch closer to the snail's jagged maw, "Why didn't we think to ask that in the first place?"

"Stop! Everyone! This is not how civilized beings enjoy a meal!" Tongue was mad. Hopping mad you might say, Krög thought ruefully to himself.

"I think I'll throw in with the uncivilized then," Legs loomed over Ydal, his chittering jaws clapping open and shut as his glittering eyes searched the princess for somewhere to bite down first.

Over the din of snarling and grumbling and quarreling and squabbling, above the cacophony of people begging not to be eaten and monsters choosing which limb to chew off first, through the sonic murk of threats, pleas, insults, screams and yells, a single, powerful voice cut past it all.

"BATTLE PRINCE!" Ashley's thunderous, booming, earth-shattering battle cry roared out, "CATCH!"

Krög looked up to see his guardian troll, the Hammer of the Southern Reach, flying through the tree branches, having leapt from unimaginable distances away, and hurtling towards them with single purpose. In Ashley's grasp was a glittering sword, Thundersteel, which the troll hurled at the young ruler as he flew towards the encampment. It sailed, end over end towards Krög, who stretched out his hand to catch the weapon and finally strike back at their attackers.

When Ash landed, it was directly on top of Legs. The enormous cockroach exploded apart like one of its smaller cousins being stomped out. Bits of shell, jointed legs, antennae and wing fragments flew in absolutely every direction. A shower of pale green foam erupted out of the shattered carapace of the gigantic bug, and covered Ydal from head to toe in its hot, fetid mess. It was accompanied by a crunch and splatter noise that very much sounded akin to a tree branch breaking loose, and splashing into a pool of mud. Ashley barely seemed to notice he had just squashed the massive insect, and whipped around to start beating the snot out of the ogres with his brick-hard fists.

While the troll clobbered Crunch, Snort, and Lurch, Krög snatched Thundersteel out of the air and concentrated as hard as he could as fast as he could. Hoping snails did not conduct electricity especially well, and also praying a bolt of lighting would be enough to break the huge creature's grip on Lee, the Battle Prince took careful aim and swung his sword through the air. It sang brilliantly as it cut, and out of the bright blue skies above, a clap of thunder rang out. It was followed by a bolt of lightning that raced down out of the heavens towards the young ruler's foes. He missed completely.

Instead, the lightning bolt slammed into Tongue with incredible force, who in turn exploded like a festering blister. Brown and green chunks of toad-flesh, bones and eyeballs, and curtains of blood, burst apart in a spectacular geyser, the vast majority of which rained back down on the Battle Prince. The huge toad's abominable tongue cartwheeled into the trees and wrapped twice around a branch, before dangling like a grotesque vine from the limb, dripping with spit and blood. Eventually, the crimson and glaucous mist settled, and there was only a disgusting crater of vaporized toad left where Tongue had been squatting.

Ashley on the other hand was absolutely clobbering the ogres who, though strong, were nowhere near as fast as the troll, and came across like scrawny kittens against Ash's brute force. Even without his hammer, Very Convincing Argument, or his gnarled club, Really Big Words, the troll was a terribly ferocious warrior, and his punches could have broken through marble columns and his kicks could have splintered tree trunks to kindling. Instead, the blows were landing with impassioned brutality on the trio of ogres who could do little but crumple and grovel in the troll's wake. They tried to run from his fury, but every time one would get a few steps away, Ashley would wrangle them back in and land another crushing blow against their thick noggins or blubbery bodies. Krög almost would have felt bad for them if he was not so exultantly glad to be alive and uneaten.

"Hey!" Lee's voice was hedging towards shrill, "Still kind of in trouble here!"

Nothing the snail did was with any manner of rapidity, but despite the rushing chaos around him, Shell had just managed to get the small girl's ankles to his teeth, still determined to eat the young woman as his companions were blasted to dust.

Krög's eyes shot around the encampment until they settled on a truly insidious, but effective, offensive option to free the girl and slay the snail. He sprinted towards the cooking fire, grabbed up a flour-bag sized sack of seasoning and ran towards Shell. The Battle Prince raised the bag labelled "Salt" over his head, and bellowing the most harrowing battle cry he could possibly muster from the depths of his lungs, smashed the bag down on the soft body of the snail.

With an awful ripping noise the sack of salt split open and rained down on the snail, whose eyes bugged out at the end of their stalks as the sea of grains sizzled through his gooey body and slowly dissolved him. Shell screamed in agony as he melted, waves of slime spilling out of his spiraled husk. Lee squirmed and writhed, and tore free of the viscous creature, peeling herself off the underside of her captor and away from his disintegrating face. Even as she slithered away from the dying monster, tentacles of dripping slop oozed over her athletic form and squeezed into every space it could. Ears to toenails, every conceivable gap on Lee was filled with the remnants of Shell. Slowly the snail's cries of pain gurgled away to nothing as the salt burned and seared its way through the last of his body, and Shell melted away entirely.

In a succinct conclusion of blows, Ashley laid out all three ogres who collapsed into a blobby, misshapen heap, unconscious and drooling, at least one of which was snoring. The troll growled in his throat as though disappointed in the fight they had put up, and took an unusual moment to preen his wild black mane a bit, like the battle had managed to only barely dishevel him. He watched the sleeping forms of the big monsters for a moment longer before turning around to survey the rest of the scene. A revolting mess of carnage and gore was splattered throughout the campsite, not the least of which had bathed the three other companions in its steaming, stomach churning mess.

Panting, and with a seemingly permanent look of shock and abhorrence etched in her countenance, Ydal was still kneeling next to the remaining bits and pieces of Legs, the green foam of his innards caked on to her skin and drying into a vomit-inducing crust. Next to the scorched hole where Tongue had been, Krög was wiping the toad's blood and viscera off his face, and brushing it out of his tangled hair. The goop stuck offensively to his fingers no matter how much he tried to shake it off. Seated cross-legged with a pouting look on her face next to the empty husk of Shell, Lee dripped with slime that ran like syrup down her body and squelched grotesquely with every subtle movement she made as she shifted uncomfortably. Bags and crates of spices were shattered apart in the brawl, and their contents still floated like dust in the breeze, making the air *almost* fragrant against the pungent stench of charred, exploded toad.

Ydal was the first to break the hanging silence and let loose another brain numbing scream, though more from total skin-crawling loathing, than fear. As the piercing, howling shriek split through the forest, Lee just quietly sat, nodding her head slowly as though begrudgingly agreeing with the princess's one-note appraisal of things. Krög winced, but did not dare plug his fingers into his ears for fear of stuffing toad guts further into their depths, which was something he absolutely did not want to have to clean out later. Though, admittedly, the athletic young woman crouched next to the shell of the dissolved snail was in far worse state, absolutely cocooned in the putrid slime of her former captor. Ashley was almost completely clean, save for some ogre blood and slobber on his knuckles, and he grimaced visibly at the Lady's screech.

Eventually Ydal let off and stormed away from the campsite, the occasional twist and wriggle interrupting her normally catlike stride as though she was offended by her own movements, foamy innards of the cockroach creeping slowly down her face and shoulders. Krög nodded at Ash who took off after the princess to keep watch over her, wherever it was she was headed off without saying another word. The Battle Prince walked gingerly over to Lee, who was still seated, a blank expression on her face. He reached out a hand to help the small girl to her feet, which she turned gradually towards and stared at vacantly for a few moments.

Krög knelt next to her, "Hey, are you okay?"

As soon as he dropped to her level, Lee stood abruptly, to which the young ruler did the same, confused by her sharp movement. She curled her fingers a few times and squared her shoulders, before lightly pulling her palms across her bright hair as though gently grooming herself despite the revolting slop she was covered in. The youthful woman then pursed her lips and narrowed her eyes as though very much in thought.

"Do you feel better?" the Battle Prince asked quietly, wondering if the whole experience had really traumatized her, "Is there anything you need?"

Lee raised a single finger to cut him off and started to walk away. She took a few steps before pausing, wheeling around on her heels, and proudly striding back over to him. Her crystalline blue eyes searched his for a long moment, and she took in a long deep breath. With remarkable speed and passion she pulled the Battle Prince close and planted a kiss of fervor on his lips, which was an exceptionally disgusting experience given her own mouth was still slimed with snail goo. Lee pulled quickly away from Krög, a strand of slop hanging between their faces, and slapped him.

Hard. He opened his mouth to object, at which point she struck the Battle Prince again from the opposite side and gave the young ruler an expectant stare that practically dared him to say anything else. Krög shut his mouth and raised his hands in surrender. Confident he had no intention to say anything else, Lee tiptoed in a circle and daintily waltzed in the direction Ash and Ydal had gone.

Krög rubbed the side of his face. On the one other occasion he had said something truly offensive enough for Lee to lay into him, he had a whole previous evening's worth of alcohol still surging through his veins to dull the blow. Quite awake, adrenaline receding, and amplified by a layer of toad guts and snail glue, the smarting on his cheek hung there for longer than he liked, but maybe not quite as long as he deserved. He could not even wipe the snail slop off his lips, or the toad gore on his hands would have gotten in his mouth. All he could do was drip fetid fluids and take a final look around at the carnage. The Battle Prince sighed through his nose, which precipitated a bubble of some substance he did not want to think about forming at his nostril and popping in his face. It felt like a suitable conclusion to the moment.

Lee's singsongy voice called back to him from the tree line, "Oh, prince," she hung on to the words and drew them out playfully, "Waiting on you now. And someone has some new responsibilities to make up for his total lack of heroism today. Responsibilities involving pampering a certain someone until she decides he's paid his due. Responsibilities that start now!"

Krög was already in the doghouse, so to speak, for trying to split his affections between Lee and Ydal, the later of whom he was more *obligated* to get along with than he actually did. He had no interest in adding more to the bright young woman's twisted, though humorous, sense of justice and retribution.

"Coming, dearest," the Battle Prince yelled back with no small amount of snark, something he immediately regretted as a glob of toad fell into his mouth.

"I hope that's not sarcasm," Lee's voice never broke its chipper, youthful cadence, "I'd hate to have to add to your new, fun list of chores."

"Yeah," Krög grumbled under his breath, "I'll bet you would."

At last, the young ruler abandoned the site of the unfortunate picnic in Troll Country and headed off after his friends, clothes and sword dripping with unpleasant souvenirs of the afternoon romp. He wondered quietly to himself whether they would be able to clean up suitably to hide the evidence of the uncomfortable adventure from his father. Krög did not fancy walking into the Great Hall still covered crown to boots in gore, and having to explain himself to the Battle King and anyone else who happened to be visiting the court. For more reasons than one, the Battle Prince could not recall a time in his life he more wanted to be clean. The thought of plunging into a riverside oasis of the Swordsong's crisp, clear waters was like ambrosia to his mind. Even just imagining the torrid pools of icy water racing through his clothes and over his skin made the Battle Prince almost hysterical to bathe the afternoon away.

Not far ahead, the young ruler finally rejoined the rest of his company, a hideous trail of garments, boots, belts and adornments still caked in nastiness preceding them. Only a short distance below Krög, in the pool they had originally stumbled upon, Lee and Ydal were already scrubbing gunk out of their hair and off of their flesh. A thin film of unimaginable filth and scum had already formed on the surface of the oasis around the two women, but it was being quickly whisked away by the tides of the Swordsong. The princess had clearly forgotten her earlier shame and was just as bereft of clothing as the spritely, athletic girl in the waters with her. Both appeared to be tolerating each other's presence for the simple, refreshing pleasure of getting clean. Ashley was nearby, though facing the opposite direction, doing his utmost to respect the privacy of the two women, but standing guard all the same.

A weary, but delighted smile crawled over Krög's countenance, and he could not be sure whether he was more excited to see teasing glimpses of tantalizing skin, or the prospect of cleaning the crap out of his own crevices. It almost did not matter; he just wanted to be out of his clothing and in the pool, whether the girls were there or not, so he could soak away the crusted toad guts and snail goo. Before he was even down the embankment the Battle Prince was already tugging off his boots as he stumbled across the soft, mossy grounds, and working to undo the buckles of his belts and baldric. Lee spotted him starting to disrobe and raised a declarative hand as her voice crescendoed to declamatory level.

"Nope," the bright girl stopped the young ruler in his tracks, "Not even a little, not even a lot. You stay right there until we have decided we are done."

"Lee," Krög huffed, "I'm disgusting, I just want to get clean."

"Let me explain to you how this works," Lee yelled from the water, "Heroes of legend come back bloody and dirty from battle and are bathed clean by their servants and concubines while they relish in feasts and lavish comforts. You are neither hero, nor legend, and princess and I are neither your servants nor your concubines. And since this whole little mess has deprived us all of anything resembling feasting or *minor* comforts, you do not get the pleasure of bathing in our company. You wait your turn."

The Battle Prince's shoulders dropped, "You cannot be serious."

"Oh, I'm serious," the small young woman nodded vigorously, "And I'm betting if princess here hadn't shouted herself hoarse, she'd tell you how serious she was as well."

Ydal turned halfway towards the prince and nodded curtly at him over her shoulder.

"See?" Lee said, "Sit your ass down in the mud and pout if you must, but stay out of the water until we've had enough time to decide whether or not to ever leave the city with you again."

Krög dejectedly settled into the loam and put his head in his hands, "I still don't see how this is *my* fault."

"TWICE" Lee laughed loudly, "They recaptured you TWICE, stupid prince."

"It could have happened to anyone," the young ruler scoffed.

"And yet it happened to you," the athletic girl sang, "But never you mind that, King Mopey. Just stretch out your hands and get your best grovel ready- I imagine Ydal and I will have some fun ways for you to make up."

Krög snorted indignantly, and then wondered if the glint in Lee's eyes was more suggestive than sadistic. He let himself laugh a little and decided his star with her was not yet extinguished after all. Was she frustrated? Put out? Haphazardly disappointed and yet wryly unsurprised? Yes, she was likely all of those things. And yet she was also intriguingly finding ways for him to continue to spend time around her, even if it was at the expense of his pride. Though, the Battle Prince reasoned, he more than deserved it given he could barely handle outwitting three block-headed ogres and a scuttle of oversized vermin. Some days, being an up and coming champion of the realm was more work than he liked.

Ashley lumbered over to his friend and sat down heavily next to the prince, still trying to keep from looking at the women in the water, "Will talk to Lèanbh. Am sure she has things little wrong in head. Probably just fear of being eaten make her remember not so good."

"Oh, she's pretty close to being right on this one, buddy," Krög sighed, "They're not exactly going to raise a statue of me in the town square for deeds of high valor today."

The troll rocked a bit, "Still, no doubt you try you hardest against much daunting odds and defended ladies with great courage."

"Daunting odds, maybe," the young ruler agreed, "I don't know about the courage part- I was pretty much scared witless myself."

"You fight when I arrive," Ashley pointed out, "You slay big toad and big snail all by you self, and never even flinch when things get messy."

Krög laughed, "Buddy, I think you did the heavy lifting when you pounded the slobber out of those ogres. I'm not sure I was all that much help."

Ash shrugged, "Would have been very hard wrestle down ogres with tongue of giant toad holding back. You intervention was necessary."

The young ruler smiled faintly, "You're absolutely determined to see me in a positive light, aren't you?"

"Know there much good in you heart, much courage in you soul," the troll scratched his head and tried to think of a tactful way to phrase his follow up, "It just... sometimes... maybe you move feet faster than ground can catch up. That okay though, you find you stride eventually. *Then* we boot evil to ground *together*."

Krög laughed out loud, "Yeah, we will indeed, my friend."

Lee called liltingly, "Prince, having fun is for heroes. That's enough laughing for one afternoon."

The Battle Prince snickered, but lowered his voice, "She's going to be mad at me for a while."

"Maybe not so long as you think," Ash rumbled, "The Lady might be another story, but Lèanbh only play mad. Can hear in her voice. She think whole thing one big, funny adventure."

"Right," the young ruler rolled his eyes, "Because walking through an enchanted forest only to be beset by gigantic magical animals and their ogre lackeys who are intent on eating you for lunch constitutes adventure," Krög immediately halted as dawning realization connected, "Eh, never mind, she might be right."

"Always right," Lee sang from the pool, a mischievous look in her gaze as though she had somehow heard the entire conversation between the prince and his troll.

Ashley grimaced, "Maybe is best we take this elsewhere."

"I'm starting to think that's a good idea," Krög stood uneasily to his feet, squirming a little as something cold and slimy slid down his back, and sticky gore squelched at his movements, "What are we going to do about those ogres, by the way? We just knocked them out and left. Shouldn't we, I don't know... slay them?"

"Ogres very stupid," the troll appraised, "VERY stupid. They not so good hunters and they not so good thinkers. Probably got talked into whole thing by big toad. Good bet a little threatening and stern talking-to set them on the right path."

"You want to lecture the things that tried to eat me today?" the Battle Prince raised an eyebrow suspiciously.

"Short lecture," Ash promised, "Have very convincing argument for them stay away from eating peoples."

"And that is?" Krög pressed.

"Very Convincing Argument," the troll explained.

"A which…" the young ruler started to ask before realizing his Honor Guard's very convincing argument was in fact Very Convincing Argument, the name of Ashley's hammer, "Oh, right. Got it now. Yeah, that'll probably work."

"You keep eye on girls," Ash advised as he rose to full height and headed back in the direction of the ruined campsite, "Only, not literally. That not prince like. Stand guard, don't stare hard, hrm," the troll chuckled at his rhyme.

Even Krög snorted a sarcastic little laugh, "Sure thing, buddy. Don't be long though, they'll leave me out here," he flipped his head towards the women in the pool over his shoulder.

"Damn right we will," Lee yelled, her uncanny hearing not missing a single thing.

The young ruler stiffened and narrowed his eyes, "How the hell does she do that?"

"She listen," Ashley winked, "Be back soon."

Krög sat by the crystal clear pool while his friend lumbered back into the woods to dispense teachings of justice, honor and dignity to a group of creatures notorious for accusing mushrooms of having extraordinarily caustic argumentative tendencies. The young ruler relaxed knowing the mighty troll was at the very least in earshot, ready to come to their rescue again… if need be. He let the cool evening breeze of the waning days of summer wash over him and carry the scent of cooked toad and melted snail far away. The Battle Prince took in a long series of breaths as the afternoon receded to early twilight, and the sky took on the hue of blushed rose, turning the swirling pool's surface a giddy crimson. It had been a long afternoon, and if he was not careful, they would be late for dinner.

As soon as the thought of the evening meal crossed Krög's mind, he immediately became conscious of how hungry he was. Their carefully laid, if hastily executed, plans for a secret picnic among the quiet majesty of River Glen had never been fully realized, and the prince realized he was absolutely ravenous. It made the young ruler laugh, how they had been so distracted by the things trying to eat them, even after the ordeal was over they had forgotten to eat themselves. Life is funny sometimes, he decided.

Over the rumblings of his stomach, the Battle Prince did eventually hear Ashley return, and Lee and Ydal were at last considerate enough to relinquish the oasis to allow the young ruler to clean himself up. Of course, they stood at the edge of the water, made a few inappropriate comments about his physicality and hurried him along the whole time, robbing Krög of the relaxing bath he had been hoping for. At the very least, however, he did end up clean enough he did not feel as though he had taken a dip in entrails, and there was just enough remaining sunlight to dry his clothes on the walk back to the Fortress City, which would conceal the last evidence of their ill advised jaunt through the Thorn Rift Forest. The Battle Prince brushed the last of the toad skin out of his tangled hair, and pulled on his boots just as Lee and the princess's respective patiences expired.

"Come on, stupid prince," Lee moaned, though mostly sarcastically, "Daddy Battle King is going to be worried if we don't get home soon."

"If your father asks, I'm going to tell him *exactly* what happened," Ydal crossed her arms haughtily, her voice a rough, husky tone after all her screaming, "*If* he asks, that is."

It was as close to the Lady offering to cover for Krög as he was going to get.

Together, the troupe set off briskly and waltzed back out of the tree-line and across the wild, open fields north of the Fortress City. Already the sun had sunk low on the western horizon and autumn's creep tried to muscle in an early night of brisk air, born in on the easterly mountain wind. It was a perfect late summer evening, clear and sharp, the few early stars to show their faces twinkling madly above as the moon just started to crest over the edge of the world. All around them tiny, dancing lights of firefly tails winked on and off, and the musical lilt of cricket song chirped quietly among the tall grasses. All things considered, it was a wonderfully serene ending to an otherwise eccentrically bizarre day.

The four friends trotted along, talking and humming amongst themselves here and there as the immense walls of the Fortress City and the Great Hall finally broke into view. It was a welcome sight to weary eyes and a comforting monument to souls rattled a little with fear. Krög sighed almost audibly when the roaring torches of the home fires along each watchtower greeted them from a distance, and he knew he was home. Rarely was he so excited to be so.

Lee's hand in his pleasantly interrupted the Battle Prince's thoughts, "Hey," she whispered so neither Ash nor Ydal would hear, "Meet me at the Hill tonight?" she referred to their favorite spot to sneak out together: at the darkened peak of the Scorched Hill behind the Great Hall.

"You really ready to slip out again already?" Krög lightly squeezed her hand, "Aren't you afraid you'll end up baking on the grasses?"

"I'll take my chances," she winked at him, "Just thought maybe you'd want something those creeps back there never got from me."

"Oh yeah," he nudged her with his hips, "What's that?"

Lee raised her eyebrows excitedly, a playful, flirtatious gleam in her crystalline eyes, "Dessert."

Krög allowed himself to glance down at her, not really shocked at her candor but certainly at how bold she was being in such close proximity to the others- normally Lee reserved her more explicit chiding for their quiet moments alone.

She added, "And just so we're clear, you *will* have to earn it this time."

With little more than an over-the-shoulder smile, Lee bounded off ahead of the group to do a few flips and cartwheels as they approached the city gates, if just to feel the rush of wind on her face. Krög laughed quietly through his nose. He would never understand the young woman's tides, and the more he got to know her, the less he *wanted* the entirety of her mystery understood and explained. The Battle Prince liked her freewheeling, mysterious, here-now, there-then ways. She was hysterically unpredictable and yet steadily of bright disposition. Lee was an enigma, and one the young ruler genuinely enjoyed having to toil over.

As if he could sense Krög's thoughts, Ashley put a massive paw on the Battle Prince's shoulders and smiled crookedly between his tusks. The young ruler returned the grin and slapped his mighty troll on the back as they strode under the heavy iron grating of the gates back into the Fortress City. Lee vanished into the shadows somewhere before them, and Ydal swayed pointedly towards the Battle Queen's House of Waiting where she no doubt would seek a velvet pillow to lay on and a hand maiden to gripe to. Krög and Ash made their way through the city and up the stairs of the Great Hall, where the inviting fires of the throne room lit the long chamber warmly beyond. The Battle King was pacing about the hall. He was unusually frantic given his typically even-keeled demeanor.

"There you are," his gravelly voice creaked and thundered when Krög and the troll approached, "Where have you been all day, boy?"

"Well..." the Battle Prince began, realizing he had not taken time to think up a suitable lie to cover his absence.

"Never mind, never mind," the Battle King said hurriedly, "There has been a turn in the war up north. Merchant Lord Berun will be joining us this very evening for a celebratory dinner, and I need you looking your finest and acting on your best behavior when he arrives."

"Yes, of course, father," Krög was relieved his disappearance had been distracted by other matters.

"I mean it, son," the old man said sternly, "He's not exactly thrilled you and his daughter get along like a fish and a thorn bush," the young ruler could not be exactly sure what the Battle King meant by the odd turn of phrase, "So I'm expecting you to be nothing less than absolutely charming tonight. He's even bringing his own personal chef to prepare a special meal tonight."

The Battle Prince wrinkled his nose, "What exactly are they making?"

"Some Northern delicacy, I imagine," the old man waved his hand dismissively and started back to the business of straightening the Great Hall for company, "Frog legs or the like."

Krög and Ashley shifted uncomfortably.

"Um, frog legs..." the Battle Prince protested meekly, "Can I sit this one out?"

The Battle Prince and the Magnificent Octopus

Krög, the Battle Prince, barely had time to roll out of the way of the swinging axe. It came down with the force of a thousand-pound guillotine blade, carving out a deep trench in the dirt where the prince had just been. In the moment it took for the wielder to dislodge the weapon from the grip of the earth, the young ruler managed to flip back to his feet and set himself to receive another attack. Two more vicious swings came within mere inches of Krög's skin, and a shockingly quick third blow clipped a lock of his hair off as the axe blade sailed over the prince's scalp. With a twist and a tumble Krög shuffled past his foe and came wheeling back into the fight. Thundersteel was ready to strike back.

Sweat flew from the prince's brow and flicked from his wrists as he hammered at his opponent in return. His attacker deftly caught each strike on the edge of his axe, but the keen blade of the young ruler's mystic sword succeeded in shattering the opposing weapon. Steel shards of the axe's head splintered dangerously in every direction as it broke apart, and both Krög and his foe were forced to retreat from one another, lest they catch one of the iron fragments in their flesh. It was just enough an opportunity for the prince's opponent to snatch up a discarded sword laying in the sand nearby. The young ruler drew back a hair to reset himself. His breath came in ragged pants and his heart thundered in his chest. Already, the fight had gone on much longer than he had expected, and he was wearing down.

Across from him, however, Krög's opponent showed absolutely no signs of tiring. Though perspiration dripped in gleaming rivulets along enormous muscles decorated with twisting, spiraling tattoos, the foe's breathing was even and calm. There was an unyielding ferocity in his eyes, and the prince knew the attacker did not intend to make their contest an easily decided one. Somehow, Krög had to figure out how to win before exhaustion broke his grip and crumpled his stance. Losing was not an option. Not with so much on the line.

If it were possible, the prince's opponent was even faster and more savage with a sword in his hands than with an axe. Quickly, Krög was rocked back on his heels as the slashes and thrusts came dangerously close to his vital spots. He barely squirmed out of the way of one stab that came so close to landing, the young ruler could feel the flat of the blade cold on his chest. Cursing he did not have armor on, the prince spun along the length of his opponent's weapon and landed behind him. Krög planted his shoulder in the small of his foe's back and lifted with everything he had. The attacker flipped backwards over the prince and slammed heavily to the ground. Before he could recover, Krög whirled around and placed the edge of Thundersteel under his foe's chin.

For several terse moments, the attacker glared fiercely at the prince, before his eyes relaxed and he grunted a single word.

"Yield."

Around the practice yard, a chorus of applause and hoots of approval rang out as the prince let out a breath he did not realize he had been holding in, and relaxed as well.

Krög reached out a hand to help the warrior up, "Damn, Detlev, you almost had me that time."

"I would have, too, if it weren't for that bloody blade of yours," the tattooed barbarian snarled, looking woefully at what was left of his axe scattered around the sandy pit.

Behind them, coins jingled and clinked as money exchanged hands among the onlookers and new wagers were placed. Krög popped his eyebrows and looked proudly at Detlev.

"What'd I win?" he asked slyly.

Detlev waved over a scorekeeper and riffled through the scraps of paper he was handed. The barbarian glowered at the results.

"A week's worth of stable duties," the warrior reported grouchily, "And since it was your third win straight today, all of next month's artifact polishing in the Great Hall. The weapon break also gets you tomorrow's sweeping of the throne room."

Despite how the others ran their wagers, Krög never bet money against his father's barbarians- it was crass and uncouth given the riches the Battle Family possessed. He would gladly, however, bet them chores and responsibilities any day of the week.

The prince laughed loudly and proudly, "And suddenly the weekend was filled with free time and leisure. Is that the best the Warbrands can offer up?"

He threw a cocky challenge at the other tattooed warriors hanging around the practice yard.

For the sake of those unfamiliar with the ranks and regiments of the Southern Reach, the barbarian hordes actually had a fair degree of organization. Of all the squadrons and batteries of wild-eyed, sturdy warriors, none were tougher, none were meaner, none were nastier, and none were more victorious than the Battle King's personal legion, the Warbrands. Earning a place among the Warbrands meant being a head and shoulders above all the other barbarians in the whole country, both in brutal skill and bloody battlefield triumphs.

Detlev, the prince's sparring partner, was one of their number. Years before, he and Krög had been close friends in War School. At one time, the two were nearly inseparable, getting into all manner of trouble and raising their fair share of hell as teenagers with too much time and energy on their hands. Truly, had things played out a bit differently, Detlev would have made a smart choice for one of the prince's Honor Guards. However, after joining the barbarian legions, he swiftly found himself on the frontline of the eastern defenses where his surgical skill with an axe at first earned him the nickname "the Destroyer," followed soon by the full Warbrand honor. As with all their members, the entire right side of his body was covered with violet tattoos to mark him as one of the most dangerous warriors in the Three Known Kingdoms. And he had just been toppled by the Battle Prince.

Krög was undaunted, "Anyone? Is somebody going to step up and defend the honor of the Warbrands?"

There was more clanking of coinage as new bets were placed, and a hushed murmur among the onlookers as they waited for someone else to step up and answer the young ruler's challenge. Given the apparent pummeling he had just laid out on a Warbrand, no one seemed particularly anxious.

"Oh, *please*," a lone dissenting, unimpressed voice pipped up, "He *let* you win."

Lee hopped the ropes surrounding the practice yard and tagged Detlev out. She smiled slyly at the Warbrand as they passed each other, giving the hulking warrior an affectionate slap, before planting herself in front of Krög, crossing her arms and raising an eyebrow expectantly at the prince.

"Warbrands don't let anyone win," the young ruler stood resolutely by his victory.

"*He* did," Lee maintained, "And so did the two bantams before him."

Bantam was perhaps an unfair way to describe the massive barbarians the prince had bested in earlier matches, and somewhat ironic given Lee was less than half the size of the smallest warrior around the yard.

Krög rested his sword on his shoulder and eyed her, annoyed, "I suppose you think *you* could do better?"

She laughed musically, "Prince, I taught you practically every move you just used out there."

He shook it off, "Well, I've gotten better since our last lesson."

Bemused shock took her countenance, "Oh, is that so?"

Krög pressed his luck, "Plus, I'm stronger than you are."

Lee did not blanch. At most, her eyes took on a quiet confidence reserved for someone out of the league of the person they were speaking too. She chewed her tongue thoughtfully for a moment.

"Alright, you're on," she smiled broadly "A lesson, and a match."

The prince hefted his sword forward and leaned on it casually, "Stakes?"

"Double or nothing," Lee replied, "Everything you just won from Detlev twice over. Plus, if I get you flawlessly, then you resume your role as my dedicated servant until the leaves change."

A flawless victory was one defined as when your opponent fails to knock you to the ground or disarm you at any point in the match.

And Krög had only just recently gotten out from under the yoke of Lee's twisted sense of penance in remittance for her silence regarding the nature of the prince's haphazard victory over the dragon, Raicleach, followed closely by his debt to her for being a bumbling idiot during their ill-fated picnic weeks earlier. Mostly, her idea of payment involved an absolutely staggering amount of massage and pampering, but she occasionally leveled him with a task of such preposterous and inappropriate design, it strained his humility to the near breaking point. While he enjoyed being at Lee's beck and call more than he was willing to admit, the prince was also anxious to be free of her conniving mind.

Still, he did not know when to quit. Wisdom did not become the Battle Prince.

"You're on," he smiled, a swagger in his voice, "I am going to love having a personal servant for the next few weeks."

Again, she giggled melodically, "As if you don't already. Though, I think maybe you overestimate your chances. And for the record, so do *they*."

Lee motioned at the hurried exchanges occurring as the prince accepted her challenge, and the wagers turned rapidly against him. Extraordinary sums of coin went whipping the opposite direction they had just come, and everyone settled in to watch the young ruler get absolutely trounced.

Krög rolled his eyes and shook off his frustration, "Get ready to be disappointed," he scoffed at her.

She grinned all the wider, "I could say the same thing to you, but I think the taste of sand will say it better."

Lee flitted to the weapons rack on the edge of the practice yard and selected a slender sword matched for her stature. After snapping it around a few times, she discarded the weapon in favor of something heavier and longer. A lesser person of her diminutive form would have needed two hands to use the blade she settled on. The lithe young woman held it steadily in one.

"Now then," she raised the sword and took her stance, "Lessons first. Do you remember this waltz, prince?"

Krög brandished his own blade, and placed its flat against the side of Lee's.

"Refresh my memory," he said overweeningly.

Lee's lips returned his boastful sneer, "As you wish. Ready? Follow me, I'll count us in. One, two, thirteen."

Her attacks came as light taps in groups of three at a cadence she rattled off as she tested Krög's memory of her exercises.

"Quick, quick, slow," she called the pacing of each strike, "Quick, quick, slow. And cha cha cha, and cha cha cha. Not bad," she admonished, "Faster now. Quick, quick, slow. Quick, quick, slow."

The prince snapped Thundersteel into place with each 'quick' count, and swept it through each of her binds on every 'slow' count. As their blades came together, the ringing of steel against steel chimed in chorus to the clip she set. With every repetition, Lee sped up the pace and tightened her form. Her attacks started to come in irrationally small spaces, and Krög quickly found himself on the very real defensive. Just when he was certain he could not keep up and worried he was about to get all too quickly embarrassed, Lee let off.

"Excellent," she quipped, "Your footwork is much better and your parries are getting cleaner. You still need to watch your weak side attacks, but that will come with practice. Again?"

From the corner of Krög's eyes, he could see money subtly changing hands as a few early wagers were won and lost, and the stakes of several others changed. He was winning back some of his decriers.

"After you, Blademaster," he joked.

"Good," she responded curtly, "This time, you lead me. I'll count us back in. And, five, six, twenty eight."

Krög called the attacks, "Quick, quick, slow. Quick, quick, slow."

"Very nice," Lee nodded, "Faster."

"Quick, quick, slow," the prince repeated the forms, "Quick, quick, slow."

"Faster," she urged.

"Cha cha cha," the young ruler pushed his muscles harder, "Cha cha cha!"

A cloud of sand billowed under the stomping of Krög's boots and the prancing of Lee's toes as they, assuredly, danced through the exercise. The young woman's fighting style was just as flashy and entertaining as it was mortally effective. Again, just before the prince was exhausted by the pace, Lee withdrew.

"Well!" she said excitedly, "Someone's been practicing!"

"I told you I had gotten better," Krög came back, trying to keep his hurried breathing in check.

"Mhm," she looked at him both amusedly and patronizingly, "You're just about ready to take on a sheep at full strength, aren't you?"

"Hey, that was pretty damn good!" the prince defended vehemently.

"Okay, prince," Lee raised her sword again, "Match me."

Krög placed the edge of his blade next to her's, and set himself.

She popped her eyebrows, "Game on."

In less than the space it took for the prince to blink, Lee vaulted over him completely and landed behind the young ruler. She kicked him hard between the shoulders. Krög went sailing through the air as though someone had tied one end of a rope to his chest, and the other end to a charging mustang. He skidded face first in the sand, but recovered just enough to twist into a forward roll and get quickly back to his feet. It was not a moment too soon, as Lee had closed the distance between them in hardly two springing leaps. He deflected her next attack with his sword, and jumped over her following blow just before she managed to kneecap him. Lee thrust out swiftly as Krög landed, but the young ruler pivoted and spun out of the way. The point of her blade went sailing by, and the prince came pummeling after the agile girl.

Everything Krög threw at Lee was met with empty air. She positively defied the human limitations of grace and speed. Her movements were fluid and mercurial, and her blocks were practically in place before it seemed the prince had even decided to attack. No matter how hard he swung, nothing shivered the athletic young woman's grasp on her sword despite Krög's best attempts to batter it away. Her face was all playful delight, in stark contrast to the young ruler's look of intense concentration. Lee was light, airy and effervescent- Krög was by contrast heavy, fervent and more than a little frustrated.

The prince committed to a particularly disorderly strike, and the limber girl swatted it aside casually. She followed with a closed-fisted blow that landed on Krög's teeth with the proximate sensation of an avalanche against his jaw. He about blacked out completely, but somehow managed to maintain his footing and narrowly skirt aside the swinging sword that trailed behind the rattling knock. Barely aware of what he was doing, the young ruler lashed out quickly just to try and rock Lee away from him. By a small miracle, his blade connected with hers, and the weapon flew out of her hand. Not pausing, she backflipped the direction it had flown, and caught the sword before it clattered into the sand. Her flawless victory was still within reach.

While it had been fun, Lee was done toying with the prince. She struck four times in quick succession, breaking the rhythm of three they had established and forcing Krög into a hurried, unexpected parry. Using the opportunity Krög gave her as his fourth block came up a little awkwardly, the young woman spun quickly and snapped her leg out behind the young ruler. She drove her shoulder against his chest, and rammed Krög out of his stance. He tumbled over her extended leg, and she swept him to the ground. With a flourish, she placed the tip of her sword under the prince's chin and pressed it lightly against his neck.

The Battle Prince huffed a few times, "Yield."

An absolutely deafening chorus of applause and hollers went up from the onlookers. The accompanying clanging of coins being thrown every which way as scores of wagers and bets were settled up only put an exclamation point on the absurdity of the prince being cast aside by the slight girl. Lee smirked at him as he lay sprawled in the sand, and flitted to where Detlev was watching the match. She snatched the pages the Warbrand was holding and skipped over to deliver them to Krög.

"Artifact polishing, stable duty, and throne room sweeping," she read off each as she flipped through the earlier wagers, "Yep. Everything seems to be accounted for."

Lee handed the scraps of paper to the prince, who begrudgingly reached out and accepted them. She smiled broadly, and then offered her other hand to help the young ruler back to a stand.

"Maybe next time, prince," she tousled his hair as he stood, and brushed off the sand sticking to the sweat on his chest, "It's okay. I used to fight like that, too- and then I had my first bottle of milk."

Uproarious laughter broke loose from the watching warriors.

"I hate you," the prince carped, not really meaning it, but definitely feeling the need to say it.

"Awe, sweetheart," she cooed in response, "Such a way with words you have. You need to get better at losing- it's going to keep happening."

Krög opened his mouth to retort. Lee raised her brow expectantly, and waited for him to say something stupid. In a remarkably aware moment, the prince just shut his jaw, sheathed Thundersteel, and started to limp to the edge of the practice ring where the circle of barbarian spectators were waiting to help him out of the pit.

Burly hands grasped him around his shoulders and hauled the exhausted Battle Prince out of the practice yard, and slapped him jovially in acknowledgement of the spectacular matches he had put on. Not one of them would say a word about the prince losing to Lee. On the one hand, he was the son of the Battle King, and even the most hard-headed of the lot was not dumb enough to make a sideways comment at their future lord. On the other hand, Lee had only the other day knocked two of the warriors unconscious, and relieved another of several of his teeth- all in the same match. How she managed to flatten so many of them was just part of the alluring mystery that was Lèanbh.

A rough hand gave the young ruler a damp towel, and Krög went about cleaning himself up. He had barely spit a mouthful of bloody sand into the rag and partially dusted off his shoulders when Lee whistled from the sandy pit.

"Oh, prince," she waved at him, "You know, I have to concede," the lithe girl twisted at the trunk a few times and worked her shoulders around, "I'm a little sore after our workout. And my feet are pretty tired from all this dancing. Hm. If only I had a dedicated servant who owed me complete acquiescence. Wait a minute, that's right! I do!"

Krög sighed and his shoulders dropped. Several low hoots and stifled chuckles surrounded him. The young ruler glared in the direction he had thought they came from, but all of the barbarians standing around him were doing a fantastic job of avoiding his gaze. Even his old buddy Detlev did not dare make eye contact.

The prince sighed, "Let's get this over with."

"You mean let's get started," Lee corrected gleefully, "I'm counting on a late autumn this year."

She pranced to the edge of the practice yard. The onlooking warriors practically fell over themselves to be the one to help her out of the ring, several even roughly shoving Krög aside for the honor- or maybe pleasure. Lee paused and rolled her eyes, though lovingly.

"Now, boys," she crossed her arms, "Not all at once. You," Lee pointed at Krög, and then turned her extended hand over for him to pull her out of the yard, "Help a lady?"

Everyone smiled knowingly at the prince. Krög snorted, but a smile cracked his countenance and he reached out to take Lee's hand. She grinned as he did so, but proceeded to flip over the ropes of the yard without his aid. Again, everyone laughed and crowed.

"Where were we?" she asked, her crystalline eyes pretending to search the young ruler for a cue, "Oh, that's right. On our way back to my room so you can start working off your debt."

Every single barbarian whooped lewdly.

Again, Lee gave them all a playful look of shock and exasperation, "Not like that!" she side-eyed the prince, "He's not that lucky. Come along, prince," the small young woman brushed past him and beckoned with one finger over her shoulder, "Follow."

As she made her way through the crowd of onlookers, Krög sent a burning, smoldering, seething gaze at the surrounding crowd.

"Any one of you tells my father *or* Ydal about this," he said just loud enough for them to hear, "And you're on third shift guard duty until winter. NEXT winter."

The crowd of barbarians nodded vigorously and coughed or cleared their throats in quiet acknowledgement. Mostly, they did so to keep from breaking into hysterical smiles or fits of snickering.

Lee whistled again, "Princey-poo, where are you?"

At once, the crowd parted swiftly to allow Krög to follow her unhindered.

The prince shot them another look, "Wow, you guys are just... so helpful."

Hushed chuckles followed him out, before shouts announcing the next series of challenges and the song of ringing steel ushered the resumption of sparring matches. Krög trudged his way to Lee's arranged quarters. She had managed to con her way into a private room just off the Battle Queen's House of Waiting- they were among the more luxurious accommodations in the Fortress City. Her room was ideally situated to keep her right in the thick of things: equidistant to the Great Hall as it was the practice yards and also the nearest tavern and clothier. Lee could bounce from fighting, to drinking, to the Southern Reach's version of finery, and always be next door to her little "home." How she had acquired it was beyond Krög's reasoning, but that was Lee.

By the time the prince arrived, she was already partway through disrobing. She smiled coyly as he stumbled in and turned a number of incredible crimsons at seeing her half naked. Lee had proven on a number of occasions she was almost completely without shame, and it amused her to no end that a barbarian like the young ruler had an odd sensibility about such scruples. While

Krög was not above stripping down to jump in a river and go for a summer swim, there was something entirely different about walking in on a woman in a candlelit room as she peeled off layers of leather and hides. Of course, while he might have been mortifyingly embarrassed at catching her in the act of, ahem, getting more comfortable, the prince's more atavistic proclivities held his gaze a moment or two too long. His eyes ran the length of her flawless skin and lingered on the delicate curve of her back and the athletic ridges in her shoulders.

"Excuse me," Lee said, feigning offense, "Mind your manners, barbarian."

Krög shook himself and immediately turned around. He awkwardly pulled the door to her little cottage closed the rest of the way, and cursed to himself in chagrin. Over his shoulder, he could hear the girl snickering at him.

"Okay, prince, it's safe now," she teased.

The young ruler turned back around to face her. She was stretched languidly on her bed, covered only in a loose silk skirt from the waist down. Had she been lying face up, it would have challenged Krög's ability to find new palettes of burgundy to flush. Her electric locks were free from the ties she normally kept them wound up in, and the fair mane cascaded over her bare shoulders like a curtain of platinum velveteen. She rested her chin on her hands and smiled pleasantly at the prince.

"You may begin," Lee both demanded and invited.

Krög snorted at her commanding nature, but climbed on to the bed and sat across her hips. His grip was exhausted from wheeling Thundersteel around all morning during his sparring exercises, but he set about kneading the sinews of the athletic girl's back as best he could. Several of her joints cracked and popped as the prince dug his fingers and palms against her back, and Lee moaned contentedly as though relieved of a burdensome load. The touch of her skin was a complicated, disparate experience- it was like satin steel. Krög could never quite figure out how she could feel so delicate and yet so ironclad at the same time.

Lee yawned, "You should lose bets to me more often. I could get used to this."

The young ruler scoffed, "You're enjoying this way too much."

"No, no," she disagreed lightly, "I think I am enjoying it just exactly the right amount."

"I can't tell what you're getting more of a thrill out of," Krög retorted, "The massage, or the fact that you've got a royal tending to your whims."

She snuggled against her pillow and lazily replied, "Maybe equal parts both. Who knows? I'm complex."

"You're twisted and incorrigible is what you are," the prince shot back.

"Probably," Lee yawned again, "Neck, please."

Krög threw her a look she could not see, but brushed her fair, feathery hair off the top of her back, and readjusted his grip to gently squeeze just behind the girl's ears down to her shoulders. Lee rocked her head back and forth with his grasp and smiled, pleased.

She made a snarky suggestion, "You know, if the whole Battle Prince thing doesn't work out for you, I think you have solid career potential as a personal attendant."

"Thanks for that," he replied tritely, "I'll keep it in mind after my father disowns me for shirking household duties again. I do have other things I need to be doing, you realize- thanks to you, my chores load over the next month just doubled."

"Please," she giggled, "You avoid responsibility and duty like plague festered boils."

"Yeah, well," Krög came back at about par for his typical level of maturity, "So do you."

Lee chuckled in the way that sounded like a lively melody, "Prince, that's because I don't have any. Nobody needs anything from me," she pulled away from his grip a moment to look up over her shoulder at the young ruler directly, "You, on the other hand, actually have a place in this world," the girl settled her head back against the pillow before concluding, "And if you would quit dragging your heels all the time, you might actually be proud of that fact for once."

The prince absolutely did not want to hear it, "Ugh, now you sound like my dad."

"See? I could be a Battle Queen," Lee quipped, "Mm, then everyone would *have* to listen to my sage wisdom, and I could have a whole team of barbarians assuring my comfort and pleasure."

Krög paused a moment, unsure whether or not the lithe girl had just made a sideways suggestion or implication that, once again, she should be at the prince's side, and not Ydal. Then again, it might have just been another of Lee's egocentric musing in a mind jestingly convinced of its own superiority- if with good cause, all the same.

The young ruler tried to roll over the moment, "Being a member of the Battle Family isn't exactly filled with the luxurious trappings I feel like you think it is. My father is as much a warrior as he is a monarch, and my mother governs the municipalities more than she ever gets her hair fussed with. I'm next, and only, in line for the throne, and I don't even have someone waiting on me hand and foot."

"Speaking of," Lee kicked backwards and tapped Krög on the shoulder with her toes, "Feet."

Again, the prince rolled his eyes out of the young woman's view and cursed internally at giving her nifty ideas, but obediently shifted positions to satisfy her request.

"So, what?" the lithe girl went on, "You don't think I could run this country better than you could?"

"When I'm Battle King, I won't directly run the kingdom," Krög explained, "The king of the Southern Reach leads the barbarian hordes and manages our relationships with the other Three Known Kingdoms, while the queen reigns over the country itself. So, your question of comparison is baseless and invalid."

For half a beat, the prince actually felt like he had made a coherent, intelligent argument.

"What I'm hearing is they'll trust you to do things that are loud and destructive, but when it comes to anything regarding subtly or tact, it's left up to a better mind- namely a woman's," until, of course, Lee responded.

Krög tried to defend his future title, "I'd hardly qualify the treaties and diplomatic accords my father has arranged as 'loud and destructive.' What the hell does it matter to you, anyway? It's not like… I mean we don't… We aren't…" the prince tripped over several attempts at avoiding being coarse and offensive.

There was an awkward pause as the young ruler's betrothal interjected itself between him and Lee without being outright stated.

She lifted her other leg, "Other one."

The prince resumed, and desperately looked around the room for inspiration to change the topic of conversation. His eyes settled on a flower in a simple vase on her bedside table. Though its petals had drained their brilliant orange color to give over to a snowy white, the young ruler recognized the bloom as the Spring's Tears blossom he had plucked for her on the side of the mountain by Raicleach's cavern. Despite its pallor it did not droop, but continued to stand tall and proud.

"Your flower died," Krög said quietly.

"It didn't die, it changed," Lee corrected, "It's a Ghost Rose now. When Spring's Tears get pulled out of the earth they become a Ghost Rose, but they don't wither. That's why I like them so much. I kinda want to be like that one day," she laughed uncomfortably, "Sorry, that was silly."

"No it wasn't," the prince assured her quietly, "It was kind of beautiful. Just like…" he drifted.

Lee turned over suddenly, and fixed the young ruler with a particularly thoughtful stare that came bursting out of the depths of her crystalline eyes. Krög considered her in return, intense rumination carved into his own brow. She scrambled out from underneath the prince and threw her arms around his neck. The lithe girl pulled Krög close and passionately kissed him. In turn, the prince ran his hands up the velvety skin of her back and through her fine hair, returning the embrace. They sank into each other for a moment.

Just as swiftly, Lee shoved him away and scampered to the corner of her bed. A confused look of anger and longing pooled in her stare as she pulled a sheet around her shoulders to cover up.

"Get out," she said softly.

Krög held still, just as confused and stunned as she was.

"Lee, what?" he could barely stammer out a question.

"You can't talk to me about being betrothed and how things will be with your future wife, and then kiss me like that," she snapped.

"*You* kissed *me*!" the young ruler came back, shocked.

"And you kissed me back!" Lee retorted, somewhat irrationally, "You kissed me back like no one has…" she stopped and pulled at her hair, "Gods, you make me crazy, you know that?"

"You could be a little clearer about what you want too, Lee," Krög growled.

She looked at him, wide-eyed, "You really *don't* have a concept of subtly, do you? Like, at all. You're *that* stupid."

"What in the nine hells is that supposed to mean?" the prince argued back.

"It means, how big a damn signpost do I have to clobber you with before you start getting it?!" the lithe girl almost shouted in frustration.

"So you get to make eyes at anything that moves and I'm the one doing something wrong? Is that about the long and short of it?" Krög snapped.

"Do you even hear yourself? Do you understand how ridiculous that just sounded?" Lee came rocking back, "Prince. We've been over this. I'm not attached to anyone. I'd like for that to change with present company included, but, oh yeah, you're getting married! So, yes, I do get to 'make eyes' at whoever the hell I want until you stop talking out of both sides of your mouth and make a damn decision!"

"What do you want me to do?!" the young ruler barked, "Go up to my father and say 'Sorry, dad, but everything you've worked for to tie two kingdoms together just doesn't work for me. Let's call the marriage off.' Would that do it?!"

"It'd help!" Lee fired.

"You're unbelievable, you know that?" Krög's frustration was palpable, "Why do you get to do the 'subtle' thing, and I have to make some giant, grand gesture before you trust I feel the same way about you?"

She looked at him in abject shock and disbelief, "Because. YOU'RE. GETTING. MARRIED! Believe me, if I could do something as grandiose as upending an engagement to get my point across, I would, if for no other reason than I don't think you would understand a smaller gesture!"

The prince crossed his arms, "I'll call off the wedding when you stop flirting with Iolar."

Her look of astonishment only spread, "Are you for real?! Let me get this straight- while you make up your mind over which girl you want, I have to wait patiently on the ropes and not even see what else might be out there for me? Do know how disgustingly selfish that makes you sound, PRINCE?"

"Selfish?" Krög asked incredulously, "Selfish people get whatever they want. I barely have a choice in what clothes I get to wear! It's all about what's good for my family, what's good for the kingdom. YOU'RE the one who gets to do whatever whenever and just live free. You're the one who can do whatever you want!"

"Well what do you want?!" Lee gestured wildly.

"I want you!" the young ruler yelled without thinking.

"Then prove it!" she challenged.

"I can't!" Krög roared, before immediately quieting, "I can't. And you know I can't."

Lee buried her face in her hands before running her fingers through her hair in exasperation, "Get out," she repeated, "Come back when you find your spine. If you find it."

At last, the prince sighed and left, too frustrated to argue further and too confused to even know what to say anyway.

A squadron of Griffin Riders went screeching over the prince's head in practice formations as the young ruler stomped back into the streets of the Fortress City. He grumbled noisomely under his breath in vexation not only at the shifting tides of Lee's affection, but also at the grandeur of the impossibly arrogant Captain Iolar's personal dispatch of Riders. Though Krög would never admit it, they looked incredibly regal and awe-inspiring as they raced over the seeping crimson of dawn, dragging victory flags behind them as they prepared for an immense parade about to get underway. Even if it had been his idea to send the Griffin Riders north to the Ivory City to flush out Mordenall and his pirates, the prince absolutely regretted the decision as it now meant having to put up with at least a week's worth of celebration in the Captain's triumphant honor.

Only just a few days prior, the conflict north of the Swordsong River had been declared over, with success owed to the swift actions of the Southern Reach's snarling barbarian hordes. Barely qualifiable as a war, given the fighting had lasted only the tailing summer months and did not stretch on for years at a time as they were known to, everyone was none the less in quite the mood to celebrate the return of the all-conquering Griffin Riders. Everyone, that is, except for Krög, who practically exploded with jealous rage at the idea of Iolar getting to be the center of attention. The Battle Prince had begged to be the one to lock horns with Mordenall a second time, and was still stinging that he had been left out of the entire campaign. Add to that Lee's brusque dismissal of his company, and the young ruler was in absolutely no mood to celebrate anything at all. In fact, if he could find a way to avoid the whole thing altogether, he determined he would just spend the next week camping in the Thorn Rift Forest.

Of course, the Fortress City was not about to let the prince forget that it was poised to explode with a cavalcade of heroic proportion. Every time he turned a corner to dodge away from the growing throngs of excited revelers, the young ruler ran smack into an even larger collection of them. They all wanted to shake his hand or embrace him warmly for his 'tactical genius'- somehow the entire kingdom had become convinced Krög had single-handedly planned the downfall of the invading marauders. Largely, the truth of the matter was when his father had handed down final refusal to allow the prince to lead the assault, the young ruler had immaturely yelled out, 'Well then why don't you give Iolar something to do?! Everyone likes him more anyway!' Somehow that translated into selecting the most elite corp of Riders to lead the charge against the psychopathic Captain of the pirates, and a proclamation of Krög's brilliance in warfare and battle planning.

Only weeks earlier, the Battle Prince had returned from his perilous misadventure in Troll Country to the arrival of the Merchant Lord who was excitedly, if a bit begrudgingly, there to announce victory. It took less than the space of ten days to recall the majority of the Southern Reach's forces for the purpose of a success festival, and suddenly the whole city was abuzz with talk of righteous slaying and glorious violence. Krög had managed to avoid most of it by burying himself in chores or practicing furtively with the Warbrands, but the atmosphere was closing around him like a constricting serpent.   He was beginning to realize, rather unfortunately, that he would not be able to avoid it much longer unless he came up with a brilliant means of escape.   And, frankly, his brain was too sloshed with thoughts of the young woman he had just left to cohesively plot a convincing and effective getaway.

With really nowhere else to hide, the Battle Prince dodged his way to the Great Hall and hoped against hope he would find it largely abandoned, that he might have some peace to pontificate what idiotic misstep he had just managed with Lee.   Instead, he found his father seated at one of the long tables of the hall, pouring over pages and pages of documents that looked positively attention-killing.

Before the young ruler could wheel around and find somewhere else to go, the Battle King called out to him, "There you are!   Where have you been all morning, son?"

Krög huffed out of sight of the old man and turned to tread back into the throne room, "Practicing with the Warbrands."

The Battle King narrowed his eyes at his son, "You've been spending an awful lot of time with them lately."

"Shouldn't I be?" the young ruler could not help himself from rolling his eyes, "I mean, isn't that the point?   I need to become a great warrior, or something like that?"

"Given your present attitude and your marked history of a proclivity for avoidance and disinterest," the old man glowered at Krög, "I think perhaps I am not totally off base in questioning your recent commitment to training. Or is it, perhaps, simply another creative method you've concocted to slip free of your other responsibilities?"

The Battle Prince squirmed in his seat and changed the subject quickly, "What're you working on, dad?"

"Treaties," the Battle King did not drop his suspicious gaze at first, but eventually turned to the papers scattered before him, "Thanks to our intervention, the Merchant Lord has seen fit to amend some of the arrangements we had laid out originally."

"Amend in our favor, I hope," the young ruler lazily pushed some of the documents around, "We would deserve it after saving his ass."

"My son," Bröghue hastily replaced the pages Krög had disorganized, "For the last six generations, truly since Battle King Slamdrö, our country has been regarded as savages and war-mongers, interested only in our own barbaric conquests and with little inclination to joining the rest of the Three Known Kingdoms in civilized dealings. My grandfather Mögren and his father Ghömak especially made us no allies. I intend on turning the course of this kingdom a different direction- one towards prosperity. In order to change our stance in the world as a whole, we must now be willing to make sacrifices to our neighbors to prove we are in earnest- that we really do wish a peaceful coexistence. Even had there been no gain in it for our country, I still would have sent our forces north to liberate the Ivory City for that exact reason. Do you understand, boy?"

"Sacrifices," Krög sneered a little, "Like my marriage to Ydal?"

"For example," the Battle King nodded in agreement, "Though do not think for one moment you are the only one taking action you do not necessarily agree with. How do you think those who died defending the Northern Empire, and not the Southern Reach as they are sworn, felt in their last moments?"

The Battle Prince's shoulders fell a bit at that sobering thought, "Yeah. Yeah, I get it."

Bröghue studied the young ruler pensively a moment, "You know it would be invaluable experience to sit in on these discussions and negotiations. We are trying to build a future for both our kingdoms, and seeing as you will be an integral part of that one day, it would do you well to take part in the planning."

Krög winced, "Maybe next time, yeah?"

The Battle King sighed heavily, "When you are ready, I suppose," his voice carried with it a twinge of disappointment, "I can no more force you to desire your destiny than I can kill a yak with naught but the power of my mind."

The young ruler blinked at his father a few times, "What exactly do those two things have to do with each other?"

"Too much time spent with my brother, I suppose," the old man shrugged, "All the same. Understand, boy, I truly wait with rapt anticipation for the day you hear fate's call and become the Battle Prince I know you can be. The one I have seen flashes of, yet who seems to retreat every time some erstwhile daydream plows through the field of your mind. I wish I knew what it would take, but your mind and your motivations remain, forever, your own."

"It's not like I'm not trying, dad," Krög sprawled himself a bit dramatically on the table, "I mean, I went back to War School, I've been trying to keep up with my duties around the Great Hall, I've even tried to be friends with Ydal. I honestly don't know what else you're looking for."

"Child, it has absolutely nothing to do with what *I* am looking for," the Battle King tried to explain, "And everything to do with what *you* are looking for. And you can act the part of the Battle Prince all you want, but until you seek to be him *truly*, it will always be just that- an act. I can encourage you in the right direction, show you the steps you must take, even command you as your king to deeds of greatness, but until you *commit* to the path, it will *all* be hollow."

Krög let a heavy silence hang between them for a few moments before asking, "What did it for you? Uncle Gögan said you never wanted the throne until you went off on some adventure alone- what happened then that made you finally take the crown?"

A shadow passed over the Battle King's face, "My brother speaks out of turn, perhaps."

"So something did happen?" the young ruler pressed.

"Nothing you are yet prepared to concern yourself with, and nothing I would ever wish upon you in the meantime," the old man said sternly, "Krög, we all find our own way, and I'll be damned if the fires that forged me fall their blazes on you as well," he sighed deeply, a bone-rattling breath that sounded like he were exhaling a ghost, "Gods know I might already be..." he shook himself, "Do me this favor, my son. Stop trying to be me. For that matter, stop trying to be every other Battle King that has strode these lands. One of your greatest shortcomings is you see your position as something to be shadowed by those who have come before you. Allow yourself to be your own Battle Prince. This kingdom may not always agree with your actions, and I may not either, but at least they'll be genuine."

"Why is it every time I actually try and be *myself*, someone tells me to act more like a Battle Prince?" the young ruler could not hide his frustration.

"Because there is a balance you have to strike," the old man instructed at the last, "And because your idea of being true to yourself usually has only to do with your own self interests. Do you understand the difference? When you can put the kingdom ahead of your own desires *and* maintain your own unique presence, then you will be the Battle Prince- but not a moment sooner. And trust me, if you think for one heartbeat I run this country at all like *my* daddy did, you are sorely mistaken, son. And you know what- I'm betting if he were still around he'd be proud of the way I've done things. Just like I hope to be one day of your efforts."

Krög stared blankly at the pages laid out before them, his head a complete mess of thoughts and emotions, and his whole psyche largely overloaded. The Battle Prince took a few long, deep breaths and tried to decide how to respond.

"There's something else bothering you," the Battle King guessed, "What is it, boy?"

The young ruler's thoughts turned to Lee, "It's nothing," he hated the way it sounded referring to her as 'nothing,' "Just... long morning I guess. This is a little much right now."

"How can I help settle your tides, my son?" Bröghue asked softly.

"Dad, am I really cut out for this?" Krög huffed, "Wouldn't the kingdom be better off with someone like... hells, I don't know, Iolar?"

"I'd sooner feed my sword hand to an angry troll," the Battle King said, a smile carved into his deep brow, "It pains me that you cannot see the greatness shining within you, and yet you are arrogant and prideful in matters that are irrelevant, or in which you have not earned the right to be. Your brash hubris could be your undoing, and your disinterest will only fuel that downfall. Somehow, you need to learn to be strong for the sake of others, and not strong for the sake of appearing strong."

"Because that's not vague and confusing," the prince snorted.

The old man studied his son a moment, "Perhaps speak to your Honor Guard on the matter. If anyone understands the lessons of strength for the sake of a cause, and not for the sake of chest-thumping, it is him. Ask him how he maintains his control and his discipline... you may be surprised at just how much effort others put into their lives," he concluded, suggesting a bit sarcastically again at the young ruler's general lack of commitment to cause.

Krög was glad for the opportunity to seek out Ashley's company, "Maybe I'll do that."

"Good," the old man said brightly, "Now then, off with you. I am certain you have better things to be doing than getting lectured, yes?"

The Battle Prince chuckled a bit, "Probably. I just lost a few weeks of chores to Detlev in the pit. I should get cracking on those."

Bröghue eyed his son, "Detlev would never allow himself to win against a member of the Battle Family- he respects our lineage too much. Who did you *really* lose to?"

Krög chewed his tongue and avoided his father's gaze.

The Battle King immediately understood, and threw up his hands in exaggerated frustration, though his eyes were beaming with uproarious pleasure, "How that girl manages to lay down such a thrashing on the best my kingdom has to offer is an absolute mystery."

"She's really fast, dad," the young ruler defended Lee, "And, like, shockingly strong. You know she accidentally punched out two of Voläan's teeth yesterday during a match, right?"

"Yes, his fellows still have not let him forget it," the old man laughed, "We are blessed her wrath comes down on our side, it would seem."

"She still feels bad about that, by the way- I don't think she meant to hit him that hard… especially when they were only practicing," Krög offered.

"Warbrands routinely lose teeth practicing," the king snorted, "And hair. And quite often bones. We just anointed a new warrior to their number, Kelly Kennedy, or Kel as everyone calls her, and she shattered the ribs of her sponsor during a similar practice match. Barbarians play rough," he finished.

"I guess it's a good thing Lee does too, then," the Battle Prince laughed.

"Indeed," the old man waved and playfully dismissed the young ruler, "Get on then. And I'd appreciate it if you found something legitimately constructive to do with your time."

Krög turned to leave. He got as far as the immense doors of the Great Hall when he turned and shuffled back towards his father.

"Dad?" the prince called quietly.

"Hm?" the Battle King did not look from the treaty he was penning.

Krög swallowed all the pride he could and tried to do something dutiful and with even a hair of acknowledged responsibility, "Bęrun should see a unifed family tomorrow during the parades."

Quizzically, the old man broke his eyes away from his work, "Yes?"

"Maybe I should be standing with you during the cavalcade," the prince offered.

"I should like that," the Battle King smiled slightly, but then cast a look at his son, "It's going to be an all day affair- and as I recall you have little love for, how do you call them, 'organized mobs with absurd music.'"

Krög had absolutely used those *exact* words to refer to more than a few barbarian parades.

"All the same," the young ruler dodged, "The Merchant Lord will take the negotiations more seriously if he believes the kingdom he is entering into a pact with has a stable ruling house and stands united."

"Gods, you sound like a bad textbook on politics," the old man chortled, "So hollow. Still, I appreciate the effort. Very well. You shall be at my side for the procession. Or as long as you can stand it, anyway."

The Battle Prince nodded at his king and turned at the last to leave. He resolved in his mind to spend the entirety of the following day stridently at the side of his father- Battle King and Battle Prince, confederated. After all, how boring could it possibly be?

***

Really, really, excruciatingly boring.

Now, victory celebrations and parades of lionhearted, warriors-triumphant were done no better in all the Three Known Kingdoms than in the heart of the Southern Reach. Whenever there was cause to throw a party, be it winning a war, or felling a dragon, or finding one's lost shoelaces, the barbarians of the badlands seized upon it with almost proprietary excitement and gusto. Though normally a stoic, often drab, people of iron and leather, in a world mostly void of bright colors in favor of more utilitarian fair, those hard-chinned, broad-shouldered, pragmatic peoples really knew how to organize a soiree. Their world was transformed from one of combat and hardiness to a, practically, magical land where the citizens laughed deeply, flags wove high, and copious amounts of the strongest alcohol known to mankind would flow freely. In short, it was basically the best of times to be a barbarian.

And so it was Krög, the Battle Prince, found himself thrust neck deep into the beginning of a week-long celebration harkening the victorious return of Captain Iolar's conquering contingent of Griffin Riders. That rowdy crew had struck a withering blow to the invading bands of marauders and their slippery, psychopathic captain, Mordenall, and were returning home from the northern banks of the Swordsong River with a song and in their throats and drink in their gullet. Their success was such that the Battle King's call for a parade and festival in honor of the Captain and his Riders had been answered by a huge collection of nearby settlements, swelling the population of the Fortress City to its breaking point. While Krög normally would have delighted in the chance to be free of his usual duties, he instead found himself sulking and sullen. The thought of having to toast the arrogant, hot-headed Iolar for anything at all caused the taste of bile to leap into the young ruler's throat.

Now, it was not that the Battle Prince was not glad his fellows had returned safely on the wings of victory- certainly he was not quite so coarse or spiteful. Rather, he just really did not like Iolar. At all. Perhaps it was that the Captain was stronger and more assured in combat than the young ruler, perhaps it was that every Battle Maiden south of the Scorched Hill universally agreed Iolar was more handsome than the prince. And perhaps it was that just one young woman in particular seemed to fawn over the roughhewn, burly, brawler from Brokus. No one could argue the logic of Krög's suggestion to send the Griffin Riders into the Ivory City to purge the pirates from her streets, but had anyone paid even slightly closer attention, they certainly would have realized his intentions were colored a few shades ignoble. Yes, Iolar was competent, and the young ruler knew it. He also knew it would mean getting the Captain out of his hair and out from under the gaze of Lee for a few months.

Jealousy is an ugly shroud on anyone's shoulders, and it did the Battle Prince absolutely no favors either. It was an easier task to maintain Lee's dancing attentions when there was no competition around, and from under the yoke of envy, Krög steered as many of his would-be romantic rivals out of his path as he could. Had *he* been paying slightly closer attention, the young ruler would have realized it was unnecessary- that the impish girl often threw her eyes elsewhere just to watch him turn funny colors and make uncomfortable faces. All the same, naivety and the prince were constant companions, and he continued to allow it to direct his actions at every turn.

Ashley tried his best to calm his friend's anxiety and head off Krög's more churlish ideas. While the prince never directly abused his authority, the wise, mighty troll did talk the young ruler out of more than a few boneheaded decisions- like attempting to issue an edict that all members of the city guard be required to wear full face helmets after one winked at Lee. Krög insisted it was a safety issue. Ashley knew otherwise.

There were no secrets between the two friends, and Ash had long been privy to the prince's private conversation with the lithe, young woman in the depths of Raicleach's cavern. And from a number of other private conversations exclusively between the girl and the troll, he also knew her affections fell in exactly one direction. Still, as much as he could not stop Krög from going off half-cocked every time the prince got it into his head Lee was chasing someone else, neither could Ash stop her from pretending to do so for the thrill of getting the young ruler's goat. So it was the gentle giant found himself trying to mitigate the ridiculously immature courting between Krög and Lee that, somehow, had managed to go on in complete secrecy to everyone else.

Verily, so it was Ash found himself in a very uncomfortable place when the Griffin Riders' parade came galavanting through the streets of the Fortress City, and streaking through the blue skies overhead. While he would have liked to have been reveling in the reds and violets and yellows and greens of the victory flags that were strung in zig-zags down every alley, or listening contentedly to the booming war drums and blasting horns, instead the troll found himself trying to keep a leash on Krög. Now, to the casual observer, one would have thought it were the other way around. Always Ashley stood at the prince's side, ready to defend his charge in the face of greatest danger or, occasionally, mild, passing insult. Yet it was Ash who most often had to pull the young ruler back when Krög's inexperience and passions got the better of him. And when the Griffin Riders came home from Fanfarra, their swords still crimson with the blood of the marauders that had ravaged the Ivory City, the troll knew he would be working serious overtime.

Columns of barbarians marched staunchly along to epic songs of titanic deeds, and squadrons of raptors screeched overhead as the procession passed by the steps of the Great Hall. Krög stood next to his father, prince and king, overseeing the grand cavalcade. The Battle King smiled softly and proudly as his fighting men and women waltzed through the Fortress City, a subtle relief so many had returned alive barely perceptible on his always furrowed brow. Beside him, the younger ruler looked cooly out at the legion of muscle and steel that would one day be under his command. Krög's countenance and posture was one of stoic confidence, something he was getting better and better at presenting. It was a facade, and Ash knew it.

The troll's gaze flitted back and forth between the colorful celebration, and examining the telltale signs that belied the prince's churning angst. Both of Krög's hands were clasped tightly behind his back, and though his posture was upright and presentable, his fingers were working furiously like they would rather have been gripping the hilt of a sword, or plucking along the neck of his bowl-harp. Though the young ruler's stare was fixed straight ahead, it was clear he was straining his peripheral vision to the point his eyes felt like they might spring out of their sockets. Through superhuman ears, Ashley could hear the prince's jaw grinding in frustration, his heart pounding in unease, and his breath coming out short and choppy with aggravation. There was little wonder to the cause of it all.

Hovering over the parade with a permanent grin of total aplomb was the Grand Marshall, the lord of the sky himself, Captain "Untamed" Iolar, drunk on triumph and more than a little Trollkiller Ale. He whooped and hollered louder than anyone else as his Riders continued to race through the clouds above, and the barbarians who had accompanied them on the campaign shook the earth beneath their boots. In one hand he gripped tightly to his reins while his spirited griffin screamed through a series of showy, aerial acrobatics. His other arm was wrapped tightly around Lee, who had agreed to sit in the same saddle as the Captain just so she could be at the center of attention. She laughed and squealed as the bird spun and pitched over the procession, absolutely delighted to be cocooned in the thrill of the flight and the noise of the crowd.

Ashley sighed to himself as the prince grew more and more discontented at the sight of it all. The troll had largely hoped the matter of Lee's not-so-wandering eye would have been settled after she reassured Krög she literally was just trying to get him to admit to his jealousy. Instead, for reasons completely inexplicable outside of the young ruler's persistently sophomoric mind, he had actually seemed to have gotten worse. Ash prayed it was just a phase that would pass, but was preparing a lecture on the virtues of patience and steadiness all the same. He understood it from both sides- certainly it was not easy on Lee either, after all, to be tempting the affections of a prince betrothed to a powerful foreign princess. The troll just wished one of them would cut it out. Or both would figure it out. Whichever came first.

Doing his best to quell the young ruler, Ash put a massive paw on Krög's shoulder. Owing to his extraordinary concentration on the looping, swooping griffin and its passenger, the prince flinched at the steadying gesture at first, but then calmed visibly. He threw a look to his guardian that said 'get me the nine hells out of here,' before turning his attention back towards the parade. Despite his own disappointment at having to abandon the festivities, Ashley looked for a moment to excuse himself and his charge from the crowd, and find somewhere the prince would be somewhat more at ease. Or at the very least, far less distracted.

When a break between battalions was accompanied by a pause in the music, the troll rumbled to Krög, "You want leave?"

"Yep," the young ruler did not hesitate, though he kept his eyes on the scene.

Ash shuffled over to the Battle King, "With you permission, wish to retire for afternoon, Battle King."

The old man eyed Krög, who still did not break his gaze away from the parade, "My son? Is that your wish?"

Obviously at odds with his marginal sense of duty and roiling discontent, the Battle Prince worked his jaw a few times, "I am by your side, father, as you request and as you require."

The Battle King snorted, though his eyes were amused, "I did neither, son, you volunteered to be here."

Krög flinched at being called out, "We must present a house united."

The Battle King huffed, though in good humor, "Oh, get out of here, boy. I hardly require you to throw a party."

Still, the Battle Prince blanched, "Are you certain, father?"

"Quite," the old man laughed, "Though I appreciate you at least trying to act like you care about the affairs of my kingdom. It's a step in the right direction."

"Thanks, dad," there was visible relief in Krög's edginess, "Come on, Ash. Let's take a walk."

"Keep him out of trouble, Honor Guard," the Battle King winked up at the troll, "He seems to be gifted at discovering it these days."

"Aye, Battle King," Ashley nodded solemnly, his grasp on sarcasm and humor developing- but still tenuous at best.

Krög did not wait for further invitation or fanfare to excuse himself. He turned briskly on his heels and stalked into the Great Hall, leaving the raucous celebration and celebratory song as quickly behind him as he could manage. Ashley held back a moment longer.

One thing the troll had gotten exceedingly good at, though it caused him great mental distress and felt a lot like dereliction of duty, was finding ways to maneuver Krög and Lee together in private. Though he would never openly admit it, Ash largely preferred the spritely young woman's company to the Lady Ydal's, and despite his oath to protect the Battle Family and, by extension, the princess Krög was to marry, he quietly hoped it would be Lee on the throne one day instead. As such, if he could, Ash found ways to allow the prince and Lee to steal moments together alone. On more than one occasion he had even lied outright to Val and Xylus, the Battle King's Honor Guards, as to the whereabouts of Krög to allow the young ruler time with the fair-haired girl. Ashley cared deeply for his position as a shield knight of the Southern Reach- but he cared about his friend more.

To that end, as the young ruler disappeared into the dim depths of the torchlit Great Hall, the troll took a moment longer to consider the position of the sun and the flightpath of Iolar's griffin. The bird was spirited, but not completely unpredictable from Ashley's observations. He waited just a fraction of a moment longer before turning his enormous shoulder-armor plate towards the spiraling raptor. Gleaming and brilliant, the high afternoon sun caught the polished metal in a blinding flash. Lee's attention snapped up just in time to see Krög and Ash vanish into the hall. The troll knew she would follow. She always did.

In the meantime, Ashley still had quite a bit of Krög's surliness to smooth over.

"Doesn't that crap just bore the hells out of you?" the prince huffed as he paced around in front of the Battle King's throne.

Ash shrugged and admitted, "Thought it was good time. Music very nice."

Krög waffled, "I mean, yeah, maybe for a little bit. But then it's just all the same thing over and over."

"You very sure that all that bother you?" the troll cut to the chase, "You seem very perturbed for to be just bored."

"Why? What else would be bothering me?" the prince turned heatedly defensive.

"Nothing," Ash played at being oblivious, "Just seem like there maybe something on mind."

"You mean like *her*?" the young ruler's voice rose in pitch, "Well she's not! That girl can do whatever, and *whoever*, she damn well pleases, and we both know she's going to anyway! So what's the point in me worrying, right?! I'm not the crazy one, she is. She's crazy, and she makes *me* crazy. Except I'm not crazy! I just said that! Agh!" he finished by making a number of undignified, very frustrated noises in his throat that were otherwise unintelligible.

The troll paused, "You want talk about it?"

"No!" Krög snapped, "Yes. I don't know. I hate that she does this to me."

"Thought Lèanbh already tell you she no care for Captain- not really, anyway," Ashley offered, "Why you not listen?"

"I did. I tried," the prince continued to pace, "But come on, Ash- you saw her out there. I mean, what's that all about? Riding around on his griffin and doing that thing."

Ash wrinkled his nose, "What thing?"

"You know! *That* thing!" Krög insisted, "That thing were she... *smiles*!"

The troll chewed at his tusk, "So... you no want Lèanbh be happy...?"

"Of course I do!" the young ruler practically snarled, "But this is a different kind of smile! It's a smile like she knows. She knows what she's doing and she wants *me* to know too!"

"Maybe this something trolls not meant understand," Ash scratched at his hair awkwardly.

The Battle Prince took in a long, deep breath and blew it slowly out, "Let's pretend, for two seconds, like I am maybe, *possibly* making too big a thing out of this."

Ashley raised an eyebrow knowingly at his friend.

"I just don't get why she thinks its okay to drive me nuts, and I can't do it back," Krög huffed.

The troll grunted, "Am going to have to do something here that you *really* not going to like. Going to tell you, you wrong."

"Beg pardon?" the prince looked genuinely shocked.

"You wrong," Ash reasserted, "You talk out both sides you mouth, too. That what Lèanbh take issue with, and she told you this before. How you think it make her feel see you walk around city for all to see with Lady from Ivory City, only for to then sneak off with her later?"

Ashley was right, Krög hated being told he was wrong- especially when he was.

"That's different," the prince defended weakly.

"Is it?" the troll asked, "Right now she out there in public with someone else- but bet she going to find quiet time with prince later."

Krög crossed his arms, "*Completely* different."

Ashley squinted at his charge, "Okay, *now* you sound crazy."

The young ruler sighed, and slumped onto the throne, "I know. You're right. As always."

"Not always right," the troll shucked off the admonishment, "Just see things way I see them. Is easier, maybe, see things from the outside than from you perspective."

Krög smiled faintly, "That's nice of you to say, Ash, but I'm starting to hear how bonkers I sound."

"Well… love perhaps make do strange things," Ashley offered.

"I'm not in love with her," the prince jumped, before pausing "I hope not, anyway. That would be really complicated."

The troll cocked his head, "It not have to be. Certainly not easy with other princess still supposed to marry. But certain you could make good case to Battle King."

Krög screwed up his face, "Yeah, I'm not so sure about that. Berun would have to decide he was so indebted to us for saving his country, that he would sign my father's treaties out of thanks- rather than requiring a marriage."

Ashley tugged on his chin, suddenly deep in thought, "Will see what can do about that."

Before the prince could ask what the troll meant, Lee came bounding into the Great Hall just as carefree as she could possibly be.

"Someone's in Daddy Battle King's chair!" she sang as she danced from tabletop to tabletop, "Someone who isn't supposed to be."

Krög stood awkwardly, "Hey, Lee."

"Hi, prince," she grinned at him, before leaping gracefully onto Ashley's shoulder, "And hello to you, good sir knight."

"Hello, Lèanbh," the troll tugged her leg in greeting.

"Great, we've all said hi! Now, let's go do something," she giggled.

"Ash and I were going to go on a walk," the prince said in a way that implied Lee was not exactly invited.

"Well, now you're taking me," she refused to be left out of anything.

"Wouldn't you rather go back to the parade?" Krög taunted, arms crossed.

"I mean, it was nice of Daddy Battle King to throw me such a big party," Lee yawned like she was bored, "But, I think I'm getting a little airsick, and honestly- your barbarian music isn't all that great."

Before the prince could raise the bar of sarcasm, Ashley stepped in, "Would be very nice have Lèanbh along today."

"Thank you, good sir knight," she performed a sweeping, half bow from the troll's shoulder, "I would be most honored to accompany thee and thine pestilence," she waved at Krög, "On this most finest of afternoons, thusly and foremost."

The prince eyed her dubiously as she continued to toss about nonsense words, "Are you finished?"

She smiled broadly, "Nope- but if it means we get this show on the road, I can be for now."

"Dazzling," Krög snorted.

"Oh! King Mopey sure is Baron Grumpy today!" Lee chortled, "I can tell this is going to be a whole lotta fun."

"Can you maybe keep your, decidedly, peculiar brand of charm to yourself today?" the prince fired back.

"I would," she replied brightly, "But you're not that lucky, and I'm not that nice. Love me or leave me, prince."

Krög half gurgled, half growled in the back of his throat, and looked to Ashley for support. The poor troll, caught between his friends, just shrugged with the shoulder Lee was not occupying.

"Right," the young ruler said finally, "Let's go."

"Fantastic! He made a decision!" the bright young woman crowed, "And here I thought we were going to be stuck here all day just waiting for a thought to occur in that thick, barbarian brain of yours."

"You are such a treat," Krög mumbled under his breath as he made for the narrow passages that lead out the back of the Great Hall.

Trying to sneak out of the Fortress City in broad daylight was a task indeed, but not one Krög was not entirely up to- he had managed it on a number of occasions, and he was, when mischief depended on it, possessed of a singular, fumbling grace that afforded him a decent degree of silence and agility. He could capably scale most of the walls in Ganithen, knew all of the guard rotations well enough to slip silently by during the changes, and had enough knowledge of the watchtowers' blindspots to hop from shadow to shadow unseen. Attempting the same feat during a massively crowded parade, while accompanied by a nine foot tall tower of muscle and armor, was a slightly different experience. Ashley was, of course, far more nimble and swift than his appearance let on, but even he had limitations- namely stuffing himself into hiding places that the lean, slender, six foot frame of the Battle Prince could barely squeeze himself into.

Fortunately, Krög was at least passingly accomplished at improvisation, and he had a few ideas about how to get out of town unnoticed during the procession. While the Battle King had given him leave to step away from the celebration, it was a stretch to assume that meant the young ruler had permission to leave town altogether. It always bothered the Battle Prince that he was still, largely, treated like a teenager, even though he was approaching his third decade. Though on further reflection, he supposed his handling was not completely unwarranted given his general proclivity of ambivalence towards rules and responsibilities. And the longer he was looked upon, hawked over, and babysat, the better he got at evading surveillance and supervision. Practice does, after all, make perfect, and he was well practiced in the art of being an aloof delinquent.

Most people's appraisal of his lack of cleverness aside, Krög was at the very least quite perceptive, and he had noticed a clear pattern in the ranks of the parades as they passed through the Fortress City. With the whole of Ganithen's attention drawn towards the town center, it was therefor an almost elementary task to time their dashes between buildings and alleyways whenever the stream of squadrons occasionally paused. The young ruler held his friends back when he knew Griffin Riders would screech overhead after a regiment, and urged them quicker when he knew there was a narrower space for them to slide by. Even Lee had to admit- despite Krög's typical bumbling and awkwardness, he was pretty decent at getting out of the city unnoticed.

"You know, you're actually not a completely terrible sneak," she half-commented as they slunk through the gates, "I've seen better, of course, but this was not the disaster I thought it would be."

"You're just… too kind," Krög rolled his eyes.

"Yes, I am," Lee sighed sarcastically as though she was troubled by her own kindness, "It is absolutely a curse being this charming. Whatever is a poor girl to do?"

A deeper, gruff voice cut their banter short, "It would be nice if she kept my son out of trouble- rather than encouraging it."

Krög, Ashley, and Lee stopped dead in their tracks and exchanged funny looks.

The spritely young woman wrinkled up her nose, "Shit."

All three slowly turned to face the Battle King, his arms crossed, face stern, and their betrayer sitting delightedly on his shoulder.

"Busted," Scale pointed his wing at the three companions.

Lee turned crimson with anger, "You little twerp!"

"Don't talk to me like that, snack," the little dragon snapped back.

"How in the nine hells did you know where we were going?!" Krög groused.

"You think I can't smell that troll a mile away?" Scale snorted derisively.

"And what'd Daddy Battle King promise you in exchange for raining on OUR parade?" Lee quipped, ignoring the fact the old man was standing right there, "I doubt he's about to feed you anything you consider sufficient recompense."

"You might be surprised, entrée," the tiny monster kept at her, "Maybe you all should have invited the dragon, and you wouldn't be in this mess."

"Would the three of you cork the whine, please," the Battle King raised his hands and boomed over the arguing, "I'm guessing this isn't the first time you've pulled this, is it, son?" Krög avoided the old man's accusing eyes, "And I'm surprised at you, Honor Guard. It is not in keeping with your station to encourage this kind of thing."

Ashley lightly toed at the dirt in front of him, clearly ashamed.

The Battle King sighed deeply, "It is, perhaps, however in keeping with the bonds of friendship."

Scale moaned disgustedly, "Ugh, you're going to let them go, aren't you?"

Krög pressed, "Come on, dad. There's nothing to do during the parades. Can we please just go for a walk?"

"I imagine you planned on doing quite a bit more than going for a walk if you put in the kind of effort it would take to sneak out of MY city with all this commotion about," the old man parried, but relented, "Still. Maybe you're right. And I suppose I could have been more specific about your boundaries when I released you."

"So we can go?" the prince asked hopefully.

The Battle King rolled his eyes, "At least take the damn sword," he unhinged Thundersteel from its hanger at his side and gave it to Krög, "And try to be back by morning. I do actually have things for you to do during all of this," he waved at the parade still going on behind them, "You and the Lady Ydal are both required tomorrow at a special ceremony. Don't disappoint me."

Lee shuffled in her stance at the mention of Ydal.

Scale preyed on it, "Ha! Someone's jealous!"

Ashley had to hold the lithe girl back from strangling the tiny dragon.

Again, the Battle King sighed, "I've lived too long. That's what's happened. To see my son gallivanting about with trolls and, well," he looked at the miniature monster still seated on his shoulder, "Whatever in the nine hells you are."

Krög did not want to waste any more time, lest they draw more attention and other tagalongs decided to join their party, "Come on, Scale. This party is moving out."

"Do we really have to bring him?" Lee pouted.

The little dragon leered at her, all fangs and drool, "Step lightly, confection."

Before they could begin fighting any more, the Battle King pointed sternly at his son and repeated his directive, "Morning," he then pointed at Ashley and commanded the Honor Guard, "Watch him."

"Aye, Battle King," the mighty troll bowed reverently.

"Thank you, father," Krög knew he was being afforded an extraordinary amount of trust, "We'll be careful," he took Scale from the old man.

"You watch him too," the Battle King eyed Lee, "Something tells me you're behind half the trouble he's in lately, hm?"

She smiled coyly, "I'll never tell."

The old man guffawed, "Nay, child, I imagine you won't. Alright. Go do something stupid and juvenile, all of you. That's an order."

Lee spirited over to the aging monarch and kissed him on the cheek, "Thanks, Daddy Battle King!"

Trying desperately to not be completely enchanted by the bright young woman, the old man kept a stern face but his eyes were dazzled. He waved them off and shuffled back into the city, shaking his head at though in wonderment of his own decision to cut the younger ruler loose during such an auspicious and ceremonious occasion. Without knowing why, the Battle King chuckled to himself and dismissed it all as naught more than youthful energy and misappropriated initiative and ability.

"So," Scale asked enthusiastically, "Where are we going?"

All eyes turned vehemently towards him.

Krög growled, "If it weren't for the fact we've already burned enough daylight, I'd have Ash here turn you into an ironic pair of boots for Lee after that little stunt."

"I don't like being left out!" the little monster defended.

"Why aren't you with your princess, Lady I'm-Too-Pretty-To-Expose-My-Face-To-Noontide-Sun?" Lee was the zenith of maturity.

"For your information," Scale crossed his wings, "She actually has important things to do, unlike you losers."

"And apparently unlike you," the girl raised an eyebrow at him.

The little dragon opened his mouth to respond, but had nothing in the way of an intelligible comeback to her accurate, if slightly hurtful, assessment of his general usefulness. He narrowed his slit-like eyes at her.

"Your day is coming, toots," Scale finally threatened.

"Not as soon as you think," Krög interjected, "Can we go?"

"Gladly," Lee threw a glance over her shoulder and then skipped lightly away, humming quietly to herself.

"Maybe would have been better just stay for parades," Ashley grumbled.

"You might not be totally wrong about that, Ash," the prince agreed, his mood slightly fouled by the unwelcome appearance of the little dragon and getting subsequently caught by his father. Even though the old man had been shockingly lenient with them, it put Krög off that he had gotten discovered in the first place. It just meant the next time he tried a similar caper, it would be infinitely more difficult. His strategies were going to need some tweaking.

"Oh, you two are no fun," Scale laughed, apparently totally amused by everything, "Look at this beautiful day we all have together now! Let's go find something to eat. Preferably L-"

"Stop," Krög cut him off, "Just, stop. Your shenanigans get only half their normal tolerance today, got it? Choose your words carefully."

The little dragon sulked visibly, "Fine. Didn't know you were going to get so cranky. I just wanted to be part of the fun."

"Gods, for someone with such a superiority complex, it is ridiculous how ornery and codependent you are," the prince huffed as he started after Lee.

"That's a vocabulary word," Scale quipped, "Who taught you that? The troll?"

"Not in mood either," Ashley practically threatened, "Keep beak shut, or will shut it for you."

"Fine, fine," the miniature monster snorted, "No one's got a sense of humor today."

"We did, you ruined it," Krög fired back and motioned at Lee, "I'm going after her to see if I can find it again."

The prince kicked up his heels and jogged after the quick young woman, giving less heed to the annoying creature clinging to his shoulder, and more to the feel of the cooling summer breeze on his face. Lee noticed him following, and with a giggle and a squeal, broke into a full sprint towards the looming edge of the Thorn Rift Forest. Practically shaking the earth with his thundering footsteps Ashley strode after them, easily keeping pace with little effort thanks to his titanically powerful legs and broad stance. In no time at all the companions were deep in the grasp of the enchanted woodlands, and the Fortress City was far at their backs and farther from their thoughts.

Lazily, they strolled through sun-dappled patches of greenery and dim glades as the afternoon languished on. There was no particular direction to head, and nothing to draw their attention beyond the sights and sounds of The Strange. Lee rode giddily on Ashley's shoulder as they romped through the undergrowth, the crunch of thorns and leaves a staccato drumbeat beneath the boots of the troll and the Battle Prince. It was a perfectly pleasant afternoon, bereft of responsibility or charge, which was exactly what Krög had hoped it would turn into. Minus the miniature, man-eating monster on his shoulder, of course.

Waltzing around The Strange was always an exercise in the completely ridiculous, if not the abjectly bizarre. There was no shortage of its wondrous oddities and its oddly wondrous. Whatever crater of magic had transformed the stretch of woodland realm into a place of sincere enchantment and wild unnaturalness, it had left behind a veritable sinkhole of the unimaginable. There was never a moment something completely new and wholly unexpected did not catch Krög's eye, and he positively relished the chance to explore the weird dominion whenever there was occasion.

A flock of moths, each the proximate size and proportion of a small sailboat's rigging, whooshed almost silently over their heads between trees that glowed with a pale, blue-green iridescence. Odd beasts looking like a frightening cross between a crab and a spindly spider scuttled sideways along arbor limbs that ended in drooping fingers, which plucked at the air as though trying to play a song on an invisible stringed instrument. Thorns that should have been able to gouge through inches of flesh bent like rubber beneath the prince's treads, only to spring back with a hysterical boinging noise when relieved of his weight. Patches of sky changed wantonly from blue to deep violet and then suddenly to electric crimson, a kaleidoscope of sparkling colors. Even the swirling mists and dusts around them seemed to move of their own accord, animated and undulating with a possessed sentience.

Then there were those things that were just... well... even for The Strange, they were strange. Krög about jumped out of his skin when a war helmet atop a pair of leather gloves walked by them on the gloves' fingertips, like a creeping insect. One tree they passed clearly seemed to be having an argument with itself, which was altogether more disconcerting given the argument seemed to be between the nostrils of the tree's nose. Yes, the tree had a nose, and yes, the nostrils were arguing with one another. Perhaps just downright odd was the person they found sprawled in the thorns, completely oblivious to the piercing brambles, who was writhing his limbs about like a squid trying to propel itself through the water. This, in particular, drew Lee's attention.

"Should we, I don't know, help him or something?" she looked cockeyed at the man who continued to squirm through the thorns.

Krög shrugged, but tried to get the man's attention, "Hey! Buddy! Are you okay? Do you need a hand?"

There was no discernible response, and the man's eyes were blank like there was no thought or animation behind them.

The prince tried again, "Yo, friend. Is everything alright?"

Lee wrinkled up her nose, "I don't think he can hear you."

"I don't think he can hear anything at all," the young ruler observed, discouraged.

"Him spend too much time in Strange," Ashley surmised, "Him mind been taken over by magic. Probably not even know who him was anymore."

Lee looked saddened at the man, "Poor guy."

"Yep, too bad for him," Scale interjected, "Since he's not making much use of his body anymore, can I eat him?"

Lee gagged visibly.

Krög flicked the little dragon on the nose.

"Rude," was all Scale offered in response.

"Is there really nothing we can do to help him?" Krög asked the troll.

Ash shook his head, "Not unless you know good wizard. One of them maybe could reverse."

"There hasn't been a wizard in the Southern Reach since Battle King Nömel, the One Armed- and that was over 400 years ago," the prince replied.

"Unfortunately not much can do for him," the troll sighed, "Magic make it so, only magic for to undo it."

"That's why we stick to steel in the Reach," Krög came back almost disgustedly, "Magic's just trouble."

"Said the stupid prince with a sword that makes lightning," Lee snorted.

"Exceptions," the young ruler dismissed, "Well, I guess we... leave him?"

"Not much danger in The Strange, except for too much magics," Ashley tried to console, "Him safe enough, just stuck like so. Not much guarantee was man in first place, really. Could be was once something else that was turned into form of person."

"That makes me feel a little better," Lee still looked pained, "I just hate to think of someone imprisoned like that."

"He's not imprisoned," Krög appraised, "He's just... stuck."

Lee rolled her eyes, "Gods you're dense. Are you sure he'll be okay, Ash?"

"Reasonably," the troll nodded, "Promise would help more if could."

"Alright, let's go then," the girl relented.

"Are you sure I can't eat him?" Scale tried one more time.

"You have problems, you know that?" Lee almost snarled before addressing the prince, "Keep him away from me today, got it?"

"Got it," Krög did not argue in the slightest, and pointed a finger at the little monster on his shoulder, "You're on thin ice, ankle biter."

"Patently inaccurate," the dragon came back, "Too much gristle on the ankle, no real flavor to sink your teeth into."

"Ash!" Lee cried out in objection.

The troll intervened, "Know how there more than one way skin a cat? Maybe today we find out how many ways skin a dragon."

Scale opened his mouth as though to retort one more time, but a dark look from both Ashley and the Battle Prince precipitated him snapping his jaws shut and crossing his wings dejectedly.

Before the tiny monster could make another objectionable suggestion, and with unfortunately nothing they could truly do to help the strange man flopping his way through the carpet of thorns, the companions set off for River Glen. Everyone was agitated and wanted to let their troubles and worries slip away in the crisp, clear waters of the Swordsong River for a time. Krög could feel the carefree afternoon slipping away from them to be supplanted by ornery infighting, and for a moment he almost wished he was back at the steps of the Great Hall, woodenly waving at passing ranks of victorious barbarians. All of those thoughts evaporated when they stumbled onto a crystalline oasis just at the edge of the mighty river.

Surrounded by amazingly tall trees was a sheer embankment that dropped into a pool a short ways below. The current of the river carried around the edge of the bowl before cascading down a small waterfall over the entrance of a charming little cave. Soft mosses and plush greenery took the place of the ever-present brambles, and Lee's eyes practically glittered at the prospect of dancing through their loamy, sumptuous beds. All the sounds of the world faded out to the crashing of the water over the little falls, and the rush of the current of the nearby river that fed into the glade. It was as serene and removed as scenes came.

"Stop here?" Krög asked the group.

"Yep!" Lee did not wait for a second invitation. In a springing leap, she went sailing off of Ashley's shoulders and over the edge of the embankment. With the grace of a falcon plummeting after its prey, the athletic girl dove headlong past the waterfall before plunging into the glassy waters below. She entered the pool with barely anything resembling a splash, cutting straight through the glistening surface and vanishing beneath the current. A few moments later she bobbed to the surface, her bright hair plastered to her face and a musical laugh bubbling through her lips.

The Battle Prince tugged off the banded leather vestment on his chest and plunged Thundersteel into the dirt next to him before following after her. Krög fell more like a rock than a gliding swan, and he smacked hard against the water after a drop that was significantly higher than he anticipated. At first the shock of the cold water pummeled the wind from his lungs, and the young ruler tugged his way quickly to the surface to gulp in air. He quickly adjusted to the chill of the pool, though, and found its chilly grasp a sincere comfort after the long afternoon hike. Just as he closed his eyes to float in peace for a moment, Lee splashed him wildly, and the prince swam after her to return in kind.

All the contents of the pool were nearly emptied when Ashley shouted something in Giant Speak that sounded roughly like "boomjuwany," and threw himself, chest first, over the embankment. His splash was so tremendous Krög felt himself lift out of the water. Lee got enough of the mighty wave to rocket out of the pool entirely and flip over in the air before again piercing wakelessly back to the depths. Ash emerged with his heavy, black locks matted to his back like hackles, a rumbling chortle in his throat much like the spritely girl. Lee was right behind him, climbing up Krög to get to the surface faster- and then to shove the prince playfully under the water.

Scale screeched grandiosely, spread his wings and leapt out over the falls. He glided an embarrassingly short distance before gravity, the cruel mistress she is, took hold of the tiny dragon, and plopped him impotently into the water next to Ash.

The companions splashed and roughhoused in the pool, guffawing and hollering the whole time. Every droplet of water that went sailing through the air looked a tiny diamond glittering under the late afternoon sun. Krög could not help but notice, hopelessly romantic as he was, they all carried the same crystalline color of Lee's eyes. She would fling water at him, he would try to do the same, and she inevitably ended up hiding, and giggling, behind the mountainous form of Ashley. Of course, she also took great joy in the fact the extraordinarily strong troll could launch her into the air with one hand, where she would twist through a truly dazzling display of acrobatics before slicing back into the pool. Krög would occasionally dive after her to try and wrestle the girl before she came back to the surface, but she was as strong as she was slippery, and she always evaded his grasp, a demure, teasing look lilting in her gaze.

For what seemed like hours, the friends forgot they had a life anywhere else but in those crisp waters. Every passing thought of any manner of duty or business washed away in the current, and faded out under the late summer sun. It was an idyllic moment, the kind the Battle Prince could only remember from his days as a teenager when he truly was without onus. He breathed the experience deep, and drew it down into his spirit.

Of course, rare were the occasions Krög went out in search of adventure and did not find himself on completely the wrong end of catastrophe. And sincerely, if their afternoon was destined to be a pleasant day of frolicking in the glades of River Country, it should hardly be a tale worth telling. While there is a certain adventure and excitement in friendly courtship and unabashed flirting, verily the fair haired woman in the pool with him was not the only thing to raise the young ruler's pulse that day. As was his rather humorously unfortunate fortune, Krög's afternoon was about to be impeded upon by circumstances most remarkable, and decidedly inconvenient. It began with the Magnificent Octopus.

The Battle Prince was busy trying to toss the squirming form of Lee over his shoulder, when he noticed Ashley standing stark still, dark eyes fixed on the cave behind the waterfall. Krög turned, confused, towards where his friend was staring, and peered as intently into the dark tunnel. Lee flung water on him jokingly, but when she realized both the prince and the troll were fixated on the cavern, she too shifted her attention towards it. Even Scale fell quiet, the feathers on his head drooping hilariously with drench, as he bobbed in the waters next to Krög. All four of them gazed, unblinking, into the dark tunnel behind the falls. Something beyond the tumbling curtain of water was moving in the black.

When it unfurled, it was with slow purpose. At first, only a single tentacle slithered through the falling waters, peeling them aside like drapery. Then another, and another tentacle, each one anchoring to the rocks around the entrance to the cavern, and dragging a gargantuan, bulbous body out of the depths. Within moments the pool was dominated by the titanic creature which sat atop the waters commandingly, suspended just enough by its many arms that the terrible maw and beak underneath its mass showed. Huge, black eyes rolled over and examined the, comparatively, minuscule crew before them. For half a heartbeat, no one breathed.

In unison, Krög, Scale, Lee and even Ash screamed- though the troll's roar was perhaps more a challenging bellow than a frightened wail. Hysterically, the gargantuan octopus curled back away from them fearfully and loosed a markedly humanlike scream of its own. Several moments passed where both parties shrank from the other. They continued to keen in surprise and, at least partial, terror for several more. It was to everyone's amazement then, when the enormous creature emerging from the waterfall covered its eyes over with several of its arms and started to weep- again with a remarkably humanlike quality to its voice and actions.

"Oh, gods, please don't kill me!" it cried out, voice dripping with dread, "I'm so sorry, I didn't mean to interrupt you, just please don't hurt me!"

Krög recovered his voice, hoarse though it was, first, "Don't hurt you? I feel like we should be asking you the same thing."

"Calamari isn't even in season, I promise I wouldn't be very good, please just let me go," the impossibly large creature pleaded, whimpering.

Lee screwed up her face.

Ashley scratched his head.

Scale just stared, bug-eyed.

Again, Krög responded, "I think there's some confusion here. We're not going to hurt you," he hurriedly followed with, "Unless you try to hurt us first!"

"You won't?" the octopus peaked out from behind one of its tentacles, "And *I* won't! Really! I just heard you splashing and thought," it started to tangle up its arms like a person wringing their hands, "Oh, dear, I don't know what I thought. I never should have come out of my cave."

Scale recovered next, and rather tactlessly shouted, "What in the nine hells are you?!"

The creature winced at the noise, but tried to resplendently pose, "I'm the Magnificent Octopus."

"Are you ever!" Lee had been completely taken with awe and wonderment.

Truly, the beast was a spectacle, and unlike anything Krög had ever heard described in myth or legend. If it had stretched its arms out fully, they would have easily cleared fifty feet from tip to tip. Rather than the bland, dark, grayish colors of most of its kind, the octopus had a skin that constantly shifted colors the way a puddle of oil sitting on top of water does. Ribbons of green, red, purple, blue and silver crawled and slid over the beast's bulbous body, and crept down its eight, muscular limbs. Rather than rubbery suckers on the underside of its tentacles, the octopus had pads of glimmering jewels, each cup circled by emeralds, rubies, diamonds and sapphires. It looked more like the opulent, luxurious vision of an artisan jeweler, than a living thing. Strange and frightening though it was, it was also regal and striking.

Lee continued to plumb her curiosity, "Where are you from?"

"The city," the octopus said forlornly, "I wasn't always like this."

"No shit?" the little dragon's complete lack of manners was boundless, "So, what? You just woke up one morning and you were a huge, rainbow disaster?"

"Scale!" Krög snapped.

"He's right," the octopus cried, "I *am* a disaster. A cataclysm. I am the woe that beats in the hearts of the heartbroken, and the trudge in the heels of the downtrodden."

"Oh, is not *so* bad," Ashley tried fumblingly to be comforting, "You very nice to look at."

"You think so?" the octopus asked hopefully, "Really?"

Ash smiled crookedly and held up one thumb in approval.

"Gorgeous, you have more confidence issues than stupid prince over here," Lee nodded sideways at Krög, "You have to be the most amazing thing I've ever seen."

"Ah, well, thank you," the octopus shifted about uncomfortably as though unused to receiving compliments, "Are... are you sure you're not going to eat me?"

"Not yet I'm not," Scale quipped.

"And you're done for the day," Krög broke in on the dragon's ill mutterings before returning his attention to the octopus, "So, what did happen to you? If you weren't always like this," the prince motioned at the beast's titanic form, "What were you like? Just a regular octopus?"

"Heavens, no," the creature languished, "I was a man once. Not much of one, I suppose, just a merchant of the Ivory City. But there you have it- I was a person before I became the abomination you see before you."

"Let's stop with the 'abomination' and 'disaster' talk," Lee said, "You can't call yourself Magnificent in one breath, and then all this other mucky muck in another. I say you're just Magnificent. And if we become friends, you'll quickly learn I'm always right."

Were it possible, the octopus would have blushed, "Again, many thanks, dear lady. It is difficult to expect rational reactions from others when you look like I do."

"Do *we* look like the height of normal and balanced to you?" Krög asked dryly.

For perhaps the first time, the octopus considered the group before him, truly. The tall, slender prince. The spritely, pint-sized young woman. The miniature dragon. And the titanic troll.

It blinked a few times, "Well, no, I suppose not."

"Good- we're all a little bit left of center here," the prince chuckled, "So what *did* happen to you, then? If you were a person, what did this to you?"

The octopus sighed, "Well, as I said, I was a merchant at one time," it settled itself slightly on the cavern entrance, and propped up its 'chin' on a few of its arms while it gestured animatedly with the others as it recanted its story, "I ran a small shop in Fanfarra, selling mostly baubles and blown glass. Occasionally I would fashion a piece of jewelry. I was far from gifted, though, and wanted nothing more than to have a storefront in the High Court amongst the truly talented of the Northern Empire. Ah, what it would have been to have had the vision and wherewithal to wrought into existence the finery the likes of which would end up adorning the Merchant Lord himself. Or his exquisite daughter, oh my…"

For a moment, the octopus's voice faded longingly as though recalling some distant memory of a glimpse it once caught of Ydal.

Lee cleared her throat- annoyed.

"Alas and nevermore," the octopus went on, "It was not to be, it seemed. And then one day, the most beautiful woman ever had I laid eyes upon sashayed into my shop. There was nothing I had that was worthy of her radiance. I was a worthless worm before her winsome ways- a puddle of pathetic plague. Ah! Such statuesqueness, such perfection. What was I to present a being of singular ideal?"

Scale whispered to Krög, "Wow he can talk a lot."

The Battle Prince was inclined to agree.

Lee was growing irritated as well, "I *want* to feel bad for him- but this self deprecating crap is worse than *your* mopey moods."

Again, Krög was inclined to agree.

"So," the young ruler summarized, hoping the octopus would get to the point, "You were a guy with a shop, and a pretty girl walked in one day. Do I have all of that right so far?"

"Indeed, indeed," the creature said woefully, "I was without any suitable offering for her. So I begged her, pleaded her, threw myself at her feet and implored should she only return within the week, I would commission such a necklace as to be suited for an empress. She agreed. I knew that all my life had been leading to that point, that it was my chance to do something truly spectacular, and that I would need something that could capture her beauty and my feelings like no other jewel or ornament before. I needed something that could not be found in the depths of a mine or under a stone. Nay, I needed something truly magical."

Lee elbowed Krög under the water, "I'm getting cold."

"How much longer could he possibly go on?" the prince hissed in reply.

"You realize by asking that question, you practically *guarantee* we'll be here all night, don't you?" she snapped back.

Still, the octopus went on, "So I came south over the banks of the Swordsong River, to this enchanted forest in search of my treasure: that mystical element I would weave into my work and dazzle her with. During my searches, night and day they were, I stumbled upon a creature most foul who promised me grand treasure if I should only help him to remove a wasps' nest that was blocking the entrance to his home. Oh, such foolishness."

Ashley furrowed his brow, "Must been very, very large nest of wasps to block house entrance."

"Ah, perhaps I should have mentioned," the octopus flopped an arm against its head as though just remembering something, "The creature I stumbled upon was an imp."

"A what?" Krög asked.

"An imp," Lee repeated for him, "A fairy folk, but meaner."

"That's a little harsh," Scale defended, "I knew some HILARIOUS imps back in my day! One of them was my jester for a while. He was something. You think *I* liked how pixies tasted, I've *never* seen anyone nosh on their own kind like this guy could! You'd love him," the little dragon leered at Lee, "And boy oh boy would he love you."

She slapped a handful of water at the miniature monster, who had to hack and snort it out of his lungs after swallowing a great deal.

"Vile, disgusting creatures," the octopus went on, "And he tricked me. Laid a spell on me! CURSED ME! No sooner had I moved the nest blocking the knothole of the decaying tree he lived in, did the little horror blast me with his magics. When I awoke, my soul, my consciousness, verily all that made me me, had been swapped out of my body, and exchanged into this globulous thing. For all I know, somewhere out there, my body is inhabited by the mind of a gargantuan octopus."

Scale laughed loudly, "Holy snot! Drogomyr!"

Krög looked crossly at the little dragon, "What in the nine hells are you talking about now?"

"Drogomyr!" Scale repeated, "I *know* the imp that did this! He is just the *best*!"

"Excuse me?" Lee's voice dripped with derision.

"That's his schtick!" the little dragon continued, "He LOVES swapping minds and bodies. It's his thing!"

"And you're just... totally on board with this, aren't you?" the fair haired girl rolled her head around as though trying to decide whether to shake it disgust or nod it in revolted acceptance.

"Its jocular!" Scale insisted, "One minute you're looking at a totally normal, everyday person, the next minute they're trapped in a beetle! It's about the funniest damn thing you've ever seen!"

Everyone stared at him blankly- and more than a little angrily.

The little dragon crossed his wings, "Maybe you have to be there."

"Hey, parrot," Lee pointed out, "We ARE there. Like, right now. And something tells me *he*," she waved at the octopus, "Doesn't find it so funny!"

Scale wrinkled up his snout and offered with only a hint of sincerity, "Yeah, well, no offense."

"Perhaps I am in penance for some horrible crime I committed in another life," the octopus moaned, "How am I to take offense when the hubris and weight of some misdeed committed in another time is still an onus upon my soul?"

"You *really* don't like yourself at all, do you?" Lee asked wryly.

"No," the octopus admitted weepingly, "No I suppose I don't."

She looked over at Krög half in exasperated plea and half genuine concern, "Can we please do something to help him? This isn't right."

"Can the thing that did this to you undo it?" the Battle Prince asked.

"Most certainly," the octopus agreed, "He is the keeper of dark arts, an arbiter of magic. *If* he could be captured, you *might* convince him to return me to my old self."

"Something tells me convincing an imp to reverse what it probably thinks is a riotous practical joke is easier said than done," Krög grimaced.

"*Especially* Drogomyr," Scale followed unhelpfully, "He probably thinks of this colossal calamity like some kind of work of art."

"So, do you actually have anything of value to add to all of this?" Lee fired off.

"Sound like dragon known imp for long time," Ashley growled, "Good bet knows where this imp flits him wings. Probably can find him quick, and probably can help convince," the troll loomed over the little dragon floating meekly in the pool, "Right?"

Scale scoffed and huffed dramatically, "Oh gods, fine."

"So glad to have you on board," the prince rolled his eyes before turning back to the octopus, "Okay. We'll find this imp thing and get him to change you back. You'll stay here and wait for us?"

"Where else would an abhorrence like myself go?" the octopus drawled.

"Right, sure, whatever," Krög shrugged, "Is there anything else we need to do?"

"If it wouldn't be too much trouble, perhaps you could find my body and bring it with you," the octopus requested, "I know my way home well enough from here, though I should hate to awaken somewhere in the midst of the Thorn Rift Forest I am unfamiliar with, and not know north from upside down."

"Of course," Krög bowed lightly.

"If it's not too much trouble," the octopus repeated, "And if you are successful at all, that is," it sighed loudly, "Which I doubt you will be."

"You know it wouldn't kill you to have a slightly more positive outlook on things," Lee said brightly, "It might even help!"

The octopus just moaned loudly and massaged what would be its forehead with a few of its arms.

"Okay," the young woman was clearly dejected, "Let's just get this stupid rescue underway.   He is absolutely sucking the sunshine right out of me."

"No arguments here," Krög waded to the edge of the pool and looked at the steep embankment that lead back up to where he had left his sword and leathers, "Damn. Climbing."

"Please," the octopus reached out with a tentacle, "It is the least I can do."

With immense strength, but also restrained grace, the gargantuan beast plucked Krög, Lee and Ash out of the pool, and lightly placed them atop the bank above the waterfall. Scale clung on for dear life as the prince was pulled out of the waters and deposited back amongst the brambles.

The octopus waved, "I wish you good fortune on your quest, or so I've heard they say. Be victorious, boy-warrior and girl-sprite. Lend them your strength, mighty troll. Please don't eat them, tiny dragon. Or me, for that matter. Oh dearest, dearest, dearest me, please do not eat me."

Awkwardly waving back, the companions sidled away as quickly as they could without seeming rude or hurried, but all the while with a desire to swiftly put some distance between themselves and the, so called, Magnificent Octopus.

Lee shook herself and squirmed like something cold and slimy had climbed down her back, "Yikes. How could anything so beautiful be such a miserable, mewling mess?"

"I get the sense he was pretty much a wreck before that happened to him," Krög appraised, "Being turned into a huge, multicolored octopus was probably just the sugar in the oats."

"Is very sad," Ashley agreed, "Feel like even if can help, him never going to feel whole again."

"All we can do is what we can do," the Battle Prince said solemnly.

"Wow, insightful," Lee snorted, "Come up with that one all by yourself, or is that something Daddy Battle King taught you on a cloudy afternoon?"

Krög glared at her, "Why would it have to be cloudy?"

She side eyed him, "That's what you took away from that?"

"So we're not actually going through with this, right?" Scale broke in, "Like we just said that so we didn't risk pissing off the eight armed blob of melodrama, and now we're getting the blessed heck out of here, yeah?"

"You couldn't be more wrong," Krög shot back.

"Look, I'm not saying this is impossible," the little dragon cautioned, "But I know Drogomyr. He does *not* play in the sandbox with others. Asking him nicely to undo all of that is going to be like reaching your hand into a burrow full of scorpions because you think there might be a piece of copper in there.   Risk, reward… doesn't add up."

"What's the matter," Lee teased viciously, "Afraid he's going to put you into a caterpillar's body?"

"No, I'm afraid he's going to put me in YOUR body," the little dragon came back, "Drogomyr and I used to be buds, sure, but there's no telling what kind of mood he'll be in.   And we didn't exactly leave off on the best note."

"Shocker," Krög retorted, "What'd you do to him?   Or was it something he did to you?   Did you used to be a noble in some faraway land before he trapped you in the body of a feather dragon?"

It would have explained a lot.

"You take that back, meat-sack!" Scale demanded, "I have *always* been, and I shall *always* be.   I am one of the breaths of eternity!"

"You're a sneeze of perpetuity, at best," Lee hocked.

Before Scale could arduously object, Ashley interrupted, "This time arguing better used rescuing. Though have to say," he looked darkly at Scale, "Am very curious what you do make imp angry."

Scale crossed his wings and looked away, "I might have eaten his girlfriend."

Lee just went bug eyed.

The little dragon felt the uncomfortable silence settle with the same unwelcoming weight as a heavy wool blanket in the baking heat of midsummer in the badlands.

"Well she wasn't officially," he began, as though that made everything better, "And frankly, he was going to do the same thing anyway! She was a pixie, he was an imp, they had that whole forbidden love thing. Then he decided she was starting to look tasty, I agreed... I mean, we can all see how this isn't *entirely* my fault, right?"

"I don't..." Krög started, "I can't... You..."

"You. Are. Disgusting," Lee put words behind everyone's pause.

"I'm a dragon!" Scale defended, "How is this a surprise to *any* of you?!"

"It not," Ashley sighed, "It pretty much exactly what expect from you."

"See!" the tiny monster gestured at the troll, "Big Ugly gets it! Besides, we're getting distracted. Don't we have a cephalopod in distress to rescue or something?"

"When this is over," Krög said slowly, "We are going to have a very, very long talk about what topics are on and off limits going forward."

"Won't that be fun," Scale quipped, "Are we doing this thing or what?"

"Yes, we are," Lee urged, "And fast, before I can no longer overcome my urge to pluck every one of your feathers and toss you over the edge of the Everfrost Mountain."

Scale was not about to be threatened without returning in kind, "I was just going to go with the quick bite, but now I think you'd be more fun to slow roast."

"Scale," Krög lowered his voice, "I would do something helpful before Ashley pounds you into goo."

"Fine," the little dragon finally relented, "I just want to make sure my objections to this whole thing are on record."

"Noted," the Battle Prince huffed, "Lead on."

"Oh, I forgot to mention," Scale said as though it just occurred to him, "We're there."

Krög had barely noticed in the midst of all their arguing, that the little dragon had been leading them along the entire time through the brambles away from River Glen and back into The Strange. Just as quickly, he realized he had no idea how long or far they had wandered during the squabble. The prince cursed himself quietly for not paying closer attention to his surroundings- especially in a place as bizarre as The Strange. There, time routinely bent and broke just about as hard as all the other odd twists on the natural order that were akin to the enchanted region. Somehow, Scale had managed to navigate through the mire of their infighting away from the little oasis pool and deep back into the Thorn Rift, well away from any direction the prince recognized as 'correct.' Privately, Krög hoped Ashley had been paying attention, or at the very least knew the forest well enough to get them back.

With a flourish, Scale waved at a fetid, rotten, decaying tree trunk that was dripping sap smelling of rotted eggs, and covered in festering knotholes that bulged with putrid, yellow mold. A swarm of flies buzzed around the broken stump- only, as was par for The Strange, they did not so much buzz as they did zingzoop.

It is not really important you understand the difference in the sounds, just trust it was extremely unpleasant to listen to, which made the dead trunk an offensive assault on the eyes, ears, and nose. Krög had little desire to touch or taste it, but he imagined both experiences would be equally gut wrenching, and that qualified the stump as among the more stomach-twisting, five-sense-affronting things the prince had ever come across. The idea anything at all made a home out of such a place was beyond reproach.

Not a thing in the world would have made the Battle Prince approach the tree stump any closer than he already had under normal circumstances. Their circumstances were anything but normal, however. They were on a mission. A quest. There was rescuing to be rescued. There was hero work to be done.

"Do we really have to do this?" Krög almost whined.

"Ugh, I don't know who has less backbone," Lee scoffed, "You, or the octopus."

Ashley furrowed his brow, "Octopus. Definitely octopus. Never met one with a backbone at all, actually."

The bright haired girl patted the troll lovingly on the shoulder, "Oh boy, Big Guy, that one just went right over your head, didn't it?"

Ash's eyes shifted suspiciously skyward for a moment. Satisfied nothing had flown over his head he was not aware of, the troll turned his attention back to the stump.

"Must admit," he growled, "Not really excited about going through stump for find imp.   Not most pleasant stump ever seen."

"How do we know if he's even home?" Krög asked.

"Hey!" Scale yelled, "Drogy! You in there?"

"Do imps even speak the common tongue?" the prince inquired.

"They speak in Sprite Song, if you're going to be polite," the little dragon replied matter-of-factly, "But since none of you knuckleheads have the subtlety or linguistic grace to speak Sprite Song back, I figure common is easier."

"You're too kind," Lee dripped.

"Drogy!" Scale ignored her and tried again, "It's The Dreaded! You still hanging your wings here?"

There was a slight pause, and then one of the frighteningly large flies zipped away from the rest of the swarm and started to pinwheel towards the companion. The closer it came, the more Krög realized it was not an extremely large fly, but rather a very small being. Whirling about in zany patterns, the tiny creature finally came to a hover just in front of the Battle Prince's face, and the young ruler was able to see it in greater detail. The imp, assuming that was what it was, could not have been larger than the length of Krög's little finger from the second knuckle to the tip.   It looked well enough like a person, except covered in fine gray scales, draped in bright purple tufts of hair, and possessing a pair of bat wings sprouting from its back.   A thin tail waved around behind it, and as it began to talk, the tail moved in perfect harmony with its words, almost like a person gesturing with their hands.

"Well, I'll be damned," the creature said in a surprisingly full-bodied voice given its diminutive size, "And here I thought you pushed south permanent! What're you doing here?!"

Scale laughed, "A little of this, a little of that. How in the nine hells are you, Drogy?"

"Eh," Drogomyr shrugged and waved dismissively with his tail, "I could complain, but what would be the point? I've got my filth and foulness, what more can a guy ask for, am I right?"

"Skippy," the little dragon appeared to agree, "You heard from Ganagam lately? He still biting the ears off tourists?"

"Last I heard, anyway," Drogomyr seemed to lay sideways in the air, relaxed, as his tiny wings kept him aloft, "No pun intended. But you know Gany- he's always looking for the next big thing. Honestly, I haven't heard from the bastard since the three of us got sick on that lost fisherman."

Scale shuddered as though recalling an unpleasant meal, "I swore off anything that sailed in from New Hope forever after that."

"You and me both, buddy," the imp continued, willfully oblivious to Krög, Lee, and Ash listening in on the conversation, "How's the toe trade these days?"

"A nip here, a nibble there, nothing to scream about," the little dragon said, bored, "Not like that afternoon with the caravan from Drenin."

Drogomyr laughed heartily, like the memory struck a pleasant chord, "The baron and his two daughters! Now THAT was fine dining!" the imp's attention suddenly shifted very deviously towards Krög and Lee for the first time, "What about these two?" he sniffed the air, "That one's a barbarian isn't he? I haven't had spicy food in a while."

"Ugh," Scale almost gagged, "Too tough, too lean. I'm fixing for the other."

"That was always your problem, Red," apparently, Drogomyr's nickname for Scale was Red, "You were always after the sweet stuff. Probably why you never got any bigger than you did."

Lee finally broke in and screamed, "CAN WE PLEASE STOP TALKING ABOUT EATING PEOPLE! ESPECIALLY ME!"

Drogomyr made a face, "Unfriendly lot, aren't they?"

"Big Ugly especially," Scale nodded at Ashley.

"Well, damn it all if that isn't the puniest troll I've ever seen," the imp chortled loudly.

Ash made a face, "You do understand what irony is, right?"

"And slap the slobber out of me- it's smart!" Drogomyr admonished cruelly.

"This conversation got weird and uncomfortable a long time ago," the Battle Prince interjected, "We're not here to shoot the breeze about… whatever it is you two have been talking about. Scale? If you please?"

Drogomyr hooted, "Scale?! They call you Scale? Gods, how you've tumbled, Red."

"Oh, cork it, Drogy," the little dragon snapped back.

"So, what, you're like their pet now?" the imp persisted, "'Fixing for the other,' he says- not likely! The Dreaded *I* knew would have had that little morsel trussed up in her sleep, and begging not to be breakfast by morning!"

"What, like you've got it so great?" Scale retorted, "It's been eighty two years since I saw you last, and you're still hanging around the same old stump? How're those plans to build your treetop empire coming along, eh Drogy?"

"This not seem like accomplish much," Ashley grumbled, clearly put out with his charge being threatened and antagonized by a creature the near size of his own fingernail.

"Have to agree," Krög was about done with it all as well, "Can we move on to why we're here already? I'd like to find where my skin crawled off to before the day is over."

"Squeamish bunch too," Drogomyr guffawed louder, "Oh, Red, these kids would have been your bread, butter, meat, *and* potatoes back in the day. Wow you've gone soft and pathetic."

Scale just screeched, rather immaturely, in frustration and anger.

"Hey!" Krög desperately covered his ears against the noise, which was all the more amplified by the fact the little dragon was still seated on his shoulder, "Just ask him and we can get out of here!"

"Ask me what?" Drogomyr righted himself in the air.

"You didn't think this was a social call, did you?" Lee asked, voice drowning in snark.

"Well, Red *did* bring appetizers," the imp returned.

Ashley snarled deep in his throat.

"Before Big Ugly here gets all violent and squashing," Scale jumped back in, "I need to ask you a favor."

Drogomyr cartwheeled backwards as he laughed incredulously, "Are you serious, Red? A favor? Are you out of your mind?"

"Just put the damn octopus back in his real body and we'll get out of your fur," Scale huffed.

The imp cracked up even more, "And he wants me to undo my best work! Classic! Oh, Red, you always were good for a laugh, but this one just really takes the barbecued eyeballs!"

"Come on, Drogy," the little dragon was clearly at the end of his frayed sanity, "You know I wouldn't ask if I didn't have to."

"Do you *remember* why we haven't gone rampaging in the last eight decades?" the imp cackled, "I know you've choked down a lot of pixie in your day, Red, but it's insulting to think you've forgotten about Priscaline."

"I *knew* you'd bring Pris up!" Scale roared back, "Need I remind you, you were going to do the same thing!"

"I might not have!" Drogomyr defended poorly, though his voice was impassioned, "She was going to accept my offer of marriage!"

"You never even asked her!" the little dragon was at fever pitch, constantly slapping Krög with his wings as he gestured wildly, "The closest you got was a fumbling poem about how she smelled as sweetly as a dead dandelion, and even then, you got so flustered after reciting it to her you flew off and didn't show your face for a week!"

"She was pretty! I got embarrassed- bite me!" Drogomyr screeched.

"Drogy, come on, you cannot still be miffed about this," Scale lolled, "And if you had *half* the confidence you *think* you do, you would have gotten right back out on the scene, and enchanted some other pixie."

"There was no other pixie! There was only her!" the imp hollered.

Lee whispered to Krög, "At this point, I can't tell if this is really tragic, or really funny."

"I'm going with a little of both," the Battle Prince responded softly.

"I heard that!" Drogomyr keened.

Scale looked awkwardly at Krög, "Yeah, so, imps have like... super good hearing."

"That's it!" the imp had finality in his voice, "Screw you, Red, *and* the barbarian you rode in on! Get out of my glen, and away from my stump!"

"Not going anywhere until you undo bad magic," Ashley growled, "Put man back in right body. Is against the way of things way he is."

"It's 'against the way of things' how much gall you've all shown," Drogomyr snorted, "I've had it with all of you."

"Could make you very flat," Ash threatened.

"I could make you very pink!" the imp shot back, "Or yellow. Or half as tall but twice as broad, or put your face on upside down!"

"Hollow threats," the troll's voice was low, but furious.

"Actually not so much," Scale offered, "Drogy's pretty good with the magic and all that."

"Great, so if he's so good, why doesn't he just snap his fingers and put the octopus back?" Krög tried to be sly, "He probably doesn't have any magic left at all."

"You didn't honestly think that would trick me into saying something like 'oh I bet I could!' and changing him back, did you?" Drogomyr raised a disbelieving eyebrow.

Lee sighed and put her head in her hands, "Oi, stupid prince…"

"Okay, fine, short sighted," the Battle Prince threw up his hands, "Look, I know Scale is a righteous pain in the ass, and it sounds like he took someone pretty special from you, but can you please forgive him? Please? And just, put the octopus back and you'll never hear from us again. I promise."

For a long moment, the imp appeared to think about Krög's empathetic proposition. At least a moment longer than he had considered Scale's plea for a favor. Drogomyr looked the Battle Prince up and down a few times, for once not hungrily, but deep in thought. The tiny creature stroked his chin and twirled his tail around a few times.

After a beat, Drogomyr spoke, "Nope."

With little more warning, the imp raised his hands and tossed an impressively large ball of energy at the prince. It slammed Krög in the chest with the force of a falling tree branch. The young ruler was lifted off his feet, flew through the air and smashed backwards into Ashley. In an instant, the world went black.

When Krög opened his eyes, everything felt heavy. His arms felt like they weighed a ton, and his chest heaved with the simple effort of drawing in a breath. Everything tingled strangely. As the sensation of immense weight drained away, it was slowly replaced with the entire world sounding far too loud and smelling much too pungent. Everything felt alien and out of place. Too, his senses began to adjust, but as they did the Battle Prince realized he absolutely could smell better and hear farther than he remembered being able to. And his limbs no longer felt heavy, but extraordinarily powerful. He was also itchy, and could feel his hair in a knotted, gnarled mess under his back.

It was then it occurred to the prince, his hair absolutely did not reach his back. Not even close, in point of fact. So how could he be itchy from his hair under his back? Krög pressed himself up from where he had fallen in the brambles, and looked around.

Next to him, still lying stunned in the thorns was... him. Krög was looking at himself.

"Ugh, what in the wrath of an eggplant...?" the voice that came out of his throat was not his own. It was guttural and gravelly.

The prince raised his hand in front of his face. What met his eyes was the gigantic, gray-green, calloused paw of a troll. Namely, Ashley's. Gingerly, the young ruler began to touch his face, and found his jaw square and rock-solid, and there were two tusks growing out of the side of his mouth.

"Oh, shit," dawning realization started to take the prince.

"LET ME AT HIM!" Scale came flapping wildly out of a bush he had landed in, "Where is that revolting, disgusting, reprehensible little son-of-a..." the little dragon's, literally, fiery speech slowed to a stop when he caught sight of Lee tangled in a nearby vine, "Why am I looking at myself? Gods! Why do I look tasty?!"

Krög's eyes went wide, "Oh. Shit."

Scale held his wings up in front of his face, and it was clear the eyes looking at them were not accustomed to seeing feathers sticking out of their hands. The little dragon made a number of squeaking sounds that were probably meant to be pointed objections, had the shock of the moment not completely robbed words from the situation.

"This isn't real," Scale said, "This is not real. No. Absolutely not," the little dragon started to smack the unconscious face of the Battle Prince repeatedly, "Get up you stupid prince! Wake up and get me out of this!"

"I'm the prince!" Krög said, pointing to himself in Ashley's body, "Who are you?!"

"WHO IN THE NINE HELLS DO YOU THINK I AM?!" Scale roared, "I'M LÈANBH!" the little dragon's face suddenly sank, "Oh, no. You too?"

Lee started wriggling vehemently in the vines she was caught in, "That magic bending bastard! That's it, Drogy! I will absolutely scorch you down to cinder for this crap!" the athletic young woman's struggles slowed, "This is weird. I feel weird. What's wrong with me? Why am I soft?"

Scale whistled, "Because you're not you, dumpling."

Finally the Battle Prince sat up, "Ugh. Head hurt badly. Not can remember such bad headache ever. Feeling need to make imp paste if not-" he cut off suddenly when he ran his hand through his hair, "Uh oh. Something not right."

"No kidding?!" Scale keened, "Am I the only one who has this figured out?!"

"Drogy, you puke-brained punk!" Lee screeched, "This is SO not okay. Get your little reality twisting ass out here, and put me back so I can have my fire-breath again and spend the next two weeks toasting you into a fine powder!!!"

"Not seem like that the kind of deal get much done," the Battle Prince groaned, gingerly plucking thorns out of his skin, and wincing every time one pried loose, "Hrm. Not like this feeling."

"Sucks, doesn't it?" Krög huffed.

"I have no idea who's talking anymore," Scale put his head in his wings and burst into tears.

It took some sorting, but the companions did eventually figure out who had ended up in what bodies. Krög and Ashley had swapped forms, as did Lee and Scale. They argued for several minutes over how to refer to each other in the least confusing way possible, which was quite the task given their present circumstances and conditions. Finally, Ashley suggested they call each other by both names, but with the personality first and the body being inhabited second. Krög, trapped in the troll, became Krög-Ash. Scale, stuck in the athletic girl, was Scale-Lee. Ashley, crammed into the Battle Prince's form, was Ash-Krög. And poor Lee, forced into the tiny dragon, was Lee-Scale.

"Headache getting bigger," Ash-Krög commented over the dizzying situation.

"So *now* what brilliant, catastrophic course of action do we take?" Lee-Scale asked pointedly, "I am absolutely *not* staying like this."

"I don't know," Krög-Ash looked at his brick-like muscles, "This could work."

"Not get used to it," Ash-Krög pointed an accusing finger at the Battle Prince's personality admiring the troll's physique.

Krög-Ash ignored him, "I feel amazing! I feel like I could rip trees out of the ground!"

Eager to test out the troll's near limitless strength, Krög-Ash jumped to his feet and reached for the nearest sapling he could get his paws around. While Ashley's raw strength might have remained, his balance and poise was evidently something acquired from hundreds of years of experience. Krög-Ash had no sooner leapt out of the brambles as he did trip forward, clearly unused to the much longer limbs of the troll- or how to control them for that matter. On his way to the ground he did in fact learn he had the strength to uproot trees, as he yanked two of them completely free of their dirt anchoring before smashing face first into the thorns once again. Amazingly, it did not hurt at all.

"Whoa!" was all Krög-Ash could manage to exclaim.

"Be careful!" Ash-Krög begged, still wincing as he hurriedly pulled more thorns out of his skin to stop his friend from any more clumsy shenanigans, "That not you body you playing stupid with!"

"I am a god!" Krög-Ash was not to be deterred, clambering back to his feet and breaking several more tree trunks with his fists- just because.

"Wow. It's like watching a two year old with a sledgehammer and the requisite strength to swing it," Lee-Scale was just as vexed as Krög-Ash was excited, "Only a two year old is possessing more maturity and sophistication. Ash, sweetie, are you okay?"

Ash-Krög made a face, "Not like this form so much. Things hurt more. Feel wobbly."

Lee-Scale climbed up Ash-Krög's shoulder and patted his head lovingly with her feathered wing, "We'll figure this out, Big Guy. Once tall, dumb, and barbarian over there gets over himself."

They watched Krög-Ash break a boulder in half with his grip, and then very tentatively try to bite a chunk of the rock off, as if unsure whether his troll teeth could handle the stress of chomping through stone. A ridiculous, delighted grin spread across his face when the rock split in his jaws, and he looked supremely proud at his companions.

Lee-Scale cocked her little dragon head, "Are you finished?"

Krög-Ash dropped the rock pieces quickly as embarrassment settled in, "Yeah. Pretty much."

Lee-Scale covered her face with a wing, ashamed for him, "Oh, stupid prince."

"Not good for teeth for to do that," Ash-Krög growled, "Not see me testing if rubbery skin as bouncy as it feel."

"Yeah, you're right, sorry," Krög-Ash toed at the ground a little before his jubilance returned, "But this is really neat!"

"I'm glad *you're* having fun, some of us are not," Lee-Scale said bluntly, "Some of us would like to be less scales and feathers, and more skin and hair again- if it isn't too much trouble to start looking for a solution to this madcap little mess, that is."

"Would be very happy be a troll again," Ash-Krög agreed, "Not sure cut out to be a little folk."

"OW!" Scale-Lee, who had remained suspiciously quiet for some time, suddenly yelped in pain.

Everyone whirled around. Evidently the temptation of being trapped in Lee's body had proven too much for the sadistic Scale. He had taken clear advantage of the athletic young woman's limber flexibility, and had managed to curl one of her legs up to her face. Just above her ankle was the half-moon impression of her teeth, where Scale-Lee had clearly tried to bite down on his own leg. Just as obvious, was he was not expecting the rush of pain that accompanied trying to gnaw on the body he was in, and a look of shock and discouragement passed over his face as Scale-Lee tried to reason through how he might best go about the task of self-devouring.

Lee-Scale was at a near complete loss for words, "Did you just… are you trying to… Gods. Help. Me. Were you about to bite into yourself?"

"Well," Scale-Lee shrugged, "A little bit."

Hell-fury took Lee-Scale, "DID YOU JUST TRY TO EAT ME?!   DID YOU REALLY JUST TRY THAT?!"

"It's not as easy as it looks," Scale-Lee defended, "I wasn't expecting it to hurt that much. Maybe if I cook myself first…"

Lee-Scale unleashed a full-throated dragon roar in fervent frustration, "YOU REPELLENT LITTLE TWERP!"

She flapped wildly towards him, but forgot Scale's wings were flightless thanks to an unfortunate run in with a hero of one of the pixie kingdoms, and said pixie hero's Torch of De-feathering- as it were. Lee-Scale hovered for an unusually short second before plummeting into the thorns, rage and ire still exploding out of her ears. Scale-Lee, in the meantime, decided it was probably not best to be in the tiny dragon's path, and tried, rather clumsily, to skitter away- a process largely hindered by Lee's usual lack of boots and the painful carpet of thorns covering the forest. Scale-Lee tumbled to the ground, at which point Krög-Ash thought it was time he get involved. He scooped up the small girl's form with one hand, and pinned Scale-Lee's arms to his side. Not quite used to how rapidly his strength could be summoned, there was a distinct popping sound when he closed his fist- not so loud to suggest a bone had broken, but certainly loud enough that it was clear he cracked a few of Lee's joints on accident. Scale-Lee yelped in pain again.

"That hurt!" Scale-Lee cried out.

"Watch it, stupid prince!" Lee-Scale objected loudly as well, "That's me you're ragdolling! Be careful!"

"Sorry," Krög-Ash tried to loosen his grip a hair on the squirming young woman, "I'm trying to help."

Scale-Lee pried the troll's fingers open and slipped out of Krög-Ash's grasp, only to be tackled awkwardly to the ground by Ash-Krög, who was still getting used to his own new coordination. When Ash-Krög got up, Krög-Ash put out a single, heavy hand, and pressed Scale-Lee into the dirt, safe from the thorns, but largely immobile.

"Come on, guys!" Scale-Lee protested, "I am NEVER going to have a chance like this again!"

"You stay there," Ash-Krög commanded, "You cause enough trouble today."

"I promise I won't eat *all* of myself!" Scale-Lee kept on, "I don't think that's even possible."

Lee-Scale had heard enough, "Tie me up. Him up. Tie *that*," she waved a wing at the dragon trapped in her body, "Up! Now!"

"I'm not sure that's a great idea," Krög-Ash began hesitantly.

"Not looking for an opinion, prince," Lee-Scale said sweetly, though her voice dripped with venom, "Just looking for some cooperation."

"I'm just saying," Krög-Ash began again.

"I am not arguing this!" Lee-Scale reached fever pitch, "We have to go find an imp so I get back into my own skin, and in the meantime, I don't trust the anklebiter with *my* body!! He does NOT get to run around and come up with some twisted, creative way to bite off pieces of me while he's got the run of my limbs! No! Not happening! Now tie him up before I figure out how to use my fire breath, and give someone here a really, REALLY bad day!"

"It's through the nostrils," Scale-Lee offered brightly.

"SHUT UP!" Lee-Scale shouted.

Krög-Ash shrugged meekly at last, and moved to retrieve some rope from their packs.

"No, no, no, lunkhead, not you," Lee-Scale held up a wing to stop the fumbling troll, "You'll cut off my circulation, or break every bone in my wrists, or something. Ashley, dearest, would you please do the honors?"

Ash-Krög was clearly not comfortable with the idea, but did not want to anger her any more than she already was, "Well... can try best, suppose..."

"Thank you," Lee-Scale bowed graciously, before casting a look of pure malice at Scale-Lee, "Hold still, parrot."

"Look who's talking," Scale-Lee snapped back.

Of course, Scale-Lee had absolutely no intention of making the process of binding him easy. As soon as Krög-Ash lifted his giant paw a little for Ash-Krög to start winding rope around the lithe young woman, Scale-Lee scampered free and made a break for the tree line. Ash-Krög ran him down, but struggled visibly with containing the dragon's anger, expressed through the athletic strength of the girl.

Ash-Krög made a disappointed and frustrated face as he gave everything he had to containing the little terror, "Battle Prince need exercise more."

"Hey!" Krög-Ash objected, offended, "I don't have troll strength! Just regular barbarian strength, so cut me a break!"

Lee-Scale flitted nervously as Ash-Krög finally started to get the rope around Scale-Lee, "Be careful with me, Ash. Make sure he can't get away, but don't tie it too tight, okay?"

Ash-Krög looked over his shoulder at the tiny dragon, out of breath and losing his considerable patience, "You want do this?"

"I don't think I can," Lee-Scale admitted.

"Then maybe let me work," Ash-Krög huffed.

"Sorry, Big Guy," Lee-Scale apologized, "You're doing great."

"There, finish," Ash-Krög said finally, "For what it worth."

Ash-Krög had tied Scale-Lee into a neat little package of writhing wrath that was both totally immobile and completely furious. Ash-Krög was absolutely out of breath from wrangling the tiny monster, and Scale-Lee had a look of combined vexation and disappointment.

"Is this *absolutely* necessary?" Scale-Lee asked.

"Yes, it *absolutely* is!" Lee-Scale insisted, "I will NOT have you messing with my body while the rest of us are out trying to find the minuscule bastard who did this, and figuring out what terrible thing to do to him that will convince him to undo it!" she flopped on the ground and moaned loudly, "Gods, I'm starting to think like dragon. All I can focus on is how tangy imps taste, and how badly I want to- ugh! Never mind! Someone better do something that gets me out of this, and FAST!"

"Battle Prince, we must take action," Ash-Krög stood swiftly, "Need find magic to reverse all of this and help octopus friend."

"You're still thinking about *him*?" Scale-Lee complained from the brambles, "What is wrong with you?! Us first, then we'll figure out big, floppy and colorful."

"Can it, Scale," Krög-Ash growled, "Alright. Let's get going. How are we even going to find Drogomyr in all of-" he cut off suddenly and realized, "Wait. Wow. I can smell him. I can totally follow his scent. Ash it is AMAZING getting to be you!"

"Can't say is mutual," Ash-Krög looked at the Battle Prince's lean arms and prodded his comparatively softer flesh, "Much prefer be a troll again."

"Don't worry, buddy- for once, I've got this!" Krög-Ash insisted.

"Good, let's get going," Lee-Scale climbed up Ash-Krög's shoulder, "I was over this before it even happened."

"If I may raise a practical point," Scale-Lee pipped up as the other companions were about to abandon him in the glade, "Drogomyr is not one to leave his trunk for long. He's kind of a homebody- really attached to his little swarm of flies there. He's also mercurial, and a major pain in the ass to track down. If he gives you guys the slip and comes back to find cute-and-scrumptious here all in a sweet little package... I think we can all see how this song ends badly, right?"

Krög-Ash looked surprised, "Scale, are you actually concerned about Lee's safety?"

"Not particularly, I just don't want him getting first bite," Scale-Lee replied curtly, "I'm not big on leftovers."

"Am going to hit him, can hit him?" Ash-Krög asked.

"No, Big Guy, cause you'll actually be hitting me, remember?" Lee-Scale said, exasperated.

"Sorry," Ash-Krög stepped back in line and mussed with the Battle Prince's tangled hair, "This all very confusing keep track of," an alternative occurred to the troll stuck in a human form, "Wait, maybe I hit dragon body then! That actually hitting him!"

"It would be, but I'm trapped in here," Lee-Scale reminded him, "Which means I would feel it.

"Oh," Ash-Krög was crestfallen, "Right."

"Wait until all of this is over, and then you can pummel him, okay, Big Guy?" Lee-Scale offered in consolation.

Ash-Krög smiled crookedly, "Thanks."

"And I mean into paste," Lee-Scale went on graphically, "For all I care, you can squeeze him until his eyes pop out and he bites his own tongue in half! He deserves at least that much for all the crap he's gotten us into!"

"Hey!" Scale-Lee objected.

"Yeah, I can't believe I'm agreeing with him," Krög-Ash thumbed at Scale-Lee, "But maybe calm down just a little bit. That was… vivid."

"Ugh, dragon brain," Lee-Scale rubbed her forehead with a wing, "Honestly, it's like my internal monologue has a vocabulary reduced to three words: Eat. Burn. More."

"Right," Scale-Lee rolled his eyes, "Because it's just so much better having a million thoughts a minute go racing through my brain, the majority of which are inexplicably fixated on wonderboy over there."

There was an awkward pause as Krög-Ash and Lee-Scale made a truly valiant attempt at avoiding each other's gaze.

She recovered first, "So then here's what we're going to do. Big Guy, you're going to need stupid prince's nose over there to find our new little best friend and, prince, you're going to need Ashley's grace and subtlety to actually catch him. Let's try not to squish the imp before he changes us back, okay? I'll stay here and guard myself in case he does come back early."

"Are you sure you'll be okay alone with him?" Krög-Ash eyed Scale-Lee dubiously.

"Well I don't really trust anyone else to protect me, in our current states," Lee-Scale came back, "So I'd say our list of options is decidedly short. Are we on board, or are we going to sit around and argue with ourselves arguing with ourselves some more?"

Neither Krög-Ash or Ash-Krög had the requisite remaining mental capacity to decipher the end of her rant. They were both terribly confused and brain-tired, and both agreed it was probably long overdo everyone be returned to their rightful skins and scales, respectively.

"Good," she could see they were not about to disagree, "Then run along you two, and find the evil little stinkbug that did this to us, and bring him back here so we can threaten some sense into him, yes? Alright boys, go be heroes. Go on," she shooed them along.

The troll and Battle Prince stumbled out of the clearing, both still trying to get used to their compromised forms and get a little more comfortable in the body they were inhabiting.

"And as for you," Lee-Scale perched herself on her own heels and crossed her wings, "Don't move."

Scale-Lee squirmed a little, "Your claws are digging into me."

"Get used to it, you'll live," Lee-Scale replied dryly.

"Can you not hang out back there?" Scale-Lee asked nervously, "It's just that, I know what I would be doing if things were reversed, and I get the sense the

whole teeth and fire thing isn't going to feel so great...
So if we could avoid all of that..."

"Live in fear, you vile little pipsqueak," Lee-Scale
growled.

Ahead, Krög-Ash vivaciously sniffed at the air
like a hunting dog as he trailed after the vanished imp. It
was interesting how he experienced smell in the body of
Ashley- and perplexing at the same time. Rather than
scent coming to him in a cloud that choked its way down
his nostrils he picked up on the individual notes of each,
with a discernible direction and origin to them. It was
more like listening, really, like tracking a sound by
following the echoes. And the imp had left behind an
absolute symphony of odorous potpourris in his wake as
he went running off to wherever he had decided to
disappear after pulling his little "prank." Lee-Scale was
right: there was a tanginess to Drogomyr's smell, along
with a sharp pungency more akin to a fine cheese gone
bad. Against the background cacophony of The Strange's
more prolific and fascinating bouquets, the imp was an
obvious stand out.

The more Krög-Ash honed in on his query, the
swifter he moved, especially as he got accustomed to the
length and power of his new limbs. His strides felt more
like bounds, and he found he could easily clear ten feet
with each lengthy step. Even more so, he wanted to
know what it would be like to drop into a dead sprint with
his new muscles, and go pummeling through the
underbrush. He was fairly certain absolutely nothing
could stop him. It was an extraordinary experience being
suddenly imbued with brawn typically reserved for titans,

and the Battle Prince wanted to make use of his borrowed body if he got the chance.

Of course, as he explored his new boundlessness, he forgot about his old body's limitations. Ash-Krög, though he was learning to push his new form's athleticism, was having a very difficult time keeping up with his fellow's loping gait. The troll trapped in the Battle Prince's form found he had little taste for the burning in his lungs and the thundering of his heart as he gave chase, and even less for the way his new legs had to move twice as fast and tired out in half the time just trying to keep up. It had been literally centuries since he had broken into a sweat so quickly and, deprived of his old senses, Ash-Krög felt practically blind as he trailed farther and farther behind his companion. Everything felt like it was coming at him at once, and he could not separate out the many disparate noises and smells- or even his own thoughts for that matter. He wondered quietly to himself how it was the Battle Prince ever came to any decision, period, with such a cataract of considerations constantly pouring through his brain.

Krög-Ash's focus was singular, however, aimed by his enhanced senses and tempered by the steady stream of sound, reasoned thoughts pointed in one direction.

"Battle Prince," Ash-Krög puffed from behind, "Little legs not keep up so well. Need slow down, please."

Krög-Ash looked over his shoulder and immediately broke his hurried pace, "Sorry, buddy. I forgot how hard it is to keep up with you."

"Did not realize was so," Ash-Krög admitted, out of breath, "Well, maybe some, but getting better idea now. Will do better for to help you keep up in the future."

"Well hey now, don't go easy on me," Krög-Ash came back, "I'm getting stronger and faster thanks to you."

"Is good to hear," Ash-Krög wiped the sweat off his forehead, "But maybe little bit stronger and little bit faster be even better."

"We can work on calisthenics once this is over," Krög-Ash said, "But right now we've got to figure out how to undo all this malarky. Lee will absolutely never forgive me if she ends up stuck as Scale."

"Is very unfortunate way afternoon turn out," Ash-Krög agreed, "Had much promise," he sighed, "Now instead end up having figure out how keep dragon from eating self which really eating Leànbh while for put octopus back into right body because of imp that switch all friends into wrong places and make things all wonky."

It was the longest winded sentence Krög had ever heard the troll articulate.

"My brain is getting to you, isn't it?" Krög-Ash asked.

"Would seem that way," Ash-Krög said sheepishly, "Not really sure understand confusing speak. Just sort of came out. This always how it is for you?"

"More than you know, buddy," Krög-Ash replied, "One minute I think I've got a fix on things, the next I've just barfed up a lungful of idiotic remarks. I really need to learn how to slow down my thoughts."

"We can work on that too," Ash-Krög offered, "But first, rescuing need be done. Ours included."

"Yeah, he's getting away," Krög-Ash noticed the scent was trailing and he was losing his sharp awareness of it, "We need to keep going. Do you want to ride, or something?"

"Leànbh make very convenient rope braid," Ash-Krög waffled a moment, "Suppose would not be worst thing."

"Climb on, buddy!" Krög-Ash waved his friend on enthusiastically.

The Battle Prince stuck in the troll braced himself when Ash-Krög took ahold of the long braid Lee used to climb to the troll's shoulders. He was surprised to find he barely noticed the weight of his old body dangling from the lengthy cord of hair, and was almost completely unaware that his companion had settled on his broad back.

"Are you comfortable?" Krög-Ash looked over his shoulder to find Ash-Krög braced in place, holding onto the braid like steering reins.

"More or less," Ash-Krög grunted.

"You feel like I weigh absolutely nothing," Krög-Ash commented. He knew his body was slender and lean compared to the rest of his countrymen, but he was not small by any stretch and it was borderline disconcerting that he felt like a light shirt on the troll's shoulders.

"Yes," the Ash-Krög agreed, "Is so. Most things feel like they feather. Some things feel more like big rock. Not really sure, but never actually found anything feel very heavy. Always kind of wondered what it be like try to lift mountain. Never had opportunity. Maybe one day. Betting it feel heavy, but kind of curious what that actually feel like."

Krög-Ash listened patiently to his friend's rambling, "Yeah, so, we need to get you out of my head fast."

Ash-Krög became immediately self conscious, "Hrm. Yes. Please."

"Right, let's get back on the trail," Krög-Ash saddled up and went running after the dissipating scent of Drogomyr.

He barely got eight steps when he misjudged a low hanging branch. It clobbered Krög-Ash right in his square, troll jaw, and then rebounded and slapped Ash-Krög completely off his perch. Ash-Krög howled when he landed in a bed of thorns, and Krög-Ash lightly rubbed the sore spot where the tree branch hit him.

"You need be more careful," Ash-Krög roared as he wrenched about trying to desperately pluck the brambles out of his back, "That *my* head you bonk, and *you* back you get covered in thorns."

"I didn't realize it was this much work keeping an eye on both of us," Krög-Ash helped his friend up, "And we're just running through the forest- we're not even in a battle. Yet."

"Be a very good thing we NOT end up in a battle," Ash-Krög climbed back up the troll's shoulders, "Not sure you ready handle that. Now, little slower this time, until you figure out how tall you are."

"Got it," Krög-Ash agreed, and then added, "Maybe hold on tight. And duck down a bit. Just… keep your eyes open."

Ash-Krög grunted, "Ugh. This going to be a rough ride."

Back in the imp's glade, Lee-Scale and Scale-Lee were getting along about as well as could be expected. Lee's nervous energy was greatly antagonized by the dragon's twitchy body, and she was constantly shifting about, flitting her glance here and there looking for threats, and hefting her stance back and forth anxiously. Of course, every time she did, Scale, stuck her body, would wince, wriggle, or writhe as the dragon's many dangerous points prickled and prodded skin that was much softer than the steely scales he was used to having. The two of them were constantly shifting uncomfortably on the bed of leaves on the forest floor and, had they not been arguing, the uncomfortable silence that would have hung between them would have only been rudely interrupted by a never ending stream of crackles and snaps from the underbrush.

"Can you please sit still?" Scale-Lee begged, "Your claws feel like someone grinding needles against me. And watch your wings! The feathers feel… funny."

"Not so much fun, is it?!" Lee-Scale crossed her wings, "I should bite me just so you know what it feels like!"

"Ah! Please don't!" Scale-Lee sounded momentarily dreaded, "I mean, you wouldn't really want to do that to *yourself*, would you?"

"It might be worth it!" Lee-Scale retorted, "At this point, I'm not even sure anymore. I mean, maybe it would teach you a lesson- and maybe the smell of *me* is just starting to get to me. UGH!" she screeched loudly, "I hate that I think I look delicious! This is crazy making!!"

"I'm glad you finally appreciate my constant predicament," Scale-Lee said, completely oblivious to his own revolting insensitivity, "Do you see what it's like now? To be deprived like I am?!"

"Excuse me?" Lee-Scale was totally incredulous, "EXCUSE ME?! YOUR predicament?! You think this is about YOU?!"

"Well," Scale-Lee tried to explain as logically as he saw reasonable, "How would *you* feel if someone you travelled with walked around all the time with a bushel of sweet berries dangling from their hips all day long, and *you* weren't allowed to have any? How would that make *you* feel?"

"That is COMPLETELY different from *actually* wanting to eat a person!" Lee-Scale objected furiously.

"I mean... is it *really* though?" Scale-Lee prodded.

"By ORDERS of magnitude," Lee-Scale asserted.

"I don't think you totally believe that," Scale-Lee guessed, "I think the longer you're in my brain, the more you agree with me. Right?"

"Do NOT start with me," Lee-Scale pointed a wing at him, "We are absolutely *millennia* away from finding any kind of middle ground."

"But there is middle ground to be found!" Scale-Lee seized on her momentary lapse in argumentative decorum, "So, we'll start now. Okay- I'll admit, after spending a little time in here, maybe the full ten toe spread is asking a bit much. Can we agree on one barefoot flambé?" he followed brightly with, "I'll even let you pick which one, left or right."

If Lee-Scale could have turned any more crimson than her scales already were, she would have gone over to a place that made the fires of the abyss look like a pleasant orange sunset, "ABSOLUTELY NOT!"

"Four toes?" Scale-Lee tried again, "Two from each. I promise minimal encroachment on your existing agility and balance."

"THIS IS NOT A NEGOTIATION!" Lee-Scale was foaming with rage.

"Three. In your sleep so you don't even feel it. Final offer," Scale-Lee coaxed.

"SHUT YOUR FOUL, ODIOUS, REPUGNANT, REPULSIVE MOUTH RIGHT NOW!" feathers were literally falling out of Lee-Scale she was flapping with such impassioned fury.

"Come on now, you're not even trying," somehow Scale-Lee managed to tame her wild mind and tap into the patient antagonizer that she usually reserved for teasing the Battle Prince, "How much of the menu is on the table, so to speak?"

"MY TOES ARE NOT ON THE MENU!" Lee-Scale crowed, "NONE OF ME IS! I AM NOT A MEAL!" between panting, heated breaths, she launched into a Grand Dragon sized tirade, "You will NEVER, EVER get to bite, nibble, chew, gnaw, scratch, scrabble, torch, burn or lick one part of me! And if you somehow find a way to even ATTEMPT it, I will PERSONALLY see to it you are plucked, scaled, frozen in a block of ice and then boiled in a stew of your own guts! DO YOU UNDERSTAND ME?!" she roared, "Dammit! Why is it the *angrier* I get, the *hungrier* I get?! I HATE being you! Why are you like this?!"

Weakly, and with perhaps a certain degree of sincere shame and muted humility, Scale-Lee shrugged, "I'm a dragon. I can't help it."

Immediately, Lee-Scale calmed and dejectedly perched herself back on her own heels and slumped over, serpentine head propped exasperatedly up on one wing, "Gods, you really can't, can you?"

Scale-Lee shook his head.

Lee-Scale narrowed her eyes at him, "That does *not* excuse you, for the record. If *I* can can control you, *you* can control you. So get it together, parrot."

"You could make it a little easier on me," when she fixed him with a look of returned fury, Scale-Lee hurriedly followed with, "The taunting crap may be funny with wonderboy, but it just salts my appetite. So maybe cut it out?"

She took a long moment to answer, never quick to admit being wrong in any capacity, "I suppose I could reduce my... ahem... intentional temptation."

"Could you also loosen your grip?" Scale-Lee tried to wiggle away from the dragon, "I'm telling you, those claws hurt."

"Right, sorry," she apologized quietly and relaxed his talons a bit.

A ways away, Krög-Ash was looking confused as he sniffed at the air, and Ash-Krög was giving over to the Battle Prince's exaggerated impatience. He was unsettled and anxious, and could not understand why his companion was taking such a long time to decide where they were going next. Ash-Krög knew how sharp his senses were, and knew it should be little trouble to discern the imp's trail. So the longer they stood in place with Krög-Ash straining the troll's nose and ears, the more nipping agitation wormed its way into the normally stoic woodsman's consciousness, spurred on by the Battle Prince's complete lack of steadiness.

"What wrong, Battle Prince?" Ash-Krög finally asked, "Why we stop here?"

"Something's weird about the scent," Krög-Ash answered cryptically, "It's stronger and weaker at the same time. And I'm picking up even more of *us*- but it feels like a faint more of us. Does any of that make sense?"

Ash-Krög looked at their surroundings, "Hrm. There something familiar about these trees. Which is saying something, considering know most of the trees in this forest quite good. This more a recent familiar."

"Yeah, I can't figure it," Krög-Ash grumbled.

"Figure," Ash-Krög reasoned through, "Figure it? No. Figure *eight*. Damn. Imp double back. He lead us in circles."

"What, you think so?" Krög-Ash scratched his head.

"Very sure. He take advantage of confusion and not knowing how use senses well. He trick us again," Ash-Krög snarled, "He leading us nowhere."

"So, why? Krög-Ash posed, rather pointedly.

"Him probably think it funny. Him probably realize which of us be able follow him and probably guess our arguing get worse when we swapped around. Bet him knew we would split up, and him having good laugh over confusing group even more and getting us lost from one another. This bad," Ash-Krög postulated.

"No kidding," Krög-Ash was finding the muddled trail of scents to be even more befuddling the longer the odors mingled together, "So what do you think we should do?"

"Need get back to glade with Leànbh and dragon-come up with new plan," Ash-Krög asserted, "Not sure this going to be figured out so quick anymore."

"Lee is *not* going to be happy about this," Krög-Ash huffed, "I wonder if Scale has annoyed her into scorching herself just to shut him up. I can't imagine they're getting on well."

"Leànbh more level-headed than that," Ash-Krög reassured, "Pretty certain she not going to hurt self just to hurt dragon. Then again, dragon very annoying... anything possible suppose. Is best we not let come to that. And if imp headed back to same glade, is best we not let him cause more trouble with thems than already has."

"Agreed," Krög-Ash nodded vigorously, "If he hurts her, I'm going to spear him on your tusk and wear him like a tusk-ring!"

"Careful," Ash-Krög cautioned, "Anger easy for trolls- but *much* more difficult for to *stop* anger. And angry troll a dangerous troll... recklessly dangerous."

"Wow, you're not kidding," Krög-Ash realized his pulse had quickened considerably, and his muscles were feeling hot for the want of battle, "How do you stay so calm all the time?"

"Take very much concentration," Ash-Krög explained, "Must always stay centered. Be easy just let anger take over in battle, but that risk being destructive to friends. Cannot be so."

"It's, like, *really* tough being you, isn't it?" Krög-Ash asked.

"Some days easier than others," Ash-Krög said quietly, "Pretty sure am only troll every try for to be a knight. Have to fight hard against evil to be so, but have to fight harder against *self* sometimes for to keep monster quiet. Dark part of me always trying to get out."

Krög-Ash could feel it. He could feel an ancient power, a roiling evil coursing in the blackest, bleakest corner of his mind. It clawing to break through, what must have been, centuries of effort to lock it away. The real monster that lived in the troll, the feral beast that tried to crush the first peoples who settled south of the Swordsong, that was descendant of the mountain giants and the abyssal demons, was lurking always. It was ready to prey on a *single* weak thought. If Ashley gave in to that dark spirit for even a moment, Krög realized his friend might never come back from it. The singular battle the troll fought every moment of every day to be a noble, upright being when every fiber of his spirit cried out to be a murderous machine of annihilation… well, the Battle Prince could not imagine what it must be like. His respect for his guardian deepened.

"Let's get this sorted out before I do something stupid that lets that thing out," Krög-Ash said quietly.

"We wasting time," Ash-Krög urged, "This conversation better have other time. Or never. Not really something like to talk about."

"Sure, buddy," Krög-Ash consented softly, "Whatever you say. Let's get rolling."

As they turned around and raced back the direction they had come, Ash-Krög tried to find solidarity with his charge as he rode between the troll's shoulders like he were kneeling on the back of an upright ox.

"Is not so easy for to be Battle Prince though either, is it?" Ash-Krög offered, "Many confusing thoughts in head. Feel very strange when look at western horizon- odd pulling, like would rather be elsewhere. Or *belong* elsewhere maybe. You know feeling, right?"

"Yeah. I know it," Krög-Ash said simply as he crashed through the forest at top speed, no longer hindered by waiting for his companion to keep pace.

"Always feel like need be somewhere else, doing something different," Ash-Krög observed, "Thought maybe you just never taught for how to be patient the right way. Thinking now maybe is more than that. Thinking you has wandering spirit."

"I don't know, maybe," the topic made Krög-Ash a bit uncomfortable, "I just… never feel right. I never feel complete."

"Except when you with Leànbh," Ash-Krög said, "You care very much for her. Is very deep. Is almost like-"

"I think that's enough of us playing around in each other's heads for this little mishap," Krög-Ash cut his friend off, "Or, you know, ever. Let's just get back where we belong and try to be home by morning like my dad asked. I'm not sure he'll be so excited to have me trying to run affairs of state stuck like a troll."

"*Him* be okay with it. *Council* not so much," Ash-Krög reminded, "Him good, understanding man. Him Council of Elders need have they heads adjusted with blunt object. Several times."

Krög-Ash laughed deep, "You're not wrong, buddy."

Meanwhile, in the imp's glade, Lee-Scale twitched her snout at the air and narrowed the dragon's slit-like eyes as something pungent caught her nose. The smell was both familiar and delectable, and was slowly wafting over the almost overpowering scent of her own form's tender skin. She recognized it without knowing why she recognized it, and immediately needed to know the smell's source. Her triple forked tongue lapped idly at the air like she was trying to taste the scent and get a better bead on who, or what, was producing it. The harder she concentrated, the more mercurial the odor became.

"Can I ask you something?" Scale-Lee broke in on her thoughts.

"Oh look, you just did, I guess we're done talking now," Lee-Scale responded absentmindedly.

Scale-Lee puzzled over how to be polite for a moment longer before pressing on, "I'm going to ask you something else."

Lee-Scale sighed and momentarily broke off from plumbing her olfactory memory, "Fine, what is it?"

"Why do you give wonderboy so much headspace?" Scale-Lee asked, endeavoring to wrench his gaze over her bound shoulders to look at his dragon body while he had a conversation with the girl trapped in it. Just the thought of that concept was enough to nearly drive him nuts.

Lee-Scale turned immediately suspicious, "What do you mean?"

"I'm still a little afraid you're going to bite me. Or burn me. Or do that weird thing with my feathers," he carried on hurriedly when Lee-Scale shot him a look, "So, through all of that, I keep wondering if the kid is going to come and help me. And I want him to. And then I don't want him to at the same time. I want to be the one rescuing *him*. And then I have a bunch of wildly inappropriate thoughts that I hope I do NOT remember when I'm back in my body. So. What's with that?"

"It's complicated," Lee-Scale shot back.

"No kidding?" Scale-Lee scoffed sarcastically, "Here I thought you were measured and reasonable."

"We're people, you can't reduce our interactions to just 'eat, burn, more,'" Lee-Scale retorted, "It's tougher than that."

"Yeah, so, is it?" Scale-Lee conjectured, "You want something with him. He obviously wants something with you. How is this a difficult equation?"

"We are not going to discuss my dealings with the prince while we're like this," Lee-Scale dismissed, "Actually, we're not going to discuss my dealings with the prince *at all*. That is an off-limits subject to you."

"I mean, I've got the kid's ear, I'm on his shoulder all the time," Scale-Lee offered, "I could put in a good word, or something."

"Why in the nine hells would you do that for me?" Lee-Scale was intensely distrustful.

Scale-Lee shrugged as much as the girl's tied shoulders would allow, "Let me explain something. I've got time unending to live out my fantasies and get the things I want. Literally. I will *never* die. The universe itself will wink out of existence, and I'll *still* be floating around all the nothingness, probably bored to shit and wondering where I'm going to find a pixie to snack on."

"Is this going somewhere?" Lee-Scale was tired and out of patience- just, with everything.

"By comparison, your life is going to be over in the blink of an eye, toots," Scale-Lee came back, "You get about half a heartbeat in the cosmic sense to figure things out. The more you two dance around each other, the more of that time is simply gone. I'm pretty amazing, I can do a lot of amazing things- but even I can't wind the days back. I'm just saying. Think about it."

Lee-Scale chewed at the dragon's tongues, "I can't. With the prince. Not until he makes up his own mind. And you know what, it's a little insulting that I'm a choice for him. If he really wanted... something... he'd just make it happen."

"First, he's not you, he doesn't have that kind of spirit, and if he did I don't think you'd find him as interesting," Scale-Lee appraised, "And cut the kid a little slack, alright? On the one hand, he's caught between a lifetime of tradition and two kingdoms wanting to hinge their relationship on his marriage, and on the other he's got probably the first girl to ever *really* get him all hot and bothered. That's a lot of moving parts. Plus, I'm betting it's no picnic for him every time you make eyes at every sword-jockey this side of the Swordsong just to make him jealous. It doesn't just make him jealous- it makes him doubt. So... stop it."

Lee-Scale paused a while, "Are those your thoughts, or mine?"

"What do you think, toots?" Scale-Lee returned.

Lee-Scale shifted her weight and took a long breath, "Why are being like this? What do you care?"

Scale-Lee waffled a bit, "I thought maybe we could trade- a little of my sage advice for a few of your-"

"Oh, GODS!" Lee-Scale groaned loudly, "Let it go already!"

"Ugh, fine," Scale-Lee relented, "It doesn't change the fact I'm right, by the way. He's not going to be the anchor, you are. Make your move, make it clear, and I promise he'll stop flitting from branch to branch. You just have to stop tiptoeing around it. Which I could help with..." he added suggestively.

She slapped him with a wing.

"I deserved that," Scale-Lee admitted, "Damn, now I'm starting to think like YOU. Where the crap did wonderboy and Big Ugly go, anyway? How are we not already back in our own bodies?"

"I think they're on their way back," Lee-Scale sniffed at the air again, "I'm... I'm pretty sure I smell the prince."

"Sort of salty, with a malted sweetness to it that has a hint of dark chocolate and a venison back?" Scale-Lee guessed.

Lee-Scale really did not want to admit he was right, "Yes."

"That's him," Scale-Lee nodded, "If you get an earthy tone combined with roasted boar and spiced with pickled goose egg, that's the troll."

"There's something else," Lee-Scale threw her snout around, "Like a... zesty... kind of vinegar with a definite curdled cheese overtone."

"Drogomyr," Scale-Lee identified, "Who smells strongest?"

"He does- the imp," Lee-Scale said.

"The little bastard doubled back," Scale-Lee started to wrench her head around, searching for the imp fluttering through the branches above, "Sounds like wonderboy caught his scent too, but Drogy is capable of a whole lot of bad in a short time. We might be in a little trouble."

Lee-Scale kept sniffing, "Wait, there's one other thing too. Ugh, really funky. I'm going with mildew and moss with standing rainwater and... I don't know... dead orchids?"

Scale-Lee went pale, which was an experience he was unused to given his scales do not so much shift colors based on his perceived level of fear or anxiety.

"Willows."

"What in the nine hells are willows?" Lee-Scale asked, looking around somewhat anxiously.

"Not willows, Willows," Scale-Lee emphasized, "And they're bad. Like, bad, bad, bad, bad, bad, bad, bad. Especially since Big Ugly is stuck in wonderboy and can't deal out his usual carnage. Drogy probably counted on that."

"What are willows?!" Lee-Scale repeated.

"In the Elderhills, they call them Harvest's Bane," Scale-Lee said cryptically, speaking of countries and mythologies Lee had never heard of, "They're malicious forest spirits. You think *I'm* bad, toots, Willows are something else. They're leftovers of some demon race, and they really don't think too highly of the living. You need to get us out of here."

"We are going exactly nowhere until you start making sense," Lee-Scale planted herself.

"Trust me, this is not a good time to be principled *or* skittish," Scale-Lee's voice rose in pitch, "Drogy might take a few of your fingers, but Willows won't even leave bones. You have to cut me loose so I can get a head start on them. I'll carry you."

"How do I know you won't just run off and leave me with the imp and the willows?" Lee-Scale asked pointedly.

"WILLOWS!" Scale-Lee repeated, "Not willows! And do I sound like I'm about to leave my beautiful body hanging around here to get pasted?!"

Lee-Scale shifted uneasily as the smell grew stronger, though she still was not totally sure whether or not to trust her rival.

Scale-Lee started to writhe about- it would have been comical were the circumstances not becoming somewhat dire, "I don't think you're grasping how desperately screwed we are going to be if a few Willows show up with Drogomyr! I'm not even sure the troll at his peak could fight *one*, and if Drogy's got himself a little company of them then the best we can possibly hope to do is run like a damned east wind and pray to lady Blind Luck they don't catch us!"

"You're serious," Lee-Scale felt her little dragon stomach tie up in fiery knots.

"Deadly serious, toots," Scale-Lee practically squealed, "We need to go, now!"

"And why would you do that, Red?" Drogomyr's voice broke in on their quarreling, "Then you'd miss out on all the fun of my revenge! Although, I have to say, I didn't count on them tying you up all pretty like this. Just makes my life that much easier- although my buddies back there are going to be disappointed."

The imp was zipping around the glade, cackling and chittering, the absolute thrill of doing something terrible boiling out of his sadistic little form. Behind him, just out of view in the tree-line, something was moving in the shadows. Something very large. And by the sounds it made, something very unpleasant.

"You weren't wrong about the Willows," Drogomyr went on, "They're a gnarly bunch. Still, when it comes to having a personal goon squad, you can't really do much better."

More shapes and shadows joined the first. Even with the dragon's superiorly sharp vision, Lee-Scale could not quite make out the details of the creatures- only that they were big, and misshapen, and they made crooked, jerking movements. They were coming closer, and closer.

"I feel a little bad you're caught in the middle of our spat, girlie," the imp addressed Lee, "Truly, it's nothing personal. Red here forgets his actions have consequences sometimes, and it can mean the detriment of his friends. Too bad, really. If it makes you feel any better, you won't feel much when the Willows finish you. Red, on the other hand, you've got some back payments to make."

"What're you going to do? Talk me slowly to death with your boring anecdotes?" Scale-Lee snorted.

"No, I thought poetic justice was more in order," Drogomyr landed in front of the young woman's nose, "You ate the woman I loved, so I thought I'd spend the next couple weeks doing the same to the one you're running around with. Of course, you'll be trapped in her skin still, so I'll get to revel in you begging me to stop. Won't that be nice? Oh! I almost forgot to mention! I'm going to have the Willows stomp your body flat so there's nowhere for you escape back to. Again, really sorry about that," he turned back to Lee-Scale for a moment,

"But you'll have it a sight better than Red here, I promise you that."

"Except for the part where you'll be killing me, and then using my body as a centerpiece for the next fortnight," Lee-Scale reminded him, "All of which sounds like a lot of not fun… ESPECIALLY FOR ME!"

"Yeah, it's unfortunate," the imp had a complete lack of sincerity to his voice, "But… you know… business and all…"

Lee-Scale hopped onto her own head and towered over the hovering imp, "You want him, you have to come across me first."

"Look, sweetheart," Drogomyr patronized, "It's not that you don't got spirit. You do! But the thing about Willows… well… it's going to take a lot more than a little snort of fire to stop *one* of them. And I've got eight."

"How 'bout lightning?!" Ash-Krög shouted from the opposite side of the tree line, brandishing Thundersteel aloft, "What that do to thems?!"

Sparks were forming on the edge of the sword as the troll trapped in his friend's body held the weapon valiantly over his head, the look of intense focus Ash was known for carved into Krög's face. Over his shoulder, arms crossed and looking rakishly confident, Krög-Ash towered in the shadows of the trees, eyes glittering with excitement at having a chance to put to test the strength of his titanic guardian.

"Oh yeah," Krög-Ash winked, "You're in it deep now, critter."

Drogomyr sighed loudly, "How inconvenient. I thought I lost you two a few glens back."

"You dramatically underestimate how bombastic we are," Krög-Ash snarled proudly.

"And *you* drastically *over*estimate your grasp on language," Drogomyr replied, "So. Here's the part where I amicably give you a chance to just walk away and forget about all of this and all you'll have to deal with is being stuck in someone else's body for the rest of your lives but you get to live even though your friends are not so lucky," the imp said in one breath, "You seem like a couple of lunkheads though-"

"Good call," Lee-Scale snorted unhelpfully.

"Ahem," the imp continued after being cut off, "Right. How does this work? Are we done with the threatening and the bargaining? Can we just cut to the part where you're dead and I win?"

Krög-Ash shrugged, "What do you think, ol' buddy?"

Ash-Krög narrowed his eyes, "You take six on right, I take two on left."

"Groovy," Krög-Ash grinned.

"And I'll take the bad hair day with wings," Lee-Scale screeched.

"I guess I'll..." Scale-Lee looked around at the girl's, still very much tied up, predicament, "Well, you know where I'll be if you need anything."

Lee-Scale was the first to launch into action. Even though his wings were flightless Lee still brought a considerable acrobatic talent to Scale's tiny body, and with a series of quick flips and glides landed almost on top of Drogomyr. The imp barely had time to zip out of the way, and he looked genuinely shocked at her competency in another creature's form as she snatched at him with her dragon jaws. Drogomyr released two sizzling bolts of energy at Lee-Scale, but she easily dodged both without so much as singing a feather. She giggled noisily in full Dragonthroat as she cartwheeled over one of her wings, and slapped the imp out of the air with Scale's barbed tail. With a hack and a wheeze, the tiny creature went flailing before landing roughly in the brambles. He was within mere inches of being squashed completely flat and dead by a gigantic troll boot bearing down on him as Krög-Ash and Ash-Krög sprinted across the glade, weapons raised, and disappeared into the tree line to take on the Willows.

Scale-Lee wrenched the girl's head around to try and get a better view of the battles going on around him. Over her shoulder, he could hear Krög-Ash balk in fear as he caught sight of the beastly Willows that Drogomyr brought to the party. The Battle Prince stuck in the troll's body cursed in a number of languages before hollering loud and long in Giant Speak some age old war cry, and taking to the fight. Sounds like rending limbs and withering moans and sighs filled the air as, Scale-Lee supposed, the troll's mighty fists shattered apart the shambling monsters of the shadows. Ash-Krög could be heard grunting a few times as he, perhaps, coaxed the Battle Prince's body into a series of athletic tumbles its original owner did not know it was capable of to dodge out of the way of the looming creatures. Twin claps of thunder shook the air and rattled the ground, and the glade lit up brightly as lightning came racing down out of the clouds and decimated whatever it was the bolts touched upon. More eldritch sighs and creaks flew from the Willows as the two companions set after their foes with impassioned fury and, especially in the face of such horrifying abominations, impossible courage! Then, it was all pretty much conjecture- Scale-Lee could not actually see any of it happening.

Lee-Scale was locked in an equally dangerous game of fire and magic against Drogomyr, both ridiculously agile and supernaturally quick. Scale-Lee saw his serpentine dragon body bend and contort in ways he did not realize were possible, and watched in awe as Lee-Scale blasted lines of flame longer and hotter than he had ever managed to conjure forth. Equally, Drogomyr was raining all manner of mystic destruction down on the bearing dragon. A veritable hailstorm of magic energy and sparking conjurations rocketed back and forth as the imp tossed out every burst of wizardry he had up his sleeves in a desperate attempt to stop Lee-Scale. She shrugged all of his attacks off with a certain demented glee, taking hysterical pleasure in squeezing between assaults with gymnastic ease, always returning in kind with a destructive, searing plague of yellow flame. Drogomyr had certainly met his match in his own creation, and there was perhaps a twinge of regret nibbling at the edge of his mind for sticking the spritely young woman into an armored machine of havoc and ruin- albeit a little one.

Voices filled the air around Scale-Lee as he lost sight of his companions, and could only make out the sounds of the fighting.

"DIE, DEVIL FIREFLY!" Lee-Scale crowed.

"Battle Prince! Get down!" Ash-Krög hollered just before another lightning bolt cut through the heavens.

"I am the reaper! I am all that is decay! FEAR MY WRATH!" Krög-Ash boomed as the symphony of snapping branches and felling trees crescendoed.

"I feel like you're taking this personally," Drogomyr said almost breathlessly, "And I'm not sure how else I can say 'this isn't about you.'"

"It's the strangest thing," Lee-Scale retorted between bursts of flame, "But somehow the fact that I still end up dead does not comfort me. What else ya' got?"

"I don't suppose you'd agree to staying a feather dragon and being my jester for the next eternity?" the imp fired back.

"Let me think about it," Lee-Scale returned quickly, "Done thinking. Nope. Would rather find out what toasted imp tastes like actually. I know it's a bit hypocritical and all, but hey, I'm complicated!"

More fire and more magic flashed back and forth between the two, along with a continually dizzying series of even more wildly nimble flips, twists and spins from the young woman locked in the miniature dragon. It was clear Drogomyr had not been so singularly challenged in quite some time, and he was starting to weaken noticeably. His mystical blasts came slower and with less pizzaz and zap, and his own attempts to dodge Lee-

Scale's flaming breath skirted through narrower and narrower windows. Drogomyr was used to surprising his victims with a quick spritz of magic and then cleaning up the scraps of them afterwards. Prolonged battles were not exactly in his nature. Lee-Scale, however, was more than prepared to take all day to wear down the imp if needed.

Fortunately, it did not take all day. Drogomyr raced towards Lee-Scale to try and throw a magic blast at close enough proximity that the little dragon being controlled by the athletic woman would not be able to dip out of the way. He was not only totally wrong, but also got way too close to a way too angry miniature dragon. Lee-Scale stretched out her neck, opened the dragon's jaws, and lashed out with his triple-forked tongue. The forks wrapped around the shocked imp, and in a snap and a gulp, he disappeared down the feather dragon's throat.

There was an awkward pause as Lee-Scale and Scale-Lee realized exactly what had happened, and that their antagonist, but also potential savior, had just gone spiraling down into the dragon's stomach.

"Well NOW what in the unholy name of the abyss are we supposed to do?!" Scale-Lee screeched, "You just ATE our only chance at getting out of this mess!"

Lee-Scale did not answer right away. She returned to her perch on her own heels and wobbled there a moment or two, smacking the dragon's jaws together a few times.

"Well?!" Scale-Lee hollered again, "Are you just going to stand there?! What's wrong with you??!!"

"Um," Lee-Scale's voice was meek, "I don't feel so good."

"What-? You don't feel so good? What does that mean? What's happening?" Scale-Lee turned panicked.

"Oh, gods," Lee-Scale got the sensation of something wriggling up her throat, "Ugh. I don't think I can keep imp down."

"Do NOT throw him back up on me!" Scale-Lee tried to squirm away.

A sickly look overtook Lee-Scale's face, and it was clear she was about to lose her impromptu lunch. She shifted a few more times, like it might quell the nausea and indigestion she was clearly struggling with.

At last, Lee-Scale opened the dragon's tiny mouth and loosed an absolutely heroic burp. It rang out repulsively in full Dragonthroat, and was accompanied by a burst of magic so powerful it blasted Lee-Scale backwards off her perch and sent her flying through the air. She smashed into a tree trunk with enough force to knock her silly.

When Lee opened her eyes, she could barely move. The indigestion was gone, but her limbs felt next to useless. She took a few moments lying in the brambles to catch her breath and get her bearings again. Surprisingly, her head did not hurt as much as she was sure it was going to- given how hard she had just crashed into a tree. Finally, she tried to get up, but quickly realized part of the reason she could not move was because she was tangled up in something. With no shortage of ecstatic joy, Lee realized she was tied up. Her body was. And her mind was back in her body. Lee was Lee again.

Of course, just as quickly it dawned on her that it probably meant Scale was Scale again.

"Gods above and below, never, NEVER again..." the little dragon came stumbling through the brambles, "That's one troll of a headache. I think I've got a concussion- I feel like I need to barf."

Lee held her breath to see how long it would take Scale to realize he was back in his own skin- or scales, rather- once again.

He moved to rub his head with his wing and the sight of his own feathers caught the tiny monster's eye, "Wait. Wait."

Scale whooped and hollered and just barely caught himself from vomiting everywhere when he jumped into the air with excitement, the sickness of eating Drogomyr still persisting.

"I'm back! Oh, thank the gods!! Happy day, this is the most beautiful moment of my entire life!" Scale strutted and squawked about, just thrilled to be back as his old self again, "Return of the Dreaded! YES!!!"

Lee tried to stay as absolutely quiet and still as she could. She was counting on Ash-Krög and Krög-Ash finishing off the Willows and coming back to untie her before something truly unfortunate came to pass between her and Scale.

Unfortunately, the little dragon's senses and awareness were not quite as dulled as she was hoping, "Well, well," he turned and leered at her, "My lucky day does continue, doesn't it?"

"Okay, let's not lose our heads or anything and do something…" Lee swallowed hard and searched for the right word, "Irreversible."

A hungry glint leapt into Scale's eye. It was followed by a long line of drool from his needle-like teeth, and a sinister furrowing of his eyebrow horns.

"Scale," Lee's voice was stern, though there was anxiousness at the edges, "Do. Not. Think about it."

"Don't worry, toots," the little dragon said darkly, "I've thought about it enough. We can move past the thinking part."

Lee tried to wiggle away as Scale waddled slowly over to her, but Ash-Krög had done a sensational job with his rope work. With a short jump, he landed where she had perched on the back of her heels. She winced as his little talons dug into her skin. Scale licked his chops.

She tried one last appeal, "Please! Didn't we have a moment, or something?"

The little dragon did not respond past giving her a toothy grin of sadistic pleasure. Lee squeezed her eyes shut when he turned away and lowered his head. She waited for the sharp, rending clamp of his jaws, or the searing, roast of his fiery breath on her tender skin.

With a single, vicious snap, Scale shredded the ropes holding Lee's ankles together. He hopped up her back, intentionally digging his claws into her a little tighter than he needed to, and snapped the ropes keeping her wrists bound. Relieved and confused, Lee skittered over and looked skeptically at the little dragon.

"You could have taken off and left me when Drogy showed up," Scale said, "As far as I'm concerned, we're even now."

"Did you just do something nice?" Lee asked.

"Don't get too excited just yet, toots," the little dragon hurriedly corrected, "You'll end up on a silver platter for me one day," he sighed and considered her with a degree of, what almost passed for, human empathy, "But it's not today. Thanks for taking out Drogy."

"Thanks for not eating me," she replied sincerely.

"Ugh," Scale choked back another belch, "I'm also not about to ruin a spread as good as you when I feel like there's titan stampeding through my guts."

Lee sighed, "Moment ruined."

"Let's go find the troll and wonderboy," the little dragon clambered up to her shoulder and perched himself there uncomfortably, "I don't know how long I'm going to be puking up magic, but we should probably get them switched back before it wears off."

"You got it, Red," Lee agreed.

Scale smiled quietly at her calling him by his old nickname.

One massive purple burp later and Krög and Ash were back in their rightful forms as well. The troll looked genuinely thrilled to have his titanic arms and thick hide back- he even went so far as to fiddle about with his heavy, black mane proudly, as though he missed having the long locks as opposed to the Battle Prince's shorter, tangled mop. Ash strutted around a little while, graciously stretching out his mighty limbs and getting comfortable again with his strength and coordination. He stretched and twisted around a few times, reaching up to the sky and down low to the ground. It was about as goofy and animated as the troll ever was, accented by the stupid, crooked grin plastered between Ashley's tusks as he finally settled back into his own body.

Krög was something of a different story. Surprisingly, he did not look disappointed to be returned to his, comparatively, smaller body, or even to have his strength so stunningly truncated in contrast to the troll's immense brawn. Rather, the Battle Prince looked pensive, and borderline haunted. There was a stormy brooding behind his eyes, and he was largely silent at first. Ash put a hand on the young ruler's shoulder to gently rouse the prince from his odd stupor. Krög looked up at the troll a little glassy-eyed and distant.

"I've never seen anything like those..." he struggled to finish describing the sinister Willows, "I don't think I've ever been that afraid."

"They very rare, and is a good thing," Ash reassured, "Likely never sees them ever again. Least, not this far west of Dragon's Spine mountains. Mostly they stay in The Darks and on other side of cliffs."

Krög struggled uncomfortably a moment longer, "It wasn't just them. It was... what's in you. I felt it try to break loose. It made me feel stronger and braver, but it also felt like it could take over. I felt like I might lose control. Is that always how it feels when you fight?"

Ashley narrowed his eyes, "Sometimes."

"How do you do the things you do, Ash, and keep that thing in a cage?" the prince asked solemnly, "How do you do *any* of the things you do? Like with Thundersteel, just now... you made it do things I've never seen before..."

"I concentrate," the troll cut his young friend off, "I listen. One day, you learn how concentrate and listen too. Then, you find you own tempest inside not quite so scary thing for to weather. Yes?"

"I guess," the prince shrugged, "I don't know if I could make it as you, buddy. You're like nothing else."

"No," Ash brushed aside the admonishment, "Just am. Just like you just you. Work every day to be better you, just like I work every day be better me. Understand?"

Krög shook his head, "No- not yet. But, I get it a little better than I did before," he held out his hand to the troll, "In case I don't say it enough: thanks, Ash. You're my best friend, and you're stronger than anything else I know."

Warily and humbly, the troll took the prince's hand in his giant paw, "Battle Prince very kind."

"Can we just... go home," the prince sighed at last, "Those willow things are going to give me a whole host of nightmares tonight, and I'd rather not have them out here in the woods."

"*Willows*," Scale corrected, frustrated, from Lee's shoulder "Why can't *either* of you get that right?"

Krög regarded the little dragon with vexation, "Too bad the imp didn't mind swap you into a fungus. Then, we wouldn't have to deal with your crap anymore."

"If he'd done that, there wouldn't have been anyone to put you all back, would there have?" Scale asked brightly as he flitted awkwardly back to Krög's arm, "So, *maybe*, someone owes the dragon a bit of a thank you?"

"Not in this lifetime or the next," the Battle Prince said dryly, "You're lucky I don't let Ash crush you into fresh squeezed lizard tea after everything this afternoon."

"You're something else, you know that?" Scale came back indignantly, "I do the courtesy of putting you back in the right place while I've got the kind of heartburn that would turn you inside out, and somehow you're still unappreciative."

Krög rolled his eyes, "I'm just glad to see you and Lee didn't tear each other apart."

Lee jumped in, "Oh, don't think it didn't almost come to that. There were more than a few bracing moments."

The prince chuckled, "And I'm betting *you* were the cause of more than a few of them yourself."

Before Lee could even respond, Scale bit down on the young ruler's ear. Hard.

"YOU BE NICE TO HER!" the little dragon screeched at a dramatically inappropriate volume given he was still on the prince's shoulder.

"What the hell?!" Krög practically swatted the tiny monster off his arm and struggled with his bleeding ear where Scale's teeth had pierced straight through.

"You two kids are worse than a cliffbeast trying to ride a boarhound!" Scale huffed as he attempted, valiantly, to climb back to his perch despite the Battle Prince's efforts to keep him away.

"What does that even mean?" the young ruler was still incensed, "Damn, Scale, what has gotten into you?!"

"Me, mostly," Lee giggled, before quickly following with, "And not one of you better make the obvious joke."

"What obvious joke?" Ashley scratched his head.

She laughed louder, "Come on, Big Guy. Sweep a girl off her feet and carry her home."

The troll chuckled and leaned over to offer her the braid on the side of his head. She delightedly scaled his nine foot shoulders and settled herself back in place atop her own favored perch. Both turned towards the prince and the dragon, who were, apparently, not yet done with their disagreement. Scale had tried again to clamber up the young ruler's side, and again Krög had swatted him away.

"You're walking the rest of the way, you little twerp," the Battle Prince said.

Ashley sighed, "Remember- is not so easy keep up to longer legs when much smaller."

"Yeah!" Scale agreed, "It's not so easy!"

Krög chewed at his tongue a moment, "Bite me again, and I swear…"

"Right, right, right," the little dragon cut him off, "Hollow threat followed by hyperbolic assessment of anger- the formula is getting a bit tired. Let's just all agree the dragon is amazing, and we wouldn't be back in place if it wasn't for him, yeah?"

The prince rather aggressively rubbed his chin as though trying to decide on how to respond in a way that was not in line with exactly what the tiny monster had just detailed.

"I hate all of you," he finally decided on, "Except you, Ash," he added quickly, "And you're alright, Lee."

"I'll pretend you said something nice about me too," Scale snorted, "Can we please get the heck outta here now? I did *not* sign up for an afternoon of this kind of excitement."

"Need I remind you, we didn't invite you along- for a reason!" the prince said pointedly, "And we've got one more thing to do before we get out of here."

Between Ash and Scale's preternaturally honed senses of smell, it did not take them long to find the man who had been flopping around in the thorns, and bring him back to the oasis where the Magnificent Octopus was in hiding. Rather reluctantly, the little dragon summoned up another vile, toxic belch, and blasted the octopus and the man's body with the imp's magic. Both the merchant and the octopus were knocked cold by the force of the blast, and Scale was very nearly thrown from his perch.

The little dragon choked back the urge to vomit, "I'm going to be really, *really* glad when I stop doing that."

Within moments, the merchant recovered, "Gods above and below," he looked at his hands, human for the first time in who knows how long, "I am restored. You were successful!"

"Yep," Scale coughed, "Now you can go back to being a miserable person, instead of a miserable monster. How nice."

"Scale!" Lee scolded, "Have some damned courtesy for once."

The little dragon waved his wing somewhat dismissively, "I wish you many happy years with that woman, whoever she was, and your little shop. Luck be with you and all that crap."

Krög looked incredulously at him, "Your attempts at genuine are positively stunning."

"Nay, though he is correct," the merchant sighed sadly, "In the Ivory City, I am but a worm amongst titans, a beetle on a heap of gold and rubies."

"Battle Prince," Ashley growled suddenly.

"How melodramatic," Lee huffed, "Honestly, I would have hoped getting put back would give you a new outlook or something. Can't you be happy about anything?"

"She's right, you know," Krög admitted, "It could be a lot worse. I mean your whole situation. You didn't even take advantage of being a huge, jewel encrusted octopus when you had the chance! And that was... well... magnificent!"

"Battle Prince," the troll repeated, nudging his friend.

The merchant sighed, "I am a mote of dust in this universe. A drifting, floating, wafting crumb of dirt. Perhaps one day I might be worthy of... anything."

"Isn't there anything at all that you enjoy?!" Lee almost pleaded with the merchant, "I mean, come on, no one is this morose all the time, right? Didn't, I don't know, making stuff like you used to make you feel good?"

"I was barely able to, even at that," the merchant drawled, "It was a labor. A veritable onus of near godlike difficulty for me."

Scale laughed, "I'm starting to like this guy! I mean, the way he talks!"

"Battle Prince," Ashley said louder.

"Ash, what?" Krög's frustration with the merchant they had saved and his complete lack of gratitude was boiling over.

The troll squinted, "What you think octopus was like before had mind of man stuck in it?"

Sighing, the prince shook his head, "I don't know, buddy. Why?"

"Because," Ash half gestured towards the cave behind the waterfall, "Octopus awake."

Everyone turned, very slowly. Looming in the entrance of the cavern, in all its resplendent, multifaceted glory, but looking decidedly angrier and more sinister, was the Magnificent Octopus, tentacles raised, maw open. Its enormous, black eyes rolled towards the group, and fixed them with a decidedly unfriendly grimace. Peeling the cascades of the waterfall aside, the great, globulous beast squeezed itself out of the cave and writhed closer to the troupe. It opened up its gigantic, toothy maw, and loosed an earth-shattering roar.

As before, the entire group screamed in unison.

With lightning speed the octopus lashed out with one of its tentacles, and snatched the merchant out of the oasis. A plunging gulp later, and the titanic monster swallowed the merchant whole. Barely the sound of the man saying something along the lines of "oh, bother," as he vanished down the creature's gullet made it past the monster's teeth. As soon as the octopus gulped down the merchant, it roared again at the remaining companions.

Krög paused only an instant, "Run?"

"Run," Ashley agreed.

They went speeding into the tree-line, and racing back through the rest of The Strange. Actually, they did not stop sprinting until they had cleared the edge of The Quiets. The trees there barely had time to open a gap in their impenetrable hedge of branches and vines to let the companions space enough to escape the Thorn Rift Forest. Ragged and breathless, Krög collapsed in the tall grasses in the rolling fields just beyond the arbors, and took a few, long, heavy pants to try and steady his howling heart. Scale had tumbled from his perch, and looked at the prince indignantly.

"You need to exercise more," the little dragon appraised, brushing dirt out of his feathers.

"I think," the young ruler managed between sucking down air, "I think we lost him."

Ashley looked cautiously over his shoulder, "Fair certain octopus not behind us. Then- fair certain octopus cannot leave water either…"

"So that mad dash for freedom could have been just a short jaunt on to dry land?" Lee asked, quipping.

"Everyone shut up so I can catch my breath," the prince asked.

"Exactly what bearing does MY talking have on YOU catching YOUR breath?" the little dragon came back.

"It have bad bearing on everyone," Ash rumbled.

"You stay out of this, Big Ugly," Scale snapped.

"And I'm up," Krög jumped back to his feet, even though his heart was still actively trying to break loose of the cage that was his ribs. He was more tired of everyone arguing incessantly.

The clouds overhead were a deep crimson as twilight came hurrying down out of the western skies. Already the grasses were painted a waving auburn, rather than their noontide greens, and it was clear night was in a rush to smear its velvet brush over the land. Krög had promised his father they would be back by morning, but the prince was more than glad to instead just be back before nightfall- he had had just about enough adventuring for one long, delinquent, summer afternoon. He knew the stars would be out in force by the time they crossed the fields north of the Fortress City, and already the sting of sleep was pricking at his eyes. All the prince wanted was to settle into his bed, pull a blanket over and wake up when all the excitement was over.

Somewhere in the Fortress City the party and festivities were still going strong, and the sounds of war drums and horns hovered in the night air like a humid drape. Even the gates to the mighty city of Ganithen hung slightly ajar, as though the evening watch had forgotten to shut the door in their haste to join the rumpus. Only half of the watchtower beacons were lit, and the few guards still attending their posts were mostly lolling in drunken stupor after returning from a day of celebration. Strings of colored flags had been partially dislodged from their anchoring, and the whole town looked like someone had turned it upside down, given it a good shake, and then sloppily placed it back on its foundation. Yes, the barbarians could party.

With an exhausted and somewhat tense farewell, the companions all parted ways to return to their individual quarters for the evening. They all suddenly knew far too much about one another after the day's events, and felt like it was prudent to perhaps slip away quickly and silently, and see if a good night's sleep would turn the whole afternoon into a bad dream. Somehow, none seemed overly confident in that idea, but everyone agreed it was at least worth a shot. Under the cover of moonlight, and with the whole city distracted by the victory parade still festively thundering along, the friends parted and stumbled back to the places they had come from.

Krög almost staggered up the stairs of the Great Hall. None of the door guards were in place, and he had to coax the oxen to tug the portal open even just a few feet so he could squeeze into the palace. Most of the torches within were out, but at least one great hearth fire was still roaring. The Battle King himself was seated at a table by the comforting blaze, pouring over a scattered pile of documents and scrolls. When the mighty doors creaked open and the chains anchoring them rattled to announce the prince's entrance, the old man looked up from his work. The dim lighting made him look even more aged than he was, but the glowing coals cast a kindly look on his face when he smiled at his son's appearance.

"Ah, welcome back, boy," the Battle King's rumbling voice was unusually soft, "I trust you had a lively afternoon bereft of duty and function?"

"It was enlightening," Krög said honestly as he passed by, still anxious to get as quickly as he could to the embrace of his own bed.

"Stay thyself a moment, my son," it was always odd to hear the old man talk in the ancient prose- it usually meant he was extremely serious, or dead tired.

"Dad, I'm wiped out," the prince tousled his tangled hair, "And it sounds like you could use some sleep too. I think we should both be going to bed, yeah?"

"Indulge me," the Battle King chuckled, before muttering, "To hear the day come my own son is telling me what *my* bedtime is."

Heavily, Krög sat down next to his father, "Why are you even still working on this? It sounded like half the city was still neck deep in the party."

"They are," Bröghue nodded, "Shortly after you left, the Merchant Lord himself requested my direct audience, and we drew up the final arrangements for a new treatise of peace and cooperation between our kingdoms."

"Fascinating," the Battle Prince yawned.

"One day, son, you'll learn to tame that sarcasm," the old man grumbled, "Though, your new companions seem to have aggravated that trait of yours a degree. The young lady especially."

"I know you don't like her," Krög began.

"It is not *her* I dislike, boy," the Battle King cut him off, "It is what she has done to *your* sense of commitment to your kingdom, which is to erode it even further than I thought possible."

The last thing the prince had been looking for before bed was a lecture. He stared blankly at the papers spread out on the table, their mind-numbing content scrawled out in loopy, over-blown words like 'henceforth,' 'heretofore,' and 'absolution.'

Bröghue sighed, "She could spark greatness in you, boy, but you allow her goad you into mediocrity. What's worse, I largely suspects she *knows* what she's doing, and just thinks it's funny. You, on the other hand, seem to be her intellectual inferior."

"Thanks for that, dad," the prince scoffed.

The old man chuckled quietly, "Alright, that was a bit harsh, perhaps. All the same, it does not change the fact that girl routinely finds ways to knock your maturity back to a place of teenage equivocation, when you should be moving well beyond that. I can see in you the desire to be better for her sake, and I am appreciative someone has found that in you- but there's still the part of you that allows her to rule your tides. As I have said before, you must be the one in control of your own spirit. So, figure it out."

Exhaustion and impatience made the young ruler cranky, "What's the point? As soon as Ydal and I get married then Lee will just… well, damned if I know, but who cares what's going on between us? It won't last."

Imperceptibly, the Battle King smiled, "Well, it is a shame to hear you say it won't last, as I had grown rather fond of the girl. And seeing as you're no longer obligated to marry the Merchant Lord's daughter, I had hoped to get to know Lèanbh a bit better."

Krög looked up sharply, "What?"

The old man slid the prince one of the documents he was working on- a contract titled 'Dissolution of Marital Treaty.' The bottom had already been signed by Bęrun, Ydal, and the Battle King. It was waiting for Krög's signature.

"This is why I wanted you back by morning," the old man said, "As I have been trying to explain, we negotiated peace and trade between our kingdoms under different terms, seeing as the Merchant Lord's need for continued protection is more immediate than before. Your mission to rescue his daughter gave me the leverage to dissolve our old accord. As every Battle Prince before, you are now free to choose your own wife, my son- provided she chooses you as well, of course."

The young ruler's hands almost shook as he held the document and quickly read through its contents. By signing, he would no longer be bound to the Bęrun family line and have no commitment to joining their families for the mutuality of the two kingdoms. Peace in the Swordsong Valley was secured, and a piece of Krög's life had been given back to him.

"Dad…" the prince whispered.

"Don't get too excited, boy," the old man cautioned parentally, "If you can't figure out how to court Lèanbh in a manner more befitting your age and station, the council will never allow her to become the Lady of the Hall. If you intend to make her a part of our lineage, then she must *become* a part of our lineage- do you understand what I'm saying?"

"For the most part," the young ruler nodded, "I'll be better. I promise. And I'll make Lee better, too."

"The two of you are just fine as you are," the Battle King partially corrected, "Just- try to be a little more adult when you're in public, at least. I trust that isn't too much to ask, is it?"

"It's not," Krög agreed, "And we will."

"For the time being, until everything has settled, it would be best we continue to keep your, ahem, liaisons with the young miss quiet," the Battle King slid a quill and inkwell to his son to sign the document, "As far as most of my kingdom is still concerned, she is a rogue assassin in this country for reasons unexplained. The idea of a member of the Battle Family being so inextricably linked to a foreign agent will not be well received, especially given warriors of the Eastern Collective were counted amongst the marauders that took the Ivory City."

"Right, of course," the prince was only half listening as he hurriedly affixed his name at the bottom of the treaty.

"My son, I'm being serious now," the Battle King said sternly, "This is your first test of whether or not you can manage to carry off the correct public appearance with Miss Lèanbh. You are not to make your intentions clear until the time is right- and *I* will be the arbiter of that decision. Do we have an understanding?"

"We do," Krög nodded vigorously, "Keep it quiet. Grow up. Be less stupid. Got it," he held up one thumb in agreement.

The old man sighed again and rubbed his eyes, "Only you could reduce such a complicated lesson to ten words and a flippant gesture. I shudder for the future of the Southern Reach."

With a rakish grin, the Battle Prince replied, "Like father like son, right?"

Bröghue laughed, "More than you likely know, boy. More than you know. Right then, off to bed with us. The announcement is being made in the morning, and it will be quite the busy day seeing the royal family of Fanfarra off. I need you by my side tomorrow, so get some sleep."

"Thanks, dad," Krög said sincerely, "I really do appreciate it."

With a humored glint in his eye, the Battle King replied, "You're going to make me regret this, aren't you?"

The same look on his face, the Battle Prince spread into a full grin, "Probably."

A booming chortle from the old man followed Krög out as the young ruler retreated, at the last, to his chambers, naught but pure ecstasy and excitement in his heart and mind. Despite his weariness the young ruler flopped onto his bed of furs, but could barely close his eyes as his thoughts raced through a thousand new possibilities before him. It felt like the world had opened up to him and Lee, that it was welcoming them, and every grand, sweeping horizon was theirs for the taking.

For once, the Battle Prince felt like he had a choice in the direction to take his life- and for once he knew what direction it would be. A part of him wanted to sneak off to Lee's room right then and there to tell her, but even more he wanted to see the look of shock and surprise on her face when it was announced the next day. As much as he wanted to be next to her, the Battle Prince tried to exercise his princely restraint, for once, and keep the secret for at least one night.

Of course, as usual, Lee was already one step ahead of him- or almost, anyway.

As the young ruler lay in his bed, plucking idly at Harpbinger and summoning mystical images of the Magnificent Octopus to float around the ceiling of his room, his playing was interrupted by a quiet shuffling at his door. Krög looked up to find Lee smiling softly as he played.

"It's very pretty," she said, waving at the hovering, smokey likeness of the mighty, multicolored octopus, "But I remember it being a bit more terrifying than that. You always seem to gloss over those details."

"What? You didn't think he was a sight?" the prince asked.

Lee squeezed the pillow she was carrying and gave him a look, "I was a little distracted. Once, just *once*, I would like you to take me somewhere nice where something awful doesn't want to eat us. Is it too much to ask to stay at the top of the food chain? I've now had TWO dragons, a giant snail, and an imp try to turn me into hor'doeuvres. THAT'S what sticks out in my head."

Krög chuckled and scooted over so she could join him, "I like to remember the positive parts, what can I say?"

"No, you like to *glorify* things," she laughed, "I'll bet even Daddy Battle King had some bumbling teenage years, but you barbarians only write the high points."

"We're pretty much counting on the world forgetting about the stupid stuff we did, in favor of the heroic stuff," the prince replied, putting his arm around Lee as she tucked in next to him.

"Then you better start racking up wins, and fast," she chided, "Or someone is going to write down all the ridiculous exploits of your life, and not have anything heroic to even talk about. Wouldn't that be embarrassing?"

"No more embarrassing than you ending up sharing skin with Scale," Krög shot back smartly.

"For the record," Lee smacked him with a pillow, "The dragon had some pretty insightful things to say."

The prince tried to swat her back with his own pillow, but missed completely, "Oh really? About what, pray tell?"

"About you," Lee wrestled herself atop the prince and playfully pinned him against the bed, "And about how I should be handling you."

Krög laughed, and tried in vain to buck the girl off, though she was surprisingly strong and balanced.

"And just how exactly is it the dragon thinks you need to be handling me, dare I even ask?" the Battle Prince queried through chuckles.

Lee leaned forward and whispered in his ear. Krög turned a spectacular shade of crimson as she got more and more detailed. When the young woman finally sat back up, biting her lip bawdily, the young ruler almost could not respond.

"That was graphic," he said breathlessly, "If we're going to do that, we'd need-"

Lee cut him off when she, inexplicably, produced a pair of slender shackles from absolutely nowhere.

Krög stammered, "I would think after being tied up all day, the last thing you would want…"

She raised an eyebrow at him coyly.

The prince surrendered, "Those aren't for you, are they?"

Lee smiled broadly and shook her head.

Krög gave her a look, "Why do I feel like you put your own interpretive spin on what Scale said?"

"I might have added a few details here and there," the athletic young woman confessed brightly, "Is that a problem, prince?"

He laughed quietly, "Well before you start… you know… I have something to tell you."

She looked at him both expectantly and impatiently, "The window of opportunity on this impossibly good mood of mine is narrow, prince, especially after the day we've had."

Krög nodded, "Trust me, you'll want to hear this."

"What is it?" Lee eyed him a bit suspiciously.

The Battle Prince took in a deep breath, "So, you remember how I was supposed to get married?"

Lee did not miss it, "Was?"

"Yeah," Krög looked deep in her crystalline eyes, "Was."

The Iron Citadel, or Alone in The Dark

Though normally a grand and resplendent chamber, the ivory and marble walls of the Merchant Lord's personal, private meeting hall were only dimly lit by a few stray candles that had not yet burned down to their last ashes. Bęrun sighed heavily and drew a frail hand across his troubled brow, narrow fingers tracing deep lines before falling to the silver strands of his extraordinarily long, regal beard. His slender form was propped tiredly in a high-backed chair, exhaustion weighing heavier on his lean limbs than any weight he possibly could have carried. The dancing shadows were his company, along with a host of troubled thoughts and ancient nightmares that haunted the aged miser- psychic scars leftover of a lifetime nearly long forgotten. Nearly long forgotten, and yet suddenly fresh anew all at once, like the icy hand of a withered, dead monster groping up from the depths of the nine hells to claw at the living again.

In his lifetime, the Merchant Lord had buried a kingdom's kingdom's worth of treasures in gold and jewels and artifacts and valuables- locked them all away in vaults sealed deep below the streets of his Ivory City where prying eyes and greedier fingers could touch them all not. He sat upon a gilded throne with a scepter spear above a veritable spider's web of safes and cellars brimming with more wealth than any twelve kings could spend in all their lives and all their children's lives as well. Buried too, among those wells of treasures, were secrets.   Secrets that frightened him more than the poisoned blade of a murderous conspirator. And if there was anything Bęrun had learned in his decades of life, it was that secrets, unlike coins, were a vapor- no matter how tightly you sealed them, they most assuredly found their way back to the light.

Times long past, the Merchant Lord was once a different man.   Though he had always been a more serious, sterner individual, there was a time once he remembered what it was to laugh, to drink, and to sing. Shoulders burdened with fear once instead carried a simple pack of clothes, and a mind cracking under the onus of dread once instead pondered the mysteries of the horizon. Once, he travelled. Once, he adventured. Once, he had true friends who shared with him the joys and wonders of youth, and drew deep the breath of life. Once.

Lower the candles burned, and dimmer the room became. His company of shadows and nightmares closed their embrace tighter around the aged miser, and Bęrun's sharp, pale eyes flitted back and forth nervously amongst them, as though truly afraid one would reach out from the corners of the room and drag him down to the abyss. Even if he cherished a luxury like sleep, Bęrun would likely fear it as well, ever in horrified waiting of what dusty memories would reveal themselves when slumber took his mind. His fingers drummed idly on the polished granite table before him, their hollow thump being swallowed completely in the echoless, suffocating hall. No sound would have comforted him.   There was no symphony great enough to drown out the terrible thoughts that chased through his lonely mind.

Devilish phantoms of things that could not be unseen, and wailing banshees of things that could not be unheard gnawed at the fraying edges of his considerations. More than anything, Bẹrun wished quietude. He prayed that he might be relieved of his most despotic, tyrannical recollections, and that he could finish out his rule in silent, undisturbed calculation of his incalculable riches. It was not to be, he knew. Even only recently, things had happened on his very shores that had seen to it. Things that were echoes of phantom memories. Things that were harbinger of waking furies. The world beneath his feet rumbled as monsters shook the pillars of the earth.

When his guests entered they did not knock, and there was no crier to announce their presence- it was far too late for such unnecessary cacophonies, anyway. And truly, they did not require such pompous attentions, nor were they particularly the type to stand on such ceremonies. In another lifetime, in the days of 'once,' Bẹrun would have called them both friends. As it was, he had another word for them- one that kept with the popular appraisal of their character, but largely discredited their honorable, if rough-hewn, ways. Like the rest of the world, Bẹrun called them barbarians… even though they were the men who were responsible for his salvation.

The Battle King and his senior Honor Guard, Xylus, crept into the meeting hall as much as men of their immense stature and build could creep. Xylus especially was not one to move quietly, his mountainous frame packed beneath an iron skin of steel plates that rattled menacingly with his every step. Both lumbered along the table to take their seats on either side of the Merchant Lord, their own carved countenances shadowed grimly in the low lighting. Titans, they were, barely out of step with the gods themselves- not the hand that rocked the cradle, they were the fist that swung the sword. And seated at the table with Bęrun, all of them together represented among the greatest gathered powers in the Three Known Kingdoms. These were they who steered the winds of the world.

The aged miser. The old man. The ancient warrior.

"You're late," Bęrun quietly accused.

"Since when was there an age that time was not among the luxuries the Merchant Lord could afford?" the Battle King retorted evenly, "Perhaps your riches are not as unbridled as they are fabled to be."

"And perhaps the barbarian lords of the south are no longer as strong and swift as they are fabled to be," the Merchant Lord grumbled.

Xylus spoke up, "Unkind words given those 'barbarians' were the ones to win a war *your* troopers proved they were not strong and swift enough to do on their own," he removed the deaths-head helm that covered his face, and let a long mane of bright white hair spill out over his armored shoulders, "Wouldn't you agree?"

Bęrun snorted, "I'm still not sure why it is a servant has a voice at this table."

Xylus smiled sadly, "And to think I remember a time you didn't call me servant, but rather called me friend."

"I remember those days too," the Battle King's gravelly voice rumbled, "Days all three of us were of younger persuasion, and dared refer to the other so boldly as 'brother.'"

"Poetic," the Merchant Lord scoffed, "We are of a different epoch. *You* are no longer a prince, and *I* am no longer a duke. We decide the very fate of the world, now. And *you*," he turned back towards Xylus, "Like it or not, are a servant to that fate."

The ancient Warbrand sighed, and the tattoos on his face twisted remorsefully, "Do you no longer remember the day I saved your life?"

Bęrun narrowed his eyes and hissed, "Do *you* no longer remember the night I saved *yours*?"

Xylus's eyes turned faraway as he retreated into his own memories, "There is not an evening I do not give thanks to the gods that you did, and implore they grant you long life for doing so."

"Wasted words and futile breath," the Merchant Lord dismissed.

"Brothers, please," the Battle King's low voice called for order, "There are more pressing things at hand. We are of a sad state if no longer we can put aside such pettiness."

Xylus cast his gaze down reverently, the long strands of his pallid hair draping over his brow. Bęrun crossed his arms defiantly, but said nothing else.

Bröghue sighed as well, and removed his crown with the same tiredness Bęrun had been suffering earlier. The Battle King placed the steel coronet on the table before him, and rubbed his eyes with a certain desperation. Several long moments of silence passed between all of them.

"Perhaps you wish to speak?" Bęrun finally said impatiently at the Battle King, "I assume you have good cause for calling this meeting?"

"Bęrun, you hardly need to guess as to why I called we three, and ONLY we three together," Bröghue came back, darkness in his voice, "It may have been very nearly three decades since last we held audience together, but certainly your mind has not given over to such an occluding fog."

"I see your love for dancing speech is no less diminished," the Merchant Lord chuckled derisively, "A pity your, ahem, son did not inherit your learnedness."

"The prince is perhaps more clever than you credit him," the Battle King dryly defended, doing his best to mask his offense.

"Well, certainly more so than the animal he travels with," Bęrun went on mockingly, "Tell me, Battle King- when did the Southern Reach cease to see the trolls as their *enemies*, and started seeing them as the guardians of their children?"

Xylus cast a sideways glance at Bröghue, waiting for the old man's answer.

The Battle King shook his head, "Bęrun, old friend, had I known our adventures together would turn you so close-minded and fearful, I certainly would have pursued other ends. Perhaps I owe you an apology. And perhaps it comes twenty five years too late."

"Adventures," the Merchant Lord huffed, "To call them such a lofty word. We lived out the terrors that prowl on the edge of man's worst dreams."

Quietly, the Battle King folded his hands and looked expectantly at the aged miser, "Tell me then, Merchant Lord: what might we have done differently, knowing the things we did- veritably that we still do?"

"What would you have me say?" Bęrun's frustration was palpable, "How shall I rewrite an impossible course of action that is already woven into the loom of time, that its threads might commit a different tale?"

"There was a wolf at the gates," Bröghue growled, "There still is."

"It does not prowl so close as you think," the Merchant Lord pointed sharply at the old man, "Even still, you make too much of it. All three of us will be long for the next world by the time any of that comes to pass."

"And should that relieve us of any onus in preventing it? Are we to leave the beast to the swords of our sons," the Battle King asked, "Or daughters?"

The aged miser glowered at at Bröghue, "We did what we could. It is not our fight any more."

"It *is* our fight," Xylus barked, "It followed us the length and breadth of the world and came into our homes to remind us exactly that. It is *still* our fight."

"Conspiracy," the Merchant Lord dismissed, "Pure conjecture. You accuse me of clinging too tight to ghosts of old, and yet you are the ones who see phantoms trailing in every shadow, and monsters creeping in every soft-furred pup."

"*We* have accused you of no such thing," the Battle King pointed out, "Oft, the guiltiest mind speaks the loudest. I wonder what things troubled *your* mind before we called upon you, Merchant Lord."

"You are not so wise as you think, Battle King," Bẹrun spat.

"And you are not so opaque as you think, old friend," Bröghue returned.

"Your folksy sagacity fails to impress in my court, barbarian," the Merchant Lord sneered again.

"Just as much as spinelessness and cowardice are derided in mine," the Battle King refused to let the aged miser have the last word.

"Enough! Both of you!" Xylus interrupted the bickering, "Gods, worse than the prince and the Lady you two are. If it should be any wonder why your sons and daughters do not get along, I suggest you plumb the depths of a mirror for the answer."

Bẹrun made a sour face, "If there is to be one light in all the bleakness of the concessions I have made to your kingdom over the last few weeks, it is that Ydal would be spared the disgrace of wedding that man-child."

Both Battle King and Xylus collapsed a little, their shoulders hunched not so much in insult, but rather deep disappointment.

Bröghue spoke up first, "Have our old ties really fallen into such disrepair you would say such a thing about my son? Is there nothing left of the bonds we shared so long ago?"

"I cannot escape those bonds!" the Merchant Lord said sharply, "I am prisoner to them! These are my chains!" he held up a handful of his beard, its deathly pallor shining silver in the candlelight, "It is a constant reminder of those dark times, Bröghue! I was still a young man when your quest turned my hair white, and it reminds me of my vanished youth every day to look upon it! *You* gave this to me, Battle King, and I have never been free of it since!"

The aged miser tossed the handful of his own beard-hair back over his shoulder dejectedly, and crossed his arms in closure.

Across the table, the old man held his gaze, "Perhaps I do not wear my 'scars' so outwardly as you do, old friend, but to suggest that all three of us do not still equally suffer the terrors of that journey does a great disservice to Xylus and myself."

"What did you think was going to happen down there?!" the Merchant Lord cried, "We crawled into the tomb of the devil itself- what did you expect to find?!"

"That we might find some answers as to *why* we are, and *how* our kingdoms came to be," the Battle King replied softly, "That the shadow might be repulsed, and we could once again live without the pall of the demon hanging over us."

"You and your superstitious people are the only ones still perpetuating *that* myth," Bęrun spat, "If you exist under its mantle, it is your own doing."

Xylus looked incredulously at the Merchant Lord, "How can you be so blind? Does your denial truly run so deep as to corrupt the things you saw with your own eyes?"

"Can we all really be sure we saw those things?" the aged miser asked scathingly, "Has time not rusted our minds and corroded our memories? Exaggeration and hyperbole have festered like mold in your recollections, I think."

"I see that place as clear as the first time every night when I close my eyes," the Battle King came back quietly, "I see the blood, the bones, the chains, and I remember the pain and the screams. I can still feel the chill of that air, and smell the musty death. And unless I completely miss my mark, you do too, Merchant Lord. I'll bet your entire kingdom's fortune THAT is the reason you have not slept a full night through in twenty five years."

"You presume," Bęrun huffed, but he broke the Battle King's gaze all the same and looked somewhere else he would not be bored into by haunted eyes of a shared dread.

"We cannot hide from this, old friend," Bröghue said gently, "This is not a vial of venom we can bury beneath the garden. All it would take would be a single innocent root to dig too deep and crack the glass, and our whole world would be poisoned once again."

"Such talk full of splintered metaphors and jagged similes," the Merchant Lord chortled with disdain, "Too much time spent with that idiot brother of yours, Bröghue."

Xylus stood from his chair abruptly, "How dare you speak like that about Battle Prince Gögan?! He and his Griffin Riders are the very reason you breathe free air this eve! Were it not for his axe, this whole city might have burned."

The Battle King lifted a hand and bid his Honor Guard be seated, "Xylus does raise a good point however."

"Barely at that!" Bęrun went on ungraciously, "They made a lot of noise, assuredly, but how effective was your war, Battle King? Even your fastest and finest could not capture or kill the marauder's Captain. That failure rests on you."

"Mordenall," the old man said sternly, "Call him by his name- it makes it harder to deny who he is."

The Merchant Lord shook his head in disbelief, "You truly do believe that raving lunatic is the same one we ran into nearly thirty years ago?"

"There is no doubt in my mind," Bröghue growled, "And the more you turn a naïve eye to it, the less patience I have for this conversation."

"You have no proof!" the aged miser cackled.

"Dammit, Bęrun!" the Battle King slammed his fist on the table, cracking the granite, "He asked for your scepter by name! When my son came to rescue the Lady, he was commanded to surrender Thundersteel! And when we finally ran those ravenous dogs off your docks, they didn't sail back *west* where they came from! They went *east*! He is headed for the Everfrost, and if you don't think he has his sights set on what sleeps in that frozen mountain, then you're even more a fool than my own son! And at least my son has youthful unknowing to curtail his general lack of wisdom. *You* have absolutely no such excuse!"

"You speak of artifacts whose names should have been lost to history, and whose stories should be covered with dust," the Merchant Lord replied with an almost sinister firmness to his voice, "I do not call my spear by any frolic nomenclature, but simply call it the scepter of my rule. That your familial line still reveres the name of a sword only underscores the folly of your whole kingdom."

"I remember so that I do not repeat," Bröghue bit down on the words, "You know what they say of those who do not learn from history."

"And perhaps it is only so because they obsess over it, and refuse to let it lay in its grave," Bęrun shot back, "After all- a thing forgotten is not a thing that can become a self-fulfilling prophecy."

The Battle King shook his head, but ultimately pressed on, "Old friend, I understand your terror- I do. You should know that I, more than anyone else, realize the depths of your dread. But we cannot shy away from this monster. We must stop Mordenall before he reaches the Everfrost. If he should return with the artifact buried there…"

Before the old man could finish, the Merchant Lord cut him off, "Even IF that were his intention- which, by the way, would require logic in the ravings of a clear madman- what makes you think he is even capable of securing it, when five centuries of history's greatest treasure hunters have failed?"

"Because he is a Hunter," Bröghue insisted, "He is the Dark Retriever- chosen and anointed by the beast itself and imbued with gifts that go beyond mortality and the limitations of the flesh!"

"Bah!" the aged miser waved his hand, "You vex me with your talk of fiends and mysticism."

"Bęrun, this isn't something you can count and quantify," Xylus said desperately, "This is not a matter of logic and reason, but one of the gears in the machination of the universe itself!"

"Tell me, Battle King," the Merchant Lord turned towards the old man, "Do you still breed warriors south of the Swordsong, or poets?"

"How are you so detached?" Bröghue asked sadly.

"I wish only to lead over a quiet and prosperous empire!" Bęrun nearly shouted, "And to leave it as such in the hands of my daughter! She is deserving of such. After the throne passes to her, she may do with our lands as she wishes, just as I have done with them since inheriting this kingdom from MY mother."

"And are you so anxious to leave your daughter with a damned gift?" the old man asked, "Will you give her an empire yoked by the return of a destroyer from an age extinguished?"

Bęrun sat back in his throne and breathed out unconvincingly, "A myth."

"I can hear the disingenuousness in your voice," the Battle King said before imploring, "We can stop it all- if we act now. We can right our failures that have been rotting for twenty five years. But, we must overtake Mordenall before he reaches the Everfrost. If he is allowed to regroup with whatever allies he has made in the Eastern Collective, who knows what fate it will wrought."

"I'll tell you exactly what," the aged miser pointed at the old man, "He will bring the armies of all seven nations of the Eastern Collective against us. The might of your barbarians is storied, fading though it may be, but even in their heyday they could not withstand such a blow."

"Then you understand why we are pressed to action," Bröghue spread his hands exasperatedly.

"No, Battle King. *I* do not see it that way," the Merchant Lord responded, "*I* do not see a grand conspiracy in the tapestry as *you* do. *I* do not believe that one crazed man who sailed out of the mists of the west could possibly unify the seven nation's armies, and bring them down on us in some deranged quest to collect a few ancient relics. *I* do not believe that the wraith of a demon is chasing us. I refuse to."

The old man and his Honor Guard exchanged looks.

Xylus turned and asked Bęrun simply, "And if *you* are wrong?"

The Merchant Lord grumbled something unintelligible.

"Please, old friend," the Battle King pleaded, "Help me. Help me help both our countries. If not for me, then do this for your own lands. Call back the Northern Spear- bring the shining armies of your empire home from the tundras, and let us chase down this madman before he has time to reach his allies in the Everfrost."

Bęrun refused to look the old man in the eye, "Do it yourself."

"I can't," the Battle King said simply, "You know that. Bęrun, the blood of more of my barbarians than I care to admit wet the streets of your Ivory City. Our losses were *far* greater than my council knows, and my country is weakened. We cannot weather a full war right now. I can keep the news of the casualties from the warlords for only so long before they start to wonder why there are not as many squadrons in the camps, and why fewer griffins fly in the skies. Mordenall is already stronger and wields greater influence than we anticipated. We cannot allow that influence to grow."

"Truly, I am sorry for the loss of your warriors, but I have already given up much to repay that debt to you, Battle King," the Merchant Lord replied curtly.

"What have you given up?!" Xylus roared, "Trade agreements?! Some of your countless wealth?! A marriage pact?! You think these things equivocate to the barbarians whose flames were extinguished defending a land that was not their own?"

"You did not have to come," Bęrun turned away.

"I was not about to let the Ivory City of the Northern Empire burn beneath the flag of a demon," the Battle King growled, "That is not the kind of friend *I* am."

"This is high talk, and I find I have no taste for it," the Merchant Lord scoffed, "It is not how people speak anymore. The world is a different place now.

Monsters belong in closets and under beds where they are but the fevered dreams of small children. They do not walk among us. And I will not entertain such a juvenile idea."

Bröghue sighed deeply, "There is death on the winds of a tempest, and you believe you can hold your breath against the storm."

"More talk that should be relegated to story books and fairytales," the Merchant Lord appraised.

"I can no longer be sure we are not living in just such a ghost story," the Battle King sat back heavily.

"That, perhaps, more than anywhere else, is where we differ," the aged miser replied, "You see the world as pages to be written upon. I see it for the stone and timber that it really is."

"There is no room in your mind anymore for things beyond what you can touch and count, is there, old friend?" Bröghue asked.

"What else is there?" Berun queried sharply.

"Indeed," the Battle King nodded, no longer able to mask his terrible disappointment, "Then it would seem our business is concluded."

"Already you have kept me from this evening's rest far later than I should be," the Merchant Lord scoffed.

"If there is any rest to be had for you," the old man shrugged, "I trust our other agreements are secured still?"

"You have my signature don't you?" Berun said hollowly.

"I do," the Battle King agreed, "If that is all that is required to have cooperative rule between our nations, then I take my leave. Truly, though, I would have preferred to have your friendship... once again."

"Your romantic view of our childhood days does a disservice to your negotiations in modern rule, Battle King," the Merchant Lord said, "I am not beholden to such trite and vapid things."

The old man exhaled sharply through his nose in disbelief, "I wish I knew what to say to that, Bęrun. Perhaps it is foolish of me to assume that those who live beyond the borders of our savage, barbarian lands are bound in some way by a sense of honor- if not camaraderie. The same honor that we uncivilized peasants obey."

"Your ancient and uncouth ways are as decrepit as the crumbling tomes they come from," the aged miser said at the last.

"I see," the Battle King nodded distantly, "Xylus, would you be so kind as to get the door for me?"

"Aye, Battle King," the ancient warrior stood to his full, grand height and dragged his deaths-head helm from the table. He bowed sharp and shallow, "Merchant Lord."

Bęrun barely gestured with a few of his fingers, "Honor Guard."

Xylus swept out of the room, his long mane of white hair trailing behind him as the spiraling tattoos on his face melted into the shadows.

The Battle King held back a moment, "I remember when you were poured of a sterner mold,

Bęrun. You were a *warrior* like we were- a *champion*. My old friend, this life of counting and accumulating... this isn't you. We both had the same wanderlust, the same taste for the wind and the eye for the horizon."

"Time changes all things," the Merchant Lord replied quickly, "The mountains are weathered. The seas recede. The hearts and souls of men rot."

"Is that what you see in yourself?" the old man asked despairingly, "Rot?"

"I see in myself what I have always seen- a man with an empire to wield," Bęrun came back.

"And what will you do with that empire?" Bröghue pressed on last time, "Will you bring it against the coming darkness, or will you raise your barricades and pray the tide does not rise so high as to break on your lands?"

For a moment, the Merchant Lord was silent before he responded, "Even if the Swordsong swelled and devoured the Ivory City... my kingdom would live on. There is no flood so great, real or implied, that could swallow the Northern Empire. We will always have more land to go to."

"Some of us do not have that luxury, Merchant Lord," the Battle King said, his eyes brimming with dejection, "Some of us have our backs to the mountains, and our shield to the wolf."

"Then some of us should have spent their years increasing their holdings- rather than their glory," the aged miser accused.

"What do you plan to take with you to the next world?" Bröghue growled in response.

"What do you plan on leaving to those you leave behind?" the Merchant Lord followed quickly.

The Battle King flinched, "It's just always a need for more with you these days- isn't it?"

"I suppose now is when you *again* tell me you remember me differently?" Bęrun asked finally.

Bröghue shook his head, "Once…"

There was nothing more to be said between the venerable monarchs. The Battle King dragged his iron barbarian crown off the table and lumbered out of the room. His Honor Guard was waiting. Together, they quietly closed the door to the private meeting hall- or as quietly as warriors of their presence could manage. They left the Merchant Lord again alone with his thoughts, whatever they may be. Peace was secured in the Swordsong Valley- but only peace.

"Gods, what has happened to that man?" Xylus rumbled as they wound their way through the lofty halls of the Empire Court.

"The same thing that happened to us, brother," the old man ran his fingers through his graying hair, "He was forced to look into the shadows of the universe, and see the things lurking there."

The ancient Honor Guard tried to change the subject, "Your *real* brother would have me beaten if he knew you called me that."

Bröghue laughed out loud, "He would have ME beaten if found I called you anything less. Gögan sees all us barbarians as family."

"Aye, true enough," Xylus agreed, "Now THERE'S a man with a spine and a pair of boulders between his legs."

"Bęrun is not a coward," the old man corrected swiftly, "You know that. He is only doing what he believes is right by his country. That it is not in line with our own interests, is no reason to cast him off in the light of cowardice. It is simply frustrating."

"Our interests are the world's interests," the Honor Guard said as they strolled through the high, dark corridors, "We entertain a perspective that is not so myopic as his."

The Battle King snickered, "Myopic. It amazes me, brother, how many times you have been hit in the head, and yet you maintain such a vocabulary."

"One of us has to sound like he knows what he is talking about," Xylus offered.

"Indeed," the old man laughed again, "And glad am I that it is you. The same, we are in agreement. Time and time again it has fallen to the Southern Reach to be the line in the sand, and the great storm of our age approaches. Are we to once again tow that line, or are we to be swept away?"

"He's not wrong about your poetic speech," Xylus gave a slanted smile at the Battle King, "It is a bit much sometimes."

"Perhaps," Bröghue returned the grin, "Always I wanted to be a storyteller above all things- I never heard the warrior's call the way my grandfather did."

"A good thing too- our nation did not need another Mögren," the ancient warrior's voice turned faraway at memories of a harsher time in the Southern Reach, before he snapped quickly back to the moment, "Though I should hope you would remember exactly that the next time you grumble about your son's love for music over that of the sword."

"You're always looking out for him," the Battle King said proudly.

"Val and I both," Xylus acknowledged his junior's similar devotion, and then after a beat, "And the troll as well."

Bröghue side-eyed his guardian, "You don't trust him."

"He's a troll, my king. It is… difficult to trust one of their ilk," the ancient warrior admitted, the stories of the Great Troll War ringing in his mind.

"Were we so different?" the old man posed, "You may have been my father's junior Honor Guard, but he never trusted you. You were trained by one of Mögren's protectors- Daddy was always afraid *you* had picked up the tyrant's bent."

Xylus took a long moment to think about that, "Maybe the product of a monster determined to be honorable, is not so different from a monster-born striving for the same."

"You never left my side, brother," Bröghue reminded his guardian, "No matter how far from home I strayed, you stayed in lock step with me. You placed yourself in the path of every danger, and advised me on the things no one else dared speak to me. Sometimes *especially* so," he chuckled, "I see that in the troll. He guides my son- offers him wisdom when Krög will listen to no one else. And when threats are raised against the prince, the troll never hesitates to crush them back. You may not like him, Warbrand Xylus, but he and my son are a shadow of you and I not so very long ago."

The ancient warrior nodded slowly and repeated back in his own manner, "He sees your son as his ward, to stand beside and instruct in the ways of the world and cosmos," the Honor Guard was not quite finished propping up his own student and partner, however, "Just so, Val sees the prince as a little brother to teach in battle and protect in war- Krög will be in good hands when the throne is passed."

There was an unusually tense moment between the old friends as Bröghue took a prolonged beat to consider his own mortality.

"Was Bęrun perhaps not wrong about *that* either? the Battle King asked softly, "What kind of a world am I leaving behind for him?"

"Right... wrong..." Xylus shrugged, "What *I* know is that you're still fighting, Battle King. That's what the prince will remember. And if the nation you leave behind is one drowning in blood and burning at its roots, still the prince will remember you fought on. So too, *he* will fight on to save our country- because his father did. IF it comes to that, that is."

"That is an 'if' that looms larger and more prominent every day, it seems," the old man sighed, "We are in a dangerous position, Xylus. Make no mistake."

"Aye, Battle King," the ancient warrior nodded, "That we are."

They broke out into the cool, crisp night, as autumn already dared to breath her chill into the evening air. Distantly, over the ramparts of the High Court and Merchant Courts, they could hear the rushing of the Swordsong River as it coursed along the docks of the Ivory City. Slowly, they made their way towards the sound, its singing roar a welcome distraction to the cacophony argument they had just suffered through. Xylus and the Battle King often spent their nights in the Ivory City dockside- the shimmering chorus of the river reminded them of times long lost.

"How bad is it?" the old man asked as they walked towards the river, "What were the real losses?"

"Survivable," Xylus recounted, "Tremendous given the scope of the campaign, but nothing that we cannot recover from in a few seasons. But, therein lies the problem."

"We have neither the seasons to recover, nor the months to call back those we have guarding the frontier," the Battle King tugged absentmindedly at his beard.

"Raicleach may be back to sleep, but the far southern borders are never a secure thing," the ancient warrior waxed strategic, "The remaining squadrons of the Griffin Riders are needed there to keep the dragons in line. Our barbarian hordes have been watching the eastern mountains. And until the Warbrands can return to the Fortress City, she will be unprotected."

"Gods," the old man sighed heavily, "We are stretched so thin, Xylus."

"Mögren's war against the Grand Dragons decimated an entire generation, Battle King," the ancient warrior went on, "Your father Öx did what he could to rebuild, but the Southern Reach has been on perilous footing for as long as my memory can recall. I understand, better than anyone, why you wish to pursue Mordenall- Berun may have forgotten, but I haven't. That said…"

"That said we are in no position to begin another campaign and give chase," the Battle King finished.

"It pains me to suggest this," Xylus said, "But Mordenall may have once again slipped through our fingers."

"Aye," the old man again ran his fingers through his hair, "And a bleak thing that is. Mark me, we have not seen the last of him, and he will bring ruin when he returns. Even if it is *not* with the full might of all seven nations of the Eastern Collective, a captain as cunning as he will not show his face again unless he has either superior leverage or strength."

"Cunning is giving that madman a lot of credit," the ancient warrior rumbled.

"In only a matter of months, he sailed across the world from a vanquished empire, and leveled half of the largest city in the Three Known Kingdoms. He held our own forces off for three months thereafter before finally *retreating* east. We didn't even finish off his number! A madman he may be, but yes, brother, he is *also* cunning," the Battle King said.

"Aye…" there was little Xylus could do but silently agree, "Aye. I suppose he is."

"I don't know," as they distanced themselves from the Empire Court and drew nearer to the docks, the old man turned more casual and less thoughtful, "We're in deep shit. I wish I had the answers. They call me 'The Wise,' yet I feel more than ever 'The Fool.'"

"You're too hard on yourself, my friend," the ancient warrior dismissed, "No man has all the answers, and to presume that you possibly could really would make you a fool. There are many things you are, Battle King- never a fool, however."

"You're always good for a morale boost, you know that, Xylus?" the old man chuckled.

"It's part of the job," the Honor Guard said stoically.

Both guffawed, and their boisterous laughter called the attention of a number of bleary-eyed citizens who wondered what decent folk would be making such noise at such an hour.

Indecent folk would.

Barbarians.

"Gods, I could use a drink," the old man lamented, "There's nothing stiff enough in this town. All wine-drinkers and champagne-swillers."

"Your son is a wine-drinker," Xylus reminded the king.

"Aye, but the stripling can also hold down his Trollkiller. Makes an old man proud," the Battle King replied mistily.

"No father in the history of fathers has ever been proud his son could drink a home-brew notorious for once, under very dubious circumstances, actually causing the death of a troll," the ancient warrior laughed.

"He's a strong kid, he'll be just fine," the old man said dismissively, "No, but you're right. I suppose I should not be so thrilled with my son's ability to drink. Still. We're supposed to be an uncivilized bunch, aren't we?"

"And so we are!" Xylus shouted, just for the hilarity of watching the annoyed citizens of the Ivory City turn their furious gazes on the pair of strolling titans.

"I fear for him," the Battle King turned suddenly serious, "Not for his own ability, or his strength: he has both in abundance- though, he has difficulty recognizing it himself. I fear for the onus of the things I have left undone, and how they will weigh upon him. Certainly he will be a conqueror when his time comes, a siege-machine all his own. Never, though, will I wish the terrors of our experiences to fall on him."

The ancient warrior laughed a little, "Well what good a conqueror and siege-machine if he has nothing to rattle his sword against?"

"Krög has a wanderer in his soul, and restlessness in his heart," the Battle King looked distantly at the canyons and valleys of flickering city torchlights stretched before them, "He could expand our kingdom farther than the days of Battle King Makö. The Southern Reach would blossom and prosper in his footsteps. Alas, I do not feel it will be his fate. Leastwise, not unless we can stop this invasion before it has even truly begun."

"So, you really believe Mordenall is the leader of the Fell Legion?" Xylus posed faintly.

"You were with me in those days," the Battle King recalled, "On the far side of the world. You saw it just as clear as I did. Do you, too, doubt it now?"

The Honor Guard sighed, "Brother, I would follow you straight into the nine hells and drive my hammer through the face of every last devil that raised arms against you. And to keep the Southern Reach safe, I would lead your armies down the throat of the Dragon's Spine mountains to chase down our foes and bury them, frozen, in the snows of Everfrost. There is no one I care for deeper than you, my old friend. Just don't tell my wife I said that."

Bröghue laughed, "Assuredly. But you did not answer my question."

"I am a warrior, Battle King- not a philosopher, nor a scholar. What I believe in is my own fortitude and the thunder of my hammer. Certainly I am not eased by a foe bearing a name we heard in that place thirty years ago coming now to our shores- but my sphere of influence begins and ends with *fighting* that foe. It is not my place to conjecture that he is part of a larger conspiracy. That burden belongs to you, my king," the ancient warrior laid out.

They had reached the docks, and the damp air of the river hung heavily on a foggy breeze that rolled across the piers. It was the kind of night where ghosts would walk, waltzing from one bank of murk to the next, slipping between the shadows and lilting through the darkness. The song of the river shimmered over the soft whistle of the wind, and dozens of ships' lights slid across the surface of the water as late-night freighters came and went almost silently. Riding low on the waves, the boats, laden with their cargo, raced off towards whatever distant port they were destined for with the haste of one being chased by death. Only the snap of their flags could be heard as each vanished into the darkness.

Bröghue leaned heavily on a railing and watched the ships drift on, "*That* is the loneliness of being king."

"I do not envy the weight of your crown, brother," Xylus settled next to the old man, "Not Öx, not even Mögren were comfortable beneath its burden."

"Xylus, I am asking you as my friend, my guardian, and my wisest advisor," the Battle King drew in a long breath, "Am I completely crazy for thinking Mordenall is one of the demon's Hunters? Have I made too much out of odd coincidence?"

The ancient warrior shifted in his armor, "Not for naught the things we saw, my king. Now, as I did then, I can help you stop the terrible things men do. But the mystic... I have never seen the underlying weave the way you do."

"Then you see this as just a pirate from a dead empire searching for artifacts in our kingdoms?" the old man did his best not to make it sound like an accusation.

Xylus did not take it as such, "I do, brother. He bears an unfortunate name and flies a flag I had hoped to never see again- but he would not be the first to seek out those weapons. Their legend precedes them the world over. Hundreds of would be revolutionaries, treasure hunters and blackguards have pursued them. Certainly this enemy wields greater authority than any in my memory, but to *my* concerns he is just another in a line of obsessed raiders."

"Not the next in line of the beast's direct servants?" the Battle King asked pointedly.

"I'm sorry, my friend," the ancient warrior shook his head, "In front of Bęrun, I said what I had to so that he would see a front united between us- but my doubts that this is the will and action of a long dead demon run deep. I *will* act on your beliefs- but I will *not* adopt them as my own."

"Just as well," the old man kept his gaze on the drifting ships, "There are more and more dissenting voices in my wake. The Council of Elders is like wrangling a pack of wild dogs anymore. I can stand for those who disagree with my thoughts, as long as they carry out my edicts. My council, on the other hand, has it in their mind to wrest control of the country from me."

"Not while I'm still alive," Xylus growled, "The king's rule is the king's rule, and a Battle King is not a thing to cross lightly. If it is not too bold, your Councilmen are a raving band of idiots if they think they're going to pull the rug out from under you."

"Would they not have good cause?" Bröghue closed his eyes as the wind swept across his face, "I'm a rogue king to them- a mustang. I vanished as a prince, they practically had to force the crown on me after I returned, and now I'm the crazy old coot that thinks there are monsters in the dark still. Mögren sent most of *his* Council to their deaths fighting the Grand Dragons, and those memories have not yet faded entirely. The shields of those fallen warlords still wreathe my throne. How much of a stretch, really, is it for them to see the same brashness in my actions?"

"Madness has always been a trait of Battle Kings," the ancient warrior said, "Back to the days of Nömel and his son Lödrek. It takes a certain brand of crazy to be the warrior lord over a nation of barbarians. By orders of magnitude, old friend, you are easily the steadiest, most even-keeled Battle King to ever come to rule."

"I am complimented, to be certain," the old man replied, "But, I doubt myself. Our nation is poised precariously and my rule may be in its twilight, but it still has many years yet left. That's many years I can still lead us all to oblivion if I am not careful."

"To find a balance between the will of the council, the warlords, your people, and the other kingdoms is a juggling act I am not certain any other man in the world has the wherewithal to manage," Xylus pushed his pale mane out of his eyes as the wind played it about.

"And to somehow find time to raise a son, serve my wife and direct this country in a manner that will leave a legacy not of bloodshed but of honor..." the Battle King rubbed his eyes, "Brother, I am tired."

"No, my king- you are strong," the ancient warrior assured.

"Strong, perhaps- but not invincible," Bröghue corrected, "One day the weariness will prove too much. Maybe my greatest fear is that I wish Krög to find a king in himself just so I can be relieved of the throne. It is a selfish thing, that."

"I don't need to remind you that I, like you, look forward to the day we can both lay down arms," Xylus said, "This armor grows more cumbersome every day, and I dread the morning I rise and can no longer lift my hammer. That said, old friend, neither of us will go until it is our time, and neither of us will break in the meantime."

"Krög," the old man said his son's name with questioning and reverence all at the same time, "He could be great. He WILL be great. He just needs his moment. And then both of us can rest, brother. Whether that moment is glorious or terrible- that will be my son's trial."

"Will you ever tell him?" the ancient warrior asked quietly, "About... the West?"

"One day, eventually," the Battle King acknowledged, "But, he is not ready to hear it. Not yet. When I know he is ready to ascend the throne, then I'll tell him. Not before."

"If I may, my king," Xylus offered, "Half the reason your son has not yet taken the risks you need him to, is because you do not outwardly display your own confidence in his abilities. You say you know him to be strong, and you expect greatness of him- but you still fear telling him the stories that made YOU ready for kingship. If you cannot trust his mind to hold that weight, how can you trust his brow to hold the crown?"

"How can he be held back by what he doesn't know?" the old man challenged.

"How would you know how strong you were, unless you found the stone you could not lift?" Xylus responded quickly, "And you, brother, have not even given him a pebble to carry."

"I push him. More than ever lately, I do," the Battle King turned directly towards his Honor Guard, "Gods, I even sent him after a Grand Dragon."

"A barbarian can slay a dragon- a king must hold heavier things," the Honor Guard advised.

The old man wagged a finger at his protector, "This is why I keep you around, Xylus."

"Ha," the ancient warrior laughed, "I'd like to see you *try* to kick me out of the house. I've been the muscle in this outfit for years."

"You only think so," the Battle King jested, "I've been holding back."

Xylus snorted, "Holding back. That's a load of Boarhound shit if I ever heard it."

"Maybe so, maybe so," the old man laughed before turning his eyes back towards the forest across the waters, "I wonder just what fabulous trouble my son is getting into right now."

"Ah, have a little faith in him," the ancient warrior said, "He could be fast asleep preparing for a day's work for all you know."

Bröghue thought for a moment, "Nope. He's definitely getting himself into trouble right now."

***

In the mystic space where winter brushed her cheek of rime against the warm hand of summer, during the slow, graceful descent of autumn, in those final waning days of sunlight and long afternoons, something powerful was happening to Krög, the Battle Prince. As the leaves of the mighty arbors in the Thorn Rift Forest hinted their colors were ready to dance from green to gold and red, and the wind from the eastern mountains carried the chill of snow and frost on its back, the spirit of the young ruler was changing too. Perhaps it was the cooling air, which made everyone want to huddle just a little closer together, and perhaps it was the relentless restlessness of a wandering soul, ever in need of a new adventure and a new horizon. Perhaps it was just as real as the approaching nights of crisp chill. Whatever it was, however you explained it, one thing was certain. Krög was falling in love. He was not smitten, he was not enamored- what he was beginning to feel was something very visceral, very genuine.

Of course, the young ruler was not exactly ready to admit it. In point of fact, he likely did not even truly understand what it was he was feeling. As far as the bumbling, would-be hero was concerned, all that had changed in his life was the introduction of a spritely, untamed, youthful woman, who was without question the single most interesting and engaging person he had ever met in his whole age. Certainly, his thoughts stayed with her constantly, though not in an unseemly, over-wrought manner. More so, he found her captivating, and intriguing. He wanted to languish days away at her side, and spend his nights in her embrace. Greater than that, he wanted to be better at everything for her sake, that he might in some way become the assured, powerful champion he felt he should be for her.

Then, Lee was far from in need of a hero, and she took every available opportunity to remind Krög of just that. Whenever he threatened to outdo her at anything at all, the girl's natural competency took hold and she quickly mastered whatever it was the prince seemed to be gaining the upper hand in. She also had the distinct advantage of *already* being better at just about everything Krög wanted to do well anyway. Lee was unquestionably faster, decidedly more skilled, and might even have been stronger than the Battle Prince- though that was never proven definitively. Likely, she just liked to tease that she was so he would turn a hundred different shades of crimson, and strain himself to lift some ridiculously heavy object so as to prove otherwise. Always a step ahead, Lee was constantly turning back to goad and beckon Krög farther on. And, try as he might, the Battle Prince could never quite catch up to her.

Somedays, he *literally* could not catch her. The two would run, free-spirited and wild-hearted, across the rolling plains of the northern stretches of Krög's homeland, sprinting through the high grasses towards the mysterious reaches of the forests beyond. For all his long, lean build, the young ruler's legs would pump as fast and as hard as their strength would carry him, and Lee would still bound away effortlessly quicker, her feet barely touching the ground as she leapt and pranced. There was a mare-like grace to her movement, and even when Krög would find himself with painful stitches in his side, sweat beaded on his forehead, lungs burning and heart racing, she would smile all the broader, wink and somehow dart off faster.

Perhaps it was that elusive, improbable, mercurial grace and talent that the young ruler found so compelling about Lee- certainly it was what urged him to greater heights himself. Most of the barbarians of his country, out of sheer, moronic pride, would have been ashamed to have been bested at every turn by a young woman with bouncing, fair hair, barely over five feet tall. Rather, Krög saw it was a standard to live up to- a standard that not his father, the elders, or any other Warbrand or warrior could set. It *did* help that Lee had beaten the tar, and teeth, out of a number of rough and tumble southerners, and had been taken in as a Battle Maiden of her own class. Even still, the young ruler never felt disgraced trailing at her heels. Instead, he felt a great satisfaction at being her playful rival- it meant he had finally earned a place in her attentions that no one else occupied. And he wanted to be better. He wanted to be worthy of her.

When Krög looked at the iron crown that sat heavily on his father's brow, or took in the immense, wooden throne carved into the tree growing through the ceiling of the Great Hall, framed by the skull of a dragon and surrounded by shields of the fallen, it had never stirred to him to achieve. When the Battle Prince was schooled again and again and again in the legends of his forefathers and ancestors on how they chased the trolls and giants from the badlands and cut the dragons from the skies, it never pressed him to accomplish. When the young ruler trained constantly in the sandy, rocky pits of War School, sword in hand and action in his stance, he was never inspired to excel. Yet, when he was in the presence of Lee, all he wanted was to be greater, mightier, and swifter. She was the spark he had been missing all his life.

The cooler the nights became, the quicker the afternoons faded to twilight and evening, the shorter the season drew, the farther and farther he fell. Every little adventure, every secluded moment, every secret rendezvous twined his spirit tighter and tighter round hers. There was not a moment spent in the menial tasks of day-to-day life that he used to enjoy that he did not wish he was instead spending his time with her. To Krög, the Battle Prince, Lee shone brighter than any star in the southern sky, sparkled more dazzlingly than the sun off the rushing waters of the Swordsong River, and captured him more than the hypnotizing storm clouds that would come charging down out of the eastern mountains. Every sickeningly romantic ballad he had ever heard played endlessly in his head, suddenly bereft of their vapid, overblown, saccharine dretch, and all at once having a very sincere quality. Krög had it bad.

And just as she always did, Lee had it figured out long before he did and constantly found new, creative ways to tantalize his every sense and thought. He would slog into the stables to shoe a stallion, only to find the mustang had been draped with a wreath of Spring's Tears, her favorite flower- a gentle reminder of her considerations for the young ruler. Once, he went to the kitchen of the Great Hall to salt jerky, and discovered all of the salt he had set out for the task had been replaced with sugar- a subtle cue that she was somewhere just around the bend. There was even an afternoon Krög was supposed to lead an impossibly drawl luncheon among the elders and visiting lords from the farthest outposts of the Southern Reach, which had to be unexpectedly postponed when their caravan was delayed after following a series of road posts pointing the wrong direction for almost fifty miles. That, of course, left the young ruler free to entertain Lee's whims and fancies for the day instead, rather than reciting political lessons and practicing court manners. How she had arranged it he would never know, but he was certain the lithe young woman had been behind the whole thing.

Krög did his best to leave about small surprises or entertain jovial pranks for her as well, but no matter how clever or unexpected he thought he was being, Lee would return in kind with some shenanigan of an infinitely deeper impish brilliance. There truly was nothing he could do that she could not do better- and she always did. Never out of spite or haughty pride, her actions were always born from a frisky exuberance and childlike spontaneity, all which churned together into her own genuine affections. Though, as one would expect, she did a much better job of hiding the true depth of her feelings as well.

So it was they danced in secret, traded sparks, exchanged snarky barbs, and courted in shadow, out of the watchful eyes of a kingdom still largely expecting Krög to announce his next choice for future Battle Queen. They were never open about their developing romance- they could not be. Lee was an outsider to the Southern Reach, and though she won over just about everyone she met, the idea of a rogue Assassin Emissary from the

Eastern Collective being named the next Lady of the Hall was not going to land well. It preyed on Krög's mind occasionally that there was likely a note of finality to his time with the young woman, but through youthful naïvety, and a general lack of foresight, he dismissed the fears in favor of reveling in her beauty and presence. He enjoyed sneaking around and finding clandestine moments to spend by her side too much to let thoughts of when it would all come crashing down on them worry him. After all, summer lasted forever, and so would Lee and the Battle Prince.

Whether by grand design or complete accident, their free time was spent wholly with the other, narrowly avoiding prying minds and judging countenances. It was on one such afternoon, when the day was late and cooling, that Krög and Lee tripped headlong into a strange and frightening adventure. The day began innocently enough, as these things tend to do, in a secluded glade at the far northeastern edge of River Glen, deep in the Thorn Rift Forest. With the Battle King across the banks of the Swordsong finalizing treaties in the Ivory City of Fanfarra, it had become easier than usual for the prince to skirt his duties. In fact, on that particular day, he and Lee had managed to slip away from the Great Hall long enough to sprint across, what felt like, half of the mighty forest. After soothing their tired limbs in a crystal clear pool at the edge of the rapids, the two stretched out in the dappled sun to doze in each other's arms.

Though it was only late summer, and not truly autumn just yet, already the days had begun to shorten and the blanket of night was unfurling to settle itself over the Southern Reach. Twilight came down with a practiced elegance, and all the world started to quiet itself for the march of the stars. Already the prince could feel the air chilling, though delicately so- the summer sundown would be bathing him and the girl at his side in its opulent warmth, when the slightest eastern breeze carrying with it the breath of the mountains would trace its fingers across his skin. As it would recede, the air around them would stay just a bit cooler than before the wind had blown through, and the nip of night would seep in just a bit faster.

Krög stirred from his long afternoon snooze when such a gale of infinite softness splashed through the trees and wrested him from sleep's embrace. At first, he did not move, taking an extended moment to feel the weight of the girl at his side against his chest and listen quietly to her breathing. The prince breathed deep himself, pulling the crisp scent of the coming fall season down into his lungs as it mingled with the soft smell of Lee's wispy, fair hair. As slowly and gently as he could, the young ruler drew his arm out from under her, not daring to disturb the girl, and quietly sat up in the gloaming glade to watch the red sundown trickle between the leaves of the canopy. Its light fell especially lovely on the athletic young woman, who somehow remained deep asleep though the dusk shone on her face and the wind spirited across her form.

Though the glen was gorgeous in its natural splendor, the prince's eyes were invariably drawn to the slumbering girl. Her sharp features were exquisite, and despite the fact Krög had examined them all time and time again, he never tired of just looking at Lee. He could not understand how the world saw her as simply pretty- to the Battle Prince, she was the height of beguiling, the absolute epoch of beauty. From the curve of her slender neck, the smoothness of her fair skin, to the coiled, limber, athleticism of her shoulders and body, there was not one part of the young woman Krög did not find totally magnetic. He often felt lucky just to touch her, much less get to take part in a number of the other, far more inappropriate, things they did. Lee was a diamond in a desert of iron.

There were details to her, as well, he was still noticing and learning. For one thing, no matter how dirty the rest of her got from tumbling through the natural world as much as she did, somehow Lee always kept her hands clean. It was an apt metaphor for her lifestyle in general, but Krög could never figure out just how she did it. Then there was the zany way her hair stuck out when she got wet- sometimes it would simply mat itself to her face, but more often than not it managed to get stuck out at truly impossible lengths and angles, and the prince could never determine just how. And there was her little tattoo above her ankle, its twisting, jagged lines an enigma all its own, and one she staunchly continued to refuse to share.

The prince was no stranger to ink scars. They were commonplace in his kingdom, and certain patterns were even used to identify the most powerful and victorious of the warriors of the badlands. In particular, the Warbrands, the most elite, unyielding, and cold-hearted barbarians in the whole country, were marked from brow to sole in spiraling, twisted motifs. Krög even had a few of them himself. Lee had made fun of all of them at one point or another, but she had also asked with genuine curiosity about the meaning of each. There was the ox on the right side of his chest, emblazoned for the memory of his grandfather, Öx the Ironclad, who had disappeared mysteriously when Krög was only a child. There was a compass on the left side of his ribs, which encouraged the prince to follow his heart. He had a memorial for an old friend, Brax, son of Trax the Warbrand, whom the young ruler had trained side-by-side with with during War School, and who was killed during his first expedition into the Eastern Collective by an assassin. For Brax, the prince had added a skull with the Warbrand tattoos wreathed in roses cut into his chest opposite the ox. And of course, on his shoulder was his family's crest the guardian reaper: a skull on a shield wearing a crown.

In their secluded moments alone laying next to one another, Lee would often trace her small fingers over the lines of ink under his skin. She would lightly graze the intricate details of each, back and forth over and over, and jest him about how ridiculous it was that he had so many skulls carved into his body. It was quietly calming, a soothing exercise in intimacy that was neither lewd nor lusty, just simple and soft. Just her touch was enough to set the prince at ease, though what in particular he really had to be stressed and anxious about was subject to much debate. Especially to Lee- she often reminded the prince that he was, in fact, a prince, and that it was beyond reprehensible for him to even conceive of ever complaining about anything at all. Krög disagreed, of course, but he had little in the way of convincing arguments to refute her.

Sitting next to her in the glade, the young ruler delicately ran his fingers over the lines of Lee's mark, wondering quietly at its meaning and significance. He allowed his touch to barely brush against her skin as she slept, afraid to wake her, but transfixed and hypnotized by the tattoo- and all of the rest of her. As he slid his fingers along the curves of ink embedded in her flesh, the young woman stirred slightly, just scarcely resettling herself where she lay. At first, Krög quickly drew back, still afraid to disturb the girl. Then an altogether more mischievous thought took hold. And, at the end of the day, the prince reasoned if their places had been reversed, Lee would not have let such an opportunity pass her by.

As quietly as he could, the young ruler reached out and plucked a Boar's Tail weed. Boar's Tail grew from a thick, dark stem and ended in a bunch of stiff bristles, much like the animal's appendage it was so named for. The quills at the end of it were not as sharp as thorns, but they were prickly none the less. In the right hands, or perhaps the *wrong* hands, it was a tool of supreme irritation and ultimate annoyance. And poor, vulnerable, sleeping Lee was about to fall victim to its wrath.

Krög resumed tracing the lines of her tattoo, but with the prodding touch of the Boar's Tail weed instead of his own fingers. He scraped the plant's bristles around and around on the lines of ink, softly at first, but with increasing pressure. Lee jerked, and mumbled something indefinable, but did not awaken. The prince attacked again, slowly drawing the quills of the weed from the back of her knee, down the back of the girl's leg to her heel. Again, the young woman squirmed and her face scrunched in sleepy nettle. She loosed a mumbling series of half objections, but remained gripped by slumber. Grinning stupidly, and encouraged by her humorous reactions, the prince pressed his luck. Reaching out one more time, he stroked the bristles of the weed across her bare arch and under the curl of her toes.

Lee's foot shot out and blasted Krög right in the jaw, sending him sprawling with the same grace as tumbling sack of potatoes. She sat bolt upright, eyes only half open and hair in a ridiculous mess, and babbled out more nonsense.

"Whoozit? Whah? Whah happen?" her head flitted around quickly in sleepy confusion.

"Shit," the prince groaned from where he had fallen in the brambles, and rubbed his jaw as he tried to clear the stars from his vision.

"Prince, there's a, there's a tomato… biting me…" Lee mumbled, "It won't stop. Prince? Where am I?"

Sleep was slowly starting to retreat from the young woman's consciousness, and the black walls of being knocked nearly unconscious were receding from the Battle Prince's vision.

"There," the prince did absolutely nothing, "Did it stop now?"

"Yeah," she agreed quietly, "It did. What are you doing down there?"

"You kicked me," the young ruler replied, wondering if she yet had the mental capacity to understand what he was saying.

"Oh," Lee sounded pleasantly distant, "Sorry."

"It's okay, I'm pretty sure I had it coming," Krög sat up finally.

She looked tiredly at him, but smiled amiably, "You probably did."

The prince thought to take advantage of Lee's, presumably, slowed reactions given he assumed she was still half dozing, and playfully lunged at the young woman. With little effort, she rolled out of the way, and kicked at him again. Krög managed to catch hold of her before she connected.

Lee giggled and tugged against his grip, "Let me go, stupid prince."

"So these are what Scale has been drooling over for the last three months," the young ruler pretended to examine her toes, "I don't know, they don't look so special to me."

"That just proves everyone has better taste than you, prince," Lee teased, "At least three different monsters have tried to eat me this summer. I'm fit for fine dining."

"I have a perfectly refined palate, thank you- I'm royalty," Krög responded with mock haughtiness.

In a pinwheeling kick, Lee not only pulled loose from his grasp, but hooked her opposite knee around the prince's neck and slammed him back to the ground, pinning him under her leg. She stretched languidly, as though it were little more than a reflex. The Battle Prince snorted, but crawled next to her and tucked the small young woman under his arm again.

Lee yawned and nestled against Krög, "What time of the day is it?"

"Late," he said, "After twilight.   It'll be dark soon."

She groaned in, somewhat, pretend disappointment, "Oh. That means we're going to have to go soon, doesn't it?"

"Yeah," Krög agreed, equally let down, "With dad away, there isn't someone to always be looking for me, but that doesn't mean someone won't realize I'm gone. We should head back before they send the whole city after me."

"Mm," Lee moaned again, "Can we stay just a little longer? I'm comfortable."

The prince closed his eyes and settled himself again, "I don't see why not," the breeze kissed them again, and in his light, sleeveless summer attire, Krög shivered, "It's getting cold already."

"You don't know what cold is," Lee snickered, though she pressed herself a little closer to him anyway, "My guild is at the base of the Everfrost Mountain. We're lucky if it's sunny ten times a year there."

"It can be cloudy and hot," the prince argued.

"Not under a mountain made of ice it can't," she came back, "It's always cold there.   The wind is just a sharp as the ice, and they'll cut you to ribbons if you're not careful up there," her voice became faraway, and the prince wondered if she was still just talking about the weather.

"You're here now," he squeezed her shoulder, not really sure what it was he was being comforting against, but felt the need all the same.

"And I get to feel the sun," she smiled, "Feel that warmth on my face and the grass under my feet. I'm betting even winter here can't be so bad."

"The best part of winter here isn't even winter-it's autumn," the prince replied.

"What's autumn?" Lee asked.

"What's autumn?" Krög was almost incredulous, "It's the herald of winter. The harvest season. It's when the world turns from green to gold and red, the air cools and the wind picks up, twilight lasts for days at a time and everything starts to change. It's the season of restlessness. How have you never heard of autumn?"

She giggled, "Stupid prince. I know what autumn is- I just wanted to hear what kind of a spin you would put on it."

The young ruler snorted, but laughed, "Fine, play your games."

"I will," the young woman said delightedly.

"In my perfect world, it would be autumn all the time," Krög went on, "We would always be drinking spiced cider and celebrating the coming frost. There would always be a stiff western breeze in your face and a cool fog every night after the sun had finally gone down and a blood moon was on the rise."

"Mine would be spring," Lee countered, "There's just nothing like going splashing through a mud-bogged field after a drenching storm, or standing under wild mountain thunder as it tries to pull the sky apart at the hems. And then the sun comes out and everything is heavy and warm, and you don't have to wear practically anything at all."

"Well," the prince paused, "That last part doesn't sound so bad."

She elbowed him hard, "Manners, prince."

He laughed through a coughing fit, "Do excuse me, fair lady."

"You're excused," Lee said curtly, though with snark, "See to it you only picture me naked when I am not in your company."

"Does that mean when you *are* in my company, I get the real thing?" Krög asked hopefully.

The athletic young woman turned over and swatted him several times, "You damned barbarian," she laughed, "Really, learn how to court a girl properly!" and then followed up with, "Earn it."

"I intend to," the prince chuckled as he tried to fend her off, "Gods, I forget how strong you are. That hurt."

"For a badlands warrior, you, sir, are not so tough," Lee chided, "This is far too soft," she prodded him sharply in his side.

Given Krög was lean and at least reasonably strong, it was an unfair assessment, but the lithe girl persisted, markedly entertained by his struggles to push her away.

"Hey, cut it out," the Battle Prince laughed, "That's southern steel you're poking, forged in the fires of War School!"

"Yeah, okay," Lee chortled at his over-appraisal of his own physicality, "I didn't realize steel was so sensitive," she jabbed and pinched him again.

Krög rolled on top of the young woman to try and stifle her playfully irksome digs. With little more effort than it takes most people to lift a fork, Lee hinged at the hips and catapulted the prince over her head. As he crashed to the forest floor behind her, the lithe girl flipped backwards and landed on his chest, pinning him succinctly to the ground once again.

"That," she said, "Is for tickling me in my sleep."

The prince surrendered, smiling, "Deserved."

Lee's face brightened as well, and she leaned down and threw her arms around his neck, holding the young ruler close for a long moment.

He asked, "What was that for?"

Lee just gave him a knowing look.

Krög pulled her close again and kissed her forehead, "You're amazing, you know that?"

She looked at him mistily and sighed, "Oh, prince. That's the stupidest thing you've ever said," and then qualified, "Today."

They both laughed. Lee slid off the young ruler, and flopped back into grasses of the glen.

With a twinge of disappointment, she sat up, "Well. I guess we should get going. No more fun today," Lee put on a dramatically visible pout.

"Dad won't be home for another two days," Krög sat up and stretched, "So, we've got tomorrow at least too."

In a pointed moment, the young woman replied, "You *never* have tomorrow- it's not something you get to have until it's a *today*."

The prince looked at her quizzically.

Immediately, Lee's solemn mood broke, and she tittered wildly, "I love that face you make. Come on, prince. Take me home."

Krög stood and gathered up his sword and Harpbinger, while Lee tugged on her boots. She often loudly complained the one thing she hated about traveling alone with the prince was she did not have Ashley's shoulders to ride around on and keep her safe from the brambles of the Thorn Rift Forest. It meant suffering the, apparently, insufferable offense of wearing boots when she and Krög stole away on their walks alone. The prince was unsure how much of her grousing was genuine, and how much of it was just for the sake of getting attention- either way, she made a show of it every time they set off on an adventure that required her wear treads. As Lee sulkily finished tightening the tassels, Krög secured Thundersteel in place, and hand in hand, they went crunching through the carpet of thorns on the forest floor.

Along the way, they bantered and joked with one another, switching topics from warfare, to the cosmic, to what spices made for the best stews, about as rapidly as a hummingbird beats its wings. To the outside listener, it would have seemed a dizzying flight between subjects, with truly harrowing transitions from one to the next and completely disparate ideals being presented at each turn. Krög and Lee had begun to develop their own language, however, and could easily pitch and dive through such complicated, bizarre changes with all the ease of breathing. Neither one had too much difficulty keeping pace with the other, although Lee did occasionally drop in a puzzler that would temporarily bring Krög's mental gears to a grinding halt. All the same, their conversation was lively and distracted, winding and lilting, without any need for any manner of destination or finality.

Night crept over the edge of the horizon, and its dark tendrils wormed their way across the sky, supplanting deep blues and violets for the reds and oranges of dusk. Continuing to stumble along became a tangled and confusing task for the Battle Prince and the lithe girl without a source of light to guide their steps. The radiance of the moon had not yet spilled its pale glow wide enough to break through the canopy and give them its silvery translucence to see by. Lee curled her small fingers around Krög's belt, following close in his steps as he lead them carefully through the brambles, endeavoring not to trip or topple.

All the sounds of the nighttime forest grew symphonically around the pair. Crickets and owls sang and called to the stars above, quiet rustles of tiny creatures skittering about the underbrush sounded infinitely louder, and the wind against the trees creaked and strained them eerily. At last there was light to see by when the two crossed into The Strange, and the glowing mosses that covered the mighty arbors there threw off just enough luminescence for their eyes to adjust. It pulsed and dimmed, growing sometimes brighter and sometimes softer as though responding to an unseen heartbeat within the enormous trunks. Lee grinned broadly at the ethereal beauty of it all, her hair shifting from pale green to electric blue as the colors of the trees changed.

The longer they walked, however, the blacker the night became, and the prince became genuinely worried once they passed beyond the enchanted depths that there would not be enough light to continue to navigate by. He had been caught out in the glade at the foot of the Scorched Hill after dark enough times to know forest darkness is a different kind of gloom- it is swallowing and suffocating, engulfing and impenetrable. Even that small glen was a veritable labyrinth once the sun went down, and it started to worry Krög what it would be like to get lost in the sylvan desert of the Thorn Rift Forest. He had slept in the forest before, but he had never tried to find his way out of it after twilight gave over to the great ink.

He suggested it to Lee, "We may have to stop here for the night. I can already barely see, and it's only going to get worse."

"Keep going, scaredy-cat," Lee teased, "It's hardly after dark, we can keep this up a little while longer. Besides, I want to sleep in a bed tonight. My bed, your bed, I don't care which, but I'm not in love with the idea of lying down in the thorns."

"I'm just saying," the prince tried again, "It's going to be tough to figure out where to go once we're out of The Strange. We can always sneak back once dawn breaks."

"Move it, you pansy," she giggled again, "Honestly. The Battle Prince afraid of the dark? Whoever heard of such a thing."

While only feeling partially emasculated by Lee's incessant joking derision, the young ruler still felt a degree of hesitancy drive itself into his heels as they continued to march through the forest. On the one hand, he hated being accused of being afraid of absolutely anything. Krög learned early on that being considered scrawny in his kingdom meant he had to pick a lot of unnecessary fights with much larger opponents for the sake of his honor. He liked to think that made him courageous, and not abjectly prideful or stupid. On the other hand, a genuine apprehension of getting hopelessly lost in the woodlands had taken root, and the Battle Prince was sincerely concerned he would not be able to find his way out. Truly, though the forest was practically on the front doorstep of the Fortress City, Krög had only been able to explore it on his own in recent months, and he did not know its glens and glades as well as he knew the rocky badlands south of his home.

Colder and colder air slipped between the trunks of the trees, along with a creeping fog that only served to further obscure the prince's vision and degrade his sense of direction. Silence was settling heavily as well, which the young ruler trusted meant they had at least made it to the tree line of The Quiets. It was a narrow band, when compared to the great magic crater of The Strange or the enormous seaside sprawls of Troll Country, but that did not mean it was easy to escape if the trees did not want you to. Their will was strongest in The Quiets, and if the prince had in any way brought a transgression against them, he knew they could make it a real task to break back into the rolling fields just beyond the jungle.

Even Lee started to shiver, "You might have been right about the cold, prince. Whew, it *is* chilly."

Krög was inclined to agree, "Here, take my cloak for now. I wasn't expecting it to get this cool- we probably should have packed better."

"Well it wasn't exactly in the plan to fall asleep for half the day either," Lee gratefully took the prince's heavier jacket, "You wore me out."

"Can I get that in writing?" he jested, trying to lighten the mood.

She bumped him roughly with her shoulder, "What did I tell you about manners, prince?"

"Considering we are now neck deep in monster territory, I think we can set manners aside for now in case I have to do something loud and violent," the prince replied.

"Oh yeah, you're a real threat," Lee snickered, "Tell me again about the dragon you conked on the head by accident. That's a tale of high heroism like no other!"

Krög was really only half listening at that point. There was something altogether more sinister about their predicament, and he was just starting to realize what it was. The trees around them should have been brimming with green leaves painted silver by the dance of starlight and moon glow. Instead, they were bleakly bare, with decaying limbs and gnarled trunks. Tangled branches grabbed at the sky like the talons of some demon of old, and the fog surrounding Lee and the prince was positively pouring out of the knotholes in their boles. Krög realized that the quiet he had mistaken for the sentinel trees at the edge of the forest listening to the world was instead the gravely silence of a haunted, dead tomb of a woodland. Fear was replaced with sickening dread.

"Lee, I think we took a wrong turn somewhere," Krög swallowed hard, "We're in The Dark."

"No kidding, stupid- it's nighttime, of course it's dark," she chuckled.

"No, Lee, not it's dark, I mean *The* Dark. The Dark part of the Thorn Rift Forest," the prince insisted.

Lee paused, "How long have we been here?"

"I don't know," the young ruler admitted, "I just noticed. But this is definitely not The Quiets. The trees are all dead."

"Okay," the young woman said as calmly as she could, "Let's just... turn around, and find our way back out, right?"

Krög looked over his shoulder and instead of seeing the borders of The Strange behind them, saw only howling darkness, "I don't think it works like that here, Lee."

Despite being the almost proprietarily gutsier and more courageous of the two, she shrunk against him a bit, "Well just try, dammit. Standing here isn't going to get us out of this place."

"Ash said once you go into The Dark," the prince swallowed hard, "It tries to keep you there."

"I remember, I was there," Lee replied sharply, "And I find myself wondering why I have to repeat that we need to at least try something, because standing still is *literally* getting us nowhere!"

Something not Krög or the girl whispered, "This way."

"Follow me," another called softly.

"Over here," something else hissed, much too close for comfort.

Lee's voice hedged towards panic, "Prince."

"I know, don't listen to them," the young ruler did his best to sound brave, but his voice was wavering, "You're right. Let's back up and go back the way we came."

Another sinister hush creeped, "Wrong way."

"Take us with you," a chorus of moans begged.

"Come to me," a rasping, rattling something choked.

Krög wanted to squeeze his palms against his ears to try and drown out the voices, but for whatever reason he felt assured it would not do any good. Besides, it would mean pulling away from Lee's grasp, and the young ruler was not about to do that either. He squeezed her hand a little tighter, perhaps for her comfort and perhaps for his own, and tugged the young woman in the direction he was relatively certain they had come. She stayed as close to him as possible, and the two of them slowly started to retrace their steps out of the haunted dale. Every step against the carpet of thorns was deafening, and just the shuffle of their feet sounded like thunder against the otherwise silent scape- excepting for the slithering voices, of course. He was not sure why he wanted to make a quiet exit from The Dark, but Krög got the unsettling feeling they were being watched and he did not want to draw further attention.

With the muted fervor of a gathering storm, the voices started to intensify and multiply.

"Please help me," something seethed.

"Not that way," another cooed.

"Stay with us," came a plea.

"I want you," someone snarled.

"Follow the trees," echoed a laugh.

Krög about yelped rather un-bravely when something grabbed his shoulder opposite Lee. He twisted towards it but saw nothing at all. Something else tugged at his ankle, and again the prince jerked wildly to pull away from whatever it was that was grasping at him. In doing so, he accidentally yanked his hand out of Lee's grasp, and the young ruler was immediately filled with dread at having lost the girl's touch.

"Prince!" she shouted from nearby.

Krög ran towards the sound of her voice and wrapped his arms around her, "I've got you."

Barely above a whisper Lee quaked, "No you don't."

The prince looked down at what he had grabbed ahold of, and was met with the grin of a bleached, cracked skull sitting atop a decaying corpse, empty eye sockets staring right back at him.

"You've got me!" the thing squealed excitedly, before cackling hideously and dissolving to dust as its laughter reverberated long through the harrowing glades.

Krög leapt backwards, naught but pure horror etched in his face, and tumbled end over end when he collided with something he could not see in the blackness. Lee cried out when he fell on top of her, and they took a hard spill in the thorns. Both were so relieved to be next to the other they barely noticed when their embrace drove a number of spurs deep into one another's skin. Their elation did not last long.

"And I've got you!" a forest of hands erupted from the dirt around them, skeletal and gnarled, and grabbed madly for the young ruler and the lithe girl.

Fingers of yellowing and browned bone clutched for the companions, ripping at their clothes and clinging to whatever they could grab hold of. One tugged at Lee's fair hair, another closed around the prince's throat. Still another pulled at the young woman's wrist, and another made a frantic swipe at Thundersteel, threatening to pull the one weapon they had away from Krög and Lee. With merciless passion the lithe girl kicked and struck furiously at the groping hands, shattering them one by one. The prince tore his sword away from the ones trying to steal the blade and lashed out viciously at the jungle of boney fingers. The companions ripped loose, and with absolutely no concept where they were going, ran headlong into further darkness, just desperate to leave the clutching, grasping, clawing hands behind them.

"Come back," something over their shoulder cried, forlorn, "Come back and play."

Both had barely put any distance between them and the source of the cries, when an absolute tapestry of barbed vines erupted out of the thorns before the prince and the young woman. The vines wove themselves tightly between two trees, and blocked the companions' path.   Krög and Lee quickly spun another direction to continue their frantic flight, but again the forest floor leapt up before them and snarled their trail.   Terrified and despairing, the prince lashed out again with his sword and tried to slash his way through the offending creepers. They cleaved less like plants, and more like fleshy limbs. Ultimately, they retreated from his blade, bleeding black ichor and sobbing as the edge of the weapon snapped them apart.

"*Oh,*" the vines seemed to sigh, "Please don't *hurt* us.   Just let us *feel* you."

Aghast, Krög watched the trees and forest floor birth forth more thorn-studded vines, which grasped out towards him and Lee.   She reacted first, and grabbed the prince by the wrist.

"Just run!" Lee called and tugged him away from the squirming ramblers.

They ran until their lungs burned and their hearts were hammering against their ribs with exhaustion and terror.   They ran until their legs felt ready to give way beneath their exertions.   They ran until their vision blurred and their thoughts came in naught but a ragged, choppy flood of fear and anguish.   They ran until both were certain they could run absolutely no more, and still they ran on.   Further and further, they charged into the blackness that had settled so comfortably around them like a bloated beast cozying up to its hapless prey.

Neither was certain how long they had run, or how far, only that very suddenly, they were surrounded by a pressing, suffocating silence.   Though he could barely see her, Krög watched Lee's head bob around like she were trying to get a fix on their surroundings through the unyielding darkness.

"Did we make it?" she asked through gasps, "Are we out?"

The prince squinted hard and tried to peer through the crushing murk, endeavoring to make out the sentinel arbors of The Quiets. It had almost become too dark to see the difference between the twisted trunks of The Dark or the pillar-like trees at home at the edge of the Thorn Rift. He strained his ears, and listened for the leaves and branches above to whisper to one another, like only they did in the silent tree-line. He looked, and he listened.

Krög's stomach dropped when his eyes, instead, beheld a single, bouncing light, flitting between trees. It seemed to move along with a spritely pace, and might have seemed innocuous or even welcome to a lost traveller. He knew better. The prince had heard them called by almost a dozen names. The Demon's Fireflies. Candles of Hell. The Dead Man's Lantern. The Lost Ones.

"Gods," he gulped, "It's a Will'o'the'Wisp."

Another appeared. And then another. Each moved jauntily about, a terrifying pleasantness that belied their true nature.

"What are they?" Lee whispered.

"Wayward souls," the prince tried to keep his voice steady, "Furious spirits of the dead who lost their lives to the forest. They'll lead you round and round forever until you collapse and die."

"Great," she replied in equal fear, "So we don't follow them, right? I mean, they're just lights."

"They're malevolent," Krög said, "They want more. Just because we don't *follow* them doesn't mean they won't *herd* us somewhere."

"Prince," Lee took a deep breath, "Get me out of here."

"Okay," the young ruler nodded several times as he tried to make a decision, "Okay."

Another ball of bouncing light floated over his shoulder, and in the depths of it Krög could see a twisted, contorted, wailing face, the eyes of which bore straight through the prince's spirit. It hung there for a moment, hypnotizing the Battle Prince. Its ethereal, inaudible pleas for him to follow it further and further on writhed their way into his consciousness. Without knowing why, Krög slowly reached out to touch it, not feeling fully in control of his own movements.

Lee slapped his hand down, "Now, prince. Get me out of here."

Krög recoiled from the will'o'the'wisp and shielded the young woman from its entrancing light.

"I think that's a good idea," he drew further back from the floating light, which seemed to wail in sadness he was no longer under its brief thrall.

"No kidding," she snorted, "Now that the murderous lightning bugs have shown up, you think it's a good idea."

"Let's move," Krög was done with debating, and with sarcasm.

They had no idea where to go, but they knew there was nothing worse than waiting around for something else to creep up and take them.

Doom-laden voices and wafting fogs that might have been ghosts drifted around the prince and Lee as they pushed on through the bleak, haunted glens. Krög remembered some of Ashley's first words about The Dark: follow no lights, listen to no voices. He also remembered the troll instructing him never to draw Thundersteel in the midst of those blighted glades- that it was a well known and grossly disliked weapon, and it would only draw attention, unwanted and unneeded. Still, Krög kept a tight grip on the blade's hilt and used the tip of the weapon to feel his way through the black, like a blind man's walking stick. He did not really care who decided they were upset to be around the sword. And what the prince would have done to have his titanic troll by his side, if for no other reason than Ash would have known how to get out of The Dark and was patently able to clobber the snot out of anything that tried to harm them.

Lee seemed to echo his thoughts, "We could really use the big guy about now."

"I think even Ash gets confused in here," Krög was not sure how that was supposed to be comforting, "He just sort of... *senses* his way out. Maybe we're trying too hard to find a path. Maybe we need to sense our way out too."

"Then get with the sensing," Lee shivered, "It's super cold in here, and I'm not ashamed to say I am scared witless."

"This isn't my idea of a pleasant evening stroll either, Lee," the prince's patience was wearing thin, "I'm trying here."

"I know," she squeezed his hand, "I know you are," and then followed in her typical manner, "But you're usually pretty terrible at being a hero, and that's kind of what we need right now. So... I'd say it's time for some personal growth."

"What about you?" Krög asked, "Usually this is about the time you step in and save my ass. That would not go totally unnoticed here."

"You know what, prince," Lee returned, "As amazing and indescribably perfect as I am at all things, sometimes it would be nice if you could do something for yourself. You know? Just a little."

"Noted," Krög retorted, "I'm just saying- if you have any bright ideas, now would be the time to share them."

"Do you honestly think if I had something in mind that could get us out of here faster, I would be holding it back right now?" Lee snapped.

"To mess with me? Absolutely," the young ruler came back.

The lithe young woman scoffed, "Gods, that damn dragon was right about you. You take it so personally when I joke."

"Well- some occasional sincerity would go a long way towards convincing me *this* is what you want," the prince quipped.

"This *isn't* what I want. To be stuck in a haunted forest while we're being stalked by the living dead in the dark is precisely the *opposite* of what I want," Lee sniped.

"Not at all what I meant," Krög rolled his eyes.

"I know *exactly* what you meant," she shot, "And not only is this absolutely not the time *or* place for this conversation, I cannot believe that's still bothering you."

"Well, it does," the prince spun around to face her, though they could hardly see each other in the blackness, "There's still a lot I don't know about you, Lee, and it makes it that much harder to trust you when you're constantly blurring the lines between genuine, and snark."

Lee recoiled slightly, but was undaunted, "Meanwhile, you whisper in my ear about how much you want to be free of the life you have and go run wild, and then make a huge damn show of strolling about your city with Princess I'm-Too-Pretty-To-Be-Bothered."

"No longer an issue, remember?" Krög pointed out.

"How nice you didn't have to make *that* decision for yourself," she snapped back, "Daddy Battle King waves his scepter and, boom, there you have it, now you're relieved of a major quandary."

The Battle Prince paused, only momentarily at a loss for words, "I could have told him I still wanted to marry Ydal. Doesn't that count for *something*?"

"Oh, please," even in the dark, Krög could see Lee plant herself and cross her arms, "You're a badlands warrior- she's about as far from your type as it gets."

"You're talking in circles now," the prince felt like Lee had, in the same argument, accused him of trying to court two women at once, and simultaneously agree he was never interested in anyone but her.

"And you're walking in circles," she replied, no longer caring if she made sense.

Krög raised a finger to object further, when something very loud, and very close, growled menacingly in the darkness.

"Fight more later?" Lee asked.

"Yep," Krög agreed.

The Battle Prince reached out and found Lee's hand in the murk, and the two pressed forward with their blind stumble through The Dark.

It was a difficult thing trying to avoid the wandering lights, while simultaneously trying to keep them from driving the prince and the young woman in any particular direction. Add to that the voices, which had resumed in both pitch and fervor, and a host of gnarled trees that absolutely would occasionally change positions if Krög took his eyes off them for too long, and the hurried struggle to be free of The Dark descended into a maddeningly confused labor. The prince realized, too, in their dash to escape the hands clawing out of the ground, he and Lee had gone slanting off in any direction that seemed safe, but not one that resembled the direction they had come in. Even more than before, they were extraordinarily lost, and the will of the haunted forest was doing all it could to exacerbate their situation.

"Prince," Lee whispered, "Where are we going?"

"I don't know, Lee," he whispered back, his voice more forlorn than frustrated, "I really don't know. Just-somewhere not here."

She sighed heavily, and Krög looked over his shoulder at her. Faintly, he could make out an expression of restrained fear and determined focus on her face. Lee was trying just as hard as he was to discern some path through the forest, her complicated features framed by wispy hair, which was glowing an unreal silver in the moonlight. Of course, it was just then the prince realized there was moonlight at all to see by. Somewhere in the tangle of branches ahead, there was enough of a break to allow a few pale beams down to the forest floor. Krög hoped it was a sign of salvation, that they had somehow stumbled their way back to the edge of The Dark.

Lee let out a long breath, "What... is that?"

"Gods above and below," Krög was taken aback as well.

In the midst of an enormous clearing, jutting straight up into the starless sky above, gleaming in the eerie light of the moon was a great, iron citadel, piercing high above the dark tangle. It was a spire as unimaginable in appearance as it was unlikely in prospect. Rather than being constructed of stone and mortar, it looked as though it had been forged from a single slab of glittering steel. Jagged and furious, the tower impaled the sky itself, like a terrible needle skewering velvety soft skin. It spun to unimaginable heights, not unlike the parapets the prince had seen in the Empire Court of the Ivory City. Disparately, it stood alone, without other ramparts or belfries for support or company. Singular and terrifying, the mighty tower was a sentinel obelisk, lord over all that surrounded it-mysterious and horrible.

"How did we miss that?" the lithe young woman whispered again.

"I mean..." the prince searched for an answer, "It's *really* dark out."

"This is *not* the kind of thing that hides in the darkness," she replied, "This isn't the kind of thing that hides at *all*."

"It's the curse of this place," Krög guessed, "The blight that reveals only what it wants."

"Creepy," Lee snorted, "Come on."

"'Come on,' where?" the prince was absolutely terrified of where he was certain she wanted to go.

"In there," she pointed at the tower and validated his dread, "Let's go inside."

"Are you out of your damn mind?" the young ruler hissed.

"No more than *you* are if you think I'm staying out here when there's a perfectly good tower we could go into and sleep or hide or ask for directions!" she retorted.

"Lee- we have no idea what's in there, or who this thing belongs to," Krög insisted, "Even for you, this is a special shade of crazy."

"Call me crazy again," she fired back, "I dare you."

"Dammit, work with me here, Lee," the prince was getting strained, "*This* is not a good place. Odds are good, that means whoever or WHATEVER is in there isn't good either. Do you know what are usually *under* towers? Dungeons. Lots of chains and blood and bad things, get it?"

"Yes, thank you, prince, I know what a dungeon is. We had a lot of them in my guild and trust me when I say they make the ones in *your* kingdom look like luxury accommodations," Lee roared as quietly as one could and it still be considered roaring, "And I. Don't. Care. I'm going in there, and you can come too if you'd like, or you can stay out here and take your chances with whatever in the nine hells just made that sound!"

Not far away, something very eldritch howled low, and the underbrush nearby rustled violently as though something large and angry was charging through it.

Lee raised her eyebrows expectantly at him.

Krög waved in several different directions as though trying to decide where to motion to emphasize whatever point he thought he was about to make, "There's not even a door on this thing!"

No sooner were the words out of his mouth did the steel at the base of the tower begin to twist and writhe, and glow deep red like molten slag that was spiraling around the mouth of a whirlpool. With a deep, moaning yawn, a portal of infinite darkness appeared, leading into the inner reaches of the citadel. It wavered, like the horizon on a hot summer day, and hummed softly with sinister power. Yet, for all its bizarre and unsettling appearance- it welcomed them.

Slowly, but with purpose, Lee said, "Prince. I am going in there. Are you coming, or not?"

Krög sighed through his nose, but relented, "This is really stupid."

She half nodded, "So are you. Let's go, stupid prince."

Hand in hand, hesitantly at first, the prince and the young woman stepped into the clearing towards the iron citadel. The thorns crunched loudly under their feet, and echoed furiously like a roll of thunder through the channels of a canyon. A heavy fog hung around the base of the tower, but it parted evenly as Krög and Lee approached. Its tendrils beckoned like pale fingers, and swirled inward towards the flickering, ethereal entrance. The molten archway seemed to pull in everything around it: the fog, the air, the very moonlight were all helplessly tugged into its maw. Its hypnotic and ghostly draw fell even on the Battle Prince and the young woman at his side. Krög was no longer sure whether it was a conscious decision to enter the tower or not. All he knew was the iron citadel was dragging them in, and there was no breaking its grasp.

The closer they got to the spire, the taller it climbed into the sky, and the deeper the arch around its entrance loomed. Seeming the only light to cast off the portal that was not devoured by the doorway, the glowing, molten red breathed an icy chill on them, rather than the expected searing heat. It made Lee's fair skin and hair turn a brilliant crimson, and it reflected the wild, barbarian fierceness in Krög's eyes. The young ruler felt all the hair on his arms and neck stand up- maybe from the cold, maybe from fear. Within moments, they were swallowed in entirety by the crushing black.

For a few heartbeats, it felt as though the Battle Prince had been pulled into the rapid current of whitewater. He squeezed hard to Lee's hand as the two of them were jerked through the portal, and tossed down some river of immense power. As quickly as the harrowing ride began, it was just as suddenly over, and it left the prince and the girl standing breathlessly in a lofty antechamber within the walls of the tower. Krög tried to find his wind as the hammering in his chest slowed back to normal, and their torrid journey came to a grinding halt. Before his eyes could adjust to the dim lighting within, he heard a sound like shearing metal and turned just in time to see the portal behind them seal itself shut. Slick, steel walls surrounded the prince and Lee on all sides. They were trapped.

"I might be regretting this," Lee said, her voice a barely audible hush.

Long black sheets that dangled from gothic anchors all around the chamber flapped in a phantom wind that seemed to breathe through the tower. The polished iron floor glistened in muted moonlight, the source of which was not immediately evident- what with there being no apparent windows on the sheer walls. Other than the snapping of the oddly placed curtains and the snarling whisper of the inexplicable breeze, the tower was silent. A spiraling staircase of similar obsidian wove higher and higher into the upper reaches of the citadel. Its lustrous metal stairs were the only obvious path anywhere out of the monolithic room.

At the base of the stairs was the truly dominant and wholly strange feature of the great chamber. A pipe organ, the likes of which Krög had only heard talked about in stories, sat dusty and choked with cobwebs, but otherwise grand and impressive beyond measure. Eight rows of keys cascaded up and down its immense face, and the gargantuan pipes that would sing if put to play raced up the walls of the tower, and disappeared high into its most soaring reaches. It was odd that the rest of the room was so pristinely polished and clean, but the monolithic organ looked tattered and decrepit as though it had been there far longer than the whole of the rest of the citadel. With each ghostly breeze, the wind would glide across the openings on the lower pipes, and they would occasionally loose a faint, rumbling moan. Just in front of the first row of keys was a fluttering clutch of sheet music. Its pages were brittle and cracked, but the dancing notes were still clear on the bars. It was begging to be played, and yet at the same time it promised damnation to anyone who was so bold as to set their fingers upon its keys.

Krög did not dare take another step into the room, "Now what?"

It was not Lee who answered him, but a spine-tingling, skin-crawling voice from beyond.

"You. Have. Come."

Lee stiffened visibly, "Oh, prince, please tell me that's some cute trick you picked up."

"I would love to," the young ruler replied, "Unfortunately…"

"I. Have. Waited."

The voice spun around them from above, sailing from one side of the chamber to the other, around and around like it were born on unnatural wings.

"For what?" Lee decided to talk back to it, which the prince considered to be markedly stupid, but had lost the opportunity to convince her otherwise, "Waited for us?"

"Long. In the tower. In the shadows. In. The Dark."

"Didn't quite answer my question," Lee was far more audacious than Krög ever could have imagined.

"Lee, maybe we don't antagonize the disembodied voice of the tower that just swallowed us," the prince suggested.

Without warning, one of the black curtains fluttered away from its anchoring and floated halfway around the room where it caught suddenly on another.

"What's that all about, huh?" the lithe girl called out, "Is that supposed to mean something? Throwing a blanket around?"

"Lee!" Krög hissed.

"Not. The first. Perhaps. The last."

"Who are you?" Lee directly challenged, "I'll even settle with WHAT are you?"

Again, the loose black sheet flew free from where it had stuck and whipped around the chamber. It caught just behind the prince and the young woman, flapping loosely above their heads.

"Let's just try and find a way out of here, instead of picking a fight with the talking citadel. Or, I guess, whatever is talking *for* the citadel," Krög urged.

"Prince, it's not going to do anything-" Lee began sarcastically.

Just as she said it, the loose black sheet tore away from the wall again and went sailing right over them. It swooped low, like a great, silken bat, before slowing considerably and hovering just above the pipe organ. Hanging there in the air, it looked like a long-limbed skeleton draped in a ragged cloak, arms outstretched in ominous welcoming. Then, as though drawn on a line straight through the floor, it snapped to the ground in a crumpled heap, before sliding across the steel tiles, and shooting back up amongst the other draperies where it vanished amongst the collected black linens.

The prince exhaled a breath he did not know he was holding in, "What the...?"

A roaring wind tore through the chamber and all of the curtains shore away from their anchoring, and went racing around the room in circles. Krög ducked under them as they flew wildly back and forth, pulling Lee down under him to protect her- though he was not exactly sure what he was shielding her from. Demonic sheets? Possessed tapestries?

Violently, they all stopped and snapped back into place.

"Okay," Lee's voice quavered slightly, "I might have made a bad decision."

"Unknowing. They don't understand. They cannot see."

"Enough with the riddles!" Krög shouted back, "Just let us out, and we'll leave!"

Another hurricane gale rushed through the chamber, and the black curtains again went sailing on its raking grip. They seemed to move out of concourse with the currents of the air and dove and swooped at the prince and the young woman huddled on the floor. Krög could feel the heavy fabrics snapping across his skin, but he did not dare peer up at the scene for fear of what else he might see. There was something in the room with them. Something that did not seem like it wanted them there.

"Stop!" Lee screamed, "Stop it, please!"

As if bowing to her pleas the wind immediately ceased, and the curtains fell to the floor around her and the young ruler.

Slowly, the prince peeked out from under his curled arms. The black sheets were everywhere, slight ripples coursing over their surfaces as the occasional breeze slipped through the room.

Krög held his breath when one of the curtains *stood* up.

It rose with the majesty of a kneeling ruler climbing back to its feet- boldly, purposed, and graceful. For a heartbeat it hung in the air unmoving, before it very slowly floated over towards the young ruler, and loomed over him. He could feel an icy breath surging softly from where its head might be concealed in the deep folds of the sheet, and the unmistakable sensation of unseen eyes studying him over. Through ragged gasps, the prince held its stare as best he could, especially given he could not see a face within the depths of the curtain. It turned on its own wind, and spirited over to the pipe organ. The phantom seemed to sit down in front of the keys on an invisible seat. Stretching out with the corners of the sheet, hands that were cloaked by the black satins began to press down on the keys of the huge organ.

"A great king died here."

Gradually, the prince let Lee up as it became clear the torrent of ghosts had come to a, perhaps temporary, halt. She brushed her hair out of her face nervously, and could not take her eyes off the specter at the organ.

"He was ancient and powerful. Strength beat in his heart though age had gnawed upon his bones. First born son of a great warlord. He came with his men of steel. He came seeking. He died seeking."

Haunting, thundering notes hummed and rattled up the pipes and expelled themselves with declamatory power. Dust and webs billowed out of the throats of the tubes with each rumbling tone.

"I thought him the keeper of that which would undo. I slew him for such. Wrong, I was. Me and mine were cast out for it- thrown aside as rogues and rebels. But the price was to be paid. The sacrifice for the sake of keeping safe that which would undo."

Lee cautioned a question, "Undo what?"

The phantom hit a sour note on the organ and ceased its playing. Slowly, disquietingly, it turned to face them, whatever it was beneath the sheet still hidden in the swallowing black depths of the curtain.

"Undo all."

In a flash that barely lasted the length and breadth of a single blink, the phantom sped from its seat in front of the organ and overshadowed the prince and the young woman. Both shrank back and tried to skitter away, but the hovering thing inched closer and closer to them. The edges of its sheet snapped and cracked loudly with each breeze.

"Inextricably, you are tied to it. Indivisibly, you are linked to it. Your fates are intertwined. I must sever. I must keep safe."

The wraith reached out with a cloaked hand. Krög could see it grasping for Lee. In an impassioned burst of action, Thundersteel leapt into the prince's grip, and he swung ferociously at the hovering curtain. Barely the tip of the blade clipped the fabric of the phantom, but all the same it wailed like a screaming banshee, as though it had been mortally rent. Like it were being dragged on a taught rope, the curtain snapped into a single length and went screaming upwards into the highest reaches of the tower. As soon as it disappeared, the room returned to deathly silence.

Over the crashing of his heart, Krög managed to speak, "Lee. Do you have *any* idea what it was talking about?"

She shook her head and shrugged blankly, "No. Maybe. I don't know. Did you?"

"Possibly," the young ruler gingerly found his feet, "More than one Battle King disappeared east heading for these forests, and never came back. My grandfather, Öx, did. But he was alone when he vanished, he didn't bring anyone."

"What does that have to do with 'that which would undo all'?" Lee allowed Krög to help her up.

"Nothing," the prince admitted, looking around at the fallen curtains as if waiting for them to start moving again, "But, he mentioned the first born son of a warlord. Öx was the only son of my great-grandfather, Mögren, the Tyrant. That part fits. And it said I was tied to... well, whatever."

"How do you know it was talking to *you*?" the girl pointed out, "It reached for *me*."

"Are *you* the descendent of a lineage of warrior kings?" the young ruler asked tritely.

"As fascinating as this lesson in your family history has become," Lee carried on in a huff, "I would very much like to find a way out of here now."

"Wait," Krög held her back, a look of concern and confusion on his face, "Am I missing something here? You actually *do* think it has something to do with you."

"I didn't say that," she crossed her arms and looked away from him.

"Yeah, and you're not denying it either," the prince tried to step back in front of her as she twisted away, "What does this place mean to you, Lee? Why did you want to come in here so bad?"

"Nothing, okay?" she seethed, "I've never been here before, I've never even seen anything like this. It doesn't mean *anything*. That thing just… said something to me."

"What do you mean it said something to *you*?" he came back, "We don't know exactly who it was talking to. The ghost was a bit nonspecific in its rantings."

"No, it wasn't just talking to us," Lee bit, "It was talking to *me*. I heard it. And if you didn't hear what I did, then maybe you weren't meant to."

"Lee," Krög tugged gently at her arm, his eyes brimming with worry, "What's going on?"

She shook her head, "Look, it was a bad idea coming in here. I'm sorry. Let's just, find a way to get out and forget this ever happened, okay?"

The prince took a long moment to consider her, "Yeah. Fine. Whatever you say."

"Thank you," the young woman sighed, before making for the stairs behind the organ.

Krög waited only a beat longer before trailing after her. As they rounded the incredible instrument, it rose up even more fantastic before them. When he reflected on it, the prince decided everything about the tower seemed to grow in scope and dominance constantly, like it was not a solid thing but rather a mercurial, undulating space. He tried to glimpse the music on the sheet as they passed. Something about the long, low tones the phantom had played rang familiar in his mind, though fear and anxiety clouded his judgement and he could no longer place it. Lee, however, was on a mission, and they passed by the fluttering, yellowed sheets too quickly for the young ruler to read it in full.

Up, up, up they spiraled, the heavy treads of their boots finding little quarter on the slippery sheen of the citadel's steel stairs. Even Lee seemed to be shaky on the narrow scaffoldings, her normally unyielding balance challenged by the smooth, polished iron and the shuddering in her legs. It took everything Krög had not to tumble backwards back down or, worse, to the side and over the edge. He could not tell how high the tower went on, but it did not take them long wind their way several stories above the floor below. Adding to the difficulty of navigating the stairs, to avoid the towering pipes of the organ the steps did not proceed in a strict circular pattern- they bent back and forth as they reached higher and higher. It was a treacherous journey.

After a ways, the companions came to a landing, which they stopped on at the encouragement of Krög.

Both leaned out over the wrought iron railing and looked back down at where they had come from. The floor was easily already more than a hundred feet below, and its gleaming surface was very suddenly bare. All the black curtains and sheets had returned to their anchors along the walls, and were ruffling idly in the passing, ghostly breeze. Above, the tower stretched into never-ending darkness- the only thing piercing its reaches being the tall pipes of the organ. Krög tousled his hair as he looked back and forth between the ground and the black yonder above. All that climbing the stairs seemed to be garnering them, in his assessment, was a greater distance to fall if the phantom should return and decide to give them both a good toss. He huffed and caught his breath.

"What exactly are we looking for?" the prince asked.

Lee fixed him with a look, "Do you have a better idea?"

"Not especially," he conceded, adding, "But, we could have spent a little more time on the first floor looking for a way out. You had to go right for the stairs."

She snorted, "I couldn't help but notice that sounded a *lot* like an accusation, prince."

"I still think there's something you're not telling me," the young ruler came right out with it, "Why are you being so mysterious?"

"There's a lot I'm not telling you," Lee shot back, "I'm a woman- ergo, mysterious. Get used to it."

She moved to pass him and continue the climb, but Krög stuck his arm out and grabbed the railing, blocking her path.

"What did it say to you?" he asked directly.

"Prince," Lee replied softly, but strongly, "Get out of my way."

Krög held a moment longer, but relented, and released the railing to allow her to pass.

He asked one more time, "What did it say?"

"Not your business," she replied dryly.

The young ruler shook his head and followed after her.

Together they continued to climb in silence, both consumed by their own thoughts, and quietly wondered how far the tower went and what might be waiting for them at the top. Certainly, there had been no further signs of the phantom as they went along, but nothing about that lent any manner or sense of security to their shattered nerves. For all they knew, the sentient black curtain was lying in wait in one of the vast, inky shadows that bathed almost every corner of the citadel, with the few excepting patches of moonlight being let in from a yet unseen source. Perhaps it was hiding as an ambush predator does, ready to pounce and send them tumbling to their doom on the iron floors below. Krög swallowed hard at the thought of his broken body lying next to Lee's, the two of them forever lost in the haunted blight with no one knowing where to look to find them.

The prince shook the thought aside and fixed his eyes instead at the oppressive black above, determined to yet puncture its reaches and find the top of the tower. It was not the height of the climb that was so exhaustive, so much as it was effort of keeping his balance on the slippery stairs and avoid taking a nasty, nasty spill over the edge to the steely embrace of the floor so far below. Then, he and Lee had done an exhaustive amount of running earlier, and the young ruler realized just how tired he was from the day's earlier activities. Sleep stung at his eyes, and ache settled into his muscles. All he wanted was for their adventure to be at its conclusion, and to be in a bed, safe, somewhere.

Unnerved by the unusual silence between them, the young ruler tried a peace offering, "Hey. At least nothing is trying to eat us, right?"

Despite herself, Lee chuckled, "Alright, stupid prince. You get a win for that much."

"I mean, unless you include the tower," he slightly corrected, "Although there was a distinct lack of chewing when that happened, so... we've got that going."

"Oh, prince," she chided, "Ever the optimist."

"That's usually your role," he pointed out lightly.

Lee sighed, "I'm tired, okay? And more than a little freaked out."

Krög jogged haphazardly a few stairs to catch up to her and took the young woman's hand, "I'm here. I'm with you in this."

She gave him a look equal parts patronizing exasperation and caring consideration, "Not a huge comfort, Sir-Fumbles-A-Lot."

The prince broke her stare in frustration.

Lee giggled and pulled his face back towards hers, "Prince. You don't *always* have to defend me. We can get out of this together, alright?"

Krög's eyes were fuming, "I hate that the world expects me to be some big hero," he exhaled sharply in his throat, "But I hate it even more that you don't."

She descended a few steps so he was taller than her again and looked expectantly, and a little chastising, up at the young ruler, "Listen to me. You ARE my hero. And if you don't get that through your thick, barbarian skull, *this*," she motioned between them, "Is never going to work. You don't have to save me from imminent danger three times a day to be my hero. Just, trust me once in a while, yeah?"

He chewed at the inside of his lip, "It's a little hard when you keep so many secrets, you know?"

"Well, I'll try and be a little better about that," she agreed laughingly.

"I will too," the prince agreed, "About the whole... rescuing thing. Or whatever your point was."

Lee giggled loudly, "Gods, this is going to take a few repetitions, isn't it?"

Krög cautioned a slight smile and shrugged, "I mean... probably."

She pressed up onto her toes and kissed his chin, "My stupid prince. It's never the easy way with you, is it?"

"Yeah, yeah," he playfully pushed her away, "Let's find a way out of here."

Lee smiled broadly and scampered back up the stairs, "For the record, when I'm stuck to the underside of a giant snail that is trying to eat me, *that's* the right time to be my hero."

"Got it," the prince snorted wryly.

"Or, if I've been body swapped into a dragon, and a creature the size of my pinky has decided it's going to spend a few weeks gnawing on the real me- *that's* the right time to be my hero," she kept at him.

"Understood," he sang back at her.

"Or when there's a-" she started.

"Yes, thank you, I think I've got it," Krög chortled.

Their humorous expressions dropped when the distinct sound of something fluttering in the darkness above precipitated the shifting of shadows just over their heads.

"Something's up there," the prince whispered.

"No shit," Lee replied, "Whatever it is, we better not disappoint it."

"Right," Krög swallowed, "Let's go."

Neither could tell how long or how high they continued to climb as the stairs wound towards the stars and possibly into the very reaches of space. There was a disturbing elasticity to the citadel, and it just seemed to stretch and stretch. Truly, the ground continued to fall farther away, and the ceiling was always out of reach- always vanishing into an abyss above. The ache of the continuous, never-ending climb was starting to wear considerably on the prince, and he wondered how much farther they would have to go before coming across any clues as to how to escape the tower. It occurred to him that for all the distance they went up, they would eventually have to go back down. And he knew from enough hikes through the badlands and foothills of the

Dragon's Spine Mountains, going down on wobbly legs was just as dangerous as going up on a bad slope.

Almost as though answering his fears and desires, the stairs rather suddenly gave way to a landing at what seemed to be the decided heights of the citadel. Krög and Lee emerged into the spires of a parapet, the elaborate head of the citadel coming together like the claws of a grasping raptor. Overhead the silver, eerie moon shone brightly, and its beams bounced between the curled pillars, reflecting back down into the lower realms of the tower. Had the view before them been of a lively forest, it would have been spectacular. Instead, it was dreadful. In every direction, the great blight of The Dark raked the forest, its twisted, bent trees sprawling all the way to the distant slopes of the sheer, towering Dragon's Spine range. A heavy white fog had crawled down out of the mountains and into the jungle, and it swallowed the base of the tower completely. The air was cold, and the companions' breath hung in little white clouds like the mist around them.

Something caught the prince's eye, "Lee, look."

He pointed into the distance over the gnarled canopy.

"Look there," he practically whispered, "The trees. They're alive."

Indeed, almost at the edge of their vision, just across a narrow passing of the Swordsong River, lush, green foliage glistened in the eventide light. It was the edge of The Quiets- their way home.

"Okay," Lee sounded hopeful, "If we can figure out how to get down off this tower…"

Krög was only half listening as she went on to reason through various ways they might scale the slick surface of the iron citadel. Something else was speaking to him. Something only he could hear.

"She will lead you to ruin."

The prince's eyes flitted about as he searched the steel columns around them for the source of the voice. He looked keenly for the phantom to appear.

"To keep her close, is to burn your world."

"You're wrong," the young ruler growled quietly.

"Well I'm not saying it's going to be easy, but work with me, we've got to try something," Lee said exasperatedly, unaware Krög was not talking to her.

"I must sever. Before all can be undone."

"Lee," the Battle Prince called softly to her, "We've got company."

Her head snapped up. Between veils of moonlight, the phantom floated down from the tip of one of the spires and hovered above the young woman and Krög. As it flitted between the silvery beams of the midnight sun, the black curtain would turn weirdly translucent. Beneath the folds of the sheet, they could see a skeletal human form with great, broad wings draped in pale feathers. Ever, though, they could not see beneath the hood of the sheet, and the skeletal phantom flew with purpose to keep its face from being shown.

"Well," she hissed, "Look who's back."

"You must never leave," it spoke to them both, *"One, or both, must stay."*

"Not a great deal," Krög replied, turning in circles to stay facing the phantom.

"I must keep all safe," it continued to spiral around the young ruler and the girl, *"I must prevent. I must sever."*

The Battle Prince drew his sword, "You weren't a big fan of getting nicked by this thing the first time- what do you say I run you all the way through?"

"Good moxie," Lee admonished.

"Thank you," Krög missed her sarcasm.

"I think it's *almost* considering being afraid," she followed.

"I could use your support here," the prince said over his shoulder at her.

"My apologies," Lee heaped on the snark, "Yeah! Do you know who you're up against?! He's the Battle Prince!"

"That was almost believable," Krög snorted.

"Battle Prince? Are you sure?"

"Why does everyone ask that?!" the young ruler grunted.

"Greater have fallen. I have seen laid low bodies of heaven. Pale ye in comparison."

"And yet I couldn't help but notice, you're not getting any closer," the Battle Prince pointed out.

It was true. The phantom was certainly keeping its distance, so long as Krög held Thundersteel at full brandish. There was no mistaking the creature was doing all it could to avoid the edge of his weapon, continuing to hover in circles around Lee and the prince, but never drawing any nearer.

"Look at you," she nudged the young ruler lightly with her shoulder, "Calling out the reaper. I might actually be a little impressed."

"I've got this thing by the spine," Krög growled, encouraged.

"Test me, and I will sever. Stand and deliver, and I will assure the deliverance of all."

"Whatever that means," the prince snorted.

The phantom halted its flight, and the young ruler again heard it speak in his head, to him alone.

"Leave her. I need take only one. Abandon damnation and I will give you salvation."

"Suck steel!" the prince roared.

At the same time, Lee barked simply, "No."

Both turned and fixed the other with a look of questioning, and simultaneously asked, "What did it say to you?"

Before they could reason through what the phantom had whispered privately in their minds, it rushed straight at them. Krög, stricken with panic, grabbed Lee and leapt headfirst over the edge of the tower. He barely had time to reflect on the incredible stupidity of his reflexes, as he could have just as easily attacked with the sword he was holding in his hand and sent the phantom racing away.

Instead, he chose to dive off the top of the citadel.

Brilliant.

Fortunately, the bizarre nature of the tower did not just extend to its inner reaches, but apparently the whole grounds around it. Krög and Lee fell for a space that felt like maybe dropping ten feet, before they slammed into the polished steel floor. Without explanation or reason, they were suddenly back inside the spire. Thundersteel broke loose from the prince's grasp and slid away towards the black curtains. He kept his grip on the young woman, however, and managed to take the hardest blow from the fall, cushioning her landing.

"*That* was the right time to be a hero," she complimented, "How did we get back in here?"

"No idea," Krög groaned, "This place… it's not going to let us go."

"Are you okay?" the lithe woman turned over and searched him for signs of distress.

"No idea," the prince repeated, "I don't think I broke anything."

"Can I ask you something?" she helped him sit up.

"We seem to have a quiet moment- go for it," the young ruler stretched his joints and gingerly shifted about, testing himself to see if anything hurt more than to be expected after a fall through, apparently, time and space.

"Why did over the edge of the tower seem like a good plan?" Lee asked the obvious, "And before you say anything, 'no idea' is not an acceptable answer."

Krög sighed, and threw up his hands, "I just reacted."

She smiled a little at him, "We've *got* to work on that. Blind damn Luck, once again, proves to be your best friend."

"Don't I know it," the prince grinned, "Hard to argue with the results, though."

"Come on, let's get you up," Lee stood and pulled Krög up as well, "We're in a little bit of a quandary here, and sitting in the middle of the room isn't going to get us anywhere."

As they clambered back to their feet, the chamber began to rumble and shake. Violently, all of the curtains ripped loose from their anchors and went spinning around the walls as they had before, accompanied by an even more terrible tempest gale. Voices screeched and moaned, keened and howled as the whole room shook ferociously and the storm of black snarled over the companions' heads. Like terrible birds of prey diving at their victims, the dark sheets came racing at the young ruler and the lithe girl, swooping back and forth, in and out of the cyclonic winds. Each loosed an eldritch scream on every pass, battering the ears and rattling the hearts of the living.

Krög and Lee held their ground. They had cowered and retreated the first time, but the act was less impressive on the second viewing. It just seemed like a lot of noise and commotion. The athletic young woman said as much.

"It's getting a little tired," she yelled over the cacophony of snapping sheets and wails, "Got any other tricks?!"

Like stones, all of the curtains dropped to the floor and the wind and noise ceased. From high above, one single sheet drifted lazily down, slipping this way and that as though caught on a fair summer breeze. It settled above the organ before snapping into a vaguely human shape and settling, once again, on an invisible seat in front of the keys.

"A nocturne."

The phantom began to ply the keys, and blast portentous notes around the chamber. Instead of vomiting forth a stream of dust and cobwebs as before, the pipes started to spit out the smokey, ghostly images of bones. As the spiraling tones of the organ rang out longer and longer, the bones started to arrange themselves into forms mirroring the phantom's moonlit appearance. They melded together into long, tall, skeletal beings flying on expansive pinions coursed with pale feathers. One by one, the smokey images dove into the mess of black sheets, each one rising up an exact reflection of the phantom until no less than twelve of the things hung in the air around Krög and Lee.

For a moment, the prince chewed his tongue, "That's new."

Every note the phantom played seemed to demand a steady, wraithlike dance out of the hovering ghosts. They twisted and spun with each throaty chord or piercing high, floating around and around the young woman and Krög as their macabre waltz grew more and more complicated.

"Cast out, we were, for being judges too harsh, executors too strict. We struck down the first keeper to come this way, and every other since. We sever so that all might continue to turn. Can you not see how we are noble? Can you not understand our cause?"

The ghosts started to tighten their ring around Lee and the young ruler, constricting their dance closer and closer to the companions.

"There is desolation before you. Ruin awaits your stride. Lay down and abandon. Separate that one might never drag the other to an unending end."

Krög found Lee's hand and squeezed it tightly as the deadly waltz turned inward, pressing ever nearer.

"That which is wound together shall fray, and assurance of destiny shall be shattered. Two paths, momentarily converged, assuredly to be rent asunder again, but not before the seeds of ruination are sewn. I see fire."

The ghosts were near enough every time they floated through a beam of moonlight, Krög could practically count the shimmering, eerie feathers draping from their boney wings. Every breath felt sharp with the chilling cold that shucked off the hovering menaces, every moment felt like a year.

It spoke directly in the prince's mind, for only him to hear.

"Can you not see what she hides? Do you not see the yoke around her neck?"

Rage and frustration erupted in Krög.

"I've heard enough!" the prince thundered, "You want to play it like this?! You may be the herald of death, but I have the Harpbinger of victory!"

Krög unslung the bowl-harp strapped tightly to his back and began to unleash its jangling, ethereal notes. He kept time with the phantom, matching the abyssal waltz with his own forbidding dirge. Silvery images started to leap off the magical strings of dragon's hair that ran the length of his harp, their shape taking the form of a protector to defend the prince and Lee.

A child, alone in the dark, calls out in fright when the nightmares of the black come too close- they call out for their first guardian, their first shield. So too, did Krög summon the bravest, strongest warrior he knew.

The young ruler's father, the Battle King, sprang into existence. He was as the prince remembered him from a bygone era: upright, broad and powerful. Shoulders like the crags of mountains, eyes of fire and carrying a scepter of lightning, Krög's father stepped out of the ghostly mist birthed from the prince's harp, and stood in challenge against the company of phantoms hovering around the chamber. The Battle King opened his bearded mouth and from his lips came a war cry like the sound of a cataract colliding with a rushing river. All twelve of the phantoms fell back from him.

Lee whispered to him, "Prince. Don't stop playing."

"Another who bore the onus. Another who might have severed the thread of oblivion. His end written, his days numbered."

"You really don't know my dad," Krög rumbled.

Obeying the march flying free from the prince's fingers, the Battle King took to action. With a mighty swing, the warrior lord lashed out with his scepter of lightning and burned one of the ghosts right out of the air. It vanished in a flash of silver light and a harrowing scream, and its tattered, smoldering sheet floated lightly to the ground, still smoking from the burst of electricity.

With devastating purpose in his movements, the image of the Battle King turned towards the next closest phantom. He advanced like a tumbling avalanche, the ghosts scattering before his might, but not so fast he was not able to blast two more apart. Their scorched curtains fell impotently to the floor alongside their fellow's, and the whole company of specters suddenly fell into disarray.

The phantom at the organ played with desperation and fury to keep his small army of wraiths from flying every which way. His doom-laden nocturne turned into an impassioned requiem as he called forth more and more of the angelic wraiths. Every time the Battle King slew one of the hovering phantoms, the notes from the organ would bear forth another set of bones that would rise back up under the shredded, burning sheets that littered the floor. Krög could feel his own fingers bleeding from the effort of continuing to play and concentrate with the kind of ardor needed to keep the image of the Battle King in the fight. His mind was totally focused on the greatest legends of his father he had ever heard. Still, as fast as the immaterial warrior lord could cut down the ghosts, they were just as quickly spewed back into the battle.

Lee looked around fiercely to try and find some way to get into the thick of things. In an instant she spied the Battle Prince's sword on the other side of the room, its glittering hilt peeking out from under the folds of a discarded curtain. She made a break for the weapon, determined to join the fray. The sea of specters in the air guessed at her purpose, and they descended on the girl like flies to carrion. Each that swooped at Lee met naught but air as she tucked, rolled, flipped, and dove past the hurtling ghosts. At last, she bounded twice, spun past a charging wraith, and her small hand closed around the jeweled hilt of Thundersteel. Lee brought it up from the floor and took to the fight, at the side of the Battle King, in defense of her prince.

Krög had never seen Thundersteel move so fast. Its brilliant edge cut through the air like sunlight glinting off falling drops of water- there in an instant, and gone just as quickly. Then, the prince had never seen the sword in the hands of anyone but a burly, brawny Battle King. In Lee's grip it moved like its very namesake, with the speed and power of lightning, crashing against every enemy in its flight like thunder. The young woman turned a heavy blade meant to be thrust and swung to cleave and skewer, into a paintbrush whose canvas was annihilation and whose pigments were death. As a ranger with a machete moves through the foliage, Lee hacked her way through the company of ghosts to the phantom at the organ.

Lee and the warrior lord moved in concourse, like a twisting typhoon, circling around Krög and staying one step ahead of the ghosts as they continued to dive from the rafters and sweep across the steel floor. The lightning scepter in the Battle King's hand tore them from the air, and Lee's indescribable swordplay cut them from their flight. Against it all, the backdrop to the melee was the whirling hum of the organ, and the lilting jangle of the bowl-harp, a veritable accompaniment to what had gone from a waltz of death to a masquerade of destruction. Bursts of electricity and flashes of iron slashed open the silver moonlight, as the mists and mires of truly eldritch magic surged out of the organ and billowed off the harp. It was a clash of titanic masterpiece.

"Me and mine are forever! We are infinite! Were there but a circumstance differing by a grain of sand, you would be at our side, championing our cause!"

"I don't play nice with demons and reapers!" Krög shouted over the din of the music, as sweat poured off his face from effort and concentration.

"Demons! You don't even know what we are, foolish one."

"I know enough!" the prince yelled back, "I know you tried to hurt me and Lee. You tried to talk me into leaving her behind to die by your hand!"

As he hollered at the phantom playing, the young ruler realized he had never opened his mouth, never took the necessary breath to roar at his spectral nemesis. Their argument was private, echoing within the halls of his own consciousness, and only there. As they quarreled, the image of the Battle King wavered and faltered just a moment as the young ruler's focus was challenged. The phantom never slowed in his relentless plying of the organ's keys, boney, skeletal fingers dancing along their ivory surface with the grace and dexterity of a more sinewy grasp. Krög grit his teeth and played on, ignoring the stinging under his grip as his digits split and tore against the sharp cables of dragon's hair.

"You cannot see where your paths lead. You are not privy to our cause. The scales of all creation hang in the balance! One grain must fall to one side, one grain must go to the other. Life and death. To remain together

is to tip the scale! You do not understand. You do not understand."

"I'm not about to let some black-robed reaper that plays a mean piano talk me into abandoning someone I care about," Krög's voice rumbled in his head in reply, "Take your foul babble to a weaker mind, you devil."

"Devil! Demon! He calls us names without understanding. He does not know. We are not from below!"

Perhaps sensing the prince's struggle, Lee threw her gaze around the chamber in search of a way to expediently end the exhaustive battle. Her eyes settled on the phantom and the organ he played, and she decided in an instant what had to be done. Before Krög could object and stop her from tangling with the embodiment of death itself, the lithe, athletic woman sprinted across the room towards the musical wraith. Specters and ghosts swooped and dove at her from every direction, and not even the ethereal image of the Battle King could not keep pace enough to stop them all. Lee had things well in hand, however. She lilted and pinwheeled past them all, and leapt and spun over and under the charging wraiths, cutting them down if they dared interrupt her dash towards the phantom.

"We came from above!"

In a blinding white flash, the phantom rose up and whipped around to face Krög, its appearance suddenly drastically different. A blast of wind shattered the other ghosts apart, knocked Lee to the ground, twisted the pipes of the organ, and sent the prince careening across the chamber. His bowl-harp flew from his hands, and the misty image of the Battle King dissipated like impressions in the sand under a sweeping wave. The being floated to the center of the room, arms and wings spread resplendently.

Krög saw it for what it really was. It was pure and beautiful. Gazing upon it filled him with hope and quieted every fear he had ever held. It was a beacon, a light in the dark. And yet it was cursed. Gilded chains hung from its wrists and shackled it to the tower, forged from decisions it had made that were beyond reproach-yet perhaps justified. It was bound to the citadel for the things it had done, imprisoned for the lives it had claimed, yet it had done so thinking it acted for a cause greater than its own existence. Littered about the floor were a dozen others like it, their own chains linked to the pipes of the organ, ready to be called forth if the one they had followed so resolutely called them.

"The wheels turn. The stars align. I might have stopped, but again I have failed. Tears I will shed for you, mortal, long will I weep. No matter to desolation or to triumph..."

It raced towards Krög, hand outstretched, grasping for him. Lee swung Thundersteel from where she lay with the kind of emotion that coaxed the true nature of the blade from its hiding. A white-hot, crackling bolt of lightning split the roof of the citadel and shot into the chamber. Onyx shards of polished steel followed the bolt on its terrible trajectory, a black rain around the searing cable of the heaven's wrath. It hurtled towards the phantom, and just before colliding, the being paused in front of the Battle Prince and spoke its last words to him in a low whisper.

"Your path will be lonely."

The instant before the lightning bolt connected, the phantom's face emerged from the folds of its sheets. Whether it was some spectral version of her from another time and another place, or whether the wraith was trying to pass on some final message to Krög, the face of the being looked like Lee. And then, as the lightning split through the phantom, her face gave way to a leering skull, sockets empty and hollow, devoid of life. When the bolt disappeared, so did the phantom. The chamber was still. It was quiet.

Krög wondered how much of what he had seen and heard Lee had as well. He wondered if she had been locked in a private conversation with the specter, or if she had seen it momentarily bear her face. He wondered if she had seen in it in all its beauty, all its purity and glory. Certainly she never would have destroyed such a radiant and wonderful being, but then certainly she never would allow anything to bring harm to the prince. Who knows what she saw, what she heard, what she experienced. Even the young ruler was starting to doubt what he had seen, heard and experienced in his own right. In the hanging hush, every thought that raced through his mind was both at once the absolute truth as much as it was the reverberations of a dream.

He gave such thoughts and considerations the span of time it takes for a viper to strike, before dismissing them in favor of being close to the girl. Both hurried across the iron chamber to the other and collapsed in embrace. Krög's mind went blank the moment he felt her familiar weight against his chest and he wondered what it was he was wondering about in the first place. All he was aware of, was Lee. The young ruler clung to her just as tightly as she did to him, the silence only broken by the thunderous clamoring of their hearts and the ragged breaths they took. For time infinite, or for only moments, the machinations of the universe came to a shuddering pause, time and space peeled away, and they were totally alone together in the bowels of the iron citadel.

Without realizing he had squeezed them shut in the first place, the prince cracked his eyes open and looked around. The tower was gone. He and Lee were still in The Dark, but in a clearing. Around them, the bent, gnarled trees were twisted together in a veritable rampart of knotted branches, though it did not feel like they were trying to keep the young ruler and the girl in- but rather the rest of the forest out. Even the eerie fog had receded from the glade they were in, and the clouds overhead parted just enough to allow the faintest starlight through. It felt like an out of place sanctuary in the middle of the haunted realm... and there was little wonder as to why.

A short distance from where Krög and Lee were huddled, rising proudly and stridently where the tower had been, was a small, stone monument. It was a simple obelisk, no more than waist height, overgrown with vines and lichen, but its markings were just as clear as ever. At the base it read "Rözar: The Explorer," a name the prince knew well from his lessons. Above the epithet was the guardian reaper: the skull, crown and shield of the Southern Reach. Emblem of the Battle Kings.

Krög shook the athletic young woman, "Lee. Look."

She still had her head buried in his chest, but cautiously pulled away, "Where are we?"

"The Dark, still," the prince said reverently, "But we're safe. This place belongs to *him*."

When she spotted the headstone, Lee tried to push away, "Prince, that is a grave."

"Relax," he replied, softly, "That's Rözar. The second Battle King. I think this place," the prince glanced around at the sedate clearing, "It's *his* territory."

"So, the phantom... was it...?" she questioned whether they had just done battle with one of the young ruler's ancient forefathers.

"No," Krög dismissed, "I think that thing killed Rözar. It mentioned slaying the first born son of a great warlord. Rözar was Röm, the First Battle King's heir. I think that wraith was imprisoned in the citadel for mistaking him and his barbarians for someone else, and destroying them."

"Why would he be all the way out here in the first place?" Lee was still clearly uncomfortable with the sight of the headstone.

The prince shrugged, "Rözar was supposed to be a wanderer. According to his legend, when the time came for him to surrender the throne, he just vanished east one morning with the rising sun and was never seen again. It looks like this is where he met his end."

"He died in the dark," her voice was forlorn.

"Yeah," Krög agreed quietly, "But we didn't."

"Prince," Lee tugged at his shirt, "Will you take me home now?"

"Of course I will," he gently pulled both of them to a stand.

Whether they were in the same place the iron citadel had been, or had been magically flung somewhere else by a power unseen, neither was rightly sure. For all they had been through and for all they had bore witness, it easily could have been both- or neither. Somehow though, it did not take them long to locate Krög's bowl-harp, Harpbinger, lying in the brambles a short distance from where they had been curled up together. He slung it over his shoulder as Lee walked over to retrieve Thundersteel. The sword had fallen, appropriately enough, across Rözar's grave. She was careful not to step directly over where the fallen Battle King was likely stretched in his eternal rest, and quickly grabbed the blade to return it to the prince. Krög lightly brushed the dirt and leaves off it, and slid the weapon into its sheath on his back. Both were ready to be relieved of The Dark.

Lee took the prince's hand, and they strode evenly towards the boundary of twisted branches that held the clearing as sovereign ground to the Battle King at rest there. For a moment, both looked confused at the impenetrable wall of branches, and wondered just how they were going to get free from the clearing.

Krög naturally tried something declamatory and ridiculous.

"Part!" he commanded, "By order of the Thirteenth Son of Röm."

Lee snickered, "You didn't actually think-"

She was cut off when, with a heavy groan and the creaking of a thousand ancient doors, the branches drew apart, and a path through the brambles ahead appeared.

The prince smiled, "Every once in a while, the family name gets you something."

"However it is you are so damn lucky, I want you to share that with me," the lithe girl chuckled.

"Are you saying you want to get lucky?" Krög raised his eyebrows at her.

"Not until you get a girl home safe, barbarian," she elbowed him, "You have to drop me off at my door before I can invite you to come inside."

The prince laughed, "Alright, alright. Come on, let's go."

Gingerly at first, but with greater confidence with each step, the two companions stepped across the threshold of brambles and back into the haunted blight. Krög looked over his shoulder expectantly as they left the clearing, waiting to see the trees tighten back together and close off the mausoleum once again. He was surprised when they stayed open, as though inviting his return- or perhaps in waiting for someone else lost to take refuge in the care of the fallen Battle King. Again, the young ruler wondered if the iron citadel had sprung up around the gravesite, or if after the phantom had been defeated, he and Lee had somehow been spirited away to the deceased warrior lord's tomb. It was, perhaps, one of the many mysteries of the dark forest that had little explanation, and required even less. All that really mattered, was they were free of the clutches of the tower.

The moon cut through a break in the limbs above, and illuminated the only path the prince had ever seen in The Dark. Granted, he had only been there once before, but he never remembered ever seeing the forest floor there- always it was heaped in briars and fog. Yet, as they retreated from the glade, a faint but unmistakable way through the blight sprung up in front of the young ruler. He tread carefully, determined to stay in the narrow beam of light being cast down by the sky above, not daring to take one step out of its luminescence.

"Do you remember where to go?" Lee asked over his shoulder.

"What?" Krög had gotten lost in his thoughts.

"On the tower," she reminded him, "You said you could see the way back, where the trees were alive. Do you remember how to get there?"

"Oh, right," the young ruler had forgotten about the near magnificent view of the world from the heights of the citadel, "I'm pretty sure. I think this is the path that Rözar took when he came this way."

"What makes you think that?" Lee queried.

"Because like the clearing, it still belongs to him," Krög then pointed out, "Nothing's bothering us."

It was true. Distantly, they could still hear the terrible noises The Dark made: the creeping of monsters innumerable and the howling of ghosts unimaginable. Far at the edge of their vision they could see the shadows move, bouncing lights of damnation darting between tree trunks, and the crushing black that swallowed the light of the stars and moon. Around them, however, the forest held back. It kept its distance. It reared its ugly as though afraid to come any closer to the descendant of the Battle King who had once tamed its wilds- even if that king had eventually fallen to one of its denizens. While they were a long way from feeling safe, Krög and Lee did at least feel a bit more at ease as they made their way through The Dark.

With no voices to interrupt them, and perhaps to talk over the sound of their own receding fears, the prince and the young woman made idle, if somewhat forced, chit chat to pass the time as they escaped the blight.

"So, any plans tomorrow?" Lee asked, wrapping herself around Krög's arm.

"I'm probably going to have to clean up the Great Hall," the prince grumbled, "Dad gets home soon, and he will find nine ways to skin me if the place is a mess when he does."

"How exciting the life you lead, Battle Prince," Lee giggled.

"Ugh, honestly," Krög carped, "I should be out slaying dragons or leading the barbarians into battle somewhere. It's not fair."

She laughed out loud, "You are just the worst of both worlds, you know that? You look ten years old than you are, and then you open your mouth and you sound ten years younger. Honestly, how old are you?"

"As of two weeks ago, twenty five," he replied a little dejectedly.

"Wait, really?" Lee asked excitedly, "Did the prince have a birthday and not tell anyone about it?!"

"It kind of got forgotten about with all the celebration over Iolar's victory," the prince complained, "That guy…"

"Why didn't you say something?" Lee slapped his chest, smiling broadly, "I'd have thrown you a party- even if it was just a private one. Maybe even especially so."

Krög cracked a grin, but sighed through his nose, "Eh, I didn't think anyone really cared."

"Well I do," she assured him, "That's an important day! Tell me the next time it happens."

He chuckled, "It happens the same time every year- right on the precipice of autumn, at the tail end of summer."

"Poetic," Lee snorted, "How about a date I can write down, Master Bard?"

"Start of the ninth month," the prince chuckled, "We're usually not specific on exact days around here."

She smiled and leaned against him, "We'll call it the first just to be safe. But, for the record, twenty-five? Start acting your age."

"You're not the first person to say that to me lately," Krög rolled his eyes.

"You know what they say about the third time some one calls you a horse, right?" the girl came back.

"Yeah, yeah, I got it," he snorted.

"Okay, so, chores tomorrow," Lee went on, "That decidedly sounds not fun. How could I possibly make things more interesting?"

The prince laughed, but lightly rebuked her, "I think maybe I should actually, you know, act my age tomorrow.   The Hall needs to be ready for Ydal's departure ceremony- apparently there has to be a ceremony every time she does anything."

"Well, whatever it takes to hurry her along," Lee said brightly.

"Yeah, and rumor has it Scale is going with her," the young ruler added, "Something about making him the first dragon of the Empire Court."

The lithe girl sighed contentedly, "I am going to feel so much safer without that little twerp around."

"You and me both," Krög agreed, "I don't know what I did to get on his bad side, but he has been extra ornery around me ever since the body swapping incident."

"Well it did leave a slightly unpleasant taste in some of our mouths," Lee reminded him, "Almost literally in some cases.   And I think he's irked he inherited a few of my memories of you even after he got put back."

"What memories?" the prince asked sharply.

"Ones you would probably turn a number of hilarious colors if you knew he knew about," she giggled.

"Oh, great, wonderful," the young ruler scoffed, "That makes sense why he said what he did about... you know what, never mind.   I don't want to revisit that conversation."

"Awe, princey-poo," Lee was mockingly patronizing, "Did the mean little dragon say bad things to you? How can I make you feel better?"

"*Now* who's acting their age?" he retorted.

She laughed out loud, "That was a remarkably heads-up comeback, prince. You're getting sharper."

"Just trying to keep up," he admitted sheepishly.

"With me? Never," she popped her eyebrows at him, "It's sweet that you try, though."

"Thank the gods," the prince's voice was suddenly flush with relief, "We're out."

Around them, the trees were tall and straight, their limbs blooming with greenery, and the sinister mist had all but completely been swept away by a chilly, early autumn wind. The night was cold, but not menacingly so, and the forest was quiet, though not ominously. There was a supreme serenity, an impenetrable tranquil that bathed the underbrush in a drizzle of placidity. High above, among the canopy of the great arbors, the prince could hear the branches whispering to one another, telling tales of ages long past and singing quiet songs to the stars. They had, at last, reached The Quiets.

Krög had no idea when it happened. He did not remember the tree-line suddenly giving way, or the path suddenly widening. Just as mysteriously as one wanders into The Dark, so too do they emerge from it. It was a place one could stumble into without knowing how, or when or why- only that they suddenly were surrounded by the bleak and the blight. Their path out was not clear, but somehow with his head up and resolution in his soul, he had found the other side. Without heralding and without any declaration, the two were simply safe again. Krög wondered, if he should ever accidentally end up on the wrong side of that tree-line again, if he would be as equally able to find his way through. Then, The Dark was different every time you went in. All he could hope were the principles of escape were the same.

The prince resolved not to test fate, and simply avoid the situation altogether were it in his power.

Together, Krög and Lee had little trouble finding their way back through the silent realm of the mighty Thorn Rift Forest, and in very little time broke out of the barbed jungle entirely, and onto the rolling fields at its edge. There was no hurried, spirited sprint over the low hills and through the tall grasses that night. Both were far too exhausted, and it took all they had just to keep their legs moving back towards the watch towers of the Fortress City.

Ganithen rose up in the distance, small at first, like a ring of candles calling them home. With each step, it grew larger and larger, its stoney parapets lit brightly by the sentinel fires that were kept burning all night by the evening guard. Silhouetted against the dim, burgundy glow of the eternally smoldering Scorched Hill, it might have been a terrifying thing to come on in the night to those who dared challenge the resolve of its immense walls and iron-clad peoples. Instead, it was a warm glow on a chilly night that promised somewhere safe to sleep-somewhere to escape the creeping nightmares of the world beyond the Great Hall. It was with utter solace the prince took in the sight of the home fires, and he very nearly collapsed there on the prairies outside the gates, relieved enough just to be within reach of home.

The night guards said nothing when Krög hailed them to open the portal and let him back into the city, despite the ungodly hour. They smiled knowingly at him when the young ruler came slinking back with Lee in tow, and chuckled softly amongst themselves. Krög knew he would owe them all a big favor in the morning to pay for their silence, but he was more than glad to pay the penance to keep his ill-fated afternoon a total secret from his father. For the most part, the city guard were an agreeable lot, and if the prince could manage to secure them a few barrels of his uncle's Trollkiller Ale, he felt assured of their cooperation. And he felt just assured his uncle would be willing accomplice too- Gögan was, as of late, Krög's greatest confederate, and all too often his most inappropriate enabler.

Protected from the hedging autumn winds by the enormous walls of the Fortress City, the streets within were still. Most of the municipality had long gone to sleep. Barbarians were early risers, that they might accomplish the harshest of the day's tasks before the heat of the day came to full bear. There was relatively little effort required, then, for Lee and the prince to sneak back to the Great Hall. The young ruler decided against bothering the door-keepers to spur the oxen and open the main entrance into his father's throne room. He was indebted enough to the tower watch, and there was no need to make the excessive noise that went along with having a team of pack animals jerk a chain rigging to drag the portal ajar. Not when there were perfectly good secret side entrances and hidden escape tunnels they could make use of.

With little more than a half extinguished torch to light the passages, Krög and Lee crept into the Great Hall as silently as they could manage and, with no small amount of consolation, soon found themselves looking on the titanic hearths of the throne room. Wisps of blue smoke slithered up from beds of nearly dead coals, giving the long chamber a pleasant scent of charred wood and roasted meat. The prince realized how hungry he was, having quite missed dinner, and wondered if anyone had left anything lying around that was still passably edible. Before he could even fathom whether his pride and lax sense of decorum and convention would abide scrounging for leftovers, exhaustion won out the battle and he resolved there would be an extra big breakfast come morning. He felt lucky his legs managed to carry him even so far as his own room.

Lee slipped in with him, and the two sank deep into the bedding of furs. Krög winced when he realized he had been so tired he had forgotten to strip off his weapons, and the two chuckled as they relieved themselves of their heavier clothes and belts, and settled again. The prince leaned his head slowly against a pillow, letting its embrace wrap around his ears and neck. Favoring his chest over any cushion, the young woman nuzzled against Krög, her eyelashes brushing lightly against his skin with each lengthening blink as sleep took hold. He took a deep breath, and watched her fair hair rise and fall as he let it back out.

"Lee, can I ask you something?" the young ruler inquired quietly.

"You just did," she yawned, "Goodnight."

Krög sighed, "I need to ask you something else."

Lee groaned and rolled over on top of him so they were facing each other, "Neither you or the dragon fall for that. What's on your mind?"

"The phantom," the prince began, "What did it say to you?"

"Do we *have* to talk about that?" she balked, "Can't we just pretend this whole night basically never happened? I'm more on board with that."

"What did it say?" Krög repeated.

"You mean other than a lot of confusing things about how my flame would burn bright but short, and that *you* were the bringer of chaos?" she asked, her trademark snark finding its way into her speech despite how tired she was.

"It actually said that about me?" the prince did not know whether to be afraid or complimented.

"In *so* many words," Lee sounded bored, "Can I go to sleep now?"

"It said something else," the prince sussed, "I *know* it did."

"Well it tried awfully hard to get me to leave you behind- made a lot of noise about letting me go if I abandoned you forever," she went on, rolling over again to try and get comfortable.

"It told me something similar," Krög recalled, and was at once somewhat disappointed and more settled, "I guess it was just trying to play us against each other."

"Typical hell-spawn," Lee said sleepily, "Leave it to you to have family members who have managed to slight every specter from here to the abyss."

"So that's it?" the prince queried at the last, before concluding, "It was saying the same thing to both of us. It just wanted... death, I guess."

For a long while, neither said anything, and Krög largely assumed Lee had finally given over to slumber after his rather ominous assessment. He was just about to fall asleep himself when he felt her swallow hard a few times and rustle against him.

"It knew why I'm here," she said simply.

Krög abruptly opened his eyes, "What do you mean?"

"It said, 'it isn't safe,' and told me I didn't run far enough," Lee went on, her voice shaking slightly.

The prince felt his blood run cold, "*What* isn't safe? I don't understand."

She sat up and faced him. In the low light of the dying candle at the young ruler's bedside, infinite sadness and terrible helplessness were reflected in the girl's crystalline eyes.

Her voice raspy, Lee said, "Prince- I didn't find you by accident."

Krög's eyes narrowed, "Your mission."

They had not discussed it in some time- Lee had always been dodgy on the topic, and Krög had eventually just stopped bringing it up.

She nodded, "But, I'm not what you think I am."

"You come from an assassin guild in the Eastern Collective," he began.

"I came from one, yes," she cut him off, "But I wasn't one of them. I'm not here *looking* for something. I'm here to keep something *hidden*."

"What?" he asked quietly.

"I can't tell you," Lee's voice was torn with anguish.

"Didn't we talk about you being less mysterious?" Krög tried to lighten the mood.

"I can't," she shook her head, "I'm sorry. I can't. You just have to trust me. No one can know. But that phantom did. It looked into me, and it knew, and it told me…" Lee's voice faded for a moment, "Where else was I supposed to go? Everyone knows the strongest heroes come from the badlands south of the Swordsong. Where else was I going to be safe?"

The prince pulled back from her a bit, "So all of this… you and me?"

She smiled at him, "Well that part was kind of unplanned. I didn't exactly count on running into the Battle Prince himself."

"But you just need me because…" Krög was almost broken-hearted at the prospect of being falsely courted for his family's influence and power.

"No," Lee sensed his confusion and immediately pulled the young ruler closer, "No, it's not like that. I needed somewhere I could disappear, where no one would dare come after me. I was looking for a barbarian- a champion. Who would have guessed I would fall in with the son of the king, and he would happen to be charming and good and maybe a little stupid but also noble and strong… in his own way."

The prince cautioned a smile, "Do you really mean all that?"

"I do," she squeezed him a little tighter, "Of course I do."

"But you can't tell me what you're here protecting?" Krög sighed.

"No," she said, "You're better off *not* knowing."

"Lee…" the young ruler was yet discontented, and he felt like his trust had been strained dramatically.

In the candlelight, she fixed him with a look of vulnerability and defenselessness he had never seen in the young woman's eyes. There was a plea for faith in her gaze, an appeal for steadfast understanding in the face of truly perplexing and nebulous circumstances. Lee was not asking him for protection by the glow of the wick- only for compassion and quietude.

The prince immediately relented, "I swear to you, my kingdom is your shield and I will be your sword."

She laughed, "Oh, stupid prince. Honestly, where do you come up with these things? Your poetry is lousy."

Krög rolled his eyes, "At least you're smiling again."

"Well," Lee lay back against him, "You have yourself to thank for that. I guess I'll keep you around."

The prince snickered, "How fortunate for me."

"Damn right," she giggled, "Once again, prince, Blind Luck finds itself a truly dubious bedfellow in you."

"Do I at least get credit for figuring out how to fight off an army of ghosts with my magic harp?" he paused, "There's a sentence I never thought I'd say."

Lee laughed loudly, "Only you would ask for accolades for something so truly ridiculous. Fine," she gave in, "I'll give you that one. All my lessons on fighting go to waste on the Battle Prince that figures out how to use music to knock down a bunch of specters."

"The Bard of War strikes again," the young ruler said proudly.

"Hey, Bard of War, how about you sing a girl a song?" she requested.

It was Krög's turn to smile, "What do you want to hear?"

"The first night we met," she replied, "Sing me that song. You remember?"

"Yeah," he said distantly, "I remember," the prince was too tired to really sing the song, but he did hum the verse and recite it softly to the young woman resting on his chest, "In ashen skies o'er windy plains, we hold tall through bitter rain. As the weight of years breaks on my brow, I will hold true should fate allow. Should it take a thousand lives, if I must cross the star's divide, if I must die and be born anew, I will come to walk with you."

Lee breathed out as the prince finished the verse, "I like that song. Sing it again."

He did. As he did, he felt her breathing slow and her body relax as it released tensions and worries she maybe did not even realize she was carrying so tightly. All of her fell against him.

"Thanks, prince," her voice was barely audible as sleep at last swept the young woman away.

Krög kissed her forehead, "Goodnight, Lèanbh."

At last, the prince closed his eyes. On the other side of the stone walls of his room, he could hear the breeze whistle past a high-set, open window somewhere.

Long tendrils of chill air slipped between the bricks of his chamber, and lightly graced themselves across the young ruler's skin. He shivered slightly, and pulled a blanket and the lithe girl a little closer. There was winter on the back of the wind, and there was frost on its breath. The shadow of the season of ice had already been cast, and autumn was her coachmen. Krög and Lee lay together, alone in the dark, as the final, waning days of summer came to a close.

Krög and his friends will return in:

**The Mythical, Mystical, Magnificent Adventures of...
Krög, The Battle Prince
Volume 3- The Shadow of Winter's Pall**

Read on for a preview as our hesitant hero and his band of motley miscreants come face to face with a dark secret hidden in the icy peaks of the Dragon's Spine Mountains, at the edge of the terrible empire, the Eastern Collective...

The Third Tale: The Quest for Winter's Blade

Autumn had always been the prince's favorite season. It stirred in him a sense of deep restlessness and feral energy, and it began with the first cool day of the year. Fall descended on the Southern Reach like a sweeping wind, driving the heat of the summer away and settling low a frosty air that promised shorter days and coming snowfall. Crisp breezes were accompanied by crackling leaves and welcoming bonfires at night, and the whole of Krög's kingdom prepared for the harvest festivals. Most considered spring the season of new beginnings, but to the prince it had always been autumn.

Traditionally the Battle King went on a three month tour of his villages during that time, serving as a Grand Marshall to the fairs and festivities of the towns, and taking time to survey his countryside. Perhaps as part of his continued effort to thrust responsibility on his son, the king offered the chance to Krög to be his stead- an opportunity the prince jumped at. The last time the young ruler had occasioned to strike out into the badlands was during his odd manner of victory over the dragon Raicleach, and the prince was seasonably fitful to add to his usual wandering anxiety.

As it was, there was even more cause for celebration that fall, with a great homecoming soirée still underway to welcome back the returning barbarians who had swept the Ivory City of Fanfarra clean of Mordenall's corsairs over the summer. Against his objections, Krög had not been allowed to take part in the campaign. Still, on his recommendation Captain Iolar and a few squadrons of his Griffin Riders had been sent late in the conflict, and brought about a considerable route. While the leader of the marauders had once again managed to evade capture or death, his numbers were broken, and the few surviving pirates were seen racing eastward towards the mountain pass of the Eastern Collective. Despite Mordenall's escape, the Riders had been victorious and Krög was ecstatic his uncle would be returning to the Great Hall for a short time when the last squadron returned from the front.

Much to the prince's relief, Merchant Lord Bęrun was so grateful for the Battle King's assistance in taking back the Ivory City, the aged miser relented in his insistence on a marriage between their kingdoms. Instead, he signed treaties that guaranteed trade in exchange for the Southern Reach's continued protection. No sooner were the documents penned did Ydal return to the Northern Empire, thankful herself to be out of the rugged barbarian nation and more than a little eased she would not be bound to the badlands. Scale accompanied her, having become quite taken with being back in a position of authority- if only as a devil on the Lady's shoulder. While the prince was glad to be rid of the little monster's revolting appetite and tales of grotesque idiosyncrasies, Krög did find he missed the dragon a bit… for the occasional laugh anyway.

Ydal, however, the prince did not miss. After the confrontation with Raicleach she only became more exhaustingly demanding, and though Krög had no direct evidence of it he was fairly certain the Lady had bedded a

Griffin Rider on their last night in Brokus. Possibly several. The prince had no room to be judgmental, but it was a vindication the two of them had absolutely no business in a betrothal except for *business*. Their farewell was polite but curt, and Krög gave very little thought to the princess afterwards, save the occasional reflection on the adventure that had lead him to his companions in the first place.

While he was practically busting to become First Dragon of the Empire Court, Scale did make a bit of a scene when leaving the Southern Reach. At first his incredibly lordly goodbye was all pomp, circumstance, and arrogance, but the diminutive monster actually burst into tears, sobbing uncontrollably when Krög removed him for his shoulder for the last time. He went so far as to present the prince with his prized helmet made from the tiny ox's skull as a remembrance. Krög had a blacksmith mount it on a chain and wore it around his neck as a pendant, somewhat out of affectation, and somewhat because he had one or two fond memories of Scale.

Lace Durington of Fanfarra's Point Guard came down to the Great Hall of Ganithen himself to fetch Ydal and her pet. As Krög predicted, the Captain and the Battle King got on swimmingly, or however one would phrase the bond shared by fellow iron men. The prince was pleased himself to see Captain Durington again, and the two spent some time polishing Krög's combat skills. While the spear was Lace's favored weapon, he was no stranger with a sword and he managed to considerably expand the prince's abilities in a very short time.

After his embarrassing showing against Iolar, Krög had returned to War School of his own accord, more focused this time. He challenged anyone willing to spar with the Battle King's son and learned to overcome his hesitation to action. Mechanics and fundamentals that had been taught to him as a child, but neglected during his years studying tactics and politics, came flooding back when put to practice. His father had officially handed Thundersteel down to Krög, now that he had discovered how to unlock its power, and the prince vowed to learn its handling better than any before him.

Krög's favorite opponent was Lee, mostly because she never let him win, but also because her own depth of knowledge was astonishing. More than anything, she taught him to improvise in a fight and turn a shortcoming into a situational advantage. The prince's over-awareness of his surroundings, which caused him to take pause planning in battle, Lee shaped into adaptivity, allowing Krög to begin holding off several opponents at once. She even taught him to use two weapons at the same time, balancing the defenses of one with the strikes of another. And while Krög was nowhere near as fast and agile as she was, Lee developed a certain nimbleness in his less graceful barbarian fighting style.

She and the prince were fast falling to a place whispered about in song. While for much of the summer Krög had to carry off the masquerade of courting the Lady Ydal, Lee always managed to steal moments with him alone. Whether on long walks through the fields outside the Fortress City, during crimson sunsets on the Scorched Hill, or finding new creative ways to sneak into his room at night- if she could create a secret moment for the two to share, she did. When Krög invited her to accompany him on his goodwill march through the Southern Reach, Lee could barely contain her exuberance.

The prince's other constant companion was his stalwart and earnest Honor Guard. After the fighting men of Ganithen heard of Ashley's slaying of a Wild Dragon by turning it inside out singlehandedly, they took to Krög's suggested nickname with ferocity. Ash became known as The Hammer of the Southern Reach in no time, and most of the soldiers of the homestead just called him Hammer. His first war-sledge, Very Convincing Argument, was hung in the Great Hall in a place of honor among a small handful of other legendary weapons wielded by shield warriors past. Though he was commissioned a new one, the troll had mostly gone back to using his bizarre, gnarled club Really Big Words. Despite his affectation for the rugged, frontier weapon, the troll was never seen publicly without his glinting Honor Guard armor, which he never had finished. Ash insisted the lack of the right arm gave him better movement when swinging his weapon.

He was by Krög's side almost every minute of every day. If not teaching the prince how to be a fiercer warrior, then Ashley was sharing his boundless wisdom as the two took extended marches through The Quiets of the Thorn Rift Forest. Ash saw the world in simpler terms than the young ruler, but not in a manner that was any less insightful. Even more so, perhaps. The troll was far more even tempered, largely unhindered by Krög's questioning, indecisive consciousness, and there was a steady, resolute nature about Ashley's ways that the prince did all he could to emulate. At his behest, but to the delight of Krög, Ash also taught him how to curse in Giant Speak, which had started out in an honest lesson on the proper pronunciation of the troll's real name.

Ashley was quite astute to the secret courting being carried out between Krög and Lee. Though it likely went against every fiber of duty in the enormous shield knight's being, he would find ways to maneuver the two alone- or cover for the prince when he would disappear with the girl. In truth, Ash cared deeply for her as well, though more as a guardian to a child... even though she did not particularly need protecting. The two together were the best companions Krög had ever had in his years.

In accordance with his station, the troll also insisted on accompanying the prince on his countryside tour, though Krög would have had it no other way. Taking Ashley anywhere in the Southern Reach was a bit like bringing a hyena to a garden party; chances were good it was completely unnecessary, but the prince still liked the funny looks he got going everywhere with the troll. However, the more Ash's mythology spread through the countryside, the more he became a welcome guest wherever Krög went. And on the rare occasion the prince found himself in a tight space, no one could clear a path faster than Ashley could.

Krög himself was becoming quite the showpiece as of late, thanks to the magic melodies of his bowl-harp: Harpbinger. While met with a great deal of objection from the Battle King, the prince had taken to calling himself the Bard of War pretty much all of the time. He retold stories of his adventures with a maverick troll guardian and spritely assassin emissary to captive audiences that were totally enraptured by the floating images produced by the instrument. He could not wait to visit some of the other villages in the badlands to regale the peoples there as well, and stun them to disbelief as he plucked the silver dragon's hair strings.

For the first time in recent memory, the prince felt at ease, even carefree. While his wanderlust tugged ever at his considerations, Krög at least had Lee and Ash to keep either him grounded, or spirit him away from the Fortress City for a time when needed. Though he longed for another grand adventure in the wilds of the Southern Reach, the prince was temporarily content to be at the Battle King's side enjoying a little more autonomy than he had previously been afforded. His father still closely monitored the young ruler's development, but had at last begun to allow Krög the freedom to choose some of his own paths. Maybe the old man realized the tighter he held the prince's leash, the more his son acted out, and maybe he was at last beginning to trust the prince's judgement to find his way. However it fell in Bröghue's mind, he gradually accepted Krög's reckless, hair-brained, and too often bumbling ways still managed to end in haphazard victory, and certainly concluded the young ruler's timid hesitation could only be solved by allowing him to take action of his own accord.

In return, the prince did his best to rein in his cynicism about taking the throne one day and act, at the very least, honored to be doing so… if not enthusiastic. Truthfully, this had been quite a bit easier for Krög after the weight of his betrothal had been lifted, and while he did sulk quite a bit over being left out of the Fanfarra campaign, he did eventually admit it was better handled by those with more experience. While he still had not come to feel the call of destiny that the Battle King assured him would lead him properly to the crown one day, Krög knew the understanding between him and his father was largely dependent on showing some degree of interest in his birthright.

It was happy coincidence then the prince's new assignment was less a pulse-raising quest against some terrible foe, and more a good long wander. In many ways it satisfied the best in both father and son, giving Krög a chance to spend time in the kingdom he was to inherit on his own, and do so without the constant threat of grisly death hanging over his and his companion's heads. Granted, the Battle King would have appreciated the same level of gusto from the prince when he had handed down his previous missions, but seeing Krög energetic about anything at all was a suitable change of pace for Bröghue.

Soon the western winds carried with them the sharp chill of the creeping mountain air, and the leaves of the trees made their gradual change from green to all manner of orange, red and brown. As the blooms fell from the mighty tree the Battle King's throne was carved in to, Bröghue allowed them to carpet the floors of his Great Hall, and the crunch of them beneath boots treads released the scent of autumn intermingled with hearth fire smoke. Days grew shorter and shorter, and Krög felt the stirring ache to be running wild.

A few nights before he was to set forth, Krög snuck out of Ganithen to meet with Lee atop the Scorched Hill. While the Battle King had given the young ruler his blessing to continue to court Lee as future Lady of the Hall, Bröghue had stopped short of announcing the change in suitors to his Council of Elders and had yet forbidden Krög from revealing it as well. So, the two continued to rendezvous in secret. The Battle Prince actually enjoyed the privacy of it, finding it allowed him and the girl more candor than having to maintain a certain gallant dignity among the municipalities of the Fortress City. While there was nothing especially sordid or bawdy about how they carried on (for the most part), Krög laughed a little easier and found himself to be more relaxed when he had Lee alone.

The Scorched Hill had quickly become her favorite spot to meet, as it was yet one of the places she could still walk around without boots. As colder weather gradually breathed into the lowlands and everyone was forced to change into heavier clothing, the burning earth under the charred knoll afforded Lee an increasingly rare opportunity to go barefoot. It became their little tradition for her to leave her boots at the bottom of the hill, and Krög to leave his sword with them. As they returned to the walls of the city, each would retrieve their possessions to go about assuming the roles expected.

At the top of the hill, the prince spread out his cloak and the two lay down on it, Lee fiddling idly with the skull necklace Krög had made out of Scale's helmet.

"I cannot believe you actually wear this stupid thing," she joked.

"The little guy was so broken up over leaving," the prince laughed, "It felt like the right thing to do."

"Ugh, I'm just glad that putrid little critter is gone," Lee scoffed.

"Oh come on now, he wasn't *so* bad," Krög was not entirely sure why he defended Scale, "And besides, I know my way around a dragon. I would have kept you safe from him."

Lee snickered, "Oh yes, tell me again Battle Prince how it was you felled the mighty Grand Dragon with naught but your sword and the fury of your forefathers. Ah! Now I remember! You scared him into bumping his head on the ceiling! My hero."

"Yes, it takes a keen mind to see every solution in a tight situation," Krög boasted sarcastically, "But I saw things through- as one does when one is the stuff of legend."

Lee rolled her eyes, "Please for the sake of the gods tell me you're kidding."

"You know one day someone is actually going to give me some credit for doing something right," Krög joked back.

"Sure we will," she agreed, "When you actually start doing things *right*."

The prince tisked, "No respect."

"Complain some more Sir Fumblesalot," Lee replied, "That reminds me, your offhand defense is still weak. You need to remember to do a better job at keeping your guard up when attacking," she referred to their training earlier in the day.

"But if I keep my guard raised the whole time I can't extend all the way through my attack," Krög returned.

"You're still hesitating," she pointed out, "The movements should be fluid, each beginning the moment another finishes. You fight like a lumberjack- you need to learn to be more like a court dancer."

They went on for some time, changing topics from combat to music to philosophy and the spectrum of the stars. It never mattered what they talked about, the prince just enjoyed the pleasure of the young woman's company, and the feel of her weight on his chest. On some nights they would lose such track of time as to glimpse the first violet rays of sunlight spill over the hills as the next day took to its beginning, and would have to race back to the Fortress City to creep back in before it was discovered they had gone missing. There always seemed to be a thrill right around the corner when Krög was with Lee, and it contributed considerably to his new willingness to keep to his father's hall; if he could not be out doing exciting things, at least she would keep things exciting.

While Lee got the prince's private moments, Ash was there for everything else. As the days began to roll together and their departure drew nearer, the troll became increasingly anxious himself, which was not a side of him

Krög was accustomed to. Normally, Ashley was serious and reserved, but he was becoming downright antsy as they prepared to leave.

Krög asked him about it one afternoon, "I've never seen you like this, Ash. Is everything okay?"

The troll grumbled, "Strange feeling on wind. Stars not in right places, worried there is pall on land."

"You just haven't hit anything in a while," the prince laughed off Ash's unsettled mood, "I know how badly you wanted to take another swing at Mordenall. I did too. We'll get him next time."

Ash's eyes narrowed, "Not like leave for next time. Next time could get us," he shook his head, "Battle King make wise decision keep us back, but could have done much good."

"I agree," Krög replied, "But now we get to go have all the fun of a victory and we didn't have to risk our necks for it!"

"Many fighting men did risk necks. Many fighting men not come home. Celebration not quite earned when no struggle done," the troll counseled.

The prince sighed, "You're right. As usual. You talk like you've been around longer than I think I give you credit for sometimes. Actually, how old are you Ash?"

"Older than look, younger than feel," the troll replied, letting half a smile slip between his tusks.

"I think we made a mistake teaching you how to make jokes," Krög laughed, "Really though, are you sure you're okay?"

Ash tried to dismiss his own discontentedness, "Will surely be better back on road. Too much time within walls perhaps. Troll no belong in city."

"You and me both," the prince concluded.

While sometimes aloof to the troll's heady warnings and permanently stern countenance, Krög had learned to listen closely to Ashley. Perhaps it was a wisdom garnered from extraordinary time spent wandering alone, but he always seemed to see several steps ahead of the prince, and had an uncanny ability to reason a situation to its conclusion before things had come to pass. As they would stroll through the Thorn Rift Forest together, Ash very often travelled in complete silence, communing with the trees and breeze. He called it "listening to the way of things," and it seemed to bless him with a degree of vague foresight. Though far from a seer or soothsayer, the troll was at the very least attuned to the moods and tides of the world.

Owing to this, the prince should have been a bit unnerved by Ashley's mood, but nothing could shake his excitement as Krög and a parade of his father's most presentable barbarians prepared to set out for their cross-country march. With all the towns they were set to visit, and the somewhat delayed timing of the year's festivals due to the war in the north, they would not be returning to the Great Hall until well into winter's embrace. The prince was thrilled to be separated from the Fortress City for so long. He determined to make the trip one his companions would never forget in all their long remaining years. Especially Lee; Krög could not wait to see her face as she took in the first snowfall of the Southern Reach.

The day of their departure came, and the prince met with his father one last time before venturing out.

"I would like to remind you, son," the Battle King instructed sternly, "I am not sending you to gallivant about our kingdom and drink away your health for your own pleasure. This is a time for the ruler of the Southern Reach to walk among those he leads. Learn your people, prince. Learn their needs and their struggles. These are things you must come to understand when you take the throne from me."

"I will, father," Krög promised, hoping the conversation would have a swift conclusion so he could get to traveling, "And I appreciate your staying back this season so I might go in your place."

"Make no mistake, boy: were it still in my strength to do so, *I* would be with my warriors these next many months as I have so many years previously," the king said, "And while my bones may no longer be able to roam, my mind is still very much needed here in the Great Hall."

The prince looked at him a little confused and concerned, "Are things not well, Battle King? I thought we were celebrating victory this harvest."

"*A* victory," he replied, "But never forget, a good king's work is never through. There are yet pressing matters that require my attendance, and I am more vital here than among the country."

"What is it?" the prince asked, a little quieter.

"It is a matter for the *king*," Bröghue said smiling, "And not one you need concern yourself with. Go now. And do enjoy yourself, son! Your legs still have a great deal of wandering in them, so get on with it."

"Farewell, Battle King," the prince shook his father's hand.

"Farewell, Krög," the king returned, "Be home in time for Midwinter's Feast, or I will send Gögan after the whole lot of you."

As the first blast of wind hit them as they left, Krög pulled it deep into his lungs and let the chilled air fill his chest, and the sensation of liberty fill his soul. He and the barbarians charged together down the far side of the Scorched Hill, descending into the Southern Reach's valleys and lowlands, shouting at the top of their lungs as the Fortress City's guard sang the Battle King's Hymn to the departing number. It was good to be back on the road.

As they went along Krög sang marching songs with the aid of Harpbinger, leaving a steady trail of floating, shimmering images like chimney smoke hanging in the breeze. Lee rode gleefully on the shoulders of Ashley, who lumbered at the side of the prince as he led the whole band across the vast, stretching countryside. Every step was a step farther away from home and towards their next little tale of glory. The prince had hoped it would be, anyway. Then, for all he knew, the Battle King could be accustomed to leading a solemn line through his kingdom, and it was more a chore than a small adventure.

Undaunted, headstrong and assured he was embarking on a wonderful autumn abreast of the country, the prince guided his company boldly through the Southern Reach. With a full parade of barbarians at his back and his mighty troll, The Hammer of the land, at his side, Krög felt right immortal. The cool air spirited his worries away and they roamed carefree and light hearted.

Each town they came to was a different experience. All were dressed with the trappings of Harvest Festivals, small multi-colored flags strung between trees and down streets, pumpkins carved with ferocious faces and vats of spiced cider bubbled at each. That year, all of the villages flew additional colors: the banner of the Battle Family was raised in victory at each. And to the delight of Krög and his friends, each locality had their own way of celebrating and were eager to share it with the visiting prince and his terrible, magnificent warriors.

Brokus, home of the Griffin Riders had a predictably tawdry display of impossibly scantily clad women given the falling temperatures, all dressed suggestively as some frightening monster though with choice pieces of the garments missing. They also brewed their ciders with a process that was guaranteed to knock even a burly man on his haunches after just a few tankards. Strömlan gave tours of nearby "haunted" glens that Ashley found hysterically delightful, and wanted to describe his stories of being lost in The Darks of the Thorn Rift to make their experiences all the more realistic. Other towns played games of skill that celebrated the season, and others held extraordinary dinners with decadent deserts. Lee as it turned out, was best kept clear of sweet treats, as it somehow fortified her already boundless energy to the point of being downright irritating.

Krög found himself regaling the people of each town with modified versions of his adventure to Fanfarra, or his heart-stopping encounter with Raicleach. He was often asked to sing and play the now famous Harpbinger, the youngest members of the villages especially awestruck by the magic images. His station went unquestioned as he arrived to each municipality; the people took him in as the Battle Prince of their lands, and Krög loved every moment of it.

Days bled into weeks, which spun into a month, possibly two. There were often long periods of travel between the distant cities, but so uplifted would the company be from the happenings of the previous town, no one seemed to notice all the walking. All the prince and his companions were aware of was the crunch of the brown grass and fallen leaves beneath their feet, and the smell of the wild autumn wind. They wandered from the secluded foothills of the Dragon's Spine all the way to the coast of the Sea of Despair, marveling at its never-ending magnificence. The world was behind him and to Krög, the Great Hall was a distant, pleasant memory he thought he might one day return to fondly out of nostalgia.

It was late one evening, long after the troupe had made camp, when the first snowfall of the season whispered out of the clouds and began to shroud the valleys around them. Silently the flakes descended, hushing the rest of the sounds of the night, glittering brightly against the silver beams of the moon. Gradually the countryside disappeared under its pale, blanketing embrace and there was only the shimmering white carpet as far as the eye could see.

Lee was beside herself with giddiness watching the tiny diamonds float softly from the clouds, and made quite the spectacle rolling around in it. Krög fired off one sideways comment about her being excited about anything shiny that she made him regret after walloping him in the face with a tightly packed snowball. He chased after her, and the two went tumbling down a hillside sending billows of the drifting ice in all directions.

She laughed when they came to rest at the bottom, "You should have seen the look on your face! Honestly, I wish I had a book of the stupid expressions you pull, and I could flip through the pages and watch you go from confused to dumbstruck in a second."

Krög tossed a handful of snow at her, the majority of which she ducked, though a good deal landed in her hair, and replied, "They can't be any worse than how you look *all* the time."

"I'm holding a mirror up to you the next time you can't figure something out to prove it- and I doubt we'll be waiting long for that to happen," she laughed harder.

"Oh, you carry a mirror now? I guess you learned a trick or two from Ydal," the prince jested in return.

Lee's jaw dropped in a sarcastic and wholly over-the-top manner, though her eyes were still smiling "How *dare* you compare me to that harpy," she hit Krög with another snowball she had packed out of his sight, "The next one is going to have a rock in it."

The prince rolled one of his own and tossed it her direction. Lee caught it lightly with one hand and rebounded it back at Krög. Ice splattered all over his chest.

They wrestled and carried on for some time until both were soaked and cold. Icicles had started to form in the girl's hair, sending it to zany points in all directions. Exuberance poured out of her eyes, their crystalline hue matched only by the glistening snow. Krög gazed on her fondly, and then a feeling turned over in his mind, and he realized there was something else behind the fondness. Something stronger, and more visceral.

She could see his look change, but maintained her mischievous playfulness, "Does Mr. Serious have something to say?"

Krög paused, words caught behind his teeth, but tried anyway, "Lee, I-"

A sudden rush of wind and the wail of a griffin just above them cut the prince off before he could finish. Two more followed quickly behind as they wheeled around and landed in a cascade of drifting snow before Krög and Lee. Captain Iolar dismounted and ran over to them.

"Battle Prince, we've been looking for you," he was out of breath, and his face was chapped against the chilled wind from high above the clouds, "The King bids you return to Ganithen immediately."

Krög laughed uncomfortably, "We can't possibly be late for Midwinter's Feast already. And there's still a few more towns we haven't visited that I know my father wants me to go to."

Iolar was iron-jawed and serious, "This is something else. He would not speak on the nature of the conflict, only asked Gögan and I to bring you to the Great Hall as soon as we could find you."

The prince's expression dropped, "Where is Gögan?"

"Your uncle is back at the camp retrieving your Honor Guard. When we didn't find you there, we followed your tracks. Please Battle Prince, I believe this to be a matter of utmost urgency," Iolar implored, his usual swaggering manner of speech steely and worried.

Krög looked back at Lee, disappointed, "We'll have to finish this some other time I guess."

"She's coming too," Iolar interrupted, "Whatever it is, the king said this involves both of you."

Lee suddenly looked concerned, "What do I have to do with anything?"

"I know only what I know," the captain said spreading his hands helplessly, "And I know he insisted you both return with haste."

Krög and the girl exchanged looks of fretting. Had the Council of Elders learned of their tryst? And if so, from who while they had been gone so long? Certainly the Battle King would not have revealed it without first consulting with his son. Were they really so furious with the prince for courting Lee they would demand everyone be drawn off the parade so swiftly to debate the on the matter? There was something grave about the way Iolar was acting that made Krög's stomach turn.

The prince nodded and strode toward the captain, "Let's go."

"Aye, Battle Prince," Iolar said mounting his griffin and directing one of his escorts to help Lee on to their own.

Gögan was already circling overhead with Ashley seated behind him, awaiting their ascent.

"Longer than a snake passing a stone it took you," despite the levity of his words there was the same harsh tone as Iolar's in his voice, "With all speed now!"

The Griffin Riders pumped their reins and the beasts rocketed through the heavy gray clouds. Born with a fury of impassioned fidelity, the raptors answered the call for expediency, beating their wings and taking ragged panting breaths as they pressed. Snow and sleet stung Krög's face as they careened across the skies at breakneck speed. Beneath them, the dream world of white was a shimmering blur. Against the hand-numbing chill of the skies, the prince gripped tighter to the bridle.

For hours they flew, silence choking the group. Krög watched his white knuckles turn red and then split as the air bit cruelly into his flesh. Each breath froze on its way down his throat, and his eyes had trouble staying open with cold and fatigue. Still they flew on. Around them the wind whistled, gnawing at the prince's face and ears and sending flurries into dizzying patterns. On another night it might have been enchanting to gaze upon, but with their hurried sojourn back to the Fortress City under such a somber pallor, it made the weather itself seem anxious and unfettered.

Distantly, Krög spotted the flames of the watchtowers that circled Ganithen blinking into view. The towering stone walls of the city slowly became visible through the haze of the snowfall, gray and ever sentinel. Draped over the Great Hall, the mighty tree of the Battle King's throne hung heavy with ice, its leaves gone for some time, replaced with the sharp points of the winter. A thin trail of smoke issued from the hall's chimney, despite the fact it must have been only just before dawn. Someone was still awake in the walls of Ganithen.

With a screech, the relieved griffins were finally called to rest before the Great Hall's staircase. They all heaved with effort and threw themselves into the comforting snow to cool their aching muscles. Iolar took a moment to speak to each one, giving thanks, as the shivering oxen wrenched forward and pulled the doors of the hall open. Val was waiting at the top of the stairs, resolute and stoic as always while flakes gathered in the crevices of his armor. Krög could not see the warrior's face behind his helm's death's-head visor, but imagined it must be carved with the same look of worry that had overtaken the countenances of Iolar and Gögan.

"My lord," the Honor Guard bowed, his violet cloak and sash whipping in the wind, "Do not keep the Battle King waiting."

"Thanks, Val. Keep warm," the prince replied grimly as he and the others stepped into the blessedly warm embrace of the Great Hall.

Ashley strode swiftly ahead of Krög and announced him to the Battle King, as was part of his training as an apprentice shield warrior.

"Battle King, prince is here to answer your call," he rumbled, kneeling reverently at Bröghue's throne.

"My thanks, Aushleeyi for seeing him safely back. And to you as well, my brother. I feel your Griffin Riders are owed more gratitude than I can repay in what is left of my days," his face was solemn, and he tugged at his beard.

"He's my kin too," Gögan said, "Wouldn't leave the boy to catch his death out in this."

"Father," Krög started, "I can assure you the weather is no cause for worry. We would have taken shelter had it become too severe. There was no need to call me off the festival march."

"It was not the blizzard that incited your summoning, prince," the Battle King began to explain, "There is a caravan approaching our Hall, and one of their number demanded an audience with you."

Something about the way the king was speaking made Krög's blood run colder than it already was, "Who is it?"

"His name is Sovereign Zaren," the king replied quietly, "He is one of the seven warlords of the Eastern Collective."

As the words left Bröghue's mouth, the prince felt Lee's small fingers dig into his arm, and he distinctly heard her stifle a shriek- though it came out as a sharp exhale.

"What business does a Sovereign from their land have with me?" Krög asked. He did not yet look at Lee, but placed a comforting hand over hers.

The Battle King took a moment to answer, searching carefully for his words, "He believes you to be in possession of something that belonged to him."

Krög scoured his mind for what his father could possibly mean. He took mental inventory of all the trinkets and treasures that had come to him through his recent adventures. None of them seemed to warrant a visit from a foreign warlord, especially given the distances the travelers from the Eastern Collective needed to cross.

"I don't get it. What is it of his I am supposed to have?" the prince finally asked.

Bröghue did not answer, but cast a sorrowful gaze down to the young woman at Krög's side. Confused, the prince looked over at her to find Lee with her eyes cast down at the stone floor, silent.

At first, Krög recoiled, "You were married?!"

She shook her head without saying a word and brushed an errant tear away from her eye.

Still confused, the prince looked back at his father, who took a long breath, "Lèanbh here was owned by Zaren's Assassin Guild before she came to the Southern Reach. Evidently, the terms of her service were never concluded," it was the most tactful way he could put it.

Krög half whispered to the girl, "You were a slave?"

Lee at last looked up at him, a heartbreaking stare of agony and shame driving forth from her eyes under the shadow of her matted hair, "Yes."

Brave the blizzard… face the storm… save Lee.
Join in the quest for Winter's Blade and weather the
Long Journey Home in…

"The Mythical, Mystical, Magnificent Adventures of Krög, The Battle Prince: The Shadow of Winter's Pall"

THE WANING DAYS OF SUMMER

-Appendix: The Bestiary-

Contained herein is a chapter fragment from one of Krög's textbooks that is required reading at Warschool, so titled: "Denizens of the Southern Reach: The Many Things That Wish to Maim, Kill, and Devour You Horribly, and How To Best Survive." While the full text is a rather comprehensive study in wilderness navigation, geography, extended survival and improvised combat, this excerpt comes from a chapter aimed explicitly at preparing young barbarians for the many beasts and monsters encountered in their nation. Though lacking in instruction on how to actually defeat these creatures (those details are spelled out in later sections of the book), it does provide rudimentary descriptions of the most common monsters, and gives a loose idea of how these creatures tend to organize themselves.

It is worth reinforcing these are the more common of the beasts... abominations, fiends, ghosts, apparitions, specters, the walking dead, abyssal leviathans, demons, and mutations, either magical or natural, defy categorization and therefor are not present. I can offer only a most sincere apology for their omission.

Giant Kin

Ogres: Ogres are the smallest of the giant kin- though they are far from small or harmless, for that matter. Most ogres stand between seven and nine feet tall, with the largest at just under ten foot.   Unlike their sturdier brethren, ogres have a slovenly, un-athletic, and altogether malformed look to them, which has lead many to believe their origin lies in a mutated cast-off of either trolls or cliffbeasts. Typically, they have sloping backs and narrow shoulders, with long, spindly arms, short, stumpy legs, and a bulging gut. Ogres are also fairly ugly, even by giant standards, with asymmetrical faces comprised of bulbous, drooping noses, flapping ears, and crooked jaws filled with teeth pointing at odd angles. Intelligence is not a blessing of ogres, and they have an only tenuous grasp on language of any kind. Both the common tongue and their native giant speak prove equally difficult for the dimwitted beasts. All the same, they manage to organize themselves in loose clans or raiding parties, though it does not take much to leverage control of such a band- especially by a more intelligent, stronger troll, or an equally devious, powerful outside influence. Ogres are simple-minded and lean on focus. Typically, they are easily distracted either by something that smells like food (which is basically anything with a beating heart), or a shiny object. Obsessed with jewels and treasure, ogres usually are found overseeing an odd collection of baubles of ranging value, occasionally amassing truly extravagant treasure hordes by sheer accident. Most often, they are found wandering aimlessly through the trees of the Thorn Rift Forest, antagonizing the gentler forest folk and preying upon the truly unlucky.

Trolls: Larger than ogres, but smaller than true, full-blooded giants, trolls are handedly the most dangerous, most insidious of the giant kin. Unlike their smaller cousins, trolls are well formed, muscular, and atavistically regal. They have broad shoulders, powerful arms, and great, barrel-like chests that sit atop legs not far removed from tree trunks. The smallest trolls are around nine feet tall, while the largest approach close to fourteen, giving them the largest proportional disparity of all giant kin. Trolls have square heads that boast heavy black manes, and a truly unique quality among their brethren- a small pair of tusks that jut from the inside of their jaws. Possessing greater than rudimentary intelligence, trolls tend to be devious in their dealings, and extremely well organized, forming large clans and even entire societies with complex systems of governance and municipality- though complex is a relative term in the case of giant kin. All the same, they are known to master several woodland languages along with giant speak and the common tongue. By virtue of their intelligence they tend to be the cruelest of the giant kin, preying on weaker beings with glee, and devising sadistic methods of torture and execution for their victims. It is rumored they were born from an unnatural union between a demon and a true giant, wherein they gained their, comparatively, sharper intelligence and organizational structure. Trolls haunt a number of environments, and can be cave and cliff dwellers as well as frequenting forests and plains.

Giants: True giants are the largest of the giant kin, and perhaps the structural archetype for their subspecies. They most resemble mankind facially and in physical frame, though they are usually fit and lean and stand between twenty two and twenty five feet tall. Height seems to have very little direct affect on their strength, and giants are massively strong- almost peerlessly so. Most giants are fair or red haired, and they tend to grow extremely long coiffure and proud beards. Somewhere between trolls and ogres in intelligence, giants can none the less learn almost no languages beyond giant speak, though this may be a physiological oddity as their lungs and vocal chords are suited only for their own booming vocalizations. All the same, giants are fantastic craftsman, and are known for being impressive blacksmiths and masons, fashioning grand suits of armor and enormous living quarters deep in the heart of mountain ranges. Their organization is a bit amorphous and loose, usually comprised of small clans or villages, and often lead by a singular chief of above average strength. In truth, very little is known about giants as they tend to be reclusive and mysterious, keeping to the absolute deepest of the mountains and canyons, far from other civilization. When ruffled, giants have absolutely unerring accuracy, attributed to extremely sharp, hawk-like vision, and can throw boulders close to a mile with very little margin for error.

Dragons

Wild Dragons: Without question the most animalistic of dragons, Wild Dragons fall between Grand Dragons and Feather Dragons in terms of size. Still fairly enormous, so called "Wilds" typically reach between ninety and one hundred feet in length, with the largest growing nearly twenty feet longer still over the course of an extremely long-lived life. Wilds are scaled and winged, and the color of their scales seems to be nearly random, covering every hue of the known spectrum with no apparent genealogy for passing them on. Almost all of them have a pair of horns set behind reptilian eyes, large, black talons on their wingtips and feet, and a hooked barb at the end of their tail. Though not immortal like their cousins, Wilds are no less of extraordinary longevity, living somewhere between eight hundred and a thousand years from hatchling to death. The longest lived are rumored to be around a millennia and a half, give or take a century. Wilds possess only animal intelligence, though they fall on the keener side, similar in organization and hunting ability to wolves and orcas. All dragons require actually very little food to survive, but still are possessed of boundless appetites. So too are Wilds pack hunters, usually preying on caveling hordes or corralling giant villages, using their ability to fly agilely and breath fire to great advantage. While they are fairly indiscriminate about what they eat, they absolutely avoid trolls at all costs- apparently troll flesh causes severe indigestion and vomiting in dragons. Despite this, Wilds are not outwardly evil or sinister as much as one would call a lion or crocodile evil. They are predatory, and dangerous, but do not have a measurable moral compass.

Grand Dragons: The largest, most impressively regal and most intelligent of the dragons are the Grand Dragons, or simply Grands. Their intellect is as boundless as their lives, and most are frighteningly brilliant and cultured. Grands have complete recall of their lives starting from the moment they were wrought into existence, and most claim to be on similar footings as the gods, having been borne from the original dusts of the universe. No one has ever challenged the assertion and lived. While they appear in much the same manner as Wilds, Grands have a few differences. To begin with, they are between two to three times as long, the biggest around three hundred feet in length, the smallest still clearing two hundred thirty feet nose to tail. The horns of Grands also curl backwards and together, rather than curving outward like Wilds, and they grow immensely long beards of silver hair. Occasionally, Grands have a fanlike protrusion along their back, rather than the ridged spines typical of Wilds. Truly though, the most notable features of Grands is the depth of their intelligence-which is fathomless genius. They have been known to love art, culture, music, and especially philosophy, and love to collect jewelry and fine treasures. They can speak nearly every language ever written into existence. As well, they are patient and undying, which gives them the ability to plot and brood for centuries, sometimes millennia at a time. Grands are markedly insidious, with a temperament that borders on wickedly apathetic to outright evil. While most have some twisted sense of honor or dignity, Grands live for destruction and mayhem at their worst, or are arrogantly detached at their best. Grand Dragons are solitary creatures, detesting the presence of one another and tolerating no other living creature any longer than it takes to devour them. Most find the flesh of mankind an extreme delicacy, and will go to impressive lengths to attain it.

Feather Dragons: It is unclear whether to classify Feather Dragons amongst fairy folk or the dragons, but they have most in common with dragons, especially in disposition and appearance. Unquestionably the smallest of the dragons, Feathers rarely grow longer than two feet in length from nose to tail, with the smallest being only half so. Rather than sails of hide between the fingers of their wings, Feather dragons are so named for the course of feathers they grow, which match in color and brilliance to their scales. Feathers also have the most expressive faces of the dragons, able to manipulate the horns behind their eyes like eyebrows and twist their long snouts into emotive expressions. While they typically are inclined towards the arrogant nature of Grands, many Feathers border on delusional at their significance in the universe. Also immortal, Feathers are rumored to have been the stupid prank of some rapscallion deity on the world, rather than a dimensional pillar like Grands.   Their intelligence is narrower than their much larger cousins, but most tend to be as clever, if not more so, than most people, and they use their minds to lord over civilizations of fairy folk. While not as linguistically talented as Grands, Feathers do typically collect a number of languages over their lifetime, and inexplicably can speak the enormous vocalization of Dragonthroat, a language unique only to dragons comprised of thundering roars and squeals. The cruelty of Feathers is tempered mostly by their size, and the fact they are unable to impact the general world much at all- though they are sinister, frightening terrors of the sky to the fairy kind. While unable to amass fortunes like Grands, they are hoarders none the less, taking what trophies they are able, usually bones of the things they kill or the occasional bauble. Feathers will feed on anything they can get their jaws around, most acting like scavengers rather than true hunters, though they mightily prefer the flesh of pixies, and if they are able to find one helpless enough to eat, the softer portions of human anatomy. Like Grands, Feathers are solitary and hate the company of other dragons.

Fairy Folk

Pixies: Fairy folk on the whole are a mysterious breed, and very little is known about them, but what is shall be presented here. The virtuous and upright of the fairy folk are the pixies. Most resemble humans, except they are only around three quarters of an inch in height, have a pair of insect-like wings attached behind their shoulders, and a thin, prehensile tail protruding from their flank. They live among the treetops in, proportionately, sprawling societies that might take up an entire limb or even a full canopy in the cases of their largest city states. Pixies are purveyors of magic and illusion, live hundreds of years at a time, and encourage growth and prosperity in everything they touch. Typically they live on berries and fruit, and are known for brewing extremely potent wine spirits. Most pixie societies exist outside the realm of human knowledge, though they are often terrorized by Feather Dragons who sometimes set up terrible dictatorships over the peaceful pixies, demanding daily sacrifices and vast quantities of wine. Pixie rangers occasionally break away from their societies and serve as guiding spirits for those who become lost in their forests, if the lost souls are deemed of equitable worth and virtue. Sprites are the slightly more free spirited cousins to pixies, though they are otherwise indistinguishable minus the minor disparity in nature.

Imps: Scaly, lizard-like and with clawed bat wings, imps are the nasty, mean-spirited, mischievous brethren to pixies. Similar in size to their upright cousins, imps share basically nothing else in common aside from general frame and stature. It is spectacular how a creature the size of one's fingertip is capable of enacting enough mayhem to send an entire village of people into disarray, but imps absolutely live to cause chaos and entropy. They use their intimate knowledge of magic and mind-bending illusion to put things far outside their natural order, and generally "screw" with the ways of the universe wherever they are able. Sometimes they serve as jesters, advisors, or simple pets to Feather Dragons who find amusement in their nasty pranks, but usually they are a lonely creature that scavenges carrion or nips at the ears and fingers of people who are unfortunate enough to fall asleep near to an imp's nest. Imps prefer to live in decay as well, inhabiting rotted tree trunks or bogs. No pun intended, little more can be said on imps as little else is known- they are frightful creatures of ill disposition, and avoiding them is generally advised.

Glade Spirits

Nymphs: Nymphs are the most beautiful and pure of the woodland spirits. They appear as slender, fully grown human women, though they are rarely more than four feet tall and possessed of immaculately gorgeous features. Most have long, silver hair, pale blue or grey eyes, and flawless ivory skin with a faint blue tint to it. As mysterious as they are beautiful, almost nothing is known about nymph culture or language- they shy entirely away from all manner of civilization keeping to small communes of their own wherein they enjoy their removed company and languish in the sun all day. To even gaze upon a nymph is said to be so rare it borders on hallucination, and verily the only people to ever interact with them are the most desperately lost and dying, or, strangely enough, children. Nymphs have a motherly way about them, caring not only for the animals and plants of the forest, but also for the occasional wayward child that stumbles upon them. Impressive swimmers, nymphs are able to burst apart into whitewater rapids when necessary to escape danger. Though very little preys directly upon them, the foulest of creatures will use their hair to weave into silk and their skin for the finest of leathers. To acquire such things is as difficult a task as it is grisly, and it is said those who slay nymphs are damned to rise again after death and haunt the forests until the breaking of the earth. Nymphs are one of only two beings known to be able to ride unicorns.

Dryads: Slightly taller and more athletic cousins to the nymphs are the dryads. Dryads appear as both male and female, unlike their all female brethren, and are usually right around five feet tall. They have decidedly more bronzed skin, deep green eyes, wild chestnut hair and a sinewy build that comes from a lifetime of climbing trees and racing one another through glens. Dryads are more active and restless than nymphs, developing fine music in their free time, and are known for their shimmering, ethereal singing voices. When challenged, dryads can root themselves to the ground, extend their hair like branches and take on the unmistakable appearance of a small tree, usually to the befuddlement and confusion of their attackers. Ogres favor dryad flesh as a delicacy, and tend to be the only natural enemies of the otherwise peaceful, if playful, beings. Like nymphs, dryads can saddle and ride unicorns, and like nymphs, laying eyes on a dryad is an exceedingly rare occurrence.

Unicorns: Of all the spirits of the forest, unicorns are absolutely the most rarely seen, spoken of only in hushed legend and myth. Appearing as a fine racing horse of either dazzling ivory or shimmering obsidian, unicorns are known for their most spectacular feature: a single, brilliant white horn protruding between their eyes. Their hooves are more akin to finely forged silver than anything else, and they seem to possess the magic ability to gallop across the surface of water, sending towering curtains of it in either direction as they run. Unicorns typically keep to uninhabited regions of forests, though they seem to have a love for river banks and waterfalls, and especially caves where they are said to rest during the daytime. They are unridable by all beings except for their forest fellows the dryads and the nymphs. Unicorns appear to keep loose societies much like the mustangs of the plains and have no known enemies in the natural world as they are mercurial and uncatchable. Only the fell kind have been known to slay a unicorn, and usually only at great detriment and loss to their own number.

Mountain Beasts

Cliffbeasts: It is difficult to determine whether to categorize cliffbeasts among the giant kin or as an entirely unique subspecies. They have much in common with trolls and ogres, being about as tall as the later, but as equally broad and muscled as the former. The major difference, however, is the coat of fur cliffbeasts have, which covers very nearly their entire body. Ranging from a dirty, tawny hue to snow white, the heavy coat serves to protect them from the extreme mountain climes they live in. The hide on their hands and feet is also notably thicker than the rest of giant kin, lent mostly to the fact they entertain no clothing of any kind and spend their entire lives clambering over sharp rocks and climbing sheer cliffs. Their intelligence appears to be limited, though they speak what sounds like simple phrases in giant speak, and their clans are even more savage and loosely organized than ogre raiding bands. Cliffbeasts scavenge like ogres, eating whatever they can find, though they are actually quite adept hunters when necessary, able to climb impossibly steep mountain surfaces to pursue their prey. What could barely be called the society of cliffbeasts seems to be limited to cooperative hunting, using their overpowering numbers and strength to bring down larger prey, and occasional navigation, where their bellowing, whining cries carry from mountain top to mountain top- a frightening sound to the wayward adventurer, to be certain, but a means of travel coordination to the cliffbeasts. The pelts of cliffbeasts are prized for their extraordinary warmth and resiliency, being able to weather most natural conditions without changing its properties.

Cavelings: Hideous and revolting, cavelings are an abomination of the deepest wells of the mountains, dwelling in positively the most remote and impassable cave regions between cliffs. Resembling stalagmites and stalactites on their back, usually a tough fleshy protrusion the same color and apparent consistency of stone, and squat, muscular, three legged spiders on their underside, cavelings are well suited for clinging to the roofs of caverns where they lie in wait to ambush their prey. The most impressive feature of cavelings, by far, is their enormous, prehensile tongue that can unravel almost a full ten feet from their wide, teeth-lined maws. Much like a frog, this tongue is used to snatch unsuspecting victims from cave floors, to be dragged under the caveling's heavy bodies where they are devoured, often over the course of several hours. While primarily ambush hunters, often times cavelings cooperate to bring down larger prey, stalking in packs. Completely blind, they communicate with high pitched shrieks and squeals, like bats, and have a highly developed sense of hearing. Lacking ears, cavelings appear to pick up on sonic, and physical, vibration through the fleshy protrusion on their backs that, aside from looking convincingly like cave camouflage, is actually a highly developed sensory organ that can hone in a variety of sounds and wavelengths. Cavelings are simply animals attached to the ecosystem, and serve little use to society outside of their own existence.

Griffins: Regal and proud, griffins inhabit the cliffs and lower foothills of most mountain ranges, making their nests in shallow caves and on sheer rock walls. Griffins have an enormous wingspan in comparison to the eagles they resemble, and most are typically twice the size of their lion cousins of which their hindquarters resemble. Wingtip to wingtip, griffins usually clear twelve to fourteen feet, and stand nothing less than six feet at the shoulder. Their feathers are always jet black, though they silver with advanced age, and their hindquarters are a shimmering, crimson gold. Griffins possess a red beak and yellow raptor eyes that can see keenly for miles. Their vocalizations resemble both the roars and moans of lions, along with the chitters and screeches of hawks. Most live a lifespan slightly shorter than most people, somewhere around forty to fifty years from hatchling to death, though some have lived markedly longer, well into their eighties and nineties. Like their much larger rivals, the Wild Dragons, Griffins are exclusively pack hunters and live in small prides of twelve to twenty where there is an established pecking order of Alpha Female, Beta Male, and then the remainder of the flock. Though intelligent, griffins are able to be tamed, though they see it more as forming a limited partnership with their mount. If allowed to imprint at hatching and raised from there, griffins form fierce, ferocious companions who never let their riders fall from the sky and are willing combatants. Easily the most agile in the air of all the flying beasts, griffins are capable of spectacular aerial acrobatics, and the more maverick of their number can be downright showy. In this way, griffins have very distinct personalities, often ranging from proud and removed to social and rollicking. Griffins are naturally quizzical, and though they can only speak their own language, many often acquire an ear for other tongues and learn to communicate or take commands from those they bond with. In terms of riders, griffins bond exactly once, for life, and if their mount dies prior to the griffin, the raptor will under almost no circumstances ever acquiesce to being saddled again. They are even known to mourn the loss of their riders unto their own demise from sadness, and for this reason, griffins are absolutely prized and cared for by those who ride them. Griffin feathers can be used as the quills for fine pens, and in certain circles apparently find employ as an extremely pleasurable tool of erotic teasing.

Boarhounds: An enormously oversized amalgamation of wolf and hog, boarhounds are extraordinary predators of the rockier foothills and low mountain ranges. Pack animals by nature, boarhounds seldom travel or hunt alone, and are normally found in teams of no less than three and typically no more than six. The occasional hunting party as large as twelve has been sighted, though these are usually the scavenging groups of two disparate packs working in tandem to bring down an unusually large prey (i.e. a wounded wild dragon incapable of flight, or a family of giants that has strayed from the peaks). Simply seeing one is a terrifying experience, especially for the lone traveller who must confront such a beast. At the shoulder, the smallest of boarhounds stands around six feet tall, with the alphas and elders clearing nine to eleven feet. They possess four broad and taloned paws, which have a similar feel to bark on the pads. Boarhounds are covered by a coarse, bristly fur that is longest at the hackles, and varies from a dirty red to jet black in coloration. While their facial features are lupine in majority, their snout terminates in a flat, open nose much more akin to a boar's, and they possess a pair of wide set, hyper extended secondary canines that present as razor-sharp tusks, owing to their inverted curvature. With only tepidly measurable animal intelligence, boarhounds are notorious for being single-minded, eating machines, and are often viewed as dull when compared to the far more intelligent sum of their parts (pigs and wolves being known for displaying marked capacity for learning). This is perhaps an unfair assessment, as boarhounds are observed to be highly socialized and advanced hunters in their own circles, a trait that is likely overridden by their extreme aggression and near bottomless appetite. It is said those possessing legendary strength and will are able to tame boarhounds as mounts, though rumors of such have all but been disproven.

Serpents

River Serpents: The mystical serpents, being those notably larger and of more aggressive temperament than common snakes, are most typically classified among three varieties, the smallest of which are River Serpents. Ranging in general length between thirty and forty feet, and usually as big around as small trees, River Serpents constitute an apex predator in most river systems they inhabit. Due to their extraordinary size, only the largest of rivers can even support a population of these creatures, and this is very good for the human civilizations that settle along the banks for their access to transportation and assets. River Serpents are opportunity and ambush predators, spending the great majority of their time in muddy burrows, or dangling among the stronger tree branches of larger arbors, waiting for prey to pass by. Most are patient enough to allow their victims to partially cross a river, before using their truly superior swimming ability to overtake, and capture or kill their intended where the water is deepest. River serpents will constrict or drown anything so large they cannot swallow whole, before bogging the corpse and allowing it to rot, much like crocodiles. Their burrows are usually rife with dead and decaying ogres, who are typically too slow and dimwitted to avoid being captured and killed. River serpents move with remarkable speed through the water, able to easily overtake any sailing vessel, even against the current, though they only very rarely attack something as large as a ship.

Sea Serpents: Next largest of the serpentine family are the Sea Serpents, which are found only in the largest, open bodies of water such as continental oceans- though there are reports of the great inland sea, Titan's Wash, supporting a colony of Sea Serpents.   Due to their immense habitat and naturally mysterious disposition, not a great deal is known about Sea Serpents.   Thanks to abyssal gigantism, Sea Serpents grow nearly twice the size of their river counterparts, both in length and girth. Broad ridges of fans and spines run along their back, and when combined with their titanically powerful tails, Sea Serpents can dive and surface with remarkable speed- enough to propel them completely out of the water in jumps that are storied to be as spectacular to witness as they are destructive.   Said to feed on other giants of the seas like supermassive sharks and deep water whales, very little challenges Sea Serpents in their home habitat for superiority.   Not even the ships of man, for all their great technology with harpoon ballistas, have been known to successfully slay and tow a Sea Serpent, and attempts to do so are always met with the sinking of the offending vessel. The only perceived threat to these great lords of the open waters are the mythic leviathans that supposedly live in the darkest trenches of the lowest depths... but their existence has never been definitively verified.

Mountain Serpents: The largest, rarest, and most legendary of the great serpents are the, supposed Mountain Serpents, also called colloquially Rumblers. No living Mountain Serpent has ever been observed, but a great deal of supporting evidence to their existence has been uncovered throughout the years. Skeletal remains place them at a length rivaling wild dragons, most exceeding one hundred feet long, with rumors of the eldest of these beasts reaching twice even that. The only of the great serpents to be primarily land dwelling, Mountain Serpents, as their name suggests, live among the peaks. Their forward mandibles are uniquely designed and adapted to tunneling, and the incredible tunnels they carve through the lowest depths of the highest mountains are often used as dungeons for hiding treasures and as dwellings for families of cliffbeasts. While able to burrow straight through solid rock, most Mountain Serpents prefer softer mediums for their nests, especially glaciers and ice. When they keep to bedrock, their burrowing can cause significant erosion and land deterioration, and the tunnels of these beasts have been blamed on the spontaneous formation of lakes and inlet bays when sections of continents fall away unexpectedly. As with their smaller cousins, Mountain Serpents are absolute apex predators with no known rivals. Even entire villages of giants will go to unusual lengths to stay out of the paths of Mountain Serpents, and the skeletons of giants are occasionally found entwined around the bones of these beasts, suggesting Mountain Serpents prey upon them indiscriminately. Little more is known about these immense beings- they are as close to mythological as the mystic beasts come.   If popular rumor is to be believed, only nine ever existed in the first place, at least two of which are known to be dead leaving a remaining seven hidden somewhere throughout the world.

Follow on Social Media for more updates to Krög's world and adventures!

Twitter @Cipriani_Ryan

Instagram: @krogthebattleprince

TikTok: TheGrimSkald

www.krogthebattleprince.com

Printed in the United States of America

First printing, 2016

ISBN 978-0-9977558-2-4